THE WORLD PLAYED CHESS

Center Point
Large Print

Also by Robert Dugoni and available from Center Point Large Print:

Close to Home
A Steep Price
The Eighth Sister
A Cold Trail
The Last Agent
In Her Tracks
The Silent Sisters
What She Found

The World Played Chess

ROBERT DUGONI

CENTER POINT LARGE PRINT
THORNDIKE, MAINE

This Center Point Large Print edition
is published in the year 2023 by arrangement with
Amazon Publishing, www.apub.com.

Originally published in the United States
by Amazon Publishing, 2021.

This is a work of fiction.
Names, characters, organizations, places,
events, and incidents are either products of
the author's imagination or are used fictitiously.

The text of this Large Print edition is unabridged.
In other aspects, this book may vary
from the original edition.
Printed in the United States of America
on permanent paper sourced using
environmentally responsible foresting methods.
Set in 16-point Times New Roman type.

ISBN: 978-1-63808-639-0

The Library of Congress has cataloged this record
under Library of Congress Control Number: 2022949833

THE WORLD PLAYED CHESS

To all the men and women who
served in the Vietnam War.
Heroes. Every one of them.

The world played chess,
while I played checkers.

—Origin and attribution debated

When I was a child, I spoke like a child,
I thought like a child, I reasoned
like a child. When I became a man,
I put aside childish things.

—1 Corinthians 13:11

PROLOGUE

A purpose, I have learned, is rarely found, but revealed. Only when I do not search does the purpose become clear.

So it would be with William Goodman's journal. I had no idea why he sent it to me, but his purpose would reveal itself in time.

William mailed the journal he kept in Vietnam in a five-by-eight manila envelope addressed simply to *Vincenzo*, without my last name, Bianco. Scrawled in blue ink, the crude numbers and letters appeared rushed, as if William had quickly written the name and my Burlingame address, perhaps worried he might change his mind before he mailed the envelope. He did not provide his name or a return address, but I knew the sender. I had not heard that version of my name in nearly forty years, nor had I seen or spoken with the only person who had routinely used it.

William's package arrived on a Saturday, via regular mail, with eight American flag postage stamps in the upper-right corner. That caught my attention. I opened the envelope with more than a little curiosity and pulled out a rectangular Tiger Chewing Tobacco tin—the orange and gold leaf scratched and aged, and the four corners, one of which had a dent, displaying flakes of rust. I held the tin like a religious relic, uncertain what it could possibly contain, or if I wanted to open it.

After a moment of contemplation, I popped the lid.

Beneath a folded sheet of paper, the kind once kept by a telephone to scribble hurried notes and phone numbers, I found a three-by-five-inch black hardcover notebook, the lined sheets filled with the same harsh handwriting as on the envelope. I unfolded the sheet and noted an illustration of a birdhouse with an American flag above the round entry hole. Again, it seemed as incongruous with the William I had known as the patriotic stamps.

The note, however, was vintage William—humor, with a seriousness lurking beneath his words.

Vincenzo!
Look what I found in a box in my storage closet.

I guess it wasn't in the box I threw out with my medals and ribbons after all.

Fate, perhaps.

I was uncertain what to do with it. My wife is gone now. Cancer took her. She had a daughter from a previous marriage who, for all intents and purposes, I raised as my own. But I cannot give this to her. She wouldn't understand.

14

It's just me now. A squad of one.

I almost threw it out. Then I thought of you.

I thought of that summer. 1979? You asked about Vietnam. And you listened when others did not. You saved me from destroying my life, and you were the reason I found my life again. I don't think you knew that. I never had the chance to tell you. I should have.

I believe we both dreamed of being journalists. I see on the internet you're a successful lawyer. Dreams are hard to catch, aren't they? I didn't obtain my dream, either, not that one anyway, but I achieved so many others I never thought possible. I have no regrets, and I certainly won't complain. Every minute of every day is a gift, and growing old a privilege, not a right.

I lowered William's letter and recalled when he'd first said those words to me—in the garage of the Burlingame remodel. I had thought of his words often over the years, and I told them to my own children, though they didn't have the depth of meaning they had coming from William.

So, the journal . . .

After the marines turned down my

request to be a combat reporter, I bought this journal and decided to write my own stories. I once thought these scribblings might someday be the makings of a novel, but maybe they're just the musings of an aging man once young, a man who lived through hell on earth and somehow survived, bruised and battered, but alive. Or maybe they're just scribblings . . .

Now they belong to you.

Keep them. Use them if you see a purpose. If not, you know the drill. All I ask is that you read the passages in the order written, so you will understand.

Peace, Semper Fi,
William Goodman

Over the next year, I would endeavor to read one entry a day, as William had written them, never realizing William's stories would be as significant now as they had been thirty-six years ago, and as painful. Some entries were just a rushed sentence or two, others, longer narratives. I read each entry slowly, searching for William's hidden meanings. Some made me laugh. Some made me sad. Some were too horrible to imagine, or to live with, which explained why William sent me the journal and did not leave it to his daughter. He no longer wanted to live with the memories—I imagine reality had been hard enough—and he didn't want her to live with them, either.

But unlike the Vietnam medals William had been awarded, the journal had clearly meant something to him, and he was not yet prepared to throw away his recollections within it.

Whatever William's reason, the journal's purpose would reveal itself during my son Beau's senior year of high school, and it would remind me of that summer, 1979, before I, too, had departed for college—when I'd first met and worked with William Goodman and Todd Pearson, two Vietnam veterans who'd come home from war to find their place in the world forever altered. I had also struggled that summer, in my own way, as Beau would struggle, as all young men struggle to ascend from their teenage years to the mantle of manhood.

William called it OJT. On-the-job training.

I suppose he was right.

Like most eighteen-year-old young men, I inhabited the center of my own universe, though cosmologists steadfastly maintain the universe has no center, that it will forever expand. Try telling that to a high school senior who thinks he's immortal because he has yet to experience mortality and indestructible because nothing has harmed him, who believes he can achieve anything he puts his mind to simply because others have said he can.

17

I said as much in my valedictorian address to my classmates, 172 eighteen-year-old young men. "Good seeds," I had called them, making an analogy to a biblical psalm. Good seeds who had fallen on good ground and would achieve great things. When I had finished, my classmates stood and applauded because, like me, they believed their futures to also be inevitable and rich with promise. The realities of life had not yet popped the bubbles in which we lived. We did not know that nothing is guaranteed, not even nineteen.

Unlike for my own children, social media had not pierced holes in our naivete. My social media consisted of a rotary-dial phone on the kitchen wall, and good luck competing with four sisters to use it. At eighteen years of age, I could count on one hand the number of times I had stepped on an airplane, and I had never traveled outside the state of California, except during summer vacations at Lake Tahoe when my family crossed the border into Nevada. News of the world came only at prescribed hours of the day, only from three television networks—NBC, ABC, and CBS—and only if I chose to watch it.

I rarely did.

I learned of Richard Nixon's 1974 resignation, and of Elvis Presley's death in 1977, from important newscasts that interrupted the radio in the car. I did not have the ability to FaceTime, text, Instagram, Snapchat, or Twitter anyone about these events. Not that I'm sure I would have—except, perhaps, to tweet the death of Elvis. I was, and remain, a fan.

Russia was an evil empire, China an emerging but backward giant, and Vietnam . . . Vietnam was just an annoying country on the other side of the world that the United States had failed to liberate from the bonds of communism.

I couldn't be bothered with any of it.

I intended to make the most of my last summer before I left for college. I intended to go out every night with my high school friends and drink in—literally—what remained of my youth. I wanted to put off, for as long as possible, the responsibilities and obligations I knew would come with being an adult. I had claimed to anyone who would listen that I was Peter Pan, youthful, carefree, and without worry.

A part of me very much wanted it to be so.

But it couldn't be.

As my classmates' applause for my valedictorian address faded in the church vestibule and our principal released the class of 1979 into the world, I rushed out those bronze church doors and never saw the fist that would punch me in the face, the fist that would shatter my illusions about life, death, and my Peter Pan youth—the same fist that would punch Beau in the face his senior year.

Like William, I, too, had intended to be a

19

journalist, and I, too, had kept a journal, a present from my mother on my seventeenth birthday. I diligently kept a record of the events that transpired during the next year, including that summer, because I had also been certain my scribblings would someday be the basis for many novels.

Like William, I shoved my journal in a box and forgot about it. Like William, I gave up my dream of writing a novel.

Until the day his journal arrived in the mail.

I found that box in my attic, and in that box I found my brown leather journal beneath the plaques and medals commemorating my high school achievements. Unlike William, I never had the nerve to throw out those awards. In my attic I thumbed through my journal and read that final entry I had written before I left for college. A poem. A very poor imitation of the great Dr. Seuss. I'd written of the reality that came that summer, despite my best efforts to stop it. It came like the Christmas that Dr. Seuss's Grinch couldn't steal from the people of Whoville.

It came, just the same.

September 16, 1979

Reality came last summer without boxes
or ribbons or packages or bows.
  It came without warnings or excuses,

And gripped me from my head to my toes.

And I puzzled and puzzled till my puzzler was sore.

How could I have missed something at my essence, at my very core?

Reality came, yes it did, with its own devilish plot.

It came like a net, and I like the fish, that in it was caught.

It struck like a fist, hitting me square in the jaw.

A blow without warning, unapologetic, and savagely raw.

The pain lingered for days, then for months and, finally, years.

It lingered and lingered until its message became clear.

The world, it seemed, had been busy playing chess,

While I had played checkers . . . and ignored the rest.

PART I

I Ain't No
Senator's Son

August 26, 1967

"Don't stand out. Just blend in. Do you hear me?"

"I hear you, Mom."

My mother draped a gold chain over my head and pressed her hand to the crucifix.

"And don't be a hero. Just blend in and come home."

"I will," I told her, because I knew it was what she wanted to hear.

And I didn't want to think about the alternative.

CHAPTER 1

August 29, 2015

I walked into a wall where once had been the entry to our kitchen. I'd had my head down, flipping through the pages of the journal I'd kept at seventeen and wondering what happened to the young man who had wanted to write.

"Damn," I said.

Elizabeth looked up from the remodel plans she had spread across our dining room table and laughed. "Old habits die hard, I guess," she said.

"I guess," I said, rubbing where I had bumped my head. "When did this go in?"

"Yesterday. They're moving the staircase tomorrow."

"Moving the staircase?" I said, my tone sharpening and volume rising.

"I'm kidding."

"Very funny."

We were in the middle of a remodel that started with just removing a nonstructural wall between the kitchen and the dining room no one ever used. The kitchen had since doubled in size and shifted, to make the family room larger. Elizabeth decided a new kitchen needed new appliances, and a bay window, and, apparently, a new entry. I wasn't complaining, at least not out loud. It would be nice to have a larger family room, which meant a larger flat-screen, in my way of thinking. It was also practical. Beau, our eighteen-year-old, who would be a high school senior, brought friends home after summer football conditioning, and that would likely continue after Friday-night games in the fall. I'd warned Elizabeth that eighteen-year-old young men after an extended workout were like stray dogs. Feed them and they would keep coming back. They did. I wished I had bought stock in Costco pizza.

Mary Beth, our freshman daughter, a basketball player, would likely do the same with her friends and teammates in the winter. Elizabeth and I had decided it was better to have them at home with friends than driving all over town.

Holding both William's and my journals made me think of that lost dream—the one I had to be a writer, maybe even someday write a novel. I forsook that dream for a stable job and a stable income as an attorney. I had justified my decision to go to law school as best I could—I told myself that having a law degree would give me something to fall back on if the writing didn't work out. I then justified becoming a lawyer by telling myself I would need to save money for when I took a sabbatical to write. More recently, I told myself my savings and investments would allow me to retire young, and that I could write that novel after both our kids graduated college.

I had only been fooling myself.

I had chickened out when I went to law school. I had been afraid to write, afraid I would fail. What would people think of me? *Class valedictorian. And he's a nobody. A failure.*

And now? Well, the law was indeed a jealous mistress. Days became months and months became years and years became decades. I devoted too much time to my job. I stayed at the office late, got in early, worked too many weekends. It was easier that way, I suppose—not having the time to write, rather than admitting that I simply didn't have the heart or the courage.

I pacified myself with things like the remodel, things we could afford, but, frankly, that I didn't care about. I told myself Elizabeth and I could give our kids more than I had growing up with nine siblings, but I realize now that kids don't want much, just to know they are loved.

Someone once said that failure is easier to live with than regret, and it pierced my heart like an arrow.

Dreams are hard to catch, aren't they?

Especially if you don't have the courage to try.

"What are you reading?" Elizabeth asked.

"A journal."

She squinted, disbelieving. "Since when do you keep a journal?"

"I don't." I held it up. "I kept this one in 1979.

My mother gave it to me. She wanted me to write the great American novel."

"F. Scott Fitzgerald beat you to it," Elizabeth said.

"Harper Lee fans might disagree," I said. "As well as Hemingway fans." I changed the subject, not wanting to dwell on my failure. "What are you doing, adding a second story?"

"Ha ha. The designer is coming over to discuss wall colors."

"We have a designer?" I could see the price of the remodel increasing.

"It's part of the contractor's services," she said. "But if you're planning on quitting your day job to write novels, you might want to wait a year."

Or thirty-six, I thought, but didn't say. I considered my journal. "My mother gave this to me before my senior year in high school."

"What made you even think of it?" Elizabeth asked. "Don't tell me you were cleaning out the attic."

"In this heat? It's a hundred degrees plus up there. I'd die of heatstroke." Like the guys William told me about who fried their brains in Vietnam's heat and humidity. Another story I had not thought about in decades. "No, I got a package in the mail today from someone I knew a long time ago."

"A girlfriend? Tell her you're committed."

"No kidding," I said. "To this remodel. I might never get to retire."

Elizabeth rolled her eyes. She ran her own real estate company and made a substantial salary.

"No, from a guy I worked with on a construction crew the summer I graduated high school. You remember Mike?"

"Your sister's ex?"

"He got me the job."

"So what was in the package?"

"This." I held up William's black book. "His journal from Vietnam."

Elizabeth put down the highlighter she had been using to mark the plans. "Why did he send it to you?"

I shrugged. "I don't think he was ready to throw it out."

"That's random."

I stepped to the table, pulled out a chair, and sat. "Not really. He and I used to talk after work. We'd sit in the garage of the house we were remodeling on Castillo Avenue in Burlingame, and he would tell me about Vietnam, what it was like, the impact it had on him."

"I thought Vietnam vets never talked about Vietnam."

"Most don't."

"What are you going to do with it?"

"Read it. I think. That's what he asked, anyway, that I read it."

"You sound hesitant."

I nodded. "His stories were raw and honest," I

31

said. "He suffered from PTSD that summer, not that he or I knew it at the time, but he deteriorated pretty rapidly."

"Why haven't you mentioned him before?"

It was a good question, but I didn't have a good answer for my wife. The summer I spent with William had been one of those transformative periods of my life—one I liked to both remember and forget. It was kind of like William's journal. It was personal. It was between William and me, and I didn't feel like it was my right to share his stories, what he had been through.

Or maybe I didn't want to think of lost dreams.

"I don't know," I said.

"Where is he now?"

I shook my head. "He didn't put a return address on the envelope."

"Seems odd."

At first blush it probably did seem odd, but the lack of a return address was likely because William felt the same way about that summer as I did. It was something both to remember and to forget.

"You know that saying, the one I've told the kids about growing old being a privilege, not a right?"

"Yeah."

"That came from William. He told me that after work one day."

"I thought it was another line you plagiarized from a *Seinfeld* episode."

I smiled, but Elizabeth knew me, and she knew William sending me his journal had been one of those unexpected moments that, while they didn't exactly rock my boat, certainly made it list from side to side.

"Sounds heavy," she said.

"It was, coming from someone who learned it at just eighteen years of age."

She nodded at William's journal. "You sure you want to read it?"

"I don't know," I said. "Part of me doesn't, but part of me feels like I owe it to William."

"Why?"

Because William taught me that you can't expect to be treated as a man if you act like a child, and that every life is precious and can be lost in an instant of stupidity or bad luck. He taught me not to waste the opportunities I had, because so many young men never had a chance at them, never had the chance to grow old.

"I just do," I said.

"Might be something for Beau to read," Elizabeth said.

"Maybe," I said. "I think I'll read it first, though." I heard the doorbell and looked to the bay window. The designer held a massive book. "That's my cue to go hit a bucket of golf balls."

Elizabeth moved to answer the door. "You know, it wouldn't kill you to stay and participate a little."

"Picking out wall colors? Yeah, it would. I'd pick out purple and you'd kill me." I pecked her cheek. "Besides, it's hard enough just writing the checks."

August 27, 1967

After hours of filling out forms, I raised my right hand and was inducted into the United States Marine Corps, then boarded a bus bound for Parris Island, South Carolina, what the marines call PI. I will undergo nine weeks of boot camp. I had turned down officer candidate school, which was an extended commitment offered to me after I scored well above average on my AFQT (Armed Forces Qualification Test). I don't care about becoming an officer. I care about getting out. The sooner the better.

Parris Island in August and September is my penance. Ninety degrees and 85 percent humidity.

Every time the bus stopped in some small town, guys got on who looked just like me. Same age. Same shaggy hair. Same sporadic facial hair. Same hard stare, like we weren't scared. We were. We didn't say much to each other, but we looked each other up and down, made assessments, wondered . . . though not for too long. You didn't want to think about it. Just like you didn't want to think that you might never see your parents or your sisters and brothers again. That you might not make it home. Might not ever again drive that car you fixed up. Might not again eat at the local diner. Might not kiss your high school sweetheart, who swore she would wait for you.

You could "might not" yourself crazy.

I decided it was best to stay in the present. The present, I figured, would be hard enough to get through.

Somewhere along the fifteen-hour bus route, one of the southern states, this big guy got on the bus. A stereotype. He looked like he could play football for Bear Bryant at Alabama. Big chest. Big legs. Big head. Crew cut. Projecting forehead. I could tell that he thought he was a badass because the first thing he did was tell the little guy sitting up front to move. The guy moved without hesitation. I'm a strapping 160 pounds, and I was thinking I would have told the guy to go to hell, but that's just bullshit. New Jersey hubris. I probably would have moved.

Anyway, this guy didn't keep quiet like the rest of us. He started saying he wanted to be first. First guy off the bus. First guy to Vietnam. First guy to kill the "Gook" commies. He was laughing about it, like he was on a bus to summer camp. Said his father and his grandfather were both marines. It wasn't the first time I'd heard that word, but it was the first time I'd heard it uttered with such intent, to kill. It took on a completely different meaning, and it had a harsh reality; I was being sent to kill other human beings.

I wasn't sure I could do it.

At some point during all his bullshit, I fell asleep. I awoke when the bus stopped at a closed cyclone fence. A marine in starched camouflage nodded and waved the driver through. I looked at my watch. Two in the morning. The bus stopped a second time and immediately all hell broke loose. This guy in a Smokey Bear hat, green pants, and a khaki shirt rushed onto the bus screaming at the top of his lungs. We learned he was the receiving drill instructor during his two-minute tirade about how we will react and how we will respond. Dazed and disoriented from a lack of sleep, I couldn't think or clearly process what he was shouting at me except to get my ass off *his* damn bus. I was grabbing shit that wasn't even mine and rushing for the door.

When I got off the bus, two more drill instructors took turns yelling at me, calling me "shit bird," "scumbag," and "numb nuts." They told me to drop my civilian bag and put my civilian shoes on the yellow footprints painted on the concrete. I couldn't see in the dark, so I just stood next to the guy closest to me. Wrong again. The senior drill instructor got within an inch of my nose and screamed in my face, "Are you queer, numb nuts?"

"No, sir."

"How were you told to respond on the bus, you petulant pus-bag?"

Shit, I didn't remember. My mind was scrambled.

"You will begin and finish each sentence with 'sir.' Is that understood?"

"Sir, yes, sir," I shouted.

"So, you are queer?"

"Sir. No, sir!"

"You seem confused, numb nuts. Are you or aren't you queer?"

"Sir. I am not queer. Sir."

"Then move two paces to your left and put your feet on my yellow footprints."

I would have laughed if I hadn't been so terrified.

The DI kept barking conflicting orders. Whatever anyone answered, it was wrong. The big guy? This is the best part. He got off the bus like his shit didn't stink. He had this smirk on his face like it was all one big joke, and none of it applied to him. First thing he did was shove a guy off the yellow footprints like he owned them. The senior DI saw him do this. The DI is maybe five foot seven and 160 pounds. He got underneath this guy's chin. "Did you just push another recruit off my footprints, you shit bird?"

The big guy, he didn't know how to answer since the DI obviously saw him do it.

"Do you think those footprints belong to you?"

"Sir. No. Sir."

"Those are my footprints. Do you think you can push me off my footprints?"

"Sir. No, sir."

"Do you think you are better than me?"

"Sir, no, sir."

"Do you think you are better than this recruit?" He grabbed the shoulder of the guy who had been pushed and yanked him over.

"Sir. No, sir."

"You're damn right you aren't. You are worse than this recruit. You are the worst recruit on my bus. You will drop and give me fifty push-ups, numb nuts, and each time you go down, I want to hear you yell, 'These yellow footprints are not my yellow footprints. These yellow footprints are my senior drill instructor's footprints.' Can you hear me?"

"Sir. Yes, sir!"

"I can't hear you."

"Sir—"

"I gave you an order. Why have you not dropped? Drop."

As the big guy dropped, the drill instructor turned to the pushed guy and yelled at him, too. "Get your damn civilian shoes on my damn yellow footprints like I ordered you, shithead, and don't you ever allow anyone to knock you off your feet again. If you do, I will personally kick you in the ass so hard you'll be farting 'The Star-Spangled Banner' out of your mouth. Do you hear me?"

"Sir. Yes, sir."

"Do you all hear me?"

We shouted, "Sir. Yes, sir."

That's all it took. We figured the drill instructors really could make us fart out of our mouths. We stood on the yellow footprints. Then we marched, except for the big guy doing push-ups.

We marched into a receiving barracks, a Quonset hut, where we were issued a bucket with a toothbrush, razor, soap, washcloth, and other toiletries. The receiving DI advised that these were military, that we no longer owned anything civilian. We marched from one Quonset hut to the next, went through hours of processing, filled out endless forms, and took endless tests. They shaved our heads to the skull in less than a minute, then marched us into another building and told us to empty our pockets and put our personal belongings in a box. If you brought drugs or weapons but threw them in the trash, you would be forgiven. If you tried to keep them, you would be arrested. Guys threw out so much pot I could have been stoned for life.

We removed our civilian clothes and were told to put our right hand on the right shoulder of the recruit in front of us. We shuffled forward belly button to asshole. They handed me white undershirts and undershorts and gray sweatpants and a gray sweatshirt, with a number on each. They didn't ask what size. They determined my size. They wrote the same number on the back of my right hand.

When the sun rose, so did the temperature. Sweltering heat and humidity.

Sweat dripped down my face and my arms. Guys passed out from the heat, the disorientation, the lack of food and water. The number on my hand quickly smeared. Not good. I've spoken to marines who've made it home, so I know that number is who I am. I'm no longer a person. No longer an individual. I'm a number in a team of numbers.

More marching, my right hand on the right shoulder of the marine in front of me. I was told he is my brother. These recruits are all my brothers. We marched to our platoon and were turned over to our permanent drill instructor for the remainder of boot camp.

"Your mamas and your daddies are not here," he said. "For the next nine weeks, I am God."

I remember thinking, *Man, this should have been my first day of college.*

This is my life. I am eighteen years old.

CHAPTER 2

June 3, 1979

I braked, stopping my red Pinto, the one with 157,000 miles on the odometer and the threat of an exploding gas tank, at the top of the steep grade descending to an oval-shaped island my siblings and I called "the track." Immature trees and shrubs filled the center of the track, with houses built around the perimeter. My home, my parents' home, was three houses down on the left. Though a sign directed drivers to keep to the right, none of my driving-age siblings or my parents ever complied.

This night, I was seriously late. I had sobered up enough to drive after a six-pack night at a high school graduation party. I wasn't big, just five foot ten and 156 pounds dripping wet—which I had been earlier that evening after accepting a ten-dollar dare to jump into a swimming pool fully dressed. My friends pooled the money to laugh at my stupidity. I didn't disappoint. The rest of the crowd, including graduates from the Catholic girls' schools, looked at me like I was crazy or drunk. The latter had certainly been true. The former debatable.

After my plunge, I hurried inside my friend Ed

Grove's bedroom in a detached bungalow in his parents' backyard. He scrounged up a towel, gray sweatpants, and a gray Serra Padres sweatshirt, which was too big, and threw my clothes in the dryer, telling his mother that I had "fallen" into the pool.

"Our esteemed valedictorian," Lenny Mifton, who we called Mif, said as I toweled off and changed. "I'm so proud."

"You're an idiot," Ed said. Never one to mince words, he shook a mane of brown curls Hercules would have admired. "Why'd you do that?" His question was apparently rhetorical since he did not pause long enough for me to answer.

Everyone laughed, including me, though as the water sobered me, I, too, realized the idiocy of my actions.

"We should have switched awards," Ed continued. A golden gloves boxer, Ed had received the Joe Serra award from our classmates, an esteemed title bestowed upon the toughest senior. I had been awarded Most Likely to Succeed, which was a distant consolation prize at a school with a student body that venerated sports, fighting, and weekend drinking. Ed wasn't continuing on to college. In a few days he'd start work for his father.

If Ed had given me the chance, I would have told him the plunge was a simple way to pocket two tanks of gasoline, which, at fifty-nine cents

44

a gallon, was suddenly at a premium. My parents wouldn't pay for my gas since I was no longer driving myself and my younger brother to school, and I didn't have a summer job or any prospects. I had been let go from the gas station on the El Camino Real, where I had worked my junior year, when the owner could no longer pay his bills. Seemed he had dipped into the company till like it was a personal trust fund.

"Ten bucks is ten bucks," I said to Ed, Mif, and the others drinking beer in the room, though it had sounded like a lot more money before the water sobered me. I wondered what the girls thought of me. Girls were both a central thought and an afterthought. The annual proms were uncomfortable ordeals for those of us without girlfriends. My buddies and I did not want to miss out on a night together; on those nights, we believed history could be made, stories could become legends, and young men could become legendary.

That's what we told ourselves anyway. It rarely happened. Our nights together were usually a lot of beer, a lot of ripping on each other, a careful drive home, and a wicked hangover the following morning. If I'm being honest, maybe I saw jumping in the pool as a chance to stand out for something other than academics, to get a little attention and send a message that I could do the same crazy stuff as my friends. If so, I had not thought through my actions very well. If I had, I might have considered jumping in the pool at the start of the school year instead of the end, when everyone was leaving. So maybe it was just the beer.

I pulled my wallet from my back pocket before handing Ed my clothes and noticed it wasn't wet. "It's dry." I held up the wallet like a prop in a magic act. I didn't know the physics behind it, but I assumed it had something to do with jumping into the shallow end like a pencil, springing off the bottom and leaping back onto the pool's edge, beating most of the displaced water.

My friends shook their heads, unimpressed, and went back to the party.

A half hour later, my clothes dry, I drove home. Now, atop the hill, I faced a bigger challenge. It was two a.m. on a Sunday night. I didn't have a curfew; by the time I had reached my senior year my parents had either mellowed or been worn out by my four older siblings. Still, a Sunday night meant both my parents had to be awake early for work. I was looking at a world of hurt if I got caught, class valedictorian or not.

I turned off the engine but didn't lock the steering wheel. I went over my plan, largely making it up on the fly—like my plunge into the swimming pool—the prefrontal cortex of my brain that controlled decision-making, planning, and self-control still not fully cooked.

My options were limited. Option one had been to hope one of my older siblings was not yet home and throw them under the bus, deflecting most of my mother's wrath. Option one quickly dissipated, however, when I saw that the electric-blue Ford Falcon my brother John drove sat parked at the curb, and the Plymouth Duster and Honda Accord, driven by my sisters, were side by side in the driveway.

Option two was my only choice.

I released the brake and coasted the Pinto down the hill, guiding the car silently and carefully to the curb, behind the Falcon. Nothing screamed drunk driving louder than parking in front of the neighbor's driveway, four feet from the curb, or on the front lawn.

I slid free from the seat belt then reclipped it so it would not ping when I opened the door. After stepping out, I pressed the door handle button and eased the door shut, sneaking a peek at the windows and french doors of my parents' bedroom on the second floor.

No lights.

So far so good.

I crept up the brick walkway like a burglar. At the front door I took a breath, held it, and inserted the key ever so carefully. I turned the lock until it clicked.

Now I was committed. No time to waste.

I slipped inside the house and, just as carefully,

closed the door and turned the deadbolt. A thud, like someone falling out of bed, came from upstairs. This was never my father. My mother was the disciplinarian. I moved quickly to the room John and I shared at the bottom of the stairs, slipped inside, and gently closed the door. More noise. My mother had opened her bedroom door and was descending the stairs.

Busted.

I had learned from my older siblings that contrition worked far better than arguing, but contrition did not necessarily mean telling the truth. Not at two in the morning.

At the last minute I ditched contrition, flipped off my shoes, pulled back the covers, and jumped into my bed fully clothed, drawing the covers under my chin as the bedroom door opened.

"Vincent? Vincent?" my mother said in a hoarse whisper.

I responded in a voice so groggy Jason Robards would have been impressed. "What? Huh? What?"

"Are you sleeping?"

"What? Yeah." I sounded indignant. "What time is it?"

"Sorry," my mother said, retreating and closing the door.

A moment later the deadbolt rattled, one of her compulsive nightly rituals before she ascended the stairs. I'd like to say I felt bad waking my mom, then lying to her, but I was so impressed that my plan of action had worked, not to mention my acting ability, I smiled at my ingenuity.

"You're such a jackass," my older brother said from his bed.

And I knew I was not out of the woods.

Not yet.

March 12, 1968

They called it "going down south" in Okinawa.

I flew to Da Nang, Vietnam, on Braniff Airways, a Boeing 707 painted in designer colors—puce and canary yellow. That meant my DEROS (date of expected return from overseas) was April 13, 1969. Thirteen months and a wake-up.

I had survived nine weeks of boot camp and eight weeks of ITR (infantry training regiment). After recording the highest score on my MAT (marine aptitude test), I chose combat reporter as my MOS (military occupational specialty). (In the military you learn acronyms quickly. They become a second language.) The marines denied my first MOS choice, so I chose combat photographer. I figured I could build a portfolio and land a job as a photojournalist after the war, then work my way up to reporter. In the meantime, I'll keep a record of my military time in this journal, in case someday, maybe, it's worth writing about.

Ironically, my combat photographer classes were at Fort Monmouth, which is just an hour from Elizabeth. For those two months, and the thirty-day leave that followed, I got to go home and see my family before I left for Vietnam.

At boot camp I learned the history and tradition of the marines, how to march, how to polish floors, how to clean the barrack and make my rack with the covers tucked at forty-five-degree angles. I learned discipline, and when I graduated, I was a rifle-carrying marine—because every marine carries a rifle and knows how to use one. At ITR I learned how to kill. Claymore mines filled with BBs, booby traps, the M-60 machine gun, a grenade launcher, .45-caliber pistol, and the M-16 rifle. I learned jungle warfare in the Okefenokee Swamp.

I held out hope the war would end before I had to go. War protests at home had intensified, and Robert McNamara, defense secretary, had resigned. But then, in January, the North Vietnamese Army and the Viet Cong launched what they're calling the Tet Offensive. They attacked dozens of South Vietnam cities, believing the South Vietnamese would rise up against the government. They didn't. US and South Vietnamese forces repelled the monthlong offensive and inflicted devastating military losses on both the NVA and the Viet Cong. Word coming back home was we had the NVA on the run, but LBJ made overtures of peace talks instead of finishing the job. The NVA refused.

So there I sat on the final leg of what would be a twenty-hour journey to Vietnam.

Many marines on board the 707 went through boot camp and ITR with me, so we were all yelling and shouting, like we were starting a vacation and planned to raise hell. Stewardesses handed out hot dogs and Cokes. It was all fun and games until we started our descent in-country. Then everyone got quiet. Out the window I saw land. Vietnam. My future for, hopefully, the next thirteen months. It still seems surreal to be here.

But there it was.

As we descended, escort fighter jets strafed the jungle canopy of a mountain to the north of the airstrip. Marines crowded the windows to watch. An instant later the trees went up in a whoosh of black-and-orange balls of flames.

Napalm.

We erupted in cheers, and I felt a rush of adrenaline and excitement, but the smile on my face was hesitant, and similar to the smiles on most of the other faces. We were all wondering why the F-4 Phantoms were strafing the bush and dropping napalm so close to our base.

The plane landed at Da Nang with a hard jolt that would get a private pilot fired and a combat pilot a medal. Get in quick. Get out quicker. The doors opened the second the plane stopped rolling. Marines boarded and ordered us to quickly deplane, though not in such polite terms. It was just like boot camp all over, except I wasn't called "shit bird" or "numb nuts." I was called "marine." "Marines, grab your gear and haul ass. Saddle up and move out."

Apparently the airport had been under mortar attack most of the morning. Charlie was hiding on Monkey Mountain, which I assumed to be the mountain to the north of the airstrip. "We're sending out kill patrols," said a sergeant who greeted us.

I stepped to the door and the first thing to hit me was the heat, like the heat in South Carolina, but on steroids—felt like a hundred and change, with 100 percent humidity. The only time I ever felt heat like this was during a summer visit to relatives in Dallas. The airport doors slid apart, and for a moment, I couldn't breathe. The heat just sucks the air from your lungs, and you feel like you're burning from the inside out. Beads of sweat popped from every pore and rolled down my face and my forearms, making my hands slick. The uniform clung to my skin, and I realized why they gave me salt tablets and told me to take two a day, every day, no matter what.

The second thing that hit me was the smell.

My first whiff of the Nam, and it smelled like shit.

Think about it. You've got five hundred thousand men and no sewage system. The army collects the human waste in these metal barrels, soaks it in diesel and gasoline, then lights the barrels on fire. The marines who made it home called it shit detail. They said somebody has to stir the shit to ensure it burns, and when the wind shifts direction, the smell of burning shit blows right into camp, which gives all new meaning to the phrase "We're in the shit now."

CHAPTER 3

June 4, 1979

I awoke the following morning, morning being relative, with a nasty hangover. My brother had long since departed to work his summer job at the hospital, making so much noise it had to have been payback for waking him at two a.m. My father and my mother had also left for work, though I did not hear them leave. I awoke to the sound of the television in the family room down the hall. A soap opera. My three older sisters were big-time followers of *All My Children* with Susan Lucci. Summers, they alternated working as cashiers at my father's pharmacy to help pay their college tuition and updating each other about that day's episode.

I got up, stumbled to the bathroom, then made my way into the kitchen to grab a tall glass of water. Mike, my sister Maureen's boyfriend, sat on the couch in the family room eating a sandwich. He wore headphones, the cord attached to a Walkman, a portable cassette player I had heard about but never seen. Maureen was at work, but my sister Bethany sat in a chair close to the television. My younger siblings were still in school.

Mike had become a part of the family since

moving to California from New York during his junior year in high school. He spent holidays with us, often sleeping on the couch, and endured endless ribbing from me and my five brothers for his thick Long Island accent and shoulder-length blond hair. He looked like a guitarist in a rock band. I gave him a bad time, but Mike had become a big brother to me, one I looked up to. Mike never treated me like a kid. He taught me how to snow-ski in Tahoe and water-ski in the Foster City lagoons.

"Big Vinny." He removed the earphones and chuckled at my obvious condition. "Rough night? Little graduation party?"

"Shh," Bethany said.

I smiled, more interested in the portable cassette player. "Is that a Walkman?"

"I just bought it yesterday," he said.

A Walkman was two hundred dollars, which was almost the average monthly rent for an apartment in Burlingame, but Mike always had the newest things, clothes, shoes, gadgets. "What are you listening to?"

"Tom Petty," he said through a mouth full of sandwich. He handed the headphones to me.

I set down my glass of water and slipped the foam pads over my ears. Mike hit the play button and watched me for a reaction. I'd never heard music so clear—like the band was playing in the room.

"Wow," I said, a few decibels too loud.

"Shh," Bethany said again and turned up the television volume.

Mike laughed, and I handed back the headphones. "What are you doing here? I thought you were interviewing for jobs."

"Lunch break. William got me a job working on a remodel just down the hill while I interview. The foreman said they're still looking for a laborer. You interested?"

I knew William Goodman only tangentially, having watched him and Mike play softball together that spring. They played with a group of East Coast transplants living at the Northpark apartments in Burlingame. The Northpark Yankees.

"How much are they paying?" I asked, which was ballsy, given I was unemployed and had no prospects. I had worked summers since I was fourteen, all the money I earned going into the bank to pay for college. I wanted to go to Stanford and had applied at the behest of my high school counselor without telling my parents, figuring I'd never get in. But I had been accepted. It was a bittersweet moment opening the telegram the admissions office sent to our house. My mother and father, the hardest-working people I knew, simply couldn't afford four years of Stanford tuition while also paying college and professional school tuition for my four older siblings, and private school tuition for my five younger siblings. It had been too much for me to ask. I was headed to a community college with a journalism program and would reapply to Stanford before my junior year—if we could afford it and I still had the grades to get in.

Mike laughed. "More than you're making sleeping. Five bucks an hour, under the table."

That was serious money. Minimum wage was just under three bucks and you had to pay taxes. "Yeah. I'll do it."

"Get dressed."

"Today?" My head pounded.

"They're looking *now*. I already talked to Todd about you."

"Who's Todd?"

"Your boss if you don't screw it up."

I took a cold shower, which made my hangover worse, the cold water reminding my body of the abuse from the prior evening. I threw on a T-shirt and jeans and a pair of scuffed military jungle boots. I had bought the boots at an Army-Navy surplus store in San Mateo when I pumped gas at the Chevron station on the El Camino Real. Gas, I had learned quickly, ruins tennis shoes. Just eats up the rubber. The jungle boots were used, meaning priced within my budget, which was as close to free as possible. Black, with a thick sole, they gave me an inch in height and a foot in attitude. The uppers, pea-green cloth, extended six inches above my ankle.

Mike did not wait for me or leave the address, but he said the remodel was on Castillo Avenue, just three blocks east of Hillside Circle, where Hillside Drive climbed into the Burlingame Hills. "You can't miss it. You'll see my car parked in the street."

Less than two miles from home, the job location would be good for gas consumption and allow me to sleep as long as humanly possible, since I intended to make the most of my summer nights before college.

I jumped into the Pinto and drove down the hill, turning left on Castillo, and parked just past Mike's MG Midget. The sun burned bright, the temperature hovering around eighty degrees, which was warm in Burlingame for early June. I figured I'd meet Todd, get approved, and start work the following morning. Then I could go home, eat something to settle my stomach, take two more Tylenol, and go back to bed.

I didn't see anyone in the front yard, so I walked down a sloped driveway recently jack-hammered into chunks of concrete that now sat in a pile. I passed through a shaded garage to the backyard where Mike and William stood knee-deep in a three-sided rectangular trench extending off the back of the house. They wore cargo shorts and had ditched their shirts. A third man, who I deduced to be Todd, stood watching them. He didn't appear much older than Mike or William—maybe late twenties or early thirties. He combed his red hair in a pompadour, the way my dad wore his hair. A thin red beard and mustache covered much of his mouth and chin.

"Vincenzo!" William set down a pickax and greeted me in the glib manner he greeted me after softball games—smiling and with a chuckle in his voice. William had curly brown hair that extended to his shoulders and a Fu Manchu mustache, both already showing gray strands despite his being only thirty. His face was tanned and weathered from too much sun. From what Mike had told me, William was a Vietnam vet, and a free spirit who smoked a lot of pot and didn't take life or anything else too seriously.

Todd gave me a look that was less than welcoming. "You Vincent?" He flicked a toothpick from one side of his mouth to the other, displaying small teeth, like a piranha's. He didn't offer his hand, just eyeballed me up and down with his thumbs hitched at his belt. In a long-sleeve cotton shirt, jeans, and pointed cowboy boots, he looked like a Montana rancher appraising a steer. He stood a couple inches shorter than me, at least in my jungle boots, but he carried himself much bigger. Silver-framed glasses, which must have been a strong prescription, magnified his blue eyes, reminding me of my grandmother's eyes. Fair skin with freckles likely explained the long sleeves and pants.

"Yes," I said, still uncertain about the protocol, whether to extend a hand or not.

"You want a job?" Todd asked, his voice so soft I barely heard him.

"I do," I said.

"We start at seven."

"Okay." I figured I would start in the morning.

Todd now looked to be suppressing a smile, a joke only he had heard. It was like he knew I was hungover. Maybe Mike had told him?

"You got work gloves?" Todd asked.

"Yeah." I pulled a pair of my mother's gardening gloves from my back pocket. Mike had brought his work gloves up to the house and told me I would need a pair. I had hoped the gardening gloves, like the jungle boots, would help me look the part.

Todd's grin became something between derisive and disgusted. "Those aren't work gloves." He walked into the garage and rummaged through a five-gallon white bucket, handing me a pair of well-worn, stained leather gloves. "Those are work gloves." His tone made me feel like an idiot.

"I'll get a pair," I said.

Todd flicked his toothpick to the other side of his mouth. "You got a pair."

He walked to the front of the house, and I noticed he had a bowlegged gait, a cocky strut. Maybe he was trying to intimidate me? I deduced I should follow, though for what reason I did not know. Todd pointed to the busted-up concrete that had once been the driveway. I looked more closely. The chunks were about four inches thick. "You see that pile?"

"Sure," I said.

"I need it in the back, in the foundation trench."

Sounded easy enough.

Todd walked up the driveway to a gold-colored Chevy stepside truck and pulled a sledgehammer from the bed. Maybe not that easy. He handed me the sledgehammer, and I followed him into the backyard. He pointed to the trench Mike and William worked in. I noticed pieces of gray steel, maybe half an inch in diameter, bent and tied with wire to create a cage-like structure.

"The cement goes in there. No piece bigger than about this." Todd held up his hand and made a three-inch-diameter circle with his thumb and index finger. I was beginning to get the picture. No, not easy at all.

"You understand?"

I did. "Sure."

"Backfill the foundation under the rebar."

"Rebar?" I asked.

The corner of Todd's lip lifted again. Amused. "Ask William. I need it done by end of today."

I tried not to blanch.

He looked down at my shoes, then back at my face with that same bemused smile, but he didn't say another word. He sauntered through the garage to the truck, pulled himself into the cab, and fired up the engine, which gave a throaty rumble. A blast of black smoke escaped the tailpipe as he backed into the street, staring at me like I was something alien.

Well, crap. I had not anticipated this. Still feeling like hell, I slipped on my gloves and swung the sledgehammer. When the metal hammer hit the concrete, the reverberation and pain extended up my arms to my shoulders and my aching head. All I had managed to do was drive several pieces of the concrete into the dirt.

Someone laughed. William and Mike stood in the garage watching. After a moment William said, "You're not going to get far like that." He walked over. "Build a platform with those two big pieces over there."

The chunks he pointed to were flat and about a foot in length and width. I put them together. "You put a smaller piece on there." William did so. "Then let the hammer do the work." He swung it, and the hammer splintered the concrete into smaller rocks. "Otherwise you'll wear out in an hour. You got it?"

"I got it," I said.

Unfortunately, the bending and lifting in the

summer sun made me nauseated and dizzy. I stepped around the garage to the side yard and threw up what little I had in my stomach. Mike and William found amusement in my misery, but Mike handed me a plastic bottle of water the second time I walked back from the side of the house. I got a routine down and learned how to let the weight of the sledgehammer do the brunt of the work. When I had a pile of rock, I shoveled it into a wheelbarrow and pushed it into the backyard, tipping the contents into the trench. After that first load, I felt like the job would take days, not hours.

Mike and William remained busy but would occasionally stop to give me a hard time.

"You're working on the chain gang now, Vincenzo," William would say. "Swing that sledgehammer, son."

The afternoon sun beat on me. The more water I drank, the more I perspired. I had never perspired so much, not even playing sports. I took off my sweatshirt, then my shirt. Both were drenched. With my olive complexion, I didn't worry about a sunburn, and with my lack of knowledge, skin cancer would not enter my thoughts until thirty-some years later when my father was diagnosed with melanoma. I just kept beating on chunks of concrete, like I really was on a chain gang.

At three o'clock William and Mike stopped for a break. We gathered in the garage and I was grateful for the cool shade. I had concrete dust all over my forearms and my chest. I was beat, but I was also eighteen, which meant I had energy and stamina. I also had pride. I had a sense that Todd had given me a shit job thinking I was some entitled kid who would quit. When you're one of ten, you learn quickly you're not entitled to anything but the necessities, hand-me-downs, and cars with 157,000 miles on them and the possibility of exploding gas tanks. And I was no kid. I was heading off to college, and I wanted to be treated like a man.

"You smell like a brewery," William said. He handed me a Coke and squatted low, his butt nearly touching the ground.

Mike and I sat on turned-over five-gallon buckets. William and Mike smoked Marlboros. "Don't tell your sister," Mike said. My family had been after him to quit smoking given reports of a correlation between smoking and cancer. He was working on it, but I figured being around another smoker made it too hard to resist. "How's your head?" Mike asked, and he and William laughed.

I got the sense that had I not come down to the jobsite with Mike after lunch, the task of breaking up the concrete would have fallen to him.

I pointed to the rock in the driveway. "Did you have to do this stuff?"

He shook his head emphatically. "Not a chance. I told you it would be grunt labor."

"And you're the grunt." William blew out a cloud of Marlboro smoke. "Don't worry about it. I was once the grunt. Todd's testing you."

"To see if I'll quit?"

"To see if you're up to the work." William leaned his head back and blew more smoke into the air, then flicked his cigarette ashes into an empty Coors can he used as an ashtray.

"What's with him?" I asked. "He looks at me like I'm missing the joke."

William laughed. "You are the joke, Vincenzo, but it ain't personal. I was the joke once and then it was Mike. Like I said, he's just testing you."

"Did he test you?"

William shook his head. "No need. In Vietnam you're asked to do shit work all the time, and you do it."

"Did he serve in Vietnam, too?"

William nodded.

"Is that how you know him?"

"No. We served at different times and in different places."

"How long were you there?"

William paused to flick his ashes. "Thirteen months and a wake-up."

"Army?"

"Marines. Todd was army. Both of us straight out of high school. About your age."

I didn't know much about the Vietnam War. I knew it ended sometime in 1973 with peace talks, and I recalled a 1975 news film of a helicopter taking off from the rooftop of a building and leaving behind desperate South Vietnamese trying to flee the Viet Cong before they overran Saigon. I knew about the boat people as well; our parish had taken in a couple of families. I knew Vietnam was the first war the United States had lost, though we didn't really lose the war, the country just lost interest. I mean, what did we want with a country in Southeast Asia anyway? It wasn't like World War II, where the Germans had invaded countries. We'd gone in to stop the spread of communism by the Soviet Union and China, which I guess was a big deal. Just not to me. I figured if the Vietnamese wanted to live in a backward society and be told what to do and how to do it, let them. It didn't impact me.

I knew William was from someplace back east. "How did you end up out here in California?"

"Long story. Another time." William stubbed his cigarette and deposited the butt into the can, then rose seemingly without effort. "You got a sledgehammer to swing."

All afternoon I toiled in the sun, making slow but steady progress. Eventually my nausea improved, though my headache felt like someone kept tightening a vise at my temples. Mike and William built the foundation cages out of the rebar—which I learned was the gray steel bars. The rebar would support the foundation for a room at the back of the house. William said we were also adding a second story. I kept breaking up concrete and filling the trench until Todd came back with a truck bed of lumber, buckets of nails, additional rebar, and other supplies. I took a break to help Mike unload the truck and put the materials in the garage.

Todd walked past my work and gave it a simple nod. He inspected William and Mike's foundation, making a few changes, then he and William pulled out building plans and spread them on the hood of his truck, studying them while talking things over.

I kept swinging the sledgehammer, making a game out of my work to keep it interesting, but it didn't feel like I was making progress quickly enough to finish by the end of the day. I developed blisters on my hands and went into the garage to look for something to protect the skin beneath the gloves. I found a role of duct tape and wrapped strips across my palms. When I stepped from the garage, Todd looked at me, though he didn't say a word. He returned his attention to the plans, and I slipped on my gloves and went back to work.

Todd left the jobsite at four—William said to finish a tile job in Burlingame. William and Mike took off their tool belts at five, cracked cans of beer, and smoked in the garage.

"Vinny," William called out. "Come have a beer."

I had more concrete to break up, but I could finally see a light at the end of the long, dark tunnel. Besides, I could not pass up a cold beer. "Hair of the dog," as my friends liked to say, and a chance to maybe bond and be accepted as part of the crew. I again upended a five-gallon bucket and sat. William squatted, his forearms resting on his knees. He handed me a can of Coors from a small cooler.

"How can you sit like that?" I cracked open the beer and took a slug.

"Hours of practice," William said. "And fear of sitting on something that might explode or bite you in the ass." He blew smoke into the air and laughed his nervous chuckle. "How do you like the job so far?" He sounded facetious, but I didn't want him to think the work was getting to me.

"It's okay." I looked at my pile. "Why are we reusing the concrete? Why not just dump it?"

"The rock gives the concrete we're pouring something to bind to. Makes it stronger. That and the more we backfill, the less concrete we need." William flicked his ashes into the makeshift ashtray. Though young, he had a smoker's voice, deep and gravelly, to go with the wrinkles and the spots of gray in his hair and mustache. "Todd underbid the job and is trying to save money. You didn't hear that from me."

"He knows he underbid it already?" Mike asked.

William chuckled. "Shit. He bid it in three days and he was the lowest bid by thirty thousand. Yeah, he knows."

"Why did he bid it so fast?" Mike asked.

"He needed the work." William blew out smoke. "He's finishing another job and didn't have anything else lined up. He's out bidding more tile jobs—kitchens and bathrooms—to try to make up some of the anticipated loss."

"How big is the rest of his crew?" I asked.

"You're looking at his crew," William said. "We'll get pulled to other jobs when we get this place buttoned up for the subs."

I wasn't sure what that meant, but not wanting to look naive, I let it go.

After another cigarette, William and Mike got up to go home. I looked at what remained of the pile of concrete. I only had another hour or two and didn't want Todd to think I'd ignored his directive to get it done.

"It will be there tomorrow," William said.

"Todd said it needed to get done today."

William smiled. "We ain't pouring concrete tomorrow. He canceled the pump truck. The foundations haven't been inspected yet by the city, and even if the city got here in the morning, which they won't, it'll be too hot to pour in the afternoon."

I looked again at the pile that remained and thought of William's comment that Todd was testing me. Okay. I'd pass his test. "I can get it done in another hour."

"Suit yourself." William showed me how to pull down and padlock the garage door when I finished. He emphasized the importance of this since the garage held our tools and building supplies. Then he and Mike took off.

I finished at six thirty, dead tired, my hands blistered beneath the duct tape. Todd never returned. I had no idea if I had passed his test or not. Or if he even cared.

But I wasn't going to make it easy for him to fire me.

April 1, 1968

From Da Nang I flew to Chu Lai, a Marine Corps air base located near Tam Ky, the largest city in the Quang Nam Province. I spent a week in the combat center and was immediately told to pretty much forget everything I learned in boot camp and at ITR. At the combat center I learned real guerilla warfare: how to pitch grenades, how to walk through minefields and use a mine sweep, how to walk through the bush in sweltering heat they said would get worse, how to jump from a helicopter hovering off the ground and belly crawl through sniper fire, and how to identify booby traps and areas susceptible to ambush.

When finished, we filled out yet more forms and rosters and got assigned to fire teams. I showed the supply sergeant my combat photographer ID, and he helped me secure a 35 mm Pentax Spotmatic kit, which included 55 mm and 135 mm lenses and three rolls of thirty-six exposure Tri-X film. The supply sergeant also got me my combat gear—rifle, flak jacket, ammunition, helmet, helmet camouflage cover, poncho, poncho liner, rucksack, clean utilities, cigarettes, and candy, which comes in C rations. I told the supply sergeant I wouldn't need the rifle, just the .45, and that I didn't smoke and wouldn't need cigarettes. He stared at me with a queer smirk on his face, then yelled past me to the first sergeant in an adjacent room. "Private William Goodman claims he is a marine but will not need a rifle or cigarettes."

"Ask Private Goodman if he plans to invite Charlie into his foxhole for a game of Parcheesi and intends to smoke bamboo shafts as he negotiates Charlie's surrender."

"Charlie," I knew, was another derogatory term for our enemy. More psychological bullshit so we would kill without remorse. "Private Goodman, do you plan to invite Charlie into your foxhole for a game of Parcheesi and intend to negotiate his surrender smoking bamboo shafts?"

"No, Sergeant. I'll take the rifle and the cigarettes."

"Private Goodman is learning, First Sergeant."

"Tell Private Goodman, 'Oorah!' "

The first sergeant further advised that

because of Tet casualties, companies were understrength. Due to my shooting marks at ITR and at the combat center, I would be embedded with the Ninth Regiment at forward Firebase Phoenix, located at five thousand feet in the Central Highlands along the Laotian border. I had expected to be stationed at the Da Nang Combat Information Center and given assignments to fly in and out of locations, taking ceremonial photographs of dignitaries and base openings, not combat operations in the bush.

I was shipped by helicopter with four other marines to Firebase Phoenix, a spit of dirt with a landing zone. Atop the hill are radio antennas, mortars, 105 mm howitzers with beehive rounds, and other mass antipersonnel defensive weapons like .50-caliber machine guns. Hooches, canvas tents with wood-stick-and-sandbag walls, have been built below the hill.

I reported to Captain Dennis Martinez, the commanding officer of Charlie Company. Captain Martinez assigned me to a rifle team in the one-three—First Platoon, Third Squad. My squad leader is Corporal Victor Cruz, a Puerto Rican from Spanish Harlem, New York, serving his second tour of duty. Cruz is called Clemente because he resembles the Pittsburgh Pirates baseball great. His head is shaved except for a patch of growth along the crown, and the tips of his ears are pointed like a pit bull's. He found me a rack in his bunker with six other guys, also from the East Coast, and told me my bunk was vacated by a marine who reached his DEROS and returned home.

"That's good luck," he said, leaving the alternative unspoken.

I feel sort of like a high school freshman on the varsity wrestling team. The other marines aren't unfriendly, but they also see me as lower than whale shit. Cruz told me the squad, platoon, and company have suffered significant casualties. The squad is down to eight marines from the standard thirteen, which explains what I am doing here. However, I have yet to fire a rifle in combat or step outside the wire, which is why they call me Cherry and FNG (fucking new guy).

Cruz also told me a supply helicopter brought news that President Johnson has put a halt to the bombing of targets north of the twentieth parallel, and they're all pissed because they believe the bombing would have destroyed the NVA and the Viet Cong supply and escape routes.

Meaning they might have gotten to go home.

"Morale right now is not good," Cruz said. "So don't come in here with a gung-ho GI Joe attitude."

No problem there, Corporal.

Cruz advised that because of the moratorium, no marines at Firebase Phoenix are going outside the wire. He said President Johnson is trying to entice the north with not-so-confidential peace talks. He then cackled and said the whole thing is a joke, a publicity stunt to appease the protestors back home.

"Don't worry about it though. I'll make sure you get outside the wire and get your feet wet as soon as possible, so you're not sitting around worrying about it."

Again, don't go to any trouble on my account, Corporal.

Cruz told me that up here in the triple canopy, we won't be fighting the VC—the ragtag Viet Cong who do mostly hit-and-runs. Up here, along the Laotian border, we'll get the NVA First Division, who Cruz described as determined and well trained. "They'll hit us with ambushes that are sudden, violent, and deadly, and they will stand and fight. So will we."

Well, shit.

"Stow your stuff and I'll show you around the firebase."

I grabbed my camera and headed out from the bunker with Cruz. Marines were playing guitars, getting stoned, and drinking beer. The military banned marijuana, but the sweet smell was everywhere. At first, everyone was leery of my camera, but after I explained I was a marine photographer, they let their guard down. Some even encouraged me to take their picture smoking weed and being out of uniform.

"What they gonna do, send me to the Nam?" was the common refrain.

Someone had cut a metal drum in half and they were using it to barbecue steaks, which Cruz explained were flown in that morning as a morale booster. The atmosphere was like a somber summer camp. We were all the same age and we were wearing the same clothes, though not in the same way. Some guys had cut the sleeves from their shirts. Others were shirtless. One guy was wearing shorts. We were just guys hanging out. No pretenses. No one trying to impress. Just being. Existing. After months of having every minute scheduled, just hanging out was a relief.

"Yeah, we're grunts," Cruz said, "but we take pride in being grunts. You dig?"

I nodded.

"Okay, first lesson. In my squad you do not talk about home when you're in-country. You don't even think about it. It's bad luck. *Comprende*?"

"*Comprende*."

"Second lesson. You don't discuss how much time you have left in-country."

"Okay," I said and thought of the calendar my mother gave me to mark off the days until I returned home. I had put it on a nail in the post by my rack.

Cruz and I continued to wander, and he continued to educate. "Inside the wire it can be long hours doing nothing day after day. It becomes monotonous. You forget the day of the week and sometimes the month 'cause it don't matter. You have nothing scheduled and nothing urgent to do. You start to think the only thing you're going to die from over here is boredom. But don't be fooled." He used his cigarette to point to the hooches. "Look a little closer," he said. "You notice anything?"

"They're empty."

"Damn straight. Officers use them during the day. Not at night."

In between each hooch, there was a trench in the ground surrounded by sandbags. The bunkers. "No one sleeps above ground. You don't tempt fate. Next lesson. Look at the perimeter."

I looked to the thick green bush that surrounded the firebase in every direction, and I saw rolls of concertina wire.

"The wire and the claymores are to keep Charlie out," Cruz said. "The trip flares on the wire are to let us know if Charlie decides to pay us a visit."

"Does he?" I asked.

Cruz laughed. "First month here, Charlie was inside the wire the first night. The next day, after they flew out the dead, they couldn't find where Charlie came through the wire. He didn't trip no flares. He didn't cut no wire. A mystery. A week later Charlie came again. More killed. This time they found a tunnel entrance, inside the wire."

"He dug under?" I asked.

Cruz laughed and shook his head. "They built the damn firebase on top of a whole series of tunnels already here."

We kept walking. I saw crude holes scratched into the red clay and rock, about two meters apart and reinforced with sandbags. Foxholes. One had a .50-caliber machine gun. Cruz saw me staring and grinned, though it wasn't really a grin. It was just a small upturn at the corners of his mouth, like I amused him. I realized he was laughing at me, at my naivete. "You'll learn, Shutter," he said.

"Shutter? At Da Nang, combat photographers were called Shooter."

Cruz laughed. "Hey, Bean," he called out to a shirtless marine filling sandbags with dirt. "What do you say? Shutter or Shooter?"

Bean is a large Black guy I met in our bunker. He flicked the butt of his cigarette. "We had a photographer in camp about a month ago," Bean said. "I didn't see him do no shooting, Corporal Cruz. So I say Shutter."

Cruz shrugged like that's the end of it. My name, what everyone will call me from here on out, had been decided.

I spent the rest of the afternoon doing a PMCS (preventive maintenance check) of my camera, drinking Pabst Blue Ribbon, and eating steak.

The sun lowered, a brilliant orange ball I photographed just before it slipped below the tree line. I put away my camera. It wasn't the beauty that struck me, it was the silence the sunset brought. Everyone and everything got quiet, tense, like something was about to happen. The bush outside the wire shimmered and buzzed; I swear I could hear it breathing, billions of insects beating their wings. The tree leaves shook, but I didn't feel a breeze. Eerie.

As darkness fell, I sat outside the bunker with the others shooting the shit. In the distance we could hear the boom of artillery fire and the occasional pop of M-60 machine gun fire. Cruz said it was likely another firebase probing their perimeter. As I started to relax, I heard a whistle, and in the time it took me to turn toward the sound, Cruz had yelled "Incoming" and shoved me into the bunker as the first loud explosion detonated. The ground rocked and shuddered, like an earthquake. Inside the bunker, dust fell from the ceiling beams. My adrenaline spiked. My breathing quickened. My joints tingled with anticipation.

"You just got another lesson, Shutter," Cruz said, smiling. I could barely hear him. It felt like my ears were plugged with water.

He spoke louder. "Charlie comes at night."

CHAPTER 4

June 4, 1979

High school had been a crucible of eight hundred young men from different cities, different socio-economic backgrounds, different cultures, and different races competing to wear the blue-and-gold uniform and earn the right to fight side by side against our perceived enemies. Those of us who did not make the athletic cut became rear support. We learned instead the intricacies of each cheer and each fight song, and we shouted them out to our brothers on the battlefields, believing those cheers mattered not just to us, but to the rest of the world.

They didn't.

And in a few months, I was sure they would not matter to me, or to many of the young men I had gone to school with. I'd watched my brother John drift apart from his high school friends; and guys in the class ahead of me, who swore they'd be best friends for life, did not even speak. My friends and I were also going our separate ways, some of us to college, some into the workforce, a few into the military. We would make new friends, get jobs, get married, have kids, move away. We would all invariably change. Some of us for the worse. Some for the better. But all certainly different. It seemed odd to think that the guys I'd spent every day with for the past four years, guys I'd studied with, taken tests with, played some sports with, and worked with on the newspaper, would soon be only a memory.

It was why, when I returned home from work, I allowed my friends to talk me into going to the drive-in theater in Burlingame. I was dog tired from the concrete work, and I had initially rejected the idea, but they hounded me until I relented.

"It's our last summer together," Mif said, in a tacit admission that he, too, recognized change was coming. "Come on, you'll be home by midnight."

I doubted the veracity of that last statement, but Mif was earnest. Eric Capitola, who we called Cap, wasn't so diplomatic. He called and questioned my manhood, my gender, and my sexuality, which was how we usually attacked one another.

In the end, I figured sitting in a car watching a movie wasn't much different than sitting at home watching TV. Plus, I could drink beer. Billy Holland lived close by, and since the Pinto was a hatchback and prevented us from hiding anyone, I didn't have to drive. Billy picked me up in his parents' station wagon. We met Mif and Cap, along with Ed and Mickey, each with a carload of our friends, in the parking lot behind a warehouse on the road weaving along San Francisco Bay. We met for two reasons. One was to hide as many guys as we could. The second was to meet Scotty, a graduate who worked in a liquor store and had purchased beer for us. We settled with Scotty, then Mif and Cap hid under the tarp in the back of the station wagon.

Who got to hide was always hotly debated. Ideally, we were to split the cost of the movie four ways, but it was never that simple getting restitution from unemployed young men. Someone always owed someone for beer bought a prior weekend, or for the cost of a burger at a drive-through. The minutiae got ridiculous, and some nights the argument would continue throughout the movie. The only real leverage we had if someone refused to pay his share was to not let him out of the trunk of the car, which could be a problem when you're trying to be sneaky and a loud voice is screaming from the trunk.

We usually just ended up eating the difference and taking turns hiding.

We had also argued over seeing *Alien* or some film called *The Prisoner of Zenda*. I voted for *Zenda*, knowing that *Alien* would lose much of its tension playing on a mammoth outdoor screen, the sound nasal and faint through a squawk box, while four of us argued over inane subjects—our stupidity a direct correlation to the number of beers we drank. This night, I drank slowly, the self-inflicted punishment I had endured at work still vivid. I also had to be at the job by seven. If I still had a job. I figured I'd have a few beers, watch *The Prisoner of Zenda*, which did not start off very good, go home, and go to sleep. I'd bring the leftover beer and put it in William's cooler, which I hoped would both ingratiate me with the guys and make them see me as more than just Mike's kid brother.

From the back seat, in the midst of some inane conversation, Cap said, "Holland, give me one of your beers."

"I'm not giving you one of my beers. You still owe me for the movie."

"Come on, just give me a beer."

"Drink your own," Billy said.

"I did."

"You drank a six-pack already?" I asked. Not believing Cap, I turned and looked over the back of the front seat at empty cans littering the floor, along with the empty cardboard box. "Holy crap."

"What?" Cap said. "How many do you have left?"

"Four, and I just cracked the second."

"What, are you nursing up there?"

"I'm drinking like a normal person. How have you not had to pee?"

"Don't mention peeing," Mif said. "We'll all have to go."

"Yeah, we wouldn't want to miss the plot of the movie," Billy said. He'd voted for *Alien*.

"Vinny B., let me have a beer," Cap said, turning his attention to the guy with the most.

"I was going to bring them down to the jobsite tomorrow. They keep a cooler and drink beer after work."

"Wait a minute." Mif laughed. "They're paying you and giving you beer? Do they need another laborer?"

"Shit, I'll do that job," Cap said. "Give me a beer, Vinny B., come on."

I handed back the remains of my six-pack. It was easier than arguing the rest of the night.

Cap immediately appropriated the box. "What do you want for them?"

"Nothing."

"Bullshit."

"I can't drink them. I told you, I got to work in the morning. Just leave me a couple to put in the cooler so I don't look like a mooch."

"Like Cap," Billy said.

"Where are you working?" Mif asked.

"A remodel in Burlingame. Five bucks an hour under the table."

"What?" Mif's voice again rose in inflection and volume. "Seriously, can you get me a job?"

"It's a small crew."

"Ask them if they got any more openings. Five bucks an hour and beer." Mif also came from a large family and, like me, what he made went toward paying his college tuition. Unlike me, he was not headed to a community college, but to Cal Berkeley to play rugby. Billy was headed to Santa Clara to play baseball and Cap would play baseball at San Diego State. I felt like the odd man out. For the graduation brochure, I'd opted to put "undecided" beside my name as my college choice, too embarrassed to put "community college."

"I could have used you today." I told them what my job had been. "I threw up twice and nearly passed out."

"Our esteemed editor in chief, jumping in pools fully dressed and throwing up on the job," Mif said.

"I got to piss." Cap shoved open the back door.

"You think?" Billy said. "Your back teeth must be floating."

"Damn it," Mif said. "Now I got to piss. I told you not to talk about it."

I reached for the door handle, but Billy stopped me. "You've only had one beer."

"You're telling me I can't pee?"

"Come on, man, don't leave me here alone. People will think I'm beating off to Peter Sellers."

I laughed and shut the door. Billy and I could

hear Ed singing Serra fight songs outside the car. Billy looked out his window and laughed. I looked over. Ed was doing push-ups in the parking lot.

"Great," I said. "That shouldn't attract any attention."

An explosion echoed on the pavement. "M-80," Billy said. "A quarter of a stick of dynamite." Smoke filtered between two rows of cars to our left. Overhead, five or six bottle rockets exploded, leaving red-and-white trails before snapping and popping near the movie screen. Horns honked.

"When does Santa Clara start?" I asked Billy.

"Orientation is late August."

"You get a roommate yet?"

"Nah. Later in the summer."

I envied my friends going off to college, even if they were not traveling very far. I envied them having just a single roommate. I had shared a room big enough for two with three of my brothers—until my parents added on a family room at the back of the house and turned the downstairs room into a bedroom. I got it after my three older sisters and John moved on to college.

"My brother John had a roommate at Davis who became catatonic and cut off his hand," I said.

"Bullshit."

"Swear to God."

"He cut off his hand? That's impossible. He'd pass out before he finished."

"No. He put it on a train track."

"Oh shit."

"I know. Right? At least my brother had a room to himself for half the year."

"And nightmares," Billy said.

Ed sang the "Padre Whisper," a fight song that culminated in his spelling out "P-A-D-R-E-S" at the top of his lungs. Our friends in the two adjacent cars were now sufficiently inebriated to join in the chorus. People yelled at them to shut up, which only caused our friends to yell louder. More bottle rockets went off over cars and another M-80 exploded nearby. I had experienced this too many times to not know how it was going to end.

Car doors flew open and grown men stepped from their cars. I couldn't blame them, but in a pack about to get in a fight, you take on a pack mentality.

"Just once I'd like to actually see the movie," I said and pushed open the door.

"This movie sucks anyway," Billy said. "At least this will be entertaining."

The unwritten code mandated you didn't stay in your car when your buddies got in a fight. You backed them up. That was easier for Cap and Mif, who had played football and were well over six feet and more than two hundred pounds. Mif had stunned the Serra weight room that year by being the first student to bench press more than three hundred pounds. Neither of them, however, was anywhere near the car at the moment, and Billy and I were no match for the four lumberjacks coming down the aisle.

Ed sang, largely ignoring the approaching platoon. Mickey Giusti, who had driven the second car, and Pat O'Flynn, who didn't care if the Forty-Niners' offensive line approached, always welcomed a fight.

It started with the usual. "You're a bunch of punks."

"What did you say?"

"You heard me."

And it escalated from there.

Ed still looked largely disinterested. He laughed and continued to sing Serra fight songs, which elicited the obvious and unimaginative refrains from our enemies that we were all homos and faggots. Big mistake. Nothing was more sacred at an all-male high school than loyalty to one's school and protecting one's sexuality.

Punches flew.

The fight became a brawl.

Billy and I largely stayed on the periphery, out of the melee, while trying to look like we were in the thick of the battle. This was an art form we had learned over four years. The goal was not to get punched in the face and get your nose broken, or lose a tooth, but to become disheveled enough to make the others believe you were in the fight.

As the fight developed, we watched to see if anyone got knocked down, in which case it would be our duty to jump his opponent. I was looking over my shoulder, hoping to see Mif and Cap returning, when one of the lumberjacks pointed at Ed. "I want the loudmouth doing push-ups."

Big mistake.

Ed got to his feet and smiled, which I thought stunned the lumberjack. The guy should have taken the hint and left, but now committed, he stepped into a left jab and a right cross that dropped him like a bag of cement. Ed then slid into the heart of the battle. A few more combinations and two more guys went down. The fourth guy separated from Pat O'Flynn, who had pulled the guy's shirt over his head and pummeled him. I thought it a great skill, one I hoped to never have to use, but which might come in handy someday.

Bright lights from the stanchions flooded the concrete lot, the film stopped, and even louder protests erupted. People wanted us thrown out. Drive-in security came running, high school guys with flashlights who were not looking for a fight when getting paid less than three bucks an hour. They just called the Burlingame police.

To underage boys with open beer cans in their cars, this was an alarm to flee. Billy and I rushed back to his car. By this time Mif and Cap had returned from the bathroom. We didn't have time to explain what had happened, and they didn't really need us to. They, too, knew the drill all too well. They flung themselves into the back seat. Billy tossed the speaker hanging from the window, and I chucked empty and semiempty beer cans out of the car as Billy backed down the cement rise.

"That one's full," Cap said.

"Screw that," Billy said. "They called the police."

I threw the can out the window and looked for others.

"Throw out the rest of the six-pack," Billy shouted over his shoulder at Cap.

"No way," Cap said.

We approached the exit. Billy pled, "I'm serious, Cap. Get rid of the beer."

"I'm not wasting them."

"You didn't even buy them."

"I hear sirens," Mif said.

"Lights," I said, and pointed to police coming around the perimeter road.

"Stop the car," Cap said.

"No way. I'm not—"

"Stop the car." Cap had the door open like he was about to jump. Billy stopped the car, and Cap got out clutching what remained of the six-pack. He ran for the cyclone fence that enclosed the drive-in and hid until the cop cars drove around the bend in the road behind the movie screen.

"What the hell is he doing?" I said.

Cap tossed the beer over the cyclone fence, beer cans falling from the pack like hand grenades. He then threw his jacket over a strand of barbed wire atop the fence and followed the beer, getting his jeans stuck for a moment before falling over the side, much to our glee.

"He ripped his pants." Mif laughed.

We reached the exit as the police cars sped toward us from the opposite direction, then thankfully blew past. Mif had his head turned, looking out the back window for our friends.

"Are they coming?" I asked.

"Not yet. Wait. I see Mickey's truck."

When we drove the road around to the back of the gigantic movie screen, Cap emerged from behind one of the wood struts holding it up and stepped into the road holding the remains of the six-pack. Billy slowed and Mif flung open the back door. Cap tossed the six-pack inside. Big mistake. Never let the beer go first. Billy wanted retribution for Cap refusing to give up the beer and for refusing to split the cost of the movie. As Cap attempted to jump in, Billy hit the gas. The car lurched forward, and Cap barely got out of the way. Billy and Cap played this cat and mouse game twice more. Ordinarily, Cap would have given up, but we now had the beer. Still, with police to consider, Cap jumped into the back of Mickey's truck.

We decided it best to hide out in the parking lot behind the warehouse until the police left the area. We popped beers, our adrenaline pumping, and sped away like thieves in the night, laughing and shouting the "Padre Whisper" at full volume—heroes who had never thrown a punch, never gotten hit, never been in danger. Never in the fight. None of that would stop us from embellishing the story at school to those who had not been present. We would tell them we were right in the thick of the battle. We would relate how Ed had dropped three guys, each with a combination of punches. Bam. Bam. Bam. We'd laugh about how Cap had saved the beer, then had foolishly given it up, and how Billy had driven past screaming police sirens and flashing lights as calm as a man on his way to Sunday mass.

Except . . . as we regrouped in the warehouse parking lot, I realized there wouldn't be another day at school to share our story. We had only ourselves to bullshit and that was nowhere near as much fun. Graduation had done what none of us would do on our own; it had shattered our glass illusion of who we were. Everything that had happened in high school was now in my past, and none of it would matter to the people I would meet in college.

At some point I stepped away from the group to contemplate this. I sat on the hood of Billy's station wagon at the edge of the bay. In the distance, lights shimmered in the high-rise buildings of downtown San Francisco and reflected off the dark water's calm surface. Overhead, lights flashed as airplanes approached the San Francisco Airport runways.

As my friends recounted our night, the enemy got bigger, increased in number, and became more fierce in their attack. But what struck me was that we had just provoked a fight that served absolutely no purpose and for no good reason. We paid for a movie we didn't see and beer we didn't drink, and we disrupted the night of hundreds of others.

For what?

I turned at the sound of approaching footsteps in gravel. Mif had two beers in hand, one opened. Of all my friends, Mif was the most in tune with me, and the most honest. He was also a paradox. A man who could bench press more than three hundred pounds at eighteen, run a five-minute mile, and hit opposing players like a ton of bricks, he was also the first to pick them up, pat them on the back, and shake their hand.

He held out the unopened beer. "Nah," I said, no longer interested in getting drunk just to get drunk. "I got to work in the morning."

"What's going on?" Mif asked, but in a soft

voice that told me he already knew what was going on, because he, too, had walked away from the crowing and the boasting.

"Nothing," I said. "Just thinking about what's next."

He slid onto the hood and stared out at the same lights, and in that moment of silence, I knew he, too, had no idea, though he did know change was definitely coming.

April 7, 1968

It just got real.

I was in a foxhole with Kenny. We rotated into Firebase Phoenix together, which I guess is why we were paired together. Cruz wanted to get us experience. He was going to put me with Bean, but Bean protested. There's been some racial tension at the firebase since we learned from a resupply helicopter pilot that Martin Luther King Jr. had been assassinated. Cruz told me it will blow over in a few days, but I'm not so sure. Morale seems to be at an all-time low.

Inside our foxhole I had my M-16 rifle and my .45 and several additional magazines. I also had frag grenades. My Ka-Bar was hanging from the suspenders of my war belt for easy access. I didn't have my camera since I couldn't take photographs at night. I tried to tell Cruz I was embedded as a marine photographer, that I was here to document the war and get classified photographs for the D-II shop back in Da Nang.

Cruz laughed and gave me the same

look the supply sergeant gave me, like I keep missing the joke. "You go to boot camp, Shutter?"

"Yeah."

"Your primary MOS is 0311, infantry rifleman, just like the rest of us grunts."

"Yeah, but I'm also—"

"A marine photographer. Yeah, I know, but it's your secondary MOS, not your primary. You're a marine, Shutter. You're a grunt, a stone-cold killer, just like the rest of us." Cruz let loose another of his cackles. "There ain't no senators' sons here in the bush, Shutter; that's why we're in the bush. You're a brother now. We're all brothers. We all got the same skin color. You'll see."

Well, shit, I thought for the third time. I thought my photographs would get published on the front page of *Stars and Stripes* and would someday be my portfolio to land me a job at the *New York Times*. I didn't think I'd be pulling guard duty.

I looked at Kenny in the fading light, and I thought, *The blind leading the blind.* Kenny told Cruz he hunted in Kentucky and he's itching to shoot a couple of Gooks. Cruz looked at him with an expression that was part derision, part disparagement. "Take it easy, Haybale," Cruz said. "Just keep your head down and try not to get yourself killed."

Haybale. Shutter was sounding better and better.

But Kenny was amped on adrenaline. He was all gung ho, apple pie, and God bless America. I was spending my first night on guard duty in a hole with private Gomer Pyle.

Cruz smiled. "Look. Don't be heroes."

I thought of the last words my mother said to me before I boarded the bus to South Carolina. *Don't be a hero. Don't stand out. Just blend in. Blend in and come home.*

"If Charlie comes through the wire, he'll trip a flare. If he trips the flare, guys will set off the claymores and the machine guns will end it. You stick your rifle over the sandbags and spray at the wire. You do not stick your head up like you're fucking John Wayne storming Omaha Beach. You get me? That's just bullshit. You got that?"

"Yes, sir," Haybale said.

"And don't call me 'sir.' And you damn well better not salute me. Charlie kills the officers. I'm Cruz or Clemente. Take your pick." Kenny and I both nodded. "If your

M-16 jams, throw your grenades." Cruz turned to leave.

"The M-16 jams?" I asked, uncertain I'd heard Cruz correctly. I still couldn't hear well out of my left ear from the shelling the prior night. Cruz said it would pass.

"Hell yeah, it jams. Didn't they teach you boys anything? Hand me your magazines." We did as instructed and Cruz started removing bullets. "It's a thirty-round magazine, but thirty puts too much pressure on the spring, so you remove two rounds, which relieves the pressure, and it will work just fine."

He handed me back my magazine, and I pulled out my other magazines to do the same.

"Sleep in two-hour shifts," Cruz said. "You both go to sleep, you both might die, along with the rest of us. If we all happen to live, I'll be the first to kill you."

I nodded.

"You got that, Haybale?"

Kenny nodded. "Yes, sir."

Cruz again rolled his eyes. "And no smoking. You flick a lighter and it might be the last thing you do. Charlie shoots at the light."

I knew I wouldn't sleep, and I figured there was no way Haybale would. He looked like he could run, and win, an Olympic marathon. It wasn't drugs, either. Haybale told me on the transport that he didn't drink or smoke. He said he was going through his tour sober so he could remember every minute, tell the family back home. Staying sober sounded smart; I thought it might also help keep me alive. Not sure about the remembering every minute though; there are already parts I'd like to forget.

Cruz started to leave. "That's it?" I asked, thinking our welcome to the bush was *Don't be John Wayne, because that's just bullshit.*

Cruz smiled. "OJT, Shutter." On-the-job training. He laughed. "Relax. Charlie hasn't come to the wire for weeks. It's mostly hit-and-run shit and random sniper fire. Keep your head down and it'll be over in five minutes. We don't use passwords and counterpasswords out here because Charlie has big ears, but given you're new and I don't want to get shot, the password for tonight is 'Penny.' The counterpassword is 'Lane.' "

I didn't know if Charlie not coming for weeks was good news or bad news. I guessed we'd find out.

I told Haybale I'd take first watch,

figuring he wouldn't sleep and would keep me company. He took out a poncho, tucked it tight all around his body, then pulled it over his head, including his face, and put his helmet on. "What are you doing?" I asked.

He pulled down the plastic. "Guys told me the rats over here are big as cats and would give a dog a good fight. Said they come right up when you're sleeping and take a hunk of flesh out of your face."

I didn't know if that was truth or urban myth to scare the FNGs. I couldn't imagine Vietnamese rats being bigger than New York City rats, or any meaner. Didn't matter though. Haybale had put the idea of getting a chunk of flesh ripped from my face into my head. So much for sleeping. He, on the other hand, was out in seconds. I could hear him snoring. All Charlie had to do was follow the slumbering *z*'s to find our foxhole.

As the light faded, I waited for the moonlight but instead got a deepening darkness until I couldn't see my hand in front of my face. It was so dark I felt like I'd been struck blind.

Blind, still partially deaf from the shelling the other night, with a gun that jams instead of a camera that shoots, and Private Haybale Pyle sound asleep beside me.

And I was on guard. Well, shit.

CHAPTER 5

June 5, 1979

The morning after the drive-in, I awoke at six thirty, pulled the jungle boots from the closet, then remembered Todd's scornful and bemused look. I put them back. I hadn't bought them as a statement. I just didn't want to ruin my tennis shoes. The used jungle boots had been affordable; steel-toed work boots were too expensive on my limited budget. As I reasoned and rationalized, I had a morbid thought. Why were the boots used? Had someone just traded them in, or had the person who had worn them died?

I set the boots down with a different appreciation of Todd's scornful look; someone who had worn those boots every day for a year, under the conditions Todd and William had worn them, likely didn't appreciate some punk high school kid using them as a fashion statement.

I put on my white Converse high-tops instead.

I didn't know if I was getting dressed for work or to just pick up my one-day paycheck, but I figured twenty-five dollars was twenty-five dollars and I had passed Todd's test. I left home at a quarter to seven, wanting to be on time . . . if I still had a job.

I arrived at the jobsite before anyone else. Since I knew the padlock combination on the garage door, I unlocked it. Not sure what to do, I put on the leather gloves Todd had given me and picked up stray pieces of rebar, organizing them by size. I put other tools and supplies in the white five-gallon buckets, and with the garage floor relatively clear of debris, I picked up the push broom and swept until a throaty rumble announced the Chevy's arrival. Todd parked in front of the house and came down the dirt driveway with his toothpick in place. He stopped to look about, then came into the garage and did the same thing. Finally, he looked at me.

"William said you stayed late to finish up."

"I didn't get it all done by five."

"I know. I came back to make sure you locked up."

Which meant he didn't trust me to do it right.

"Well." He cleared his throat and shifted the toothpick. I fully expected to be fired. "I figure a guy who would hump concrete in the hot sun all day is willing to work hard. You want a job?"

It took me a moment to find my voice. "Yes, sir."

"Don't call me 'sir.' My name's Todd."

"Okay."

Todd smiled, this time like I had no idea what I was getting into. He turned on the heels of his boots and walked to the front yard. I followed.

He removed the toothpick and used it to point to the roof of the house. "I'm going to need you to tear off the roof." Todd explained we were adding a second story to the single-story home. "I don't have a harness, so you're going to have to do it from inside the attic."

"Okay." I assumed a harness was something I'd wear to keep from falling off the roof. The pitch was steep. I still wondered how I'd remove the shingles from the inside.

Todd returned to the garage and grabbed a crowbar. "Grab the Sawzall," he said.

He spared me further embarrassment by pointing to a machine that looked like a sawed-off shotgun with a long blade at the end. William had used it the day before. The blade cut like a handsaw on speed.

"You ever used one before?" Todd asked.

"No."

He plugged the saw into an extension cord and gave me a fifteen-second crash course. Seemed simple enough. I grabbed the saw and the extension cord and followed Todd through the kitchen door into the house. The family that owned the property had moved out during the remodel. In the hallway, Todd pulled down a collapsible ladder using a string hanging from the ceiling. I followed him up the rungs into the attic. A single bulb attached to one of the rafters provided a dull light. Though it was still early morning, the temperature already bordered on hot and the air, suffocating. I could only imagine how hot the attic would get in the heat of the day and how difficult it would be to breathe.

Todd moved to the pitch of the roof, which was only about five feet in height and required that we hunch over. "You tear out the insulation," he said. The insulation looked like pink cotton candy with a brown paper backing stapled between the roof joists. "Then you punch a hole in the shingles using the crowbar. Once you've removed the insulation and knocked off the shingles and tar paper, you can use the Sawzall to cut the one-by-four slats, then the roof joists. Got it?"

"Got it," I said, realizing I wasn't just removing the shingles but the entire roof.

"Don't kill yourself or cut off a finger. I'm not bonded, and I don't have health insurance."

I wasn't sure what that meant or what to say, so I just said, "Okay."

"Get it done by the end of tomorrow. I have a dumpster coming midmorning and I don't want to pay to keep it another day," Todd said. "Everything gets thrown in the dumpster."

That was it. Those were my instructions. On-the-job training, I guess.

Years later, as a lawyer representing Monsanto, which produced a spray-on asbestos fire retardant, I learned more than I ever wanted to know about the harm asbestos could do to the human body, including mesothelioma, a cancer that causes the lungs to lose elasticity and the person to suffocate. Experts say the disease could be caused by a single asbestos fiber inhaled into the lungs. I didn't know this back in 1979, but given the year and the age of the house, I would worry that the insulation in the attic was asbestos, and I never took a deposition of a dying former asbestos worker without thinking of that hot summer day in the attic of that home in Burlingame. I feared I might someday sit in that same chair answering the same questions.

Todd's truck departed, and a moment later, William's El Camino arrived. I descended the accordion ladder and walked into the garage. William looked like I had felt the prior morning, tired and hungover. Bags, too large for a man his age, protruded beneath his eyes, and he moved with lethargy as he alternately sipped from a Styrofoam cup and inhaled a cigarette dangling from his lips.

"Vincenzo," he said in his deep voice, but this time without humor or excitement. "You still working here?"

"I guess so," I said.

"Too bad. You had a chance to get out while you still could. I thought for sure Todd would fire you."

"What? Why?"

William smiled, squinting as the cigarette

smoke wafted up to his blue eyes. "I'm just giving you shit. Todd called me last night. Said he couldn't believe you got all that rock broken up and into the foundation ditch. He said anybody that would do what you did with a hangover and without complaint had to be a good worker."

"How'd he know I was hungover?"

"Experience," William said with his distinct chuckle. "You looked like shit. Todd doesn't care what you do on your own time so long as the work gets done. Because you got the work done, he was able to schedule the foundation inspector for tomorrow morning, and the concrete pour for the afternoon. That puts us ahead of schedule. What's he got you doing this morning?"

"Tearing off the roof," I said.

William's eyes widened. "Oh shit. From the frying pan into the fire." He laughed and took off the long-sleeve cotton shirt he wore over a stained T-shirt and handed it to me. "Wear this," he said.

"It's already hot up there."

"Forget the heat. That insulation itches like a bitch. Don't touch it. Don't let it touch your skin." William pulled out a crumpled blue bandana and a pair of plastic goggles from one of the white buckets. "Tie this around your nose and mouth and wear the goggles. Trust me. Or you'll scratch your skin off."

William went back to work preparing the foundation for inspection and, hopefully, the cement pour. I went up the ladder with the handkerchief and the goggles and pulled down insulation for about fifteen minutes. It was already warm and humid inside the attic; my goggles kept fogging and I could hardly breathe through the bandana. The temperature felt hotter by the minute, and now that William had gotten me thinking about itching, I was itchy.

After pulling down several batts of insulation, I better understood Todd's instruction about cutting the nailing slats. The framing looked like what I imagined a whale's skeleton would look like from the inside. The two-by-six beams formed the backbone. In between the framing were the one-by-four nailing slats, the rib bones. The tar paper, shingles, and insulation—what I imagined to be the blubber and skin—were nailed to the slats. I stopped and thought for a minute. There had to be a better way to do this job.

I took an end of my crowbar and banged on a place where I had removed insulation. Dust fell, further choking the air, but eventually I poked a hole in the tar paper and shingles. The hole allowed bright light and a puff of fresh air. I enlarged the hole enough to insert my head, pulled down the bandana, and took a deep breath of cool morning air. I knew how Todd wanted the work done, but I contemplated a way that would save time, save lumber, and most importantly, provide me breathable air.

I stuck the blade of the Sawzall through the hole I had punched near one of the ridge beams and hit the trigger. The saw jumped from my hands like a rifle and I dropped it, putting a small gash through the top of my Converse. A quick check confirmed I had not cut off my toe. I swore, took a breath, and tried again, this time with a firm grip on the machine. The blade ripped through the tar paper and shingles as well as the rib bones. I cut a four-foot-long gash, then stepped to the adjacent two-by-six and repeated the process. When I had finished, I busted through the shingles at the top of the two gashes. I then used the crowbar to lift the square I had cut until momentum, gravity, and its weight caused the cut section to tumble end over end down the roof. It crashed in the front yard with a bang.

William cursed a blue streak, and he and Mike, who had arrived earlier, came running from the garage looking like they expected to find me sprawled on the front lawn.

William swore a string of expletives. In between he said, "I thought you fell off the roof." He looked at the roof section on the front lawn. "I guess that's one way to do it. Just don't kill yourself."

Killing myself was the furthest thing from my mind. I was only thinking about breathing. With William's tacit blessing, I cut out bigger and bigger sections of the roof and pitched them over the side. Some I could angle so they would slide from the roof directly into the blue dumpster, which alleviated the chore of having to clean up the yard. Most importantly, I could breathe.

By the time Todd got back, just a few hours after he'd left, I had ripped off nearly the entire roof, but for the larger skeleton. I figured I could pry it apart and he could reuse the wood for the new roof. Made sense anyway. Todd stepped from the cab of his truck and considered the minimal debris in the yard. Then gazed up at me. I couldn't tell if he was pissed or pleased.

"We can reuse these boards for the new roof." I slapped at a two-by-six board making up the framework of the roof.

Todd pursed his lips and nodded. Then went into the garage.

The next thing I knew, he had climbed the ladder with a sledgehammer and a crowbar.

"Good idea saving the lumber," he said. He showed me how to separate the boards nailed together using the crowbar. Once the board was down, he handed me something called a "cat's paw" and a hammer to pull up the nail heads. "You raise the nail head. Then use this." He handed me a "Superbar" to pry out the nails.

I cleaned up the yard first so the company could haul away the dumpster at the end of the day, saving a second day's rental, then worked with Todd to salvage the wood. Mike came out at five to get me, but I knew Todd needed a hand disassembling the roof beams, so I told Mike I was going to stay. Todd and I got the beams down. Then he, too, took off while I stayed to de-nail them and stack the boards according to size. William also worked late, to get the foundation trenches finalized for inspection. At six o'clock he called me down to the garage. With Mike not there I felt a bit awkward, but William handed me a beer and I sat on the bucket. He again crouched, smoked, and drank.

"Doesn't that hurt your knees?" I asked.

"The opposite," William said, swallowing his beer and shaking his head.

"I don't think I can bend that far."

"I didn't have much choice. You didn't want to sit on anything in the bush. You'd have ants and termites crawling up your ass and in your pants. I knew a guy who sat with his ass hanging over a log and got bit by a coral snake camouflaged on the other side."

I laughed at the visual. "Was it poisonous?" I asked.

"Hell yeah. 'Red on yellow kills a fellow. Red on black, venom lack.' This one was red on yellow."

"Did the guy die?"

William sucked in nicotine, and when he raised the cigarette, I noticed a tremor in his hand. He tilted back his head and blew out a stream of smoke. "Nah. The corpsman got the antidote in him, and they helicoptered him to a military hospital. They took out a chunk of his ass about that big though." William held his hands together to indicate a rough circle the size of a baseball. "When he came back, guys called him Rawlings." I knew Rawlings to be a baseball brand. He chuckled. "After that everyone was looking for logs to crap over."

I shook my head. "Wait. What? You mean so they wouldn't get bit?"

"No. So they would get bit. You get bit and you're flown back to base and get two weeks of R & R. That beats the shit out of humping your ass all day in the bush." I didn't know a lot, but I knew R & R meant rest and relaxation. "They had snakes all over that damn place," William said. "If you weren't looking for land mines and trip wires, you were looking for snakes. We called one 'two-step.' You know why?"

I shook my head.

"Because if you got bit you took two steps before you died."

"No shit?"

"No shit. Another time, this guy got bit in the ass and the corpsman is reading the manual to determine what to do. The manual says, suck the venom out of the wound with your mouth. The guy who got bit gets anxious and says to the corpsman, 'What does the journal say?' Medic looks at him and says, 'It says you're going to die.' "

William laughed.

I laughed with him, but asked, "Did that really happen?"

"Nah, that's an old joke that went around after Rawlings got bit."

I took a slug of beer. "How old were you when you got drafted?"

William tilted the can to his lips. After swallowing, he said, "Eighteen. And technically I didn't get drafted. I volunteered."

This surprised me. "Why?"

"Because I knew I was going, sure as shit."

I gave that a moment of thought. We had a classmate volunteer for the marines, and we all thought that was about the stupidest thing ever. The marines were always in the shit. "Why'd you volunteer for the marines?"

William dropped the cigarette butt into the beer can and tossed it aside, opening a second beer. He offered a second to me.

I declined. "I'm good."

"I was a wrestler in high school," William said. "My junior year I won state in my weight class. I had scholarship offers, which I needed to pay tuition. My parents didn't have the money."

"Mine don't, either. I'm heading to community college."

"Mikey told me. I wasn't that lucky. My senior

year I tore my shoulder and the scholarships went bye-bye. Without wrestling I lost focus, screwed around, and almost didn't graduate. College was no longer in the equation, so I wasn't going to get a deferral. I got my draft notice and went down to the draft board to take my physical. The line for the army was out the door and it was about ninety degrees on the blacktop. I wasn't going to stand in that heat all day. I looked over at the Marine Corps office in the same strip mall and there was no line. I mean no one. So I asked the guy in line behind me to hold my place and I walked over and asked the marine recruiter, 'How long do I have to enlist for?'

"Recruiter says, 'If you volunteer, two years active, one reserve.'

" 'How much time in Vietnam?'

"He says, 'Thirteen months.'

"The army was two years active with twelve months in-country, so I figured it wasn't any different and I wouldn't have to spend all day on that asphalt. Plus, I was told if I did well on my AFQT—that's the Armed Forces Qualification Test—I could choose my MOS."

"What's MOS?"

"Military occupational specialty."

"What did you choose?"

"I got the highest score you can achieve, so I chose MOS 4341, combat correspondent." My interest was piqued. I intended to study

116

journalism and creative writing in college. "But they ended up denying my first choice—I think because I turned down OCS. They made me a combat photographer. I figured maybe I could put together a portfolio to get my foot in the door at a newspaper somewhere."

"That's what I want to do."

William nodded. "Mikey told me. He told me you were valedictorian. I figured you had to be smart."

"I haven't felt like it the past two days. Todd looks at me like I'm a moron."

"Nah, he don't feel that way. If he did, he would have fired you." William lit another cigarette and blew smoke over his head. "Todd doesn't care how smart you are. He cares how hard you work. You've saved him time and money getting the driveway and the roof done this quickly. Reusing the roof beams was also smart. Those boards are expensive."

I felt good about that. "How come you didn't pursue photography?" I asked, thinking maybe I would like to see William's photographs.

William lost the grin and the chuckle. "Didn't work out," he said, and I got the impression he didn't want to talk about it. Then he said, "I got a camera and training on how to use it, but I also got a rifle, because a marine always carries a rifle. Always. I thought that I'd be working out of the combat information center at Da Nang, but the marines were down in numbers because of casualties, and I had high shooting marks. So they embedded me at a firebase along the Laotian border. I got combat photographs published in *Stars and Stripes*, but those were the photographs the military wanted people to see. They didn't want people to see the others I took—like me sitting on an armed personnel carrier strewn with dead bodies."

"Vietnamese bodies?"

William shook his head. "Americans. Marines."

The gravity of the situation hit me. "That happened to you?"

"More than once." William gave me a faux salute. "A marine never leaves a man on the battlefield." My silence probably spoke volumes because William shrugged. "You get immune to it," he said, but it didn't sound like he had gotten immune to it. It sounded like the thought I'd had the prior night, with my friends, that we were only bullshitting ourselves.

William motioned to my chest. "I saw your cross."

I touched it. "My mom gave it to me when I got confirmed."

"Good Italian Catholic boy. My mom gave me one just like it before I shipped out to boot camp."

"Are you Catholic?"

"I was." He brought the cigarette to his lips.

"When I first got to Vietnam, I used to take out that cross and kiss it all the time."

I did not see a chain and cross around his neck and didn't recall seeing either when he and Mike worked without shirts. "What happened to it?"

William took another drag. His hand shook. "I lost it," he said, looking away, and again I felt something, that there was more to tell but William wasn't about to tell me. William shrugged. "It wasn't doing me any good anyway. I figured if God wasn't going to listen in Vietnam, when I needed him most, I wasn't gonna keep asking."

Again, I gave the comment a moment of thought, covering the pause with a drink from the beer can. Finally, I asked, "So are you an atheist?"

William tilted his head, as if thinking about it. "I don't know what I am. I don't put too much stock in that 'praise Jesus' stuff. I've been to hell, and I didn't see any sign of God. After a while you stop looking. You figure it out on your own."

For the life of me I don't know what compelled me to say what I said next, maybe that underdeveloped frontal lobe. "But you lived. That had to mean something."

William gave me a pensive smile. "You know what it meant? It meant I got lucky. That's all. Dumb, blind luck. Guy in front of me steps on a land mine that was meant for me. Bad luck for him. Good luck for me."

William snubbed out his cigarette and stood, and I was glad he did. I thought I knew about the Vietnam War. I had heard and read about all the young men who had lost their lives, about what they had experienced, and what they had perpetrated. I knew about the My Lai Massacre, about soldiers coming home to protests and people calling them "baby killers." I also knew we'd lost a lot of young men who were my age when they died to stop the spread of communism in Southeast Asia, and that when we had pulled out of the country, it had fallen to the communists anyway, and everything American soldiers fought and died for seemed to have been a waste. I recalled the publication of the Pentagon Papers, which indicated the war had not been driven by idealism and that the US government had lied to the public and to Congress, which made the deaths of those young men all the more senseless. But those were impersonal snippets learned from news articles. William had been there. He had lived it.

When William spoke of Vietnam, he was like a live electrical wire I had gripped. His stories sent a current through my body. But then, just as quickly, William flipped a switch and the current turned off, leaving me drained and tired.

Like my high school friends who embellished our stories to perpetrate an illusion, I sensed William held back information about Vietnam, about what he had truly experienced, to perpetrate his own illusion—that the war hadn't affected him. But I sensed it had.

After four years of high school, I didn't feel like I really knew my friends, not at their core; I had never gotten past the veneer we all erected to protect ourselves. And I didn't feel like I knew William. Not in the least. I knew the happy-go-lucky William with the chuckle in his voice, but not the Vietnam William who had, somehow, managed to survive and make it back alive.

I wasn't sure I wanted to know that William.

PART II

Never, Neverland

April 7, 1968

I was wearing my helmet and flak jacket and cradling my M-16 like it was a lover. I couldn't see Kenny, but I could hear his muffled snoring beneath his poncho. At times he choked and coughed, as if he had sucked in the plastic. In the darkness, the sound was magnified. Every sound was magnified. I wanted to punch Kenny and tell him to shut up, but he couldn't very well roll over.

I couldn't see jack shit. The night was ink-black darkness, the darkest darkness I'd ever experienced. I know now what it's like to go blind. One minute you see things. The next, nothing. I kept telling myself I was in a John Wayne movie. Victor Cruz put that thought in my head, but it was better than thinking of a rat pouncing on my face and ripping out my flesh. I looked around for the movie cameras and the overhead boom microphone—'cause that shit couldn't have been real.

But it was real.

I don't want to be here, and I just got here. I've got a whole year, plus a month.

I miss New Jersey. I miss my parents and my brothers and sisters. I just want to go home, like Dorothy in *The Wizard of Oz*. I want to get to Oz, click my heels three times, and go home. And when I get back, I sure as shit won't run away again.

Trickles of sweat rolled down my face. It was humid, even at night. I told myself sweating meant I was alive, was proof I hadn't died and slipped into the great dark abyss. I assumed I wouldn't have been sweating after I died; would I? I didn't think so. I didn't know.

I heard a noise, a scratching sound, and I grabbed the handle of my Ka-Bar. I thought maybe it was one of Kenny's rats, big as a cat. Even with my eyes now adjusted, I couldn't see past the rim of the sandbags surrounding our foxhole. I heard the scratching again. Then a click. Leaves rustled but there was no wind. A pop, a bright white light flashed, and the night came alive in a brilliant burst. Another pop. Another flash. More light. Claymores were being detonated.

Charlie.

I heard the rattle of machine gun fire and heard and felt the explosions.

Kenny struggled to free himself from his poncho. He'd become entangled in the plastic and started to scream in frustration. I reached down and helped pull the poncho off him as additional bursts of M-16 gunfire rattled overhead and red tracers flew in every direction. Red is friendly fire. Green is Charlie.

I was uncertain what to do. The sound was deafening and disorienting.

Kenny wasn't uncertain. Freed from his poncho, he grabbed his M-16, and despite Cruz's warning, he crawled atop the sandbags and started shooting, at what, I had no idea. I stuck my head up. Red trails crisscrossed the firebase. Illumination flares continued to light up the ground.

I aimed at the razor wire and fired a burst with my M-16 on semiautomatic. A mortar detonated. The ground shook, dirt clods rained down on my foxhole.

I was certain we were about to be overrun by NVA. I was going to look up and see Charlie dropping down on top of me, sticking me with a bayonet. That was my perception of war. Those were the movies I watched as a kid.

I heard Kenny firing on fully automatic. He slapped in a new magazine. I still had no idea what he was shooting at. Now he was snapping off bursts. He didn't spray. He was deliberate. Hunting.

I imagined just like he hunted in the hills of Kentucky.

My ass quivered. My butt cheeks shook. I couldn't control them. I couldn't keep them from shaking.

The fighting ended as suddenly as it began. Five minutes, just like Cruz had said, but it felt like five hours.

I heard shouting. "Cease fire. Cease fire, you assholes." Cruz. The corporal came down the line yelling obscenities. I stayed in our foxhole, listening. Waiting. Cruz came up behind us, like a ghost in the glare from the illumination. He nearly gave me a heart attack.

"Penny," he said.

"What?"

"Penny, Shutter. Penny."

I didn't know what he was talking about. Then I remembered. "Lane," I said. "Lane."

"You good?" he asked.

"I'm good," I said, but he didn't wait before he turned to Kenny. "Haybale, you good?"

Kenny didn't answer.

"Haybale?"

Cruz went to Haybale, shook him, then swore. "Shit." He yelled, "Corpsman!" in a loud voice. "Corpsman!"

A navy corpsman is attached to our platoon. The company actually has four because we are light artillery. It is not something I like to think about.

I checked my clothing. I didn't feel blood. Did I get hit? Was I dying?

Guys rushed forward, boots pounding the ground. The corpsman, a pudgy twenty-year-old named Hayes, dropped beside Kenny. He's not a doctor. He received eight weeks of training in battlefield injuries. I thought, *Just like you're not a photographer.*

I watched, paralyzed, unable to look away. Cruz spoke to me, but I couldn't hear him. His lips moved, but I couldn't hear his voice. My ass continued to shake. I tried to stop it, to not look so scared. But I was scared. I was having these weird thoughts, flashbacks of my life, thinking I got hit, that I was dead, and I just didn't know it yet. They say that happens. They say when you die, you don't know you're dead, not right away. You walk the earth wondering why nobody pays any attention to you.

I think again of *The Wizard of Oz*, of Dorothy talking to Toto, the little black dog that started all her damn problems.

Like Dorothy, I have a feeling we're not in Kansas anymore.

Nor Kentucky, Haybale.

I'm thinking Dorothy should have shot Toto.

She should have just shot the damn dog.

Maybe then she could have just stayed home.

CHAPTER 6

October 23, 2015

Football season Beau's senior year meant Friday nights playing under the lights. We had sent Beau to Serra after much debate. From my own experience, there were things about the school I had not liked, but Serra had changed in the intervening years. It had improved its academics, worked hard to change the culture from a "jock" school, and collaborated with the all-girls schools to have classes and other nondating events together. Unlike me, Beau would meet girls in normal high school settings and, hopefully, make friends. Beau's best friend, Chris Carpenter, also chose to attend Serra, which more or less sealed the deal.

Beau had been named a team captain, and Elizabeth and I decided to make the season memorable. Elizabeth became a team mom and helped put together the team dinners on game day as well as the special night for senior players. I decided to organize tailgate parties for the parents before the home games to promote camaraderie. With the games on Friday night, I could escape the clutches of the law, at least for a few hours, and I was determined to be at each of Beau's games.

I bought a portable grill to do the tailgates up right, and I barbecued chicken, hot dogs, and hamburgers, and other parents brought side dishes to share. The tailgates were a chance to get to know the parents of Beau's teammates, especially the underclassmen moving up to varsity. Some we knew from prior seasons and some, like Chris, we had known since grammar school. The Carpenters lived just a few blocks from us in Burlingame, and we had carpooled before the boys could drive. Chris was a big kid who became an even bigger young man. At six foot four and 290 pounds, he was a beast on the football field but a gentle soul off it. He played both ways at offensive and defensive tackle, and not surprisingly his play was generating letters of interest from nearly every Pac-12 school as well as Notre Dame, Oklahoma, and Michigan.

Chris and Beau's relationship was symbiotic, as were their positions on the football field. Beau played fullback and usually ran directly behind Chris, who opened holes like a bulldozer. On defense, Beau played middle linebacker and Chris, a defensive tackle, tied up offensive linemen, which allowed Beau to split the gaps and make tackles and sacks behind the line of scrimmage. Beau had heart and strength and stellar statistics, but not size. Six feet tall, he struggled just to reach two hundred pounds. As happy as I was for all the interest Chris had generated, I felt bad for my son.

Beau's junior year, Serra won the Northern California championship but lost the state championship to a Southern California school. Serra had brought back a lot of starters on offense and defense, but their archrival, Bellarmine Prep, brought back even more, including an all-American running back who had already committed to Alabama. The two teams were undefeated heading into a showdown on Serra's home field.

Elizabeth and I gathered with the Carpenters and other parents in the parking lot two hours before game time to prepare the tailgate. Mary Beth, who attended Mercy, an all-girls school in Burlingame, didn't stick around long, finding friends and disappearing.

"Chris heard from Stanford," Art Carpenter said to me as we set up tables and unloaded food from the back of his Suburban and my Subaru.

"Yeah?" I said.

"They're interested," Art said. "But they're waiting for his SAT scores before they offer him a scholarship." Like my parents, the Carpenters needed a scholarship for Chris to attend Stanford. Art owned an appliance store in Burlingame and Josephine taught at a public elementary school. With four kids, money was tight.

"That's terrific," I said, but I again thought of Beau. Though he had better grades than Chris, he would not have nearly the same options; football would not get him a scholarship. It wasn't fair, but neither was the real world.

"Do you realize what a Stanford education could do for Chris?" Art continued.

I did.

Art pulled out a pack of hot dogs and handed them to me. "He could do whatever he wanted. I'm more nervous now than I've ever been."

"Why?"

"Because Chris is one bad tackle or bad play away from an injury. I hate to say this, but I'm hoping he just gets through this season healthy and gets in."

I almost said, *You can't think that way,* but I'd been reading William's journal and it had spurred my memory of the conversations William and I had shared during those summer months. William had told me the only difference between him and all those young men who died in Vietnam was bad luck. They took one step in the wrong place, stuck their head up at the wrong time, got on the wrong chopper, or slept in the wrong bunker.

"Chris is a big kid," I said, putting the hot dogs beside a row of hamburgers. "He can take care of himself."

"I hope you're right," Art said.

As game time approached, an electricity filled the parking lot and the stands. We cleaned up the tables, put away the food, and made our way to the bleachers in time to see both teams exit the locker rooms and storm onto the field. Serra had put money and resources into their field, but it was far from a stadium. It was a high school football field with bleachers. As we stood in the parents' section, I looked around and noticed a lot of young men I didn't recognize.

"Scouts," Art said, catching my gaze. "Chris got phone calls they'd be here."

Maybe they'd see Beau, I contemplated, then immediately tried to dismiss the thought. Still . . .

Serra got off to a fast start. Beau ran well behind Chris, and on a third down, Beau plunged into the end zone from the one-yard line, followed by a successful extra point to put Serra up 7–0. The game plan was to have Beau, as linebacker, spy on Phillips, the running back, and follow him all over the field. Beau had several tackles behind the line of scrimmage and held Phillips more or less in check on offense, but Phillips also played defensive safety, and just before halftime he picked off an errant throw and ran it to the end zone. Bellarmine made the extra point to tie the score 7–7.

I'd like to tell you that it was just a game, that the score, the outcome, didn't matter. You'd think I would have understood that better than anyone—reading the journal of a young man who for a year struggled daily to stay alive and watched so many of his friends die—but it's hard to be objective when it's your son on the field and you know what the game means to him. I wanted Beau to have the chance to celebrate on the field.

In the third quarter Serra scored on a pass to the tight end. With the successful point after, they led 14–7. The defense hadn't given up a score. Beau made tackle after tackle, and I couldn't help but glance over my shoulder at the college scouts, wondering if any paid attention.

As the clock ticked down to the end of the third quarter, Beau made another tackle, but a Bellarmine player dove at the pile after the play, spearing Beau in the back of the head with his helmet. The referees, deciding the hit had been intentional, ejected the Bellarmine player, but I didn't care. Beau was on the ground, not moving.

Elizabeth had her hands over her mouth in silent prayer as the team doctor tended to Beau, then, unable to stand there, she bolted from the bleachers. Beau was her baby boy, and he and Elizabeth had always had a special relationship. She taught him to snow-ski when he was eighteen months, to water-ski in Lake Tahoe, and to ride horseback on his grandparents' farm. I hurried after her as Beau was helped to the sideline, clearly groggy. The team doctor examined Beau under a tent. Elizabeth and I went inside. I heard Beau say, "I'm fine. Where's my helmet? Give me my helmet."

The doctor looked at me. "His pupils are dilated and his eyes are not focusing. He could have a concussion."

"I'm fine," Beau said again. "Dad, I'm fine."

The doctor stared at me. Elizabeth stared at me. Beau tried to get off the table, stumbled off balance, and nearly fell over. "I can play. I'm fine. Where's my helmet?"

In my day, guys played through concussions all the time, because we could not diagnose them as well, and we didn't know the repercussions of head trauma caused by football. Elizabeth had been reluctant to let Beau play, but he had been adamant he wanted to play with Chris, and we had relented.

I looked at Beau. "I'm sorry, son." To the trainer I said, "Take his helmet."

Beau looked at me in disbelief. "Dad. No."

"Take his helmet," I said again, struggling with emotion. I knew what this game meant to Beau and to his teammates, but I knew what my son meant to me and Elizabeth, and I couldn't live with myself if anything happened to him. I thought again of William, and of what had transpired that summer we'd worked together, how one instant could have forever changed his life and the lives of others.

"I'm sorry, Beau. I know—"

But Beau turned away and stumbled from the tent, without his helmet. He stood on the sidelines watching the game as Elizabeth and I returned to the stands and told the other parents what had happened.

Without Beau spying on Phillips from his middle linebacker position, Bellarmine's running back gained huge yardage. He scored twice in the fourth quarter to give Bellarmine the win, 21–14.

I watched our son walk off the field with his head down, utterly dejected. The team doctor came to the sideline and put a hand on my shoulder. "I'll check him in the locker room. But you made the right decision," he said.

I nodded.

"Keep an eye on him. If he gets sick, starts to vomit, can't answer simple questions, take him to the emergency room." He handed us a card. "This is the concussion clinic at Mills hospital. Call that number and give them my name. They'll get Beau in tomorrow."

Beau exited the locker room with Chris. They had shed their pads and jerseys, carrying them with their helmets. Each wore cutoff T-shirts, football pants, and flip-flops. Both looked dejected, but particularly Beau.

"Hey, Mr. B. Hey, Mrs. B.," Chris said. "Hey, Mary Beth."

"Sorry about the loss, Chris," I said as Elizabeth and Mary Beth tried to console Beau.

"We played well," Chris said. "If it wasn't for the cheap shot, we would have won." He put his hand on Beau's shoulder. "We have more games to play. The season isn't over."

I knew for Chris there would be many more games, but for Beau that was far from a certainty.

"I'll drive Beau's car," Chris said.

"We'll follow you to our house and I'll drop you off," I said. "Let's go, Beau."

Beau never looked at me. He looked to his mother. "I'll ride with Chris."

I started to object, but Elizabeth gave me a quick head shake. Then to Beau she said, "We'll meet you at home."

In the car, I said to Elizabeth, "Did I do the right thing?"

She looked at me like I was crazy. "Of course you did the right thing. If you hadn't told them to take his helmet, I would have hit you over the head with it."

"I'm not sure he's going to get over this. I know what this game meant to him."

"It was a game, Vince. Just a high school football game. Don't make it out to be more than it is. He'll get over it. If this is his biggest disappointment in life, he'll be damn lucky."

"Tell that to Beau."

"I will," she said, defiant. "And someday he'll realize I'm right. No one died out there. No one was seriously hurt. Beau's coming home tonight. That's all that matters."

I blew out a held breath. She was right, of course. William's journal reinforced that.

She continued. "You know Beau. He never

139

stays mad long. He'll get through this, and he'll forgive you."

"Forgive me?" I said, indignant. "For what?"

"He's just disappointed, Vince. Don't make this personal."

I shook my head. "Of course it's personal. That's my son."

"Our son," she said. "And no one is saying you made the wrong decision."

"He doesn't know what disappointment or loss is," I said. We had given Beau and his sister a lot more than I ever had. Vacations to Europe and places like Disney World in Orlando, Florida, and like Scottsdale, Arizona. We could afford to send Beau and Mary Beth to whatever college they chose. I lost my best friend to a heart attack at forty. I lost my dad to cancer at just seventy-six. I never even met my grandfather, and I never got the chance . . . I stopped. I'd had the chance to write, but I'd chosen money and stability instead of the dream. I couldn't lay that at anyone's feet but my own. "He has no idea what loss is," I repeated.

"Did you at that age?" she asked.

I hated when she used common sense.

I did not, of course. Not before the end of that summer when I worked with William. I would get a painful lesson on loss, and a perspective that eluded most young men at eighteen years of age.

April 7, 1968

I thought the hardest part would be making it through that first night on guard duty, wondering if I would even awake to a tomorrow. I figured I'd never again be so happy to see a sunrise and the light of a new day, that bright orange ball rising above the treetops, that strip of fuchsia on the horizon, ribbons of pink and yellow painting the underside of the persistent haze. Color would mean I'd survived; I'd lived another day in-country.

Kenny had not.

Daylight has brought a harsh reality.

Kenny is dead.

Though I say the words, I don't believe them, not fully. Kenny took a bullet in the eye that blew out the back of his head inside his helmet. A one in a million shot, Cruz said. Just bad luck. Kenny never cried out. Never made a sound. He just lay there, with his M-16 pointed toward the wire. Like he was hunting.

He was the hunted.

"Why'd he leave the foxhole?" Cruz asked.

"I don't know," I responded.

"Goddamn it. It's your job to know. You're a team. Didn't I say don't leave the damn foxhole. Didn't I say that?"

"You said it."

"Then why did he leave? You should have drug his ass back down." Cruz swears. "Goddamn FNG."

I wish I hadn't called Kenny "Haybale" or thought of him as Gomer Pyle. I feel bad about it, and now it's too late to apologize. What did my mother say about words being like arrows? Once you shoot them, you can't take them back. Not from Kenny. Not ever.

I also can't take back seeing Kenny dead. I'd never seen a dead man before, at least not one who was not already in a coffin and shit. My grandparents are alive. I've never lost an aunt or an uncle. Never lost a cousin. I've never lost a friend. Never really contemplated death. Never had to. I was going to live forever. Aren't we all at eighteen?

Not Kenny.

Maybe not me. It sinks in, the reality. *Maybe not me.*

I didn't know Kenny. We weren't friends. They put us in the same foxhole. They put us together. I didn't ask them to. I had no say in it. The blind leading the damn blind. Maybe that's why Cruz is pissed, because he knows he fucked up and now it's too late to do anything about it.

Cruz and the corpsman are matter-of-fact. It scares me how matter-of-fact they are about death, guys still in their early twenties. It scares me to know they've been through this enough to know the drill so well. To not even flinch. They went through Kenny's pockets for things to send home. They removed one of his dog tags, bagged it, and taped it to his wrist for military records. We put Kenny in a green body bag and zipped it closed, then carried the bag to the LZ, and a helicopter carried Kenny off, along with the other two marines who died last night.

I didn't even have the chance to get to know them.

And that was it. The helicopter lifted and Kenny was gone. And we were expected to get on with our day. "Do your jobs," Cruz said.

Someone said Kenny was lucky, that if you had to go, better to go right away than live through this shit only to die at the end. I bet Kenny doesn't feel the same.

He slept right beside me. I heard him snoring. The next moment, he was gone.

It changes everything. I realize now, truly understand, that I could die here. I could be the guy they load in a green body bag, zip it closed, and put it on the helicopter. I wandered around the LZ taking photographs. It felt morbid, but that's my job. Right? I'm supposed to snap photographs. That's my job. *Do your job.* I find that looking through the camera lens somehow makes it seem less real. Makes it seem like maybe it's just a movie I am shooting frame by frame— something that will be watched on a movie screen or television.

A somberness permeated the camp.

Cruz walked over to me. I lowered the camera. He said, "Growing old is a privilege, not a right, Shutter. You learn that quickly here in Nam, and the sooner the better. What happened today is over. You're here. You still got a job to do. *Comprende?*"

"*Comprende.*"

"Take photographs. Do your job."

The guys who've been here awhile called out to those of us who haven't as we dragged our tired asses back in—I hadn't slept a wink. I'm not sure anyone had, other than Kenny.

"You got that cherry popped now?" Bean

sat on sandbags, smoking a cigarette. He had his shirt off, dog tags dangling between his pudgy breasts. I don't know Bean's real name. Everyone just calls him Jelly Bean or Bean. He didn't wait for an answer. "Yeah. You know I'm talking to you, Shutter." He nodded to the camera in my hand. "A lot more real now, ain't it? Yes, sir. A lot different than looking through that camera lens, when it's up close and personal, ain't it?" I wondered how he knows. Experience, I guess. "You're a veteran now. A veteran of the Nam. No more FNG."

I raised the camera, focused the lens, and snapped several pictures of Bean. He stared, like he was looking past me. The million-mile stare they call it. He didn't smile. He didn't frown. He had no expression. He just existed.

I lowered the camera and Bean spoke:

You give boys guns and vests,
throw them into general chaos and hope
    for the best.
Vietnam is *Lord of the Flies*, a brutal
    Neverland that doesn't lie.
Outside both time and space;
a place where marines die without grace.
Real or unreal? I can't tell.

145

So hot you think, this must be hell.
You don't have time to grow up here.
You just grow old from all the fear.
Bean blew out cigarette smoke. I could
  see his poetry in his lifeless eyes. And I
  understood.

CHAPTER 7

June 6, 1979

Mike had call-back interviews with an insurance company, and a job in that industry seemed imminent. When Mike wasn't on the remodel, I was number three in the crew. William called me down from my work on the second level and told me the building inspector had signed off on the foundations and Todd had scheduled a concrete pour that afternoon. He said we would have a long day and asked if I could work late; Todd couldn't pay overtime but William said he'd appreciate the help. I thought it was a trick question. I figured more hours meant more money, regardless of if I got paid overtime, and I got the impression they would both appreciate my willingness to do what needed to be done to finish the job, so I said, "Yes."

"You ever pour concrete?" William asked.

"No. Not really. Not ever actually."

William told me my job would be to keep a path clear for the long pump hose that would extend from the cement truck in the street to the foundation at the back of the house, to make sure the hose didn't pinch. To save on money, I suppose, we'd do the pour ourselves. Todd would handle the nozzle. William and I would hold the hose farther up the line and manipulate it as Todd instructed with hand signals. My job was to pass those signals to the pump-truck operator. An open hand meant let it pour. A closed fist or slash sign across the throat meant stop.

"Miss a signal and we step on a land mine," William said.

I underestimated how much a hose filled with wet concrete weighed. The minute the truck started pumping the cement, holding on to the hose was like trying to hold the neck of a dragon that didn't want to be held, but we soon fell into a good rhythm. As we poured, two young women drove slowly past the jobsite in a red 1965 Mustang, the windows down and Donna Summer's "Hot Stuff" blasting from the speakers. The dark-haired passenger lowered her sunglasses to the tip of her nose and checked me out, then broke into laughter. Feeling cocky, I returned the smile and checked her out, figuring I'd never see her again. What did I care? I was surprised and a little nervous when the driver turned into the driveway two houses down on the same side of the street as the remodel.

"Vincent," William yelled with urgency. He had his fist closed.

"Shit." I turned to the cement-truck operator and closed my fist, yelling, "Cut. Cut."

I was late, but we hadn't stepped on a land mine.

I had literally perspired through my shirt, but I didn't have time to rest. As Todd and William worked hand trowels over the concrete, my job was to clean off cement overspray, particularly in the street. At the end of the day, Todd took off to bid a small tile job, leaving William and me to finish cleaning up the site, the trowels, and other tools. When we were done, William handed me a beer and I collapsed on my bucket. We BS'd again. I purposefully avoided Vietnam, but eventually the conversation got back around to his photography, so I assumed it was safe to ask a question.

"Why are you working construction with Todd? Why aren't you working as a reporter or a photographer at a newspaper?"

William sucked on his cigarette. Smoke escaped his nose and mouth. Something about the blank expression on William's face, the way he looked at me but also looked past me, made me uneasy.

William dropped his cigarette butt into his beer can. I thought he was going to get up and leave. Part of me wished he would. Instead, he said, "Because dreams are hard to catch."

Uncertain what to say and not wanting to direct the conversation to Vietnam, I remained silent. William went there anyway.

"My platoon had been pulled back from our firebase to defend a city called Dak To during

149

another offensive by the North Vietnamese. We were fighting street to street and door to door. In the middle of all this chaos, a Jeep comes whipping down the road and slams on the brakes. The driver talks to some marines, and I see them point to where I'm standing. The Jeep jerks forward and barrels toward me. The driver again slams on the brakes. He's young, clean shaven. Clean uniform. He looks terrified.

"He says, 'William Goodman?'

" 'Yeah.'

" 'You're leaving. Now. Get in.'

"I was confused because I still had something like twelve weeks before my DEROS. I thought it was a mistake."

"What did you do?" A stupid question I regretted the minute it left my mouth.

"You know," William said, a wistful smile spreading on his lips, "I almost stayed."

"Are you serious?"

"As a heart attack. It sounds crazy, doesn't it?"

It didn't sound like a question, and even if it had, I figured it was rhetorical. For once the frontal lobe kicked in and I kept my mouth shut.

"But in the midst of all that craziness, crazy is the only reality you know." William shrugged. He lit another cigarette, blew out the smoke, and sipped another beer. "I was amped on adrenaline and all the drugs I'd been doing, and I was thinking that what I had known in New Jersey, what I had left behind, was no longer real. Vietnam was real. It was where I belonged."

"So you stayed?" I asked, thinking it the craziest thing I'd heard.

"This Polish guy from Philadelphia, who we called Cheesesteak, punched me, hard, in the shoulder and said, 'Shutter, get in the fucking Jeep, man. Don't be a hero.' That was something my mother said to me the morning I boarded the bus to boot camp. 'Don't be a hero.' It was like she was calling me home. So I got in the Jeep. I still wonder what I would have done if Cheesesteak hadn't knocked some sense into me. The driver took me straight to the transport helicopter and wished me Godspeed. When I got on the helicopter, I realized I didn't have my ditty bag."

"What's a ditty bag?"

"A duffel bag. When I was embedded at Firebase Phoenix, I'd been sending my film rolls to a lab in Da Nang. I had a buddy from film school, a lab rat working there. He made me copies of the best photos and sent them back to me in these canisters. He said mine were the best photographs he'd seen from military or civilian photographers. I kept the cans in my ditty bag."

"And you didn't have it," I said, the picture becoming clear.

"But I didn't want to ask anyone about it because I was worried they'd realize they made a mistake, that they sent me home from Nam before my DEROS, and they'd send me back, or that I'd draw attention to the cans and they'd take them."

"So what did you do?"

"I kept my mouth shut, went home, and waited four months until my stuff arrived. I figured I'd be working as a reporter and photographer at the *New York Times* in a matter of days." He smiled, but it was wistful. "They didn't send the cans."

I was aghast, and angry. "Why not?"

William took another drag, blew out the smoke, and took a swig of beer. "Initially they said they didn't know what I was talking about. They said the cans must have been lost." He shook his head. "Guys had been trying to ship home all kinds of shit—their rifles, pistols, knives. The military got wind of it and started searching bags. If they found stuff, they confiscated it and threatened to prosecute."

"Why would they take photographs?"

"Because they didn't want them to wind up in the press. The war was getting enough bad publicity at home from civilian photographers embedded over there. The marines didn't need one of their own embarrassing them."

"But they were yours."

William shook his head and pointed the cigarette at me. "The military said I didn't own the photographs because I took them during my service. Therefore, the marines owned them."

"That's bullshit."

Another shrug. "Maybe, but they said I signed something that said I forfeited all rights to the photographs. Didn't matter what they said; the photographs were gone."

I couldn't get past the loss. I knew that without those photographs, William was just a guy with a camera. "Did you ever find out if they took them or if they were really lost?"

He nodded. "I kept the cans with the photographs in the same bag with my medals, and my medals made it home." He took another drag on his cigarette. "It was my own fault. I had contemplated mailing the photographs home, but sending home a package from the bush wasn't that easy, and it's likely they would have searched the cans before shipping them and found the photographs anyway. I thought it safest to carry them home with me."

"You must have been pissed," I said.

William smiled like I was the most naive person on the planet. "I was home, man. I was home. And I had all my body parts. I never thought that would happen. I figured that if they wanted their photographs of their war, they could keep them. I was done with it. I was done with them. I was done with Vietnam. The way I looked at it, I beat Vietnam. I made it home."

I guessed that was true, and I was sure it was

paramount, but I kept thinking there had to be a way to fix the situation. After a few moments, I asked, "What medals did you get?" I thought the medals would have improved his chances of getting a job at a newspaper.

William shrugged. "The Combat Action Ribbon is the one that really counts. That says you fought, that you were in the shit, that you weren't just support at the rear. That and a Purple Heart."

I knew the significance of a Purple Heart. "You were wounded?"

William pulled down his T-shirt and showed me a puckered scar on the left side of his chest just below the collarbone. About the size of a quarter, it looked like a spider's web. "I still don't have full motion in my shoulder. It's why I can't throw a softball worth a shit."

I recalled from softball games that William's throws looked like wounded ducks. Now I knew why. "What did you do with the medals?"

"They sat in a box marked VIETNAM in the basement of my parents' house until I left New Jersey to come out to California. I threw out the box without bothering to open it."

"Did you know the medals and ribbons were inside?"

"I knew."

"And you threw them out?" I didn't understand.

He gave me another shrug. "I didn't have any use for them in California, which meant

154

somebody—my mother or father, someone—was going to have to throw them out. I just saved them the trouble."

I thought of the awards I had won in high school, the plaques for being class valedictorian and for winning the California Newspaper Journalism Scholarship that would help pay my first-year college tuition. They hung proudly on my bedroom wall.

"Didn't they mean something to you?"

"Yeah. They meant a lot of bad memories." He shook his head and stubbed out the cigarette. "All medals represent is where you've been and what you've done. And believe me, I didn't need any help in that department."

"But couldn't they help you get a job, I mean . . ."

William shook his head. "No, no, no. What? Go into interviews and announce you're a screwed-up Vietnam vet, a psycho baby killer?" He looked out the garage door from above the tops of his knees. "That's why I left New Jersey. I didn't want to face all those people I grew up with, the families that had been a part of my life. They didn't look at me the same when I got back."

I understood, as much as I figured I could. "Is that why you came to California?"

He smiled. "One time in Vietnam I dreamed of a sunny beach with no humidity and beautiful girls in bikinis."

I laughed.

"I'm telling you the truth. I took the trip to LA chasing a girl, but the girl was just an excuse. I was chasing the dream. After two days she was gone, but the sun was still shining, there was no humidity, and the beaches were crammed with bikinis. I put on a tank top and shorts and went to the beach every day. At night I slept on the sand or on someone's couch, and I thought they were the best days of my life."

"No family in Southern California?"

"Nope."

"No friends?"

"None."

"You went just for the sunshine and bikinis?" I said, smiling, thinking I'd never have the guts to do that. Then again, I didn't think I'd have the guts to fight a war in Vietnam, either.

William gave me a long stare, and for a moment I thought he was angry. Then he smiled. "From where I'd been . . . What else was there, man?"

I drove home hoping to talk to Mike, ask him if William had ever told him any of the stuff he'd told me, but Mike wasn't at the house. He and Maureen had gone out, and the more I thought about it, the more I realized William's story wasn't my story to share. I didn't have the right to tell it—not to Mike and not to my friends.

I never did.

I walked into my room and grabbed a change of clothes for my shower. My plaques and framed certificates hung on the wall, a road map of my past. They didn't say a thing about where I was going or what I'd do when I got there, and they had no significance to anyone but me. They'd likely go in a box when I went off to college and another sibling claimed the bedroom as his or her own, and they'd remain buried in that box until I earned enough to make a down payment on a house. Then I'd retrieve the box and store it in the basement or attic of my own home. Unlike William, I didn't have the courage to throw out those plaques, my medals. I feared I would lose a part of myself I could not yet let go of.

William had tired eyes in 1979, the eyes of a young man who had grown old well before his time. Todd did also. It was as if they had lived a decade in that one year, and when they returned home, the world passed by without so much as a pause to glance at them. Maybe that's why William had thrown out his medals. They didn't mean anything to him, because they didn't mean anything to the world that passed him by— certainly nothing positive. Vietnam was the war everyone wanted to forget. So did he, apparently.

And someday, I realized, when I'm gone, my plaques and certificates will also be just sad memories that my wife and my children will have to decide what to do with, reminders of who

I had once been. And it will hurt them to throw away the box with the mementos of my life lived.

I won't do that to them, hurt them that way. I'll throw the box out someday, just like William, so they don't have to.

April 7, 1968

The bodies of the five Viet Cong killed last night lay side by side in the center of the firebase. They laid them out like they weren't even human, like they were caught fish put on the shore before gutting. A swarm of flies covered their skin and hovered above their bodies. Barefoot, they were wearing thin black shirts and pants that looked like pajamas, not uniforms. They looked like skinny poor kids, and it was hard to imagine they could cause so much chaos, that they could have killed three marines, including Kenny.

Someone said, "We killed six Gooks," like it was a badge of honor.

I looked over at Cruz, who walked beside me as I snapped photographs. Cruz just rolled his eyes. He didn't buy it, either, but he wasn't about to say that. "Get used to it, Shutter. The military keeps on us about the body count. Westmoreland said this is going to be a war of attrition and we're winning, but I'll tell you this, it don't matter how many we kill, Charlie just keeps coming down the Ho Chi Minh Trail." He considered the bodies. "Most likely VC, not NVA," meaning the Viet Cong guerilla army which first formed to fight the French, and not the North Vietnamese Army.

The sixth confirmed kill still hung from the concertina wire, like a puppet whose puppet master has dropped the strings. A marine found a hole in the razor wire almost directly in line with my foxhole. I wondered if the bullet that killed the guy hanging from the wire came from my gun, or maybe Kenny's.

Eye for an eye.

"That boy is mine." A marine named Harris spit a brown wad of chewing tobacco juice in the direction of the dangling body. His nickname, I've been told, is Hard-On because he has a hard-on for killing Charlie. Hard-On kept saying the kill on the wire was his kill. I'd have been glad to let him have it, to not think that I had taken another life, but that kill belongs to Kenny, maybe because his dying makes some sense that way.

Eye for an eye.

I heard myself say, "No. He isn't."

"The hell he ain't, FNG. What do you know?" He laughed and looked at the others to join him. No one did. They looked to me.

"Kenny shot him," I said.

"Haybale? Haybale's dead."

"Shot him before he could get through the wire. I saw him do it. He hunted. In Kentucky."

Hard-On spit another wad of brown syrup. "Saw him do it? Bullshit. Not last night. You couldn't see your hand on your pecker."

"Saw the kill when the flare went up, the illumination." I hadn't, but Hard-On didn't know that.

"Yeah, well, I'm taking credit."

"No." I took a step forward. "You're not."

He stepped toward me, turned his head, and spit. "What'd you say, FNG?"

"You heard me. That kill belongs to Kenny." The argument was ridiculous since the marines don't give kill credits to individual marines, only to companies, but it meant something to me, to think that Kenny killed one of the enemy before he got shot. I don't know.

Hard-On looked me up and down, like he was contemplating a go. He outweighs me, but I figured I could take him down in a few moves. He smiled, but I'd seen that smile before on the wrestling mats. He was unsure of himself, nervous. Finally, he said, "Whatever you say, Shutter. No matter. Plenty more where he came from anyways." He spit and walked off.

Cruz looked at me and nodded.

Some of the other FNGs eventually pulled the body from the wire and laid him in line with the others. I have no idea what the military does with enemy bodies. Somebody said they douse them with gas and diesel and burn them with the shit. I didn't want to think about that, and I really didn't want to snap any photographs, but that's my job, and I figured if I didn't do it, they'd keep putting an M-16 in my hands.

I placed the camera to my eye and lost reality in the lens.

Cruz took out a crumpled pack of cigarettes and offered me one. "How you doing, Shutter?"

I shook my head at the cigarette. Having been an all-state wrestler, I'd never smoked, except a little weed. I'd figured if smoking was going to take years off my life, I might as well get high doing it. "I don't smoke," I said.

Cruz chuckled. "Yeah, Shutter, you do. Trust me, you do. The nicotine helps take the edge off."

I took a cigarette and Cruz lit it, then

lit one for himself. The cigarette was like drinking a tall glass of cool water. I felt the nicotine melt away the tension.

"Why didn't more come?" I asked. "Why didn't they send more than half a dozen?"

Cruz gave me a sideways glance, let out smoke, and pointed with the cigarette. "That isn't half a dozen, Shutter. Can't you count? That's twelve." He smiled. *"Comprende?"*

I nodded.

"Never take a photograph that allows them to count the actual number. You make us out to be liars." He said the last sentence smiling.

Cruz blew smoke from the corner of his mouth. "This is a psychological war, Shutter. We let Charlie control the tempo even though we got the better firepower, better artillery, and better air support. We don't get to invade Cambodia or Laos. If we could, we could end this war in a month. No. We announce these 'truces' and halt the bombings and the patrols, but Charlie? He don't pay no attention. He just keeps on keeping on. You get me?"

"So what was the point of last night? What was the point of sending just six?"

"To probe our defenses, see if we're

alert or asleep. Charlie wants to know what kind of manpower and firepower we have, how mentally prepared we are. They're testing our resolve."

"So, what then?" I motioned to the six bodies. "These guys were just bait?"

"No different than when we're out humping, Shutter. See, initially we were supposed to protect the cities to free the ARVN to fight, but they don't know their ass from a hole in the ground. So now *we* go outside the wire, but not to win terrain or seize positions. Our mission is simply to kill as many VC as possible, Viet Cong, NVA. It don't matter. If it's Vietnamese, then it must be VC." He cackled. "The military thinks they're sending us out to wear down Charlie, but that's just what Charlie wants. He's wearing us out. We go out and kill Charlie, and twice as many come down the Ho Chi Minh Trail. They're like the rats in New York City; they multiply faster than we can exterminate them. Charlie has an endless supply and the stomach to wait us out. This is his country. He's been fighting for it for almost thirty years. Charlie knows the bush, where he can snipe at us, set booby traps, detonate ambush mines. He tries to create chaos, to break down our

164

training. Then he slips out like he was never here. He leaves nothing behind. He leaves nothing for us to follow. You'll see. Soon enough." Cruz toed the ground with his boot, blew out cigarette smoke, and looked up at me. "Search and destroy. We search. Charlie destroys."

CHAPTER 8

June 7, 1979

The following morning, Todd arrived at the jobsite with his toothpick in place and told me we would begin framing the second floor while waiting for the concrete foundation to set. Mike had accepted a job at an insurance company and would no longer be working on the remodel. I was happy for him, sad for me. I'd miss not having him around, but it also meant more responsibility and maybe less grunt work.

I had the job of cutting the lumber Todd and William needed to frame the walls. Todd's instructions on the use of the miter saw had been simple, but precise. Measure twice. Cut once. Cut the board too small and I wasted the board. With the job underbid, every inch of lumber mattered, even reusing the boards we'd saved from the roof. Todd didn't tell me the latter. He didn't have to.

I also had the job of cutting and nailing in place fire blocking between the first and second floors, and in the walls being constructed. Todd and William shouted out measurements using just about every body part to describe the precision needed. "A pubic hair short of eleven and three-quarters." Or, "An inch shorter than your pecker, so three inches."

After tearing down and breaking up, seeing the walls go up felt like we were accomplishing something productive, which lifted our spirits. We laughed and smiled, even Todd. I stacked the remnants of wood by size so if William or Todd needed a shorter length, say for framing a window or a door, I didn't have to cut a new stud. I also used the remnants for my fire blocking. William said we would frame all day, then use bracing to hold up the walls. In the morning Todd would bring in a crane to lift a massive glulam roof beam in place that would form the new roof peak, and structurally tie all the walls together.

The sun blazed. William and I worked with our shirts off. Todd covered every inch of his freckled, pale skin beneath a long-sleeve cotton shirt and a floppy jungle hat.

With faded blue jeans, my boots, and a fair dose of eighteen-year-old hubris, I felt pretty cocky even before William pointed out the two young women watching us work from the bedroom window of the house next door. I recognized them to be the same women who had driven by the house and nearly caused me to screw up the concrete pour. The limbs and leaves of large maple trees obstructed a portion of the view, but we could see the women, and they could see us.

They looked about my age, maybe a couple of years older.

William said, "Vincenzo, they're definitely in your ballpark." He caught their attention and waved and smiled, and they waved and smiled back, not the least bit embarrassed to have been caught watching us.

"Well, I know they're not waving and smiling at two of us," Todd said, meaning him and William.

I smiled and tried not to look like an embarrassed idiot.

The heat turned up quickly when the two women walked out a sliding glass door onto their backyard pool deck wearing bikinis.

"Vincenzo!" William said, smiling.

Definitely not teenagers. I guessed early twenties. The one who had driven the Mustang had light-brown hair and wore a navy-blue bikini with white polka dots. The dark-haired passenger who had lowered her glasses to stare at me was built like a gymnast, with a washboard stomach that put mine to shame. I pointed this out to William, who just kept uttering my name, stringing it out like an announcer at a ball game. "Vincenzo . . . this could be your lucky day."

As we worked, I would occasionally catch Todd watching me. He didn't say anything, but his shit-eating grin was only partially hidden by his mustache and beard. I initially thought he was concerned I would get distracted and screw up the board cuts, but I soon realized Todd was assessing me, the way he had that first day when he told me to break up the concrete blocks. I suspected Todd still thought of me as a naive kid who had grown up in the Burlingame bubble, which was mostly true. Though I wouldn't admit it—none of my friends would have—I'd graduated high school a virgin, and I could count the number of dates I'd had, not including proms, on one hand. Going to an all-boys school didn't exactly foster healthy relationships with young women.

For the next few hours, the two women dove into the pool with a splash and came up shouting at one another, or listened to music as they lay in lawn chairs, acting now as if they had no idea we watched.

"Oh, they know we're here," William said. "And they know exactly what they're doing."

His comment was a spot-on imitation of Paul Newman in the movie *Cool Hand Luke*, the scene when the prison chain gang worked in the blazing heat, tantalized by a woman washing her car. Just about every eighteen-year-old young man who'd watched *Cool Hand Luke*, myself included, fantasized about Joy Harmon fondling a garden hose while wearing a skimpy sundress soon to be soaked with water and phallic suds. I figured this afternoon was the closest I would get to anything even remotely close to Joy Harmon, who the actor George Kennedy called his Lucille.

The show continued for much of the afternoon, then the two women went inside. I looked between the maple leaves to the bedroom window, hoping they'd go upstairs and take off their swimsuits, but they weren't Lucille and I wasn't Paul Newman.

We worked past five again. When we finished, I was beat. Todd looked around the tripod legs of the miter saw where I'd swept a pile of sawdust and thin scraps of leftover wood. The largest scrap was no longer than a couple of inches.

"Where's the rest of it?" Todd asked.

I didn't understand his question at first. Then I realized he was asking about the leftover lumber from the cuts I'd made.

"What did you do with them?"

"I used them for the fire blocks, or for the smaller pieces you and William needed."

Todd looked confused. He pointed to the sawdust pile. "That's all that remains?"

I worried I'd done something wrong. "No. We got more eight- and ten-footers downstairs," I said. "I didn't unsnap the final two bundles. I reused the roof beams for the longer pieces."

Todd did not look convinced. He looked like I was pulling his leg. William crouched and smiled up at me as Todd walked to the building's edge and looked down at the two bundles of wood I had not touched, then turned and peered at me like I'd just landed from outer space. After a beat he looked at William, who chuckled.

"Well, shit," Todd said. "I'll take them back to the lumberyard." He removed his gloves. "Kelley's working late." I assumed Kelley to be his wife. "Let's grab a drink at Behan's."

I knew the Irish pub on Broadway, though I'd never been inside, and I didn't want to risk having my brother's expired driver's license confiscated. "I can't get in," I said.

William stood from his crouch. "Yeah. You can. Todd and I will meet you on the sidewalk out front."

I helped clean up the tools and lock down the jobsite, slipped on my T-shirt, and walked to my car parked at the curb in front of the house where the two women had been swimming. As I unlocked the driver's-side door, the fire-engine-red Mustang backed out of the garage, the two women in it.

"Hi," the brunette said from the passenger seat. She had both arms folded on the car door, her chin resting on her hands.

"Hey," I said.

The driver leaned across the car. "You finished for the day?"

"Yeah," I said.

"You want to come out and get a drink?"

This confirmed the two women were older

than twenty-one. I was not yet close. I could just picture a scenario where I went out with them and the bouncer laughed at my fake driver's license, then the two women laughed at me.

"I'm going to Behan's," I said. "With the guys I work with."

The driver got out of the car but left the engine running. The passenger followed. "I'm Jennifer," the driver said. "This is my cousin, Amy. She's visiting from New York."

"Hey," I said. "I'm Vincent."

"You live around here?" Jennifer asked.

"Just up the hill."

"Where did you go to high school?"

"Serra," I said and realized Jennifer maybe thought I was home for the summer from college or that I worked construction full time. "I go to Stanford." I said it with purpose. I figured it was nothing more than a white lie, since I couldn't envision how it might hurt anyone. It didn't go unnoticed.

Jennifer said, "Wow," and smiled at Amy.

Not wanting her to ask me what year I was in school or for any details, I quickly asked, "How about you? Where do you go?"

"I'm a senior at UC Davis."

"My brother and sister graduated from Davis," I said.

"Amy goes to Fordham law school in New York. She's visiting and hopes to go out before she goes back to start her internship at a law firm in Manhattan."

"When do you go back?" I asked.

"Sunday."

I shrugged. Now I could be bold. "I have plans tonight, and a softball game tomorrow night." Mike had gotten me a spot playing second base for the Northpark Yankees during their summer softball season. Their regular second baseman had moved back to New York. A thought crossed my mind. "You'd probably like the guys I play with. They're all from New York."

"How do you know them?" Amy asked.

"My sister's boyfriend is from New York and plays on the team."

"Where do you play the games?" Jennifer asked.

"Washington Park. It's at—"

"I went to Burlingame High School." That's where the park was located. "What time is the game?"

I doubted either would come to a softball game. "We play at six. Afterward, we go to Village Host on Broadway."

"Maybe we'll see you there," Jennifer said.

Amy smiled.

They got back in their expensive car. Amy looked at me over her shoulder with that radiant smile that made me feel like George Kennedy watching his Lucille. Like George and the rest of the chain gang, there wasn't a chance I was going to get to know Amy any better, so, emboldened, I gave her my best Paul Newman grin, like I knew what was what, and I had enjoyed every minute of it.

Amy blushed.

If it was the last time I ever saw her, I figured at least I'd have a good memory, one in which I wasn't the embarrassed high school kid.

Todd and William stood on the sidewalk outside Behan's sucking down cigarettes. Cars lined the street, parked in slanted parking spaces, and people crowded the sidewalks, eating at restaurants and enjoying the long summer days and the warm weather. Music spilled from Behan's open windows. "Sorry," I said. I wasn't. Not in the least. I had rehearsed telling them the story in my head. "I ran into those two girls from next door as I was getting into my car."

"Vincent . . . ," William said, drawing out my name as he chuckled.

"One's visiting from New York. She attends Fordham law school and is starting an internship at a law firm in Manhattan."

William's eyes went wide. "Do you know how much money lawyers make at Manhattan law firms?"

I didn't. But I could tell from his facial

expression and the tone of his question it was significant. "The other goes to UC Davis."

"Yes, but did you ask out the one from New York who's going to be making a lot of money?" William said, laughing.

I shrugged. "I told them we have a game tomorrow night and they should stop by Village Host."

"You should have asked her out tonight," William said.

I looked at Todd, who wore his ever-pensive smile that pierced right through my facade. I decided to quit while I was ahead. "Didn't think about it," I said.

"Let me give you some advice," William said with his impish grin. "It's just as easy to fall in love with a rich girl, Vincent."

Todd dropped his cigarette butt, crushed it under the toe of his boot, and walked into the bar with his "I'm the baddest man on the planet" saunter.

Narrow, the bar had dark wood, paper shamrocks, and green-and-white décor. A crowd of young men and women filled the barstools and tables up front, drinking and talking above music playing from a jukebox. I hoped the crowd meant the waitress would be too busy to take the time to ask for my ID.

We walked to an empty table at the rear where the bar widened a bit and the sound didn't echo.

Guys played darts. On the wall, near a pay phone, hung a white sign with green lettering.

BAR PHONE FEES
$1 NOT HERE
$2 ON HIS WAY OUT
$3 JUST LEFT
$4 HAVEN'T SEEN HIM ALL DAY
$5 WHO??

A waitress approached our table and I prepared to reach for my wallet, but William put out his hand beneath the table to stop me and leaned across it. He raised his voice over the music and cacophony of other sounds. "Hey, Brenda."

"Hey, William. Hey, Todd."

"Hey," Todd said.

The woman leaned in. "You meeting Monica?" she asked William.

William cupped his ear against the music and the din of the crowd. I had bad hearing also, my father's hearing. I learned this when a bicycle tire I filled at a gas station on Broadway and El Camino exploded and my mother took me in to be tested. Brenda raised her voice and repeated her question.

"She's working late," William said. "We framed a job today and worked late also."

I looked around, nonchalant, as if relaxing after a tough workday, and realized William had just set me up to get a drink.

"What can I get you?" Brenda flipped three coasters onto the table, each depicting a leprechaun in knickers. I was in.

"Jameson's, rocks," Todd said.

William ordered the same.

I didn't know Jameson's. My only criterion for hard alcohol was cheap. "I'll have a Guinness," I said and waited for the inevitable question. It didn't come.

Minutes later, Brenda returned with our drinks and held out menus. "Are you eating?" she asked.

Todd shook his head. He had to meet his wife, but William nodded, so I did also. Brenda handed us menus and promised to return to take our food orders. We shot the shit and William kept on me for not asking out the New Yorker, but in a funny manner. Todd just smiled.

When Brenda returned, William ordered a club sandwich and a second Jameson's. I ordered a hamburger and a second Guinness. Todd bugged out.

"Springsteen," William shouted as the music changed songs. He rapped on the table edge like a drummer. "A good New Jersey boy."

Mike had turned me on to Bruce Springsteen's music. The prior Christmas he had bought me the eight-tracks *Greetings from Asbury Park* and *The Wild, the Innocent & the E Street Shuffle*.

"We used to sneak into the bars on the Jersey Shore to hear Springsteen when he was a teenager with long hair and a shitty guitar," William said. He smiled like he'd gone back to those carefree days.

I wasn't a big music guy, I didn't have money to spend on albums or eight-tracks, but I had installed an eight-track cartridge player in my Pinto; I'd even cut in the speakers in the back and run the wiring under the carpet. My tape selection was limited. The Beatles, the Rolling Stones, and the two Springsteen eight-tracks from Mike. Mif and I also liked Elvis, though I didn't have a tape and wouldn't admit it out loud. Billy called Elvis "a fat has-been" and said Springsteen was a yodeler. "Uh-uh-uh-uh-oh." It wasn't flattering.

I worried William and I would not have much to say to one another; this wasn't just sitting around after work with a beer. After Brenda returned with our food and drinks, I said, "You have bad hearing?"

William nodded.

"I do, too. I got my dad's hearing."

William grinned. "I have Vietnam hearing."

"Oh," I said.

"Blew out an eardrum during a shelling my first night in the bush." He shrugged like it was not a big deal. "You know Vietnam?" he asked.

"No," I said. "Not really."

William grabbed his napkin and pulled out a pen from his pants pocket and drew what looked like the mirror image of a longer and thinner version of California.

"Saigon is here." He put a star close to the bottom of the drawing. "I was up here near the Laos border at a firebase in the triple canopy jungle."

I figured William wanted to discuss it. "What did you do?"

He shook his head. "Went out at night on recon missions and watched guys step on land mines and get blown to pieces. Then we'd get up the next night and do it all over again, like it never happened. Stupid." He shook his head, so I did also.

William's blue eyes looked to have turned a shade of gray. "You ever watch movies where the soldier is taking aim from behind a log and shooting the enemy? John Wayne shit?"

"Yeah." I loved to watch movies with my dad. War movies had changed over the years. Movies like *The Great Escape*, *The Dirty Dozen*, and *The Guns of Navarone*, which emphasized American heroism and patriotism, had given way to movies like *The Deer Hunter*, which focused on the madness of the war in Vietnam.

"It's bullshit," William said.

"How so?"

"You don't aim. Not if you're smart. You lie down behind a log or a tree trunk or a rock— whatever you can find—lift your M-16 over

179

your head, pull the trigger, and hope the spray hits something. You lift your head up and you're dead."

He proceeded to tell me about his first night in a foxhole, and how the guy he shared the hole with, Kenny, climbed out and took a bullet in the eye. "Didn't even know he was dead," William said.

I sipped my Guinness. "Were you scared over there?" It seemed a logical and harmless question.

William eyeballed me. "Have you ever been scared?"

"Yeah," I said. "A lot of times."

"No, you haven't." William shook his head. "You don't know scared."

I didn't know what to say.

"You ever been so scared that your ass shakes? I'm not talking about shitting your pants. I'm talking about when the flesh starts quivering and you can't stop it."

"No," I said.

"Then you don't know scared." He sipped his drink, and I noticed a slight tremor in his hand. "Growing up, I got in fights because I was bored; hell, sometimes my friends and I would fight each other, and not once did my ass shake."

William finished his drink, which I took as my cue to finish my Guinness. I did and set the glass down, waiting for William to get up, but he had one more thing to say. "You know when my ass finally stopped shaking over there?"

"When you came home?"

"When I no longer cared."

"Whether we won or lost?" I asked, confused.

"We were never going to win. That wasn't the point. No. It stopped shaking when I no longer cared whether I lived or died." William stared at me with such intensity I was certain he could see right through me and was looking all the way back to Vietnam.

"And that," William said, "is when you really should be scared."

As I drove from Behan's back up the hill to home, I couldn't imagine reaching a point when I no longer cared if I lived or died. I couldn't imagine losing all hope, no matter the problem I faced, but maybe that was because, as William had said, I didn't know scared, and I'd never faced a problem so big, so terrifying, that my ass shook.

I hoped I never would.

April 28, 1968

The supposed moratorium has not stopped
Charlie from lobbing 60 mm mortars
at our firebase at night or sniping at us
during our day patrols outside the wire.
The patrols are intended to get us FNGs
acclimated to humping in the oppressive heat and humidity, help us identify
ambush areas, and educate us on how to
detect the many booby traps and ambush
mines we will encounter. I'm sure they're
also to get us past our nerves and anxiety,
as Cruz told me my first day.

I look forward to going outside the wire.
Inside the wire, the monotony, boredom,
and oppressive heat have caused a
lethargy I've never felt before. The sun
rises just before six—an orange-red
ball that turns gold around midday and
becomes a searing white globe for most
of the afternoon. I can hardly get up from
my rack, barely get moving, and do so
only to get away from the putrid smells
in the bunker that remind me of our
forty-year-old high school locker room.
Cruz said the temperature is only mid to
upper 80s and will get hotter, but with the

humidity and the lack of any breeze, it feels like 180. He also said the lethargy is not uncommon, that it will pass.

I haven't taken too many pictures inside the wire. There are only so many shots I can take of guys doing nothing before they tell me to piss off.

The military tries to keep us alert with news that the peace talks are failing and the NVA is massing in the DMZ and along the Laotian border, but they can only say that so many times before it becomes the boy crying wolf. We sit for long hours in the shade and drink warm beer or get high. I gave up my goal of making it through Vietnam sober the night Kenny got shot. Besides, I don't think I'll have any trouble remembering, drugs or no drugs.

Cruz came to me yesterday and said I was to accompany him back to Da Nang on a top-secret mission. He said it was time to put this lull in the fighting to good use. I had no idea what that meant, but I would have done just about anything to get off this firebase.

At twenty-three, Cruz is considered the old man of the platoon, which is why he says he gets the plum assignments and can choose who to accompany him. He's also tight with our captain, Dennis Martinez. They're both from New York. Both Puerto Rican. Martinez is a good officer. The platoon likes him. "He treats us like men," Cruz said. "And he never asks us to do anything he wouldn't do himself. He doesn't try to pretend he knows more than the guys who have been here in the shit."

Cruz and I hopped on the supply chopper and flew back to Da Nang. After picking up supplies for Captain Martinez, Cruz told me we were making a detour. He had a long order to buy weed, and the piastres to back it up. He also knew where to go—a particular mama-san who can be trusted. That sounded to me like a contradiction in terms.

"She'll haggle like hell and act like she's insulted, but in the end, she'll come around." Cruz was looking to buy party packs, ten rolled joints for about five dollars. This mama-san also had what Cruz calls 100s, joints as long as cigarettes soaked in opium. Those sell for a dollar a joint. Cruz once told me you don't smoke the 100s unless you're on base or at the rear. "You can't function," he said. "They will literally knock you out."

We traveled to the Hai Chau District and stopped in a hole-in-the-wall store below three-story apartments. The store had cut flowers for sale on the sidewalk. The inside was as big as my bedroom back home. An oscillating fan, a relic, did little to alleviate the suffocating heat. Maybe that explained why no one else was sitting at the two nicked and scarred tables and chairs.

The mama-san welcomed Cruz like he owned the place. Maybe he did, based on the amount of piastres he carried. The woman was plump and her face ageless. I couldn't tell if she was fifty or a hundred and fifty. I also didn't detect a drop of sweat on her, both of which led me to conclude she'd made a deal with the devil. She rarely looked directly at Cruz or at me. She did, however, have cans of Tiger beer, which were brought unopened to the table by a boy old enough to be fighting. I wondered if he could be Viet Cong and whether he was thinking this would be a good way to kill two marines. He delivered the room-temperature beers with a blank stare that only made me more nervous. I drank the beer with one eye on him and the other on the door, my spare hand on my .45.

Cruz's deal with Mama-san involved haggling in both English and Vietnamese, which Cruz has picked up on his tours. Mama-san yelled and hollered and looked aggrieved, but each time Cruz stood to leave, she waved for him to sit. She wanted the money. She nodded to the boy when the deal was done, and he and Cruz left the room to secure the merchandise while I finished my second beer.

When Cruz returned, I stood, but we weren't leaving just yet. "Shutter. That was a good day's work, and a good day's work deserves its reward. I know you're strung out waiting to meet Charlie, and Mama-san has something to help."

I expected him to light a joint, maybe one of the 100s. He took me behind the curtain covering the doorway. Two women were waiting. He explained that he'd haggled us two of Mama-san's prostitutes. In addition to liquor and weed, Mama-san runs a "boom-boom" house.

I had not yet been with a Vietnamese hooker, or any hooker for that matter, and I still remembered all the negative information fed to us during boot camp about venereal diseases so severe they will rot our peckers. Cruz assured me Mama-san had assured him that these girls had assured her that they are checked regularly by a doctor.

"Well, if she says that they say that a doctor says, then it must be the truth," I said.

"Bad for business," Mama-san said.

So is your prostitutes spending money on a doctor, I thought, but didn't offer. I also didn't offer that I had never been with a woman. I mean, there were two high school girls I fooled around with, and I reached second base with one, but that's where they put up the stop sign. The two girls Mama-san had produced for us didn't look much older than those high school girls, and far less interested. The heat looked to have zapped whatever enthusiasm they once possessed, if ever. I doubt it. They likely hate us as much as the VC, maybe more. The muscles in their faces never moved.

"Just like riding a bike, Shutter," Cruz said as his woman led him behind one of two curtains.

That comment struck me as wrong— equating sex with these two women to riding a bike. But again, I didn't say this.

The woman who took me to another bed was attractive, with a nice figure beneath a thin dress that didn't stay on long. She had small breasts and thin hips and a red scar near her shoulder from a cut badly stitched. I wanted to ask her how she got the cut. I wanted to ask her why she was a prostitute, but I sensed I knew why. She was doing what she had to do, likely to support her family during a war that has disrupted everything. But given her look of bored indifference, I concluded that was not the time for deep discussion. I tried to make small talk, because I was nervous that I was going to mess up, but that, too, went nowhere. She told me to drop my pants and get busy. So I did. I figured this wasn't going to last long when I heard someone yell, "Switch. Switch." Cruz came running into my room naked and slapped me on the back like a Saturday morning tag-team wrestler. "Double your pleasure, Shutter."

I didn't have much choice. I switched rooms to an equally disinterested woman. It didn't take long for me to complete my business, even with the sudden interruption, and based on the lack of any sound or facial expressions, I'm sure the moment was as anticlimactic for the woman as it was for me. It didn't even feel like sex. It felt more like that first cigarette Cruz handed me to calm my nerves.

I had no sooner finished my business when the woman slipped on her thin dress and left the room. I took that as my cue to leave, except Cruz was still going strong in the bed behind the blanket where my clothes lay on the floor. I hoped to hell he wouldn't yell "Switch" again. I figured I'd just wait in the room, but then the girl reappeared with another GI. She'd no doubt spent the minute in between the two of us getting a quick checkup and nod of approval from that doctor. If I didn't have the clap by nightfall, it would be a miracle.

Cruz came through the curtain ten minutes later, but I told him I'd only been waiting a minute or two. We put on our clothes, took the merchandise, and left.

"Nothing like Vietnamese boom-boom to take the edge off, am I right?" Cruz said.

I smiled and nodded and generally played my part. I know I should be grateful. Cruz could just as easily have chosen one of the other guys in our squad to accompany him, but I just can't help but be disappointed by my first experience, and to feel bad for the two young women, but mostly I fear that I'll finally be out on a long patrol and I'll suddenly be scratching like a bitch and crying when I pee.

CHAPTER 9

June 8, 1979

William moved slowly the following morning, and I deduced he hadn't stopped at three Jamesons at Behan's. Mike had told me cocaine was the drug of choice and prevalent among many of the Northpark Yankees, along with marijuana and hash.

On the other hand, I felt pretty good. I arrived home from Behan's too late to catch up with my friends, which allowed me to drink a lot of water, spend the night watching television with my dad and younger siblings, and get to bed at a reasonable hour. I'd also consumed quality beer, not the piss water my friends and I frequently drank.

Regardless of how we felt, there wasn't time for William, Todd, and me to discuss the prior evening. We had a huge glulam beam to set, and Todd said it would crush us if anything went awry. Setting the beam meant getting up on the second story, giving me a chance to peek into the bedroom window and peer down into the backyard pool for my Lucille. No such luck. My Lucille never showed. It was just as well. When the crane arrived, Todd was all business. While

Todd guided the boom operator and put the beam at the exact angle, I worked with William to attach the walls, so the structure tied together and didn't collapse. Once we had secured the framed walls, we put up joist hangers and slid two-by-six roof joists in place. Unfamiliar with the work, I had to learn on the fly watching and mimicking William. Eventually I got the hang of it. Getting the ridge beam in place, securing the walls, and framing out some joists took all day. We quit at five. William and I had a softball game to get to.

We played in the top league. The guys in this league were men. Huge. Or maybe by comparison, I wasn't. The bases extended just sixty feet from home plate, which meant the softball exploded off their bats like a screaming missile. As an infielder, I was supposed to stay in front of that howling explosive and knock it down at all costs, including playing the ball off my chest if need be. Any sane human being would have stepped out of the way, but some on the Northpark Yankees weren't sane. Far from it. Tough New Yorkers, they didn't take shit from anybody and were not averse to provoking the other team. Our left fielder, Greg, had done time for a drug charge and was quick as spit. He would stand on the edge of the outfield grass screaming at the other team in a thick Brooklyn accent, daring the hitters to hit the ball over his head. Many frustrated batters tried and failed to hit the ball over his head, then yelled at him to shut his mouth as they returned to the bench. That only egged him on. The chirping had progressed to some on-field scuffles, and we had been warned by the league that any additional complaints would result in a forfeit.

The game this night, however, finished without incident, a victory that was never in doubt.

We gathered at Village Host Pizza with wives, girlfriends, and friends, and relived each pitch and hit while eating slabs of pizza and drinking pitchers of beer. The team wouldn't let me spend a dime and, as long as I wore the Northpark Yankees jersey and hat, no one carded me.

I'd just sat down at a table with a glass of beer when I felt someone lean close and whisper in my ear. "Vincenzo," William elongated my name. "They're here."

I turned, uncertain. William wore a shit-eating grin. "Remember," he said. "Go for the rich Manhattan lawyer."

I followed his gaze to where Amy and Jennifer surveyed the crowd from the arched entry. Beside them stood a tall, preppy-looking guy in khakis, loafers, and a blue button-down. Amy wore a waist-length faux-rabbit-fur jacket, tight blue jeans, and black boots. I didn't think it possible, but she looked better than she had in her bikini. I'd had two glasses of liquid courage at this point, and quickly drained my third glass and poured another while William kept a close watch, I suppose to see how I handled myself. Then I slipped through the crowd.

"Hey," I said, offering the women my best smile. "You came."

"Sorry we didn't make it to the game," Jennifer said.

"We won," I said.

"I can see that." She turned to the guy, who looked bored and largely disinterested. "This is my boyfriend, Scott."

He gave me a half-hearted handshake. Because I was feeling magnanimous and emboldened, I said, "Can I get you a beer?"

Scott shook his head. "Jennifer and I are on our way out. Can Amy hang with you?" His tone sounded like he was dropping off his child at the sitter. Amy looked embarrassed, uncomfortable, and humiliated all at once, and I deduced she had not willingly come to Village Host. More likely she did not have much say in the matter, and with her being from New York, I was the only potential game in town.

"Yeah, sure. No problem." I turned to Amy. "I'd be happy to drive you home. Come on in and have a beer. You'll like these New Yorkers. They'll make you feel like you're *at home*." I said the last sentence while glancing at Scott.

Amy smiled. Then she and Jennifer hugged, and we said our goodbyes. I turned to Amy, still a bit uncertain, but she alleviated any concern with one question. "You said something about beer?"

I brought her into the crowd, poured her a beer, and grabbed a few slices of pizza. I would have sat at a table in the corner, but Vincenzo having a cute young female was a novelty, and William had apparently told Mike and everyone else that Amy was the girl next door and soon to be rich. My sister, who rarely stayed long at the Village Host—neither softball nor beer were her thing—was the first to come over. Mike followed. Turned out Amy had grown up in Queens, one of the boroughs where Mike had once lived. Mike and my sister asked Amy about law school and where she would be working in Manhattan, and she and Mike discussed clubs in the city where Mike used to hang out. Common ground seemingly relaxed her, and me. I was grateful for the conversation, but also worried that Mike, or more likely my sister, would spill the beans that I'd just graduated from high school, but both either were adept in this situation or never thought to bring it up.

"You're a Yankees fan then," Mike said.

"Born and raised," Amy said with pride. "I wore a Yankees pinstriped jersey home from the hospital. I have three older brothers and they're also die-hard fans. We go to about twenty games a year."

As she talked with Mike and the other New

Yorkers, Amy's accent thickened. "Father" became "Fawther." "Billy Martin (Mawtin) is coming back, that's the rumor in the Bronx, and he'll get them playing great baseball again. Guidry and Munson will take them back to the World Series."

"They may get there," I said, "but I don't see them beating the Pittsburgh Pirates with Willie Stargell, Dave Parker, and Bert Blyleven."

"You watch. Yankees will sweep them."

"Not going to happen," I said. "They'd have to get by Baltimore first."

She stuck out a hand. "Big words. How about a bet?"

I took her hand. "How am I going to recover when I win?" I said.

"You better figure out how you're going to pay when you lose. What do you want to bet?"

"Ten bucks," I said.

"Ten bucks? What, are you scared?"

By now several of the Northpark Yankees had become interested in the conversation and made clucking noises and uttered unflattering words about my manhood.

"A hundred bucks," Amy said.

Since I could not envision how this bet would ever come to fruition, I agreed. "A hundred bucks," I said to a roar of delight from the people around our table.

The conversation flowed easily now, and I went

from thinking I'd never see this woman again to imagining going to Yankees games with her and her brothers. I fantasized about living in New York City with a big-time corporate lawyer. As I said, an all-guys high school didn't exactly foster realistic expectations of relationships between men and women.

Amy asked me about Stanford, and I did my best to be vague but not avoid the subject. A few times I nearly told her the truth, but I never found the courage. So I fudged it. I told her I was studying journalism, that I hoped someday to write for one of the big newspapers, like the *New York Times*, and maybe take down a president, like Woodward and Bernstein. Yeah, I was laying it on thick, but what did I have to lose?

Amy apologized for Scott.

"What's his problem?" I said.

She said she'd been in town for two weeks and her visit had cut into Scott's time with Jennifer. "He's been sulking the whole time I've been here. He wants to get laid." Amy shrugged. "I was in the way. Dropping me off was his idea."

"I figured as much. Anyway, I'm glad he did."

Amy smiled and it looked sincere. "Yeah. So am I."

As the night wore on, and the number of glasses of beer I drank increased, the liquid courage came on stronger. "You have gorgeous eyes," I said at one point, and I meant it. Though she had a dark complexion and dark hair, Amy had these crazy blue eyes and long lashes.

"My mother is black Irish," she said.

"And your father?"

"One hundred percent Italian. No doubt about it."

"Get out of here. That's the same as my parents," I said. "Though my mom is blonde with blue eyes. Where is your father's family from in Italy?"

"Southern part of the boot," she said.

I leaned away from the table. "Your last name isn't Corleone, is it?"

She smiled coyly and said, "Are you concerned I'm going to make you an offer you can't resist?"

"I'm more worried you might have bodyguards."

"DeLuca," she said. "My father is Anthony DeLuca."

"Wait, serious?"

She looked confused. "Yeah, why?"

"My father's family is from Sicily and his last name is DeLuca."

Her face went blank. I waited a beat, then laughed. "I'm kidding. My father's family is from outside Bologna and his name is Bianco."

Amy threw her pizza crust at me. Then she said, "You're a good liar."

It gave me pause.

Amy reached across the table and touched my

hand. "Bet I can still make you an offer you can't resist."

"Refuse," I said, feeling my blood surge. "As an Italian, you should know the line is 'make you an offer you can't refuse.' "

"Refuse. Resist. You want to get out of here?"

"You don't want another beer?" I asked. The pitcher remained half-full and, as I said, picking up on subtle female cues was not exactly a strength of mine.

William, who had been standing close by, reached over and grabbed the pitcher from the table. From behind Amy he looked down at me. "Rich girl," he mouthed.

"Yeah, sure," I said, but I now faced another potential problem. What if Amy DeLuca wanted to go to another bar, or a club?

We left Village Host and walked to my car parked on Broadway. I unlocked Amy's door and held it open for her, then went around to the driver's side trying hard to think up excuses why I couldn't get into another bar. *I've drunk too much already. I can't drive.* What if Amy offered to drive?

I pulled open the car door and slid behind the wheel, going through each potential scenario. When I looked over to ask Amy where she wanted to go, she leaned across the car and kissed me. I felt her hand on the back of my head and her tongue against mine. She pulled back a bit, smiling at me with those black-Irish blue eyes.

"Let's go to my cousin's house," she said.

I relaxed. I wouldn't get carded, and I'd have Jennifer and Scott, and probably both parents, to ease any uncomfortableness. Again, subtle female cues, not one of my strengths.

Amy sat back, then quickly leaned forward and picked up an eight-track. "Oh my God. You have *Greetings from Asbury Park?*"

"Are you a Springsteen fan?"

"Are you kidding? Everyone from New York is a Springsteen fan. He's homegrown, straight from Freehold, New Jersey, and the Jersey Shore."

"I know. My sister's boyfriend, Mike, used to go sneak into bars to hear him play when Bruce was just getting started."

"The Stone Pony," she said. "Are you serious?"

"As a heart attack," I said, stealing William's line.

"I saw him and Southside Johnny play there. Will you put in the tape?"

Hell, I would have driven her to New Jersey to hear the Boss.

We drove the El Camino Real, singing "Blinded by the Light" and "Growin' Up," which was more appropriate than I realized at the time. I was never happier that I had put in speakers. Yeah, it was a Pinto, but this night it was a rolling Springsteen concert.

When we reached her cousin's street, I pulled to the curb in front of the house and noticed the dark windows. Amy leaned over and grabbed my hand before I could turn off the engine. She wanted to listen to "For You." I was happy to oblige, hoping she'd lean across the seat again, but within a minute I noticed a change in Amy's attitude. She wiped a tear from her cheek.

"You okay?" I asked.

She smiled. "Yeah. Sorry. I used to listen to this song with my boyfriend."

"Oh," I said, uncertain what else to say.

She looked at me. "We broke up at the end of the school year, just before summer. He went to DC to work for a congressman, and I chose Fordham over Georgetown because they offered me a scholarship. My parents couldn't exactly afford Georgetown tuition."

"I'm sorry," I said, "that he didn't understand." Then I had another thought. Amy was not over this boyfriend. She clearly still cared for him, which made me what exactly?

"Yeah. I guess things happen for a reason." She reached into her purse, pulled out a small compact, opened it, and removed a joint. She lit it like it was just a cigarette, inhaled, and handed me the joint. Up until this moment, I'd never smoked a joint or taken a hit on a bong. At Serra, a demarcation line existed, our own DMZ, between the jocks and the stoners. You made a

200

choice between the two and you stuck to that choice. The jocks drank beer and looked down on the stoners. The stoners considered the jocks uptight morons.

I didn't know what I wanted at that moment, except not to embarrass myself and come across as a naive kid. I took the joint, continuing the facade I had already perpetrated, took a small hit, held my breath, and passed it back without coughing up a lung. We smoked the joint while listening to Bruce's sultry voice and his poetic lyrics, and my thoughts drifted to William in the jungles of Vietnam, about how he said he used to get high to fend off reality. Maybe I was doing the same thing, fending off reality.

When "Spirit in the Night" ended, Amy pushed open her car door. I got out to walk her up the brick path, now drunk and high for the first time. She took out a key and unlocked the front door, pushing it open. Then she reached back, took my hand, and pulled me inside. Apparently, the night was not yet over.

She led me to the back of the house and down a set of stairs into a family room with a pool table, television, and bar. I could see the pool out the sliding glass doors. Amy turned on the stereo, loud enough for me to realize we were the only ones home. A new reality hit me. Where exactly was this going? Sex? A part of me was thrilled with this prospect, but that other voice kept calling out to me, telling me I was a fraud. I wasn't even in college. I didn't smoke dope, and I'd never had sex. Despite the acting job, I felt young and inexperienced and nervous. I again felt like a kid, not the man I'd pretended to be.

Amy poured rum and Cokes and I sat on a barstool and watched her. She handed me a drink. "My aunt and uncle are in Tahoe until tomorrow. Scott and Jennifer are going to his apartment in the city," she said, confirming what I had already deduced. Then she picked up a cassette and stuck it in the stereo. "This is one of the tapes I brought with me." She hit play, leading me out sliding glass doors to the pool deck while Springsteen's "Rosalita" played from the outdoor speakers.

The summer weather remained warm, but with a slight breeze. I looked from the patio up at the remodel, just a dark skeleton. Never in a million years did I think I would be looking at it from this perspective.

Amy danced and sang. She shed the rabbit-fur jacket and kicked off her black boots. Then she undid the buttons of her blouse, slowly, never taking those beautiful blue eyes from mine. The blouse came off, revealing a black lace bra. Inside I felt like I was swimming as hard as I could but still sinking. Amy unbuttoned her Levi's and shimmied from her jeans. She stepped forward, as if cold, into my embrace, and kissed me.

"Let's go for a swim," she whispered.

I was drowning. A part of me was thinking of every excuse to get out of this situation, fearful that I would mess up and look and feel a lot worse than I would have if I'd lost my fake ID at a bar. But that other part . . . that other part wanted what I saw before me.

Amy helped me remove my jean jacket, unbuttoned my Yankees softball shirt, and pulled the T-shirt over my head. I removed my tennis shoes, stumbling, but Amy held me upright. I was moving on automatic pilot, afraid to consider too deeply what I was doing. I removed my pants.

Amy led me to the pool's edge, and as Springsteen implored Rosalita to jump a little higher, Amy removed her bra, then her panties, looked over her shoulder at me with a thin, wicked smile, and dove into the water. I felt frozen on the edge of the deck. I had two choices, jump in with both feet or step back from the ledge and tell the truth. It briefly occurred to me that I should have had this type of internal discussion before I jumped in the pool at Ed's party. Maybe if I had, I would have realized there had been a lot more at stake than ten dollars.

Amy surfaced. The time for debate was over.

I dropped my shorts and dove into the water. When I came up, Amy swam to me and wrapped her arms and legs around me. I could feel that tight, muscled body against me.

"I promised you an offer you couldn't refuse," she said.

"Refuse. Resist. It's just semantics," I said, trying to make light of the situation. "Besides, do I look like I'm refusing?"

She giggled and we kissed. I knew I was just a rebound, but then I felt her hand on my groin and I was done with the debate. Amy guided me inside her. The first time didn't last long, but being eighteen, that wasn't a problem. Emboldened because I hadn't embarrassed myself, we made love a second time, allowing Springsteen's voice to float over the pool on a hot, starlit summer night. A night I would forever remember.

With time, however, the cool water chilled and sobered me. Amy, too. She climbed from the pool and grabbed towels, and we dried off. As I dressed, Amy went inside and came out wearing a terry cloth bathrobe.

"When do you go back to New York?" I asked, slipping on and buttoning my jersey.

"Sunday. I catch a red-eye."

"Maybe we could go out tomorrow night, to dinner?"

She smiled. "I better spend time with my cousin and my aunt and uncle on my last night."

"How about Sunday before you leave?"

"I think they want to take me to the ocean."

I nodded. I was desperate now, throwing out

options. "Maybe I could go to New York and visit."

She lost the smile. "I'm going to be really busy when I start my internship, Vincent, probably sixty to seventy hours a week, and then I start school so . . ." She shrugged.

She wasn't brushing me off. I know that now. She was just being practical. But I wondered again how long ago she and the boyfriend had broken up. Maybe that frontal cortex was finally starting to kick in—when I really didn't want it to.

She must have seen this inner monologue in my facial expression.

"Vincent, I'm sorry . . ." She stumbled to find words.

"Forget about it," I said using my New York accent, which made her smile. "It's fine."

But it wasn't fine and Amy could tell, which only made my pain worse. She went from looking sorry, which was bad enough, to looking at me with pity. Then her eyes widened. "This wasn't your . . . first time, was it?"

"What? No. No, of course not," I said, but it must not have been very convincing.

"Vincent, I'm so sorry. I didn't . . . Oh my God. Please tell me you're eighteen."

"Don't," I said, taking a step back. I shook my head. "Don't do that."

"Do what?"

"Don't make me feel like some kid."

"I'm not trying to, I just . . ."

"I'm not a kid," I said. But, of course, I was. And I had acted like one this night, just as I had acted like one that night at Ed's party. Act like a child and you will be treated like one. My mother's old refrain.

"You worked and played softball with those guys . . . I just thought you *looked* young."

She was right. It wasn't her fault, and I wasn't blaming her. I had given her every reason to believe I was older. I had played the lead role in this performance, and I'd done it convincingly, but now I had shed my costume and makeup and forgotten my lines, and Amy saw through the facade and my ad-libbing.

"I just thought we could have some fun," she said.

"It was. It was fun," I said. And it had been. So much so that I'd just hoped there would be more. "I better go."

"We could listen to another album," she said.

"No. I better get home."

"Spend the night," she said.

I smiled and gave away still more. "I can't."

"You're sure?"

"I wish I could." I turned for the sliding glass doors, then stopped and turned back to her. "I'm going to collect on that bet."

Now she smiled, pensive. "Never," she said.

I grabbed my jacket off the chair and stepped inside the sliding glass doors. When I turned around, Amy wasn't chasing after me, like in the movies. She remained at the pool's edge with a look of regret and both arms wrapped around the bathrobe.

From the speakers came the gentle keys and guitar strings of Springsteen's "New York City Serenade," as well as his admonition. Sometimes it's better if you just walk on. Leave the past behind.

He was right. I wasn't about to stay to hear the end of that song.

Or see Amy ever again.

So I thought.

As the years passed, I realized what it felt like to be dumped by someone you thought you loved, and I understood better what had happened with Amy that night. Amy's longtime boyfriend had dumped her, and she was in pain. Her trip to California was no doubt intended as a trip to get away, to have a little fun with her cousin, as she had said. And I'd certainly led her to believe I could provide that fun, for an evening at least.

I didn't see Amy DeLuca Monday morning when I returned to work, and I didn't tell William or Todd about what had happened in the pool. When William asked me, I said Jennifer and her parents had been home when I dropped Amy off, and now she was back in New York, going to work.

He didn't ask any more questions, like whether I'd gotten her phone number. Maybe he knew better. Maybe he knew it was just one night in a lifetime.

Ironically, I did see Amy again. Even more ironic, I was in *my* third year of law school at the time. I was dating a woman from New York, and we'd gone back east to ski. We went into Manhattan to a comedy show at Catch a Rising Star on First Avenue between East Seventy-Eighth and Seventy-Seventh Streets. I didn't know it at the time, but this was the original club where many famous comedians started their careers. On my first visit to New York, I was in awe of the entire spectacle, the snow falling between the tall buildings, all the cabs, and all the people. The evening had been great, incredible food at a hole-in-the-wall restaurant, and comedians who kept me laughing all night. One, Ronnie Shakes, made me laugh so hard he stopped his routine, bought me a drink, and asked me where I would be laughing next. I looked him up thirty years later hoping to take Elizabeth to see this comedian whose bits I could still recite. Turned out Shakes died less than a year after that show. He had a heart attack while jogging. He was just forty years old.

When the comedy show ended, I stood and

looked to my right. Sitting at the table were a woman and a man. The woman stared at me with a look of recognition. She was older, early thirties. Her hairstyle had changed, but she had those same electric-blue eyes. Her look was so certain, I was sure she had noticed me much earlier in the evening, maybe when Ronnie Shakes called me out, and perhaps she had been racking her brain until she figured out how she knew me. Maybe she'd remembered that evening also.

When her husband—she had a diamond on her left hand—turned for the door, she hesitated, as if she wanted to say hello, then likely wondered how she would explain me to her husband. She looked uncertain, then lowered her gaze.

"Excuse me," I said.

She glanced toward the door, to where her husband had been swallowed by the crowd. Then she turned back.

"I'll make you an offer you can't resist," I said.

She smiled, closemouthed but genuine. Her electric-blue eyes sparkled. "Refuse," she said. "As an Italian, you should know the line is 'I'll make you an offer you can't refuse.'"

"I should," I said.

We both smiled. Then Amy DeLuca stepped into the crowd, glancing back one final time before the mass of people also swallowed her.

"Do you know her?" my girlfriend asked.

"No," I said. "She was just correcting . . ." I was going to say "a mistake," but that would have been wrong. "She was just reciting a line from *The Godfather*."

PART III

When You Coming Home, Son?

May 1, 1968

Dying is hardest on the living.

CHAPTER 10

February 17, 2016

Eventually Beau got over their loss on the football field, though he seemed to have some lingering resentment about how their season ended. Serra had lost to a team in the Northern California playoffs, a team they had drubbed earlier in the year. This time, however, they played without Chris. Art Carpenter's fear had been a premonition. Chris tore his ACL in the second-to-last game of the year when an offensive lineman fell on the side of his leg. Chris had had surgery, and while successful, it had been involved. Doctors were optimistic Chris would be able to rehabilitate to the point of playing again, but that didn't help Serra.

Worse, the Division I schools revoked their scholarship offers or stopped calling, including Stanford. Coaches told Chris to enroll as a regular student and rehab his knee. If the knee returned to strength, and Chris returned to his prior playing level, they'd consider putting him on scholarship.

Art and Josephine Carpenter were equal parts devastated and angry that schools would be so quick to "change their tunes" and "abandon" their son. Many of the schools were no longer financially realistic.

I thought of my own college situation, my disappointment, and I thought of William Goodman losing his wrestling scholarships after injuring his shoulder and losing interest in school. Chris wouldn't end up in Vietnam, but I took Beau aside and told him to keep an eye on Chris anyway, and encourage him to keep up his grades and not give up on his dreams at such a young age.

Without Friday night football we fell into a different routine. Elizabeth and I attended Mary Beth's basketball games. I had suggested to Beau, more than once, that Mary Beth would be proud to have her big brother attend, but Beau did not want to miss a night out with his friends. Beau also had a girlfriend, which I never had in high school, and he had confided in me that sometimes he resented the commitment.

"Guys talk about what they did over the weekend, and I feel left out when I'm not there," he told me one night as we sat in our remodeled family room.

"I know the feeling," I said, and I did. "But do your friends ever do anything really epic, or is it just the same stuff every weekend?"

"I don't know. But, I mean, it's my senior year. Some of these guys, like Chris, will be my friends for life, but others I know I won't see again."

I didn't want to tell Beau that I used to think Mif, Billy, and Cap would be the best men at my wedding, and that we'd remain lifelong friends. We did not even attend each other's weddings. Like most guys, I was not good at staying in contact. Nor were they. Some friends moved away, and we all had our own commitments with spouses, children, and jobs. Beau's comment also made me think of William's journal, how his corporal, Victor Cruz, advised him not to make friends in Vietnam, that it was easier that way when those soldiers were killed.

The issue of Beau going out with his friends came to a head in late February, as Elizabeth planned Mary Beth's sixteenth birthday. I was in a protracted trial in San Mateo County and not much help. Elizabeth wanted to surprise Mary Beth and take her to Tadich Grill in San Francisco. When the kids were young and I worked in San Francisco, Elizabeth used to dress them up and they would ride BART into the city. The four of us would have dinner, usually at Tadich Grill. The 150-year-old restaurant had a special place in all our hearts, and Mary Beth thought of it as magical. Elizabeth had called six weeks in advance to get the reservation. While we were away at dinner, my older brother, John, and his wife would drive their Honda Accord to our house and leave it in the driveway affixed with a pink bow. John's four kids had driven the car

217

to school and put 158,000 miles on the odometer, but it still ran well. My brother just wanted the car off his insurance, and I just wanted Mary Beth to have wheels to get to school, as Beau had. Mary Beth's school was less than two miles from our front door, so it was not like she'd be driving the car on cross-country excursions.

I didn't want to buy either of our children something new and fancy just because we could afford it. I wanted them to know how difficult it could be to make a buck, as I'd had to learn, so they would appreciate what they had.

The problem that soon developed, however, was Elizabeth made the dinner reservation on the night of Serra's infamous Jungle Game against their basketball rivals Saint Ignatius. The inaugural Jungle Game had been in 1975, when my brother John played for Serra. The game received its name when the Saint Ignatius coach was quoted in the newspaper saying, "We have to go down to Serra, and it'll be a jungle down there." The next year the entire all-male cheering section stormed into the arena wearing white T-shirts and carrying palm leaves. They chanted, "SI. Welcome to the jungle."

The game had grown in infamy and was usually hard fought and exciting. I had been to many games over the years, and truth be told, I was sorry to miss this year. But family was family.

Beau and Chris had become Serra's head

cheerleaders for the basketball games, and they planned to make the night memorable. I felt for Beau, but I had my own problems with a complicated trial, a difficult client, and a lot of money at stake. Admittedly, my fuse was short, as it usually was when I was in trial.

The conflict came to a head in the family room when Mary Beth was out with her cousin.

"You can't miss your sister's sixteenth birthday, Beau," Elizabeth said as I entered the house after another long day. "We've had these plans for weeks."

"Change the night," Beau said.

"I can't change the night. I had to make the reservation six weeks in advance. And Friday night is her birthday."

"Then change the restaurant."

"I'm not going to change the restaurant. This is a special night and I want Mary Beth to feel special."

"Well, you should have checked with me before you made the reservation," Beau said. "This is the biggest game of the year, and I'm a head cheerleader."

I knew exactly what was going on without being filled in. I didn't like Beau's attitude with his mother, but I didn't want to escalate the situation. Softly, I said, "Beau, I understand—"

He turned, his eyes burning holes in me. He clearly had been preparing for this confrontation.

"No, Dad. You don't understand. You say you do. But you don't. You didn't play sports in high school. You were the editor of the school newspaper. It's not the same thing. You don't know what sports represent."

It was not the first time Beau had lashed out at us that year. He wasn't a child anymore, and he didn't want to be treated like one, though he still occasionally acted like one. At eighteen he could vote and he could be drafted. He wanted to make his own decisions. I tried to remember what it had been like for me, turning eighteen and being an adult chronologically, but nowhere close mentally. I used to blame my underdeveloped frontal cortex for all the stupid things I did, but it was just immaturity. As my father had once said, *If you want to be treated like an adult, then act like one.* Easier said than done for young men at eighteen.

Many times, I worried that Elizabeth and I had made Beau's landing too soft because we could. I had to grow up quickly because my parents were spread so thin. I had to care for those younger than me, as my older siblings had cared for me. That meant doing laundry, making dinner, then cleaning the house before my dad got home from work. But my landing was nothing compared to William's crash landing in the bush of Vietnam. He'd had no choice but to grow up if he wanted any chance to come home alive.

It was the conundrum of every parent with a boy becoming a young man—loving your child enough to let him make his own decisions and his own mistakes, and not stepping in to rescue him.

So while I didn't take Beau's comment personally, I wasn't about to let Beau ruin his sister's birthday.

"First of all, don't take that tone with me or your mother," I said. "Second, you're not the only one sacrificing. I'm in trial and your mother also has a lot on her plate."

"It's not the same thing," Beau said, defiant.

"You're damn right, it's not. My job pays for you to go to that school and puts food on the table and a roof over your head. You're talking about just another game."

"Like Bellarmine was just another game?" Beau said.

"Don't put that on your father, Beau," Elizabeth said. "You had a concussion."

"This is the Jungle Game," Beau said, ignoring reason and common sense.

"Bellarmine *was* just another game," I said, my voice rising in volume to match Beau's. "So, if you're trying to make me feel guilty about choosing my son's health over a game, forget it."

Elizabeth stepped in. "There will be more games, Beau. This is family. You don't sacrifice family for a game. These are memories that will last a lifetime."

221

"There won't be another Jungle Game, just like there won't be another Bellarmine football game." He turned to me. "You ruined that game for me, and now you're ruining my last Jungle Game. These are the memories I'm going to take with me for the rest of my life, not some dumbass birthday for my sister."

"Your sister has been to every one of your birthdays, Beau," Elizabeth said.

"And she attended every one of your football games," I said. "You can't even make it to one of her basketball games."

"My birthday isn't on the biggest game day of the year, and she attended my games to be with the guy she likes, not to support me."

"That's not fair, Beau," Elizabeth said.

"It is fair. You're not being fair. I'm not going. Period."

Beau started for the door and I stepped in his path. "Don't you talk to your mother that way," I said.

"Get out of my way," Beau said. "I'm done talking."

He stepped past me and I grabbed his shoulder. He swung his arm and knocked my hand away. I took a step after him, but Elizabeth stepped between us.

"You walk out that door tonight, don't come back," I said, and I regretted the words before they had left my mouth. Italian temper.

"Vincent," Elizabeth said.

"I'll sleep at Chris's," Beau said.

"You're not sleeping at Chris's," Elizabeth said.

At that moment Mary Beth and her cousin came into the room. Mary Beth had been crying and it was clear from the anguished expression on her face that she had heard the argument. "You don't have to go to my birthday, Beau," Mary Beth said. "I really don't care."

"He doesn't mean it, Mary Beth," Elizabeth said.

"Yes, he does. He never wants to do anything that involves me. I went to every one of your stupid Little League games every summer. All the stupid tournaments on the Fourth of July and all your stupid football games."

"I didn't ask you to go," Beau spit back.

"That's the point," Mary Beth said. "You didn't have to."

We stood in stunned silence. I didn't know if my daughter had ever said anything so profound. Beau didn't have to ask her to go. She went because he was her big brother and she loved him and was proud of him. He was also the only brother she'd ever have, and she his only sister. They wouldn't have nine siblings to choose from. They had only each other.

Mary Beth sobbed and went upstairs. Beau remained upset, but I could see that Mary Beth's words and her tears had pierced a hole in his shield of anger.

"You do what you want," I said.

"Don't guilt me," Beau said, but his tone had changed, now soft and regretful.

"If I wanted to guilt you, you'd know it," I said. "I mean it. You do what you want. Go or don't go. But I don't want you there if you're going to ruin your sister's birthday. We're going to make this night special for her, with or without you."

May 2, 1968

The peace talks continue, but so does the war. Our firebase has been on alert since April 30. NVA troops have engaged marines in the Battle of Dai Do along the demilitarized zone, trying to punch an invasion corridor into South Vietnam. A battalion of marines known as the Magnificent Bastards is repelling them. We are hearing rumors of another NVA offensive, what is being called a Mini-Tet.

While we wait for orders, I wrote my first letter home since being in-country. I decided it was time. I'd put if off because I didn't want my family to expect the letters, not knowing when I'd get the chance to write another or how long it would take for the letter to reach them. I have received letters from home. They come in with the Hueys that resupply our firebase and take my film back to the lab at Da Nang. My mother apparently sent a birthday package with cookies and a cake for my nineteenth birthday. I received an empty box. I don't know if the guys here ate the contents, or if they were eaten in transport. Too bad because I'm losing weight and could have used the extra calories. The heat of the bush melts the pounds off and kills your appetite, as does the thought of eating another C ration.

I kept my letter bland because, well, but for that first night when Kenny died—seems like a long time ago now—it pretty much has been bland. I told my family I missed them. I thanked them for the birthday gifts. I didn't want to say, "I'll see you soon," or that I couldn't wait to come home, remembering Cruz's admonition not to talk about home while you're in Nam. Marines have all kinds of superstitions.

"What good is talking about home going to do? You're here. You're in Nam. This is your home. This is where you live. *We* are your family. You keep your mind here and you keep your body here. You let your mind go home . . . and your body goes home. You don't think about it. Don't talk about it. *Comprende*, homie?"

I learned quickly. The calendar I hung on a nail near my bunk was torn down the first day I arrived. I never did find it or find out who took it down, but I understood why. "You don't count days until you're a short-timer sent back to the rear," Cruz said.

It's lonely here, even with all these guys. We know one another but not too deeply. Another superstition. "You don't make friends," Cruz told me on another night. "We ain't friends, Shutter. You understand? I don't have any friends in the Nam. I don't make any friends in the Nam. Most guys aren't here long enough to care about anyway. They rotate out, their DEROS comes up, or they get flown out in a body bag. That's Nam. It's easier to say goodbye when you aren't friends."

CHAPTER 11

July 9, 1979

My mother worked late, taking a seminar, something she called continuing education. The oldest at home this year, I cared for my younger siblings, as my older siblings had cared for me. After cooking and putting out a meal, I cleaned the kitchen and took a shower. My mother arrived home, and with everything in order, I told her I was headed out.

"Don't be late."

"Never," I said.

She gave me the look—she wasn't buying it. I smiled. "I won't be late. I got work in the morning."

Mif picked me up in a yellow Volkswagen bug. "Whose car?" I asked, sliding into the passenger seat.

"My sister's. My brother's home from school and has the other car."

In my house, when siblings came home, the available car often went to the oldest. The same rule applied in Mif's house.

"Where's Billy and Cap?"

"Billy's got baseball. Cap is going to meet us at Ignatti's."

Mike Ignatti, a junior, had a basement with a pool table and a pinball machine. His father was deaf in one ear. Ignatti said his dad put his good ear to the pillow and couldn't hear anything in the basement. That meant playing music and drinking beer while shooting pool, playing pinball, and throwing darts. It made me uncomfortable, drinking beer in someone's house, knowing their parents were home, but it didn't stop me.

I could only recall drinking beer with friends one time in my parents' home. My dad had walked into the family room and handed me, Mif, and Cap one can of Coors each as we debated what to do with our night. It was a small act, but it meant something to my dad, and it meant something to me. A man of few words when it came to these things, my father was no dummy. He knew I drank. He knew my older brother drank. Handing me a beer in front of my friends was his way of telling me he no longer thought of me as a child, but also that he would hold me to a higher standard and expect me to live up to that standard.

When Mif and I drove up to Ignatti's house, Cap stood out front like a thief scoping out a burglary. He bent down to speak in the driver's-side window.

"Ignatti's mother won't let him have friends over. His sister came home from college and they're having a family dinner."

"What do you want to do?" Mif said.

"I don't know." Cap walked around to the passenger side of the car. "Vinny B., get in back."

"I'm not getting in back. You get in back."

"Come on, I can't fit in the back."

"Too bad. I'm not getting in the back."

"Fine, then let me in."

I knew what was going to happen. We all knew what was going to happen. The minute I got out, Cap forced his way into the front seat, laughing. I didn't have a chance in a power struggle. He stepped out and pulled the seat forward and I sat in the back.

"What about the drive-in?" Mif asked.

I didn't want to go to the drive-in. The memory of Ed singing Padre fight songs and the ridiculous melee it caused remained fresh. We threw out and rejected three or four more options before Cap said, "My Brother's Place?"

We had stumbled onto the hole-in-the-wall bar on El Camino Real in Millbrae on a Friday night earlier that summer, after my one and only dine and dash at a Denny's restaurant. Todd paid us every Friday, cash under the table, and while most of what I earned went into the bank to help pay my future tuition, I had enough that night to pay my portion of the bill, but not the entire amount. I had no choice but to run, along with my friends.

I never told my friends, but my conscience got the better of me, and I went back to that

Denny's the next day with more money. I told the manager, who wasn't much older than me, that I'd been in the restaurant the night before and that my friends and I had forgotten to pay the bill.

"You what?" The manager wore his hair parted in the middle and had fuzz over his upper lip that would never pass for a mustache. He looked and sounded like I was speaking a foreign language.

I repeated myself and he said, "Hang on."

He went into a room at the back of the kitchen, and I thought for certain he was calling the Millbrae Police Department. When he came out, he held a bill. "Is this yours?"

I looked it over. "Yeah that's it."

"The waitress said it was a dine and dash."

"No. Just a mistake."

"You plan to pay in full?"

"Yes," I said.

He shrugged, looking more than a little confused, and rang up the bill on the cash register. I handed him cash and walked toward the door.

"Hey," he called. I turned around. "Why'd you do it?"

"I told you it was just a mistake. My—"

"No. Why'd you come back to pay?"

He knew I was lying. He knew it had been a dine and dash. "I don't know," I said.

But I did know.

I was ten when I accompanied my father to the ACE Hardware store in Millbrae. I don't recall what he purchased, but I do recall he handed the cashier a ten-dollar bill and she gave him back change for a twenty. I remember thinking we'd hit the mother lode.

"No. That's not right," my father said. "I only gave you a ten." He handed the woman back her ten-dollar bill. She cried.

"I'm sorry," she said. "We lost our nephew in Vietnam. My sister got the word last night."

My dad expressed his condolences before we walked to the parking lot. "Why are we in that damn war?" he said.

"Hey, Dad?"

"Huh?"

"Why'd you give her back the ten dollars?"

"Never take anything that doesn't belong to you or that you haven't earned," he said, sliding into the car. "You never know who you're stealing from, and what that money means to them."

I had forgotten that moment until that summer, when I worked with William.

My Brother's Place was a strategic choice. To underage drinkers, a bar's most important attributes are dark lighting and cheap beers. My Brother's Place had both. The patrons inside were sparse, even for a weeknight, and we hoped the bartender would see our money as no different from anyone else's. Cap and Mif didn't get carded because they looked twenty-five. I was eighteen and looked sixteen.

We stepped through the swinging door like we were stepping into a western saloon. Confidence was key. You walked in like you owned the place, like you belonged. You sauntered in, like Todd Pearson, a badass who showed no fear. It took a moment for my eyes to adjust to the dim lighting from the bloodred candles on the half-dozen nicked and scarred tables. My Brother's Place was well worn. I don't remember the carpet color; I just recall that it crackled beneath your feet when you walked across it. A window faced the sidewalk, but the owner had put black film on the inside. We made our way to the three empty booths with vinyl seats lining the back wall, which was painted a dark gray, or black. I couldn't tell. Flecks of white showed through where the paint had chipped. I remember thinking the walls looked like outer space.

Three patrons sat on barstools nursing cocktails and watching a black-and-white television mounted over the bar. Each looked older than dirt. The bathroom was in the back, past the bar, along with an office and a storage area. A door led to an alley. I'd learned this when I'd used the bathroom in June, just in case I ever needed a quick escape.

I'm not sure why, but My Brother's Place had a piano. The lid reflected the red, white, and blue neon Budweiser sign hanging in the window, and tonight, a piano player sat at the keyboard, playing and singing a song I recognized. I figured the guy had to be a customer, that the bar wouldn't spring for a piano man on a weeknight with so few customers, but he was really good.

Mif and Cap handed me dollar bills. "Vinny B., your turn. Get us a beer," Cap said.

"What? I'm not buying the beer. I look the youngest of all of us."

"Exactly. Bull by the horns," Cap said. "He won't expect you. If you sit here, he'll think we're hiding you and card us all."

"That's the stupidest—"

"Do it," Cap said, and I didn't have much choice. The longer we delayed, the more suspicious we all looked. *Confidence is key,* I told myself as I slid from the booth and walked to the bar. I fully expected to get shot down, and I didn't really care. I had work in the morning. "Three Buds," I said.

"Got an ID?" The bartender looked midthirties. He wore a light-blue bowling shirt and had long sideburns.

I took out my wallet and removed my brother's expired license, holding it up in the dim lighting with my finger over the expiration date. The bartender snatched it from my hand and bent closer to one of the bloodred candles. I was certainly busted. If he kept the license and turned it in to the police, I was toast. If my parents didn't ground me, my brother would kill me.

He smiled at me. "You're twenty-one?"

"No," I said. He turned his head and gave me a disbelieving look. "I'm twenty-two."

He looked back to the license, then gave me a thin smile that might have meant either *Nice try* or *Well played*. I couldn't tell. I held my ground for what felt like hours but was only seconds. The bartender handed me the license. Then he reached into a fridge below the bar and pulled out three long-neck Buds, popping the caps on a bottle opener attached to the bar. I gave him three bucks, then put a fourth on the sticky bar top, making certain he saw the gesture. The bartender handed it back and nodded to the piano. "Much obliged if you would take care of the piano player instead."

I said we would. I didn't care. We were in.

I walked to the booth like a hero. Cap and Mif just smiled. "Told you," Cap said.

I told Mif and Cap what the bartender said to me about taking care of the piano player, then walked over and put the dollar in a glass with a sign. **PLAYS FOR TIPS.**

The piano player gave me a somber smile and nod.

Mif, the most social of the three of us, made his way to the piano. The guy at the keys had long dark hair and a thick mustache. He looked like a young Freddie Mercury from Queen, and he was banging out a pretty good version of Elton John's

"Rocket Man." When he finished, Mif stuffed another dollar in the glass; we'd all decided it would keep us in the bartender's good graces.

Cap and I pulled up barstools to the piano.

Mif said, "How about 'Piano Man' by Billy Joel?"

The guy busted right into the song, and soon we were singing the tune. We took turns dropping a buck in the jar and trying, unsuccessfully, to stump the piano man. None of us liked the disco crap still getting significant airtime, so we threw out some rock 'n' roll—bands and songs, like the Rolling Stones' "Beast of Burden," the Beatles' "Yesterday," Elton John's "Yellow Brick Road," and Elvis Presley's "Always on My Mind." Whatever song we chose, the piano man played and sang the words. Our enthusiasm and inability to stump the piano man had a ripple effect. Pretty soon the three men seated at the bar came to the piano, paying a buck and throwing out songs. Someone asked for "Danny Boy" and the piano man never hesitated. The entire bar, including the three of us, sang the song at the top of our lungs. The bartender opened the swinging door to a hot summer night, and soon people ventured in off the sidewalk to see what was happening. The crowd grew to perhaps thirty.

After an hour the piano man took a break. His tip jar was full. Mif, Cap, and I decided to let others continue to fill the till and save the rest of our money for beer. I went to the bar to order three more. Cap and Mif grabbed a booth.

"Thanks," the bartender said.

"For what?"

"For breaking the ice, for being interested in my brother's music and putting some money in his till."

"He's really good. He's your brother?" I looked to the piano player and could see the familial resemblance.

"Younger brother."

"No offense intended, but why is he playing here? He should be doing shows and stuff."

The bartender smiled. "That was the dream. Then he got drafted."

"Vietnam?" I said.

"Viet-fucking-nam," the bartender said. "He had a music producer interested in his stuff and a record deal on the table. He played with a band in San Francisco. Of the four band members, three got drafted. The drummer died over there. The guitar player came back worse off than my brother. I'm hoping that letting him play here will get him back into it. Maybe get him back on his feet." The piano man turned and smiled at his brother as he sat to play a second set.

"That's gold right there," the bartender said. "I haven't seen him smile like that in a long time." He wrapped his knuckles on the bar. "Those three are on me."

"You don't have to do that," I said.

He smiled. "Yeah, I do. Thanks for bringing him some good memories. He's brought home enough bad memories."

I thought of William telling me how his ribbons didn't mean a thing to him except a lot of bad memories, and how he tried to forget the past and not think much about the future. He just lived day to day.

I retrieved the free beers, and on my way back to the booth, I stuffed the dollars in the glass jar. I handed Mif and Cap their beers and told them of my conversation with the bartender. "He's trying to get his brother back on his feet and said the good memories help."

"He's probably gay and likes you," Cap said.

I shook my head. "Seriously, he had a record deal before he got drafted."

"That sucks," Mif said.

"Do you guys realize we're the first generation this century that hasn't had a war hanging over our heads?" I asked.

Cap glanced at me like I'd lost my mind. "What the hell are you talking about, Vinny B.?"

"You're right," Mif said. "I hadn't thought of that. We don't have a war to worry about."

Cap grabbed his beer. "You guys are killing my buzz." He slid from the booth and walked back to the piano.

"Is the piano man messed up?" Mif asked.

"The bartender didn't really say." I took a sip and contemplated William, the shake in his hands and the quiver in his voice I had noticed whenever he spoke about Vietnam. "Did I tell you about the guy I work with . . . about him riding out of the jungle on a tank covered with dead American soldiers?"

"No. Really?" Mif said.

I shared William's story with Mif and told him of the shake. Then I said, "I don't know, but it seems like he's getting worse."

"How so?" Mif asked.

"Every morning, he looks tired, and hungover. And I think he's losing weight." I sipped my beer and played with the label. "He wasn't much older than us when he went over there."

"Shit, are you guys still talking about war?" Cap slid onto his seat, carrying just one beer.

"Thanks for the beer," Mif said, chuckling.

"I got the last round," Cap said.

I didn't care. I'd had enough. "If this was ten years ago, Ed and Mickey would be at the draft board instead of working for their fathers. It would be our friends getting killed."

"What are you worrying about? You're smart as shit," Cap said.

We finished our beers, thanked the piano man on the way out the door, and promised to be back. A different problem now presented itself. Cap lived in San Mateo. Mif lived thirty minutes in the opposite direction. I was a five-minute drive up the hill, but Cap had to get home, and no way he'd pay for a taxi. None of us would have.

"Shit," Mif said, knowing this would add an hour to his drive.

We drove the El Camino Real into San Mateo and dropped off Cap. We were nearly to the 280 freeway when Mif again swore. "The gas light came on. We're on empty."

I leaned over to gauge the needle. I worked on cars with my dad and fancied that I knew more about them than my friends. But *E* was *E*, and the needle was on it.

We found a gas station near the freeway entrance. Mif swore again. The gas cap was locked. The gas crisis that had followed the Iranian revolution had caused people to siphon gas tanks, which led to locked tanks.

"Where's the key?" I asked.

"I don't know," Mif said.

We checked the key ring but didn't find it. We then tore apart the glove box. No key. It wasn't there. We had no way to get ahold of Mif's sister. After fifteen minutes, we did the only thing we could. We set out for home. I told Mif he could sleep at my house and we'd get gas in the morning.

Mif jumped on the freeway. As we neared Black Mountain Road, Mif put on his blinker. "No," I said. "Go to the Trousdale exit. If we run out of gas, we can coast down the hill and get closer to my house."

It was a good plan. In theory.

The VW bug bucked as we neared the uphill grade to the exit, then it died. Mif pulled to the side of the freeway.

"We can push it," I said.

Hell, Mif had a chest like an inflatable raft. I stood at the driver's door steering and pushing. Mif went to the back, bent to the bumper, and pushed like he was hitting a football blocking sled. The bug picked up speed. As we neared the top of the grade, we gave it another push and I jumped in behind the wheel.

"Get in," I yelled, but before I knew it, I was flying down the exit. "I'll get my car and come back and get you," I shouted out the window, seeing Mif getting smaller in the bug's side mirror.

It was idiotic, really, another illustration of that underdeveloped frontal cortex, or simply beer on the brain. I should have just stopped and let Mif in. We were on a downhill slope, and I could easily have gotten rolling again, but my thought process was to not hit the brakes, to pick up as much speed as I could, and to coast as close to home as possible. And that's what I did. I ran every stop sign on the downhill grade and made it to my house. I didn't try to be stealth this night. I ran inside to the flicker of blue-gray light coming from the television in my parents' bedroom. I grabbed the keys to the Pinto from the desk in my room, ran back out the door, and made my way to Trousdale. Along the way I expected to see Mif.

I didn't.

He had to be on the exit. He wasn't.

I thought it unlikely he could still be on the freeway, but at a loss as to where else he could have gone, I drove onto the on-ramp heading south, the wrong direction, took the first exit and made my way north again. As I approached the spot where I'd left Mif, I slowed and looked along the side of the road. I didn't see him. With each passing moment I got more and more concerned.

I thought of William telling me that he didn't make friends in Vietnam, that it was easier if you didn't really know the guys who died.

"Shit."

I took the exit, scouring every shadow. I backtracked to my street. No Mif. I turned around and drove back, compulsively swearing. My mind thought of the worst-case scenarios.

What if he got hit by a car on the freeway?

What if the police picked him up wandering along the freeway?

What if somebody killed him?

I kept driving, kept looking. All the while, William Goodman's words kept flowing through my mind.

You don't make friends.
Guys can be gone in an instant.
It's just bad luck.

I had visions of driving the Pinto, Mif's battered, bleeding, and lifeless body strapped across the hood, like those soldiers on the armored personnel carrier that had carried their bodies from the jungle. I drove backstreets. I drove in circles. When I finally looked at my watch, it was one in the morning. I'd been looking for Mif for an hour. I drove home and contemplated calling Mif's house, but what would I say?

Uncertain what to do, I did the next stupid thing. I went to bed. It seemed like just minutes before my mother's voice woke me.

"Vincent?" She stood in my bedroom. "Mrs. Mifton is on the phone. She said Lenny didn't come home last night. Is that his car parked in front of the house?"

Fear gripped me. I got up and went to the phone and explained what had happened. "I got my car and went back to get him, but I couldn't find him."

I don't know what possessed me to keep talking. If Mif's mother wasn't upset before, she certainly was now. I'd just painted the worst possible scenario for her. She no doubt thought her son was dead and that I had abandoned him.

I was no marine.

I hung up the phone and tried to explain to my mom. She wasn't pleased, but she didn't have time to deal with it. She had to get to work. I showered and was getting ready for work when the phone rang.

Mif.

I swore a blue streak. "Where the hell did you go?"

Mif laughed that nervous chuckle. "You took off. You left me."

"I yelled that I was coming back."

"I didn't hear you."

"Where'd you go?"

"I ran to Ed's house and woke him."

Ed's house was a couple miles from the exit, but so was mine. I know Mif chose Ed's house because he could get into the room in the back without waking Ed's parents. Smart thinking, I suppose, except it screwed me when Mif didn't call home.

Then again, I'd screwed myself.

I picked up Mif and we got gas for the bug. He'd reached his sister. The key to the tank was on a ring on the emergency brake between the seats. We were such idiots.

I was late getting to work and decided to just come clean. Todd and William laughed their collective asses off.

"Why didn't you just hit the brakes?" William asked.

I told him my rationale. Then I said, "Shit, I thought the guy got killed."

William's grin vanished. He didn't say another word. He didn't have to. He gave me that thousand-mile stare, like the one he gave me at Behan's. I had no business mentioning the possibility of Mif dying, not to two guys who truly understood that possibility every day for a year. I had no clue what I was talking about. If I or one of my friends died at eighteen, it wouldn't be from a Viet Cong bullet, or from stepping on a land mine while I humped through a jungle. It wouldn't be bad luck.

It would be from utter and complete stupidity.

May 5, 1968

The moratorium has officially ended and so have the peace talks. The Viet Cong launched Mini-Tet, firing rockets and mortars at Saigon and more than a hundred other cities and military installations. We can hear the bombs going off and see the flashes of the explosions at night.

We've been told to expect to saddle up and go outside the wire on long-range reconnaissance patrols (LRRPs or "lurps") for weeks at a time. "Vietnam is a war of nerves, each side waiting for the other to blink first," Cruz said one night in our bunker. "The difference is, we're all waiting to blink and go home. For Charlie, this is home. He can wait forever."

I was in my bunker, throwing a blade at the wood post—I've become proficient; I can stick the blade just about every throw. In between, I was talking with Longhorn, whose DEROS had come up. He was preparing to ship out on the next Huey bringing supplies to our firebase. Longhorn's real name is Jimmy Edelson. He's from El Paso, Texas, and performs in the rodeo circuit—rides bulls, horses, the whole thing. Jimmy isn't big, but he looks like a tough little shit.

"Got something for you, Shutter." He handed me a Tiger Chewing Tobacco tin. "I kept my personal stuff in here—a picture of my girlfriend and my parents, and a medal."

"What medal?" I asked, thinking it a military medal.

The medal was now around his neck. He held it out. "Saint Jude, the saint of desperate cases and lost causes."

I laughed. "Sounds about right for Vietnam."

"I'm not taking any part of the Nam home with me. I'm leaving it all here. That tin brought me good luck. I hope it does the same for you."

I thanked him, though I've never been superstitious. I do wear the crucifix my mother gave me, and I pull it out and kiss it whenever I get the chance. Maybe say a little prayer. I figured the tin might come in handy though. I opened it and fit my journal and my pencil inside. *That'll do,* I thought.

"I kept it in the pocket of my flak jacket. Right here," Longhorn said, putting his hand over his heart. "One more thing

Charlie had to penetrate before he killed me."

I went back to throwing the knife. Cruz came in, and I nearly impaled him with the blade. Missed his shoulder by an inch. He didn't even flinch.

"Tomorrow," he said to me, "we're heading outside the wire. Search and destroy."

I nodded. I was uncertain how I felt. I'd thought I would be happy to have something to do, but now a million thoughts were running through my head. Like that night with Haybale. Shit just got real.

"We're going after the NVA, try to disrupt whatever they think they're going to start."

The NVA. I recalled Cruz's admonition—that they won't run. *They will stand and fight.*

I noticed Longhorn never looked at Cruz. Never looked at me. For him, the war was over. For me, this was just the start. I looked at the tin. I'll slip it into the pocket of my flak jacket. One more thing Charlie has to penetrate before he can kill me.

CHAPTER 12

July 12, 1979

I had progressed on the job and was handling the work well. Now that Mike was working in the insurance industry, Todd and William didn't treat me like his kid brother. They treated me like an adult and expected me to handle myself like one. I figured that was because no one had treated them like kids at eighteen, far from it.

When I left the house that morning, I noticed the sky had clouded over, or maybe it was just my mood. I was nursing a wicked hangover despite downing a tall glass of water and four Tylenol before going to bed at two a.m. I was also dog tired, and my brain was addled. I'd been out late every night of the week. As the summer progressed, my friends and I tried to compress as much fun as possible into the time we had left.

By the time I reached the jobsite, the clouds had darkened. Tendrils resembling the barren, spindly branches of winter trees reached down from the sky. It did not rain during the Burlingame summer, not that I could ever recall, but it would rain today, and from the look of those angry clouds, this would not be a mist or a sprinkle.

William knew I was hungover the moment I

stepped into the garage, but he had no sympathy for my plight. "Night is your time," William liked to say. "Come morning, your ass belongs to Todd."

His, too.

"Brought you something." He handed me a tool belt, an older one he said he'd had at home. He said it was his first belt, and I sensed the belt meant something to him, though he downplayed it. I told him how much I appreciated it. I wore the belt proudly, and, like the jungle boots, it gave me attitude.

"No time for that now," he said, not with the sky about to open and no roof on the remodel, making everything on the first level susceptible to water damage. As we opened the tarps William bought that morning, he explained that when drywall gets saturated, it loses its structural integrity, making it unsalvageable, and even if salvageable, wet walls become susceptible to infectious mold. The knob and tube wiring between the walls was at risk of shorting out, and otherwise becoming damaged, and the decades-old hardwood floors could buckle and warp and would be expensive to replace.

William moved as if in battle mode. I felt like a dull knife, barely cutting through my morning fog as I tried to keep up. Twice I went around the side of the house to throw up, first my toast and more Tylenol I took. Then dry heaves. I wanted to go home and sleep it off, but I didn't have that luxury. "Lock and load," William kept saying. "Got a job to do." We were in a fight, the enemy didn't care if I was hungover, and I didn't have the luxury of picking and choosing my battles.

"You do what has to be done, or we all suffer the consequences," William said.

William looked at the darkening sky like it was an old acquaintance, though not a friend, come back to pay him a visit. I imagined it was. William had described the weather in Vietnam as "hot, with rain, becoming hotter with still more rain, turning to sizzling with showers, and a shitload of mosquitos."

William and I fastened bungee cords to hold down the tarps. It was a lot of work getting the tarps over the new roof ridge. We finished, barely, just as the first showers fell.

The rain sounded like hail as it splattered against the blue tarps, and I noticed William looking up at the noise like it was something far more lethal. "I'm going up to check the tarp for leaks," William said, leaving me in the garage.

All the rushing around and climbing up and down ladders had caused the blood to pound at my temples like the rain pounding on the tarps. The prior day Todd had had me cutting lengths of rebar for a brick barbecue we were building at another jobsite. I think it was busywork, but it was something to do and I hadn't yet finished.

Cutting metal rebar is done by switching out the wood-cutting blade on a Skilsaw for a black carbon fiber blade that cuts metal. I'd watched William and Todd change out the blade a number of times, and I'd watched them prop the rebar over the toe of their boot to get one end off the ground when they cut.

Still moving like a dullard, I changed out the blade, plugged in the Skilsaw, put on protective goggles, measured a piece of rebar, and put it over my boot. The blade whined and screeched and threw sparks when it hit the rebar. I hesitated, thinking I should put on leather gloves, then dismissed the thought.

I was bent over, the metal blade spinning, sparks flying, when William came into the garage and shouted over the whine of the blade.

"Stop!"

I turned and looked up at him through the goggles. He put a hand to his throat and made a violent slashing motion, then reached out as if to grab me, but pulled back before he touched me. With the gray light behind him and the fingers of his hand spread wide, he looked like the ghost of Jacob Marley in *A Christmas Carol*. I released the trigger, and when the noise of the saw faded, William stepped forward, his arm still outstretched.

"Drop the rebar," he said, his voice calm but adamant. It sounded like he was telling me not to move, as if I had just stepped on one of the land mines he had described in Vietnam. I let the rebar drop. It pinged twice against the concrete, the sound tempered by the puddle of water in which I stood.

The dull blade of my mind sharpened. The cloudy haze fogging my common sense lifted, and my frontal cortex made the connection. I had gripped a metal bar in one bare hand. In the other hand I held a saw plugged into a compromised electrical outlet, while standing in a puddle of water. I flashed to my childhood, to being in a crawl space over the kitchen with my dad while he repaired a stove fan. My father had looked at me and said, "If I start to shake. Don't touch me."

I'd never been so scared.

I stepped back. William let out a held breath. He looked pale, his pupils enlarged dark circles in a sea of white. William had been scared for me. Now he was angry.

"Do you have a death wish?" He asked the question with such intensity, such brutal honesty, such piercing practicality, that I felt compelled to answer, though I knew his question to be rhetorical.

"No," I said.

He shook his head, like a father disappointed with a child. "You're standing in a puddle of water with an electric power tool and holding a piece of metal." He punctuated every other word with a profanity. "You're supposed to be smart." He pointed to his temple, a quick, decisive gesture. "Think."

Then he turned and left the garage, but not before he brought the heels of his hands to his eyes.

I looked at the tool belt William had given to me that morning and realized I had just thrown away what respect I had earned in one dull moment of stupidity.

I imagined William had experienced too many of those senseless moments and the resulting consequences, moments that could never be taken back, never changed, never forgotten. Guys were there one moment and gone the next.

If William mentioned the incident to Todd when he arrived later in the day, Todd never said anything about it. He never called me an idiot or a moron or asked how I had such a wanton lack of common sense. He never fired me.

Still, William hardly talked the remainder of the day, and after work he didn't squat in the garage to smoke a cigarette and drink a beer. He gathered his red cooler, put it in the bed of his El Camino, and drove off. I knew William had experienced far too much death for a man who had just turned thirty, and I knew I had brought him back to a place he had tried hard, though unsuccessfully, to forget. I'd brought him back to the bush.

Perhaps I was just too naive to understand that death did not discriminate because of age, and that I could die, in an instant and without any warning.

William and Todd were not that naive.

They were never given the chance.

Over the weeks of work, I'd come to learn certain other things about them. Similarities. Neither seemed to have much of a plan for their future. They both lived from one paycheck to the next. And when each day ended, they routinely grabbed a beer from the cooler. And they didn't stop at one. I knew what a hangover looked and felt like. I'd gotten that down to a science. Their tired eyes and lethargic movements as they sipped cups of black coffee like it was a tonic every morning came from too little sleep and too much alcohol. I doubted they drank to socialize, as I did. I doubted they drank to celebrate the future.

I suspected they drank to ward off demons, unforeseen enemies who haunted their sleep. It left them feeling like shit come morning, and yet they seemed to do it habitually. Their demons, I surmised, were far worse than the hangover. I could only imagine from the stories William had already told me what persistent nightmares haunted him and led him to desensitize himself, just so he could sleep.

His belt was a gesture of friendship, as much as

anything, and I had almost repaid his gesture by electrocuting myself and leaving William to care for my dead body.

"You don't make friends," William's corporal, Victor Cruz, had told him. Because someday you might be putting that friend in a body bag.

So selfish. So stupid.

May 6, 1968

I'm in my bunker, getting my pack ready to go outside the wire. We expect to be out several weeks.

Cruz gave me a list of what to take, and it's a lot of shit. A poncho, poncho liner, two pairs of socks, two towels, and toiletries. I'll be wearing a war belt, which is like a belt with suspenders. You can hang your canteen off the back and your fourteen-inch Ka-Bar off the left strap. I have an entrenching tool for digging my foxhole at night, and gun oil, bore cleaner, and a cleaning kit for my rifle; I have bug juice without any scent, iodine packets, a smoke grenade to mark positions for air support or firepower. The mortar unit can't carry everything, so mortars are spread out among the platoon. Cruz handed me a 60 mm that weighed about two and a half pounds. The 81s are almost four pounds. I will also be carrying a claymore mine filled with BBs and a communication wire to put a charge in it. Cruz gave me a bag of Willie Peter (white phosphorus used in mortar shells). The bag is waterproof, which will come in handy. He also handed me packs of black condoms. I looked at him like he'd lost his mind.

"Waterproof," he said. "You put one over the barrel of your rifle and use another to keep the extra socks dry."

I also have four star cluster flares, two quarter-pound blocks of C-4 explosive, rope, a mosquito net, an abbreviated first aid kit, a canteen cup and utensils, one trip flare, extra M-16 ammo, nine C ration meals, eight quarts of water, four grenades, and a steel helmet. I had packed underwear, but Cruz took it out. Said it was a surefire way to get crotch rot, that the foot rot would be bad enough.

He handed me parachute cord and a bag of marbles. "You can unwind the cord and use the fine strands to tie up cans along your perimeter."

"What are the marbles for? In case I lose mine?" I laughed. Cruz did not.

"You put the marbles in the can. Guys use rocks, but the Vietnamese have small hands and can get the rocks out without making noise. Not possible with the marbles. They rattle and roll."

I had difficulty swallowing.

I'm guessing my pack is fifty to sixty pounds before I add my film. My camera,

I'll wear around my neck. Cruz said, "If you can stand up with the pack on your back, you're not carrying enough."

I'll also be carrying extra ammo for the M-60 machine gun and the LAWs (light anti-armor weapons).

I turned and startled at the sight of someone standing beside me, surprised because I didn't hear anybody come in the bunker. I looked again, more closely, and I realized I was looking at a mirror, only I didn't recognize the person I was looking at. The face was gaunt and wrinkled. The hair was long and unkempt. But it was the eyes that made me walk closer to the reflection. My eyes have become like the eyes of other marines who have been here for a while—flat, gray, lifeless. I stepped still closer. The dirt on my face gives me crow's feet, like stage makeup used to age a man. I have a nineteen-year-old body with thirty-five-year-old eyes.

I am like the pencil I constantly sharpen with a knife; I am just a dull nub of the person I was.

CHAPTER 13

July 12, 1979

I went home that afternoon shaken and embarrassed at my own stupidity. At a time when I felt like I was starting to fit in, I'd painted a scarlet *A* on my forehead. "Can't be trusted. Do not befriend."

We went out that night, the boys. We had no plans, as per usual. Four guys, each without a plan, made for a cohesive group. After half an hour of bickering and rejected suggestions, we stopped at a gas station so Mif could call Ed and Mickey. When he hung up, he told us they were at the Lanai bar at the Villa Hotel in San Mateo. Like My Brother's Place, we chose the Lanai not for the décor or the ambiance, but because we could get in.

I was on the verge of bugging out, still shaken by the event that morning, and what it had done to William, how it had affected him. I knew that actions had consequences, but I'd never before thought that those consequences could be death, not until I worked on the remodel that summer. I never realized how fragile life could be. One day in the garage, as William talked to me about losing his foxhole partner the first time he was on guard duty, he said, "Growing old is a privilege, not a right."

Those words kept going through my head, as if on a loop. I looked at my friends and thought of all the dumbass things we'd done, and I wondered how long we could continue to get away with them without something bad happening. Something that could disrupt the rest of our lives and the lives of those we loved.

"Summer's almost over," Mif said as I debated whether to go out. "And we both know we're going our separate ways, and it's not going to be the same."

Mif had the courage to express what the rest of us would not. I wouldn't see these guys, not after I went off to college. Some never again.

The Lanai bar had a mystique that might have been more legend than reality. It was rumored that the famous Las Vegas Rat Pack—the name given to performers Dean Martin, Frank Sinatra, Sammy Davis Jr., Peter Lawford, and Joey Bishop—stayed at the hotel and drank in the Lanai after performing at the Circle Star Theater in Redwood City. I thought it was an ingenious promotional campaign. None of us, in our collective visits, had ever encountered anyone even remotely that famous. I did once see Jim Nabors, a.k.a. Gomer Pyle, in the Lanai men's room.

"Hey, you're Gomer Pyle," I'd said.

"Wrong guy, kid," he'd said.

But it had been him. I found out later that he was performing at the Circle Star. I also read later that he didn't answer to Gomer Pyle.

Each visit, we'd ask the Lanai waitresses, hard-working women not there to talk with boys who weren't likely to tip, if Frank or Dean had been in. They'd either blow us off or perpetuate the mystique.

"You never know. Maybe."

"I think it's bullshit," I said as Mif, Billy, Cap, and I drove the El Camino Real to the Lanai.

"Why would they make that up?" Billy asked.

"To get people to come to the bar thinking they're going to see one of those guys. They spend money on food and drinks while waiting for something that is never going to happen," I said.

"Good point," Mif said.

"Who gives a shit?" Cap said.

I think we fancied ourselves as our own rat pack. We weren't famous, had no real discernable talent, but we hung out together in bars making asinine comments and usually drank more than we should. It was hard for me to admit, but it was getting old. I didn't want to be working just to have enough money to go drink beer and play softball when I was thirty. I looked at William, and to a lesser extent at Todd, some mornings, and I realized I had an opportunity they never had. I had an opportunity to do something with my life. Too many nights I just felt like my friends and I were wasting time until college.

A large neon-green-and-pink palm tree—San Mateo's slice of Las Vegas—greeted us at the hotel like a beacon. "I wouldn't even ask for their autograph," I said. "What do I care?"

"Whose autograph would you get?" Mif asked.

"Jimmy Stewart, Jack Klugman, Elvis Presley, and Muhammad Ali."

"Little late for Elvis Presley," Billy said. "You could have asked him while he was on the toilet."

"Jack Klugman?" Cap said. "What the hell?"

"I love *The Odd Couple*," I said. "Whose autograph would you get?"

"Jim Beam and Joe Coors," Cap said, putting an end to the conversation.

We split up and went to the door in pairs. The unwritten rule was each guy was on his own. If you didn't get in, you went back to the car and waited in the parking lot. You didn't leave, especially if you drove. This night, we didn't have to worry. We knew the bouncer. If you slipped him five bucks, he looked the other way. Cap hated paying the guy, but he hated the alternative worse.

The Lanai interior was koa wood tables, a faux thatched roof, and wooden masks and other tiki décor on the walls. The coup de grâce, however, was a massive beach mural, a scene of an exotic island paradise with palm trees and the ocean lapping onto a sandy beach with Tahitian women wearing coconut bras and grass skirts. The mural hung over a 1,700-gallon fish tank. Tacky. Las Vegas. It got worse. The lighting on the mural changed from sunrise to sunset over the course of an hour. We used that mural to tell tiki time, saying things like, "Spent four days at the Lanai last night."

Once inside, we regrouped and sat in bamboo chairs around koa wood tables in the back along the perimeter wall. It didn't matter who you sat with. For that night, they became your platoon, your squad, and you spilled inane insults at the guys sitting at the table next to you.

Mickey, Ed, and Scotty sat at a table beside us. Our butts hadn't even hit the seat when the waitress slapped down coasters on the tables and asked what she could get us.

"Have you seen Frank tonight?" Mif asked. "He's singing at the Circle Star."

"Not tonight," she said with bored indifference.

We didn't need a menu of the various tiki drinks. We always ordered the biggest, strongest drink on the menu, the Double Sidewinder's Fang. The drink came in a large fishbowl—fruit juices and rums. I imagine the drink was meant to be shared, but we each ordered our own. Being high school students, and poor, we also snuck in bottles of rum. Not the airplane bottles, which would have been easy to conceal. Scotty got fifths from the liquor store, and we refilled our glasses beneath the table as we drank, eventually reaching the point of saturation, almost pure alcohol, with the expected result.

Ed, Mickey, and Scotty had already been at the Lanai for a while, and Mickey was trashed, barely able to sit up.

I drank my Fang slowly. On a few occasions, Billy offered me the bottle of rum, but each time, I shook my head. "I have to work in the morning, and I can't function when I'm hungover."

A tiki day later, Scotty showed up at our table. "We got to get Mickey out of here," he said. "He's going to puke."

"We'll catch you later," Cap said.

"Mickey drove," Scotty said. "I'm going to drive him and Ed home and drop off his truck, but I'm going to need you to follow us and give me a lift home."

I had driven that night. "That's all the way in South City," I said.

Scotty shrugged. "Don't leave me hanging."

Another of the unwritten man codes. It didn't matter that Scotty and Ed had let Mickey trash himself, though Mickey was driving. I would pay the price. Besides, Scotty was our alcohol source.

It was bullshit, but I acquiesced.

Cap stayed at the Lanai. The rest of us exited. I stepped into the bathroom before leaving. After turning from the urinal, I stopped. There stood Frank Sinatra dressed in a tuxedo, fixing his hair. He caught me staring and put a finger to his lips. Then he winked, and just before slipping out the door, he said, "No one will believe you."

"Son of a bitch," I said softly.

When I reached my Pinto, I contemplated telling the others, but Frank was right. No one would ever believe me.

We followed Scotty driving Mickey's white work truck with his father's business logo on the doors. Mickey sat propped in the middle between Scotty and Ed. We dropped Ed at his home, which was just a few miles from the warmth and comfort of my own bed, then pushed on to South City. I didn't know where Mickey lived, but Mif did. We pulled down his street just as Scotty pulled into the driveway and parked the work truck. Mif got out and helped Scotty get Mickey to the front door. Once there, they hesitated.

"What are they doing?" I asked.

It became apparent that either Mickey didn't have a key or Mif and Scotty didn't know the correct key on his key chain.

"I think they're trying to figure out where to put him," Billy said.

"What are you talking about?"

"They can't very well open the door and throw him inside," Billy said.

At that moment, Mif and Scotty did what any

eighteen-year-old would have done under similar circumstances. They propped Mickey up at the door, rang the bell, then ran. Billy hurried from the front seat, and he and Scotty jumped into the back. Mif got in the passenger seat and shut the door just as the porch light came on and the front door to the house pulled open.

"Don't move," Mif said. Then, "Oh shit. That's Mr. Giusti."

Mr. Giusti stood in a T-shirt and boxer shorts. We watched, waiting for Mickey's father to pull him inside. Instead, Mr. Giusti stepped back, and I thought, for a brief moment, he might slam the door. No such luck. He threw a right hand, a punch that hit Mickey flush in the face, knocking him backward. Mickey stumbled backward and fell onto the front lawn. I'd tell you the punch knocked Mickey cold, but I think Mickey was already out before the punch. Mr. Giusti shut the door.

"Holy shit," Mif said, laughing his nervous chuckle.

"What do we do?" I asked.

"Drive. Go," Billy said.

"Go," Scotty said. "His mother will bring him inside."

Maybe, but I didn't see any lights on inside the one-story rambler, and in that instant, I realized the stupidity of what we had just done, what I had participated in. We'd basically sent

Mr. Giusti a clear and undeniable message. By leaving Mickey alone, propped against the door, we had made Mr. Giusti reasonably assume his son had driven the company truck stone-cold drunk, likely putting everything they owned, and his company, at financial risk.

We'd acted like immature eighteen-year-olds.

And Mickey had paid the price.

The thought of standing in the puddle of water now sent chills up my spine.

Billy, Mif, and Scotty urged me to drive away, but I felt the way William had looked that afternoon, his feet rooted to the concrete floor as he reached out to try to save me from my stupidity. I realized his reach had not been to grab me, but more an attempt to dial back time so that I would not be standing in that puddle of water about to electrocute myself. I wanted to dial back time now. I wanted to handle the situation with Mickey differently.

I got out of the car.

"What the hell are you doing?" the other three said.

Mif got out of the car and followed me. "Vinny B., what are you doing?"

I grabbed Mickey under the arm. Mif grabbed the other side and we got him to his feet. He was bleeding from his nose and it ran down his chin. All the while Mif kept asking me what I was doing. We brought Mickey up to the door, and

I rang the doorbell. Mif swore under his breath.

After a moment, Mr. Giusti yanked open the door. He looked surprised, then pissed.

"Mr. Giusti, we brought Mickey home," I said. "He had too much to drink, but he didn't drive the company truck home. We drove it. We should have handed you the keys to the truck and carried Mickey inside. I'm sorry we didn't. But I wanted you to know that Mickey didn't drive drunk. He wasn't stupid. We were."

Mr. Giusti looked stunned, maybe embarrassed, maybe remorseful. With little said, he took Mickey from us and brought him inside. Then he shut the door.

I wouldn't hang out with Mickey or Ed or Scotty again that summer, or since. They didn't attend any of our high school reunions. When I'd run into Billy or Mif, I'd inquire about them. Scotty had died young. Mickey and Ed both went on to eventually run their fathers' businesses. My final image of Mickey would be of an eighteen-year-old sprawled on his back on the front lawn of his parents' house. Ed, too, would be forever eighteen, stalking across a boxing ring at Serra's Fight Night, slipping punches, then unloading his lightning-quick straight right hand. That night they became working men. A part of the real world. They learned a trade, made an income, eventually got married, started a family, and got on with the rest of their lives.

269

I guess. I don't really know.

We began the inevitable process that night of drifting apart, going our separate ways, to live our separate lives. At least we had that chance. At least I had not electrocuted myself. At least Mickey had survived his night of nearly drinking himself into a coma. At least I had not died or watched him die. At least our collective stupidity had not cost a life.

William's eighteen-year-old platoon mates weren't that lucky.

Maybe that was why William refused to call them friends—not because he didn't care about them, but because he did. And he could not stand the pain of losing them. He kept them alive, and forever young.

May 6, 1968

It was early morning, still dark. Time to fall out. I sat on the ground and slipped my arms through the straps of my ruck-sack, then held out my hands. Victor Cruz pulled me to my feet. In the bush, I use a tree to stand. I was halfway out of the bunker when I touched the pockets on my flak jacket and realized I didn't have my Tiger tin with my journal and pencils. I found it on my bunk and tucked it into the vertical pocket near my heart, where Longhorn kept the tin. One more thing for Charlie to penetrate if he wants to kill me.

Cruz assures me he does.

It rained earlier, which Cruz said was just Vietnam pissing on us, not the start of the monsoon season. The heavy rain turned the firebase into reddish-brown slop. I thought about pulling out my poncho from my pack, but that would have necessitated me dropping the pack and starting all over again. My nerves cried out for a cigarette, but we had been told no cigarettes, since we would be walking out from the firebase instead of taking the CH-46 transport helicopters.

The company, 212 marines, walked out silent, so Charlie wouldn't know we were coming.

I fall under Charlie Company, First Platoon, Third Squad (one-three). Charlie Company is commanded by Captain Dennis Martinez. Lieutenant Brad Dickson runs the First Platoon. He came on board about three weeks ago. Cruz runs the Third Squad. There's been a bit of a power struggle because Dickson has been in-country less than a month, straight out of OCS, and Cruz is in the middle of his second tour, almost all of it spent in the bush. Cruz has seen everything and anything, but Dickson seems intent on telling Cruz what to do, a playground power play. Cruz told me not to worry about it, that Captain Martinez has his back.

Bean told me if Dickson doesn't listen and puts him in danger, he'll frag his ass in the bush, which means roll a frag grenade up behind him.

The first guy from our company outside the wire was Whippet, a gung-ho marine from Idaho who asked to go first. We call him Whippet because he's built like one of those lean dogs with the pointed face and he has boundless energy. We were to fall out one at a time, three meters between us. Whippet made the sign of the cross, kissed the crucifix hanging around his neck, gave all of us a big grin and a thumbs-up, and stepped outside the wire. I'd been outside the wire, but this time felt different. This felt real. We expected to engage Charlie, to engage the NVA. I had goose bumps on my arms and tingling up and down my spine and along the nape of my neck. My entire body was a bundle of nerves, adrenaline, and anxiety.

Guys who have been here awhile say the tingling is a premonition of death. I think they're joking. I hope they're joking.

Cruz smiled when I reached the wire. "You ready, Shutter?"

I nodded.

"You got your film?"

"Yeah," I said, but my throat and mouth were dry, and the word came out as a croak.

"Let's hope you don't have to use it. I like my search-and-destroy humping the way I like my helicopter rides."

"What?" I asked, uncertain I had heard him correctly.

"Boring." He smiled.

I returned the smile, but mentally I was having images of a helicopter crashing and burning.

CHAPTER 14

July 13, 1979

During each softball game that summer, I felt like I was sitting on a keg of gunpowder about to explode. With Greg and others yelling insults at the other team's players, an explosion was inevitable and, I believe, provoked on this Friday night so that we'd forfeit the game and no longer be undefeated. Teams couldn't beat us on the field, so they took a different tack. They all knew the league had warned us about our behavior.

This night the chirping started in the second inning. I don't recall what was said by who, but the umpires warned both benches we'd forfeit if the chirping got worse. That was usually all we needed to hear. The Northpark Yankees were in first place. None of us wanted to forfeit a game and risk wrecking an undefeated season.

With a runner on first base, the opposing team's batter hit a screaming line drive to Louie, our third baseman. Louie fielded the ball cleanly and winged it to me covering second base. I grabbed the ball, turned, and fired to first base. The runner breaking toward second base, although clearly out, ducked under the ball and hit me with his shoulder, like a linebacker, planting me hard on the dirt infield. I would have yelled, but I couldn't find my voice. The guy had knocked the wind out of me.

Mike, our shortstop, dropped his glove and went after the guy, throwing punches. The benches emptied, guys raced onto the field and in from the outfield. I managed to get to my feet to keep from being trampled, then heeded my high school education and stumbled away. I was no match for the behemoths streaming onto the field when healthy. I could barely breathe, and my shoulder burned as if on fire. I vaguely heard the umpires yelling and the fans in the stands cursing and shouting obscenities. Punches were thrown, blood, ripped jerseys. This was a brawl.

In the middle of this chaos, the other team's first baseman, a bearded player as big as a mountain, came out of the dugout and jogged toward me. This guy would snap me across his leg like the toothpicks Todd chewed, but unlike in the fights with my high school buddies, I could think of no way out of this situation. I couldn't run and look like a coward, though I contemplated it. I dropped my glove and expected to get killed.

A blur caught my peripheral vision. William. My height, but William had lost weight over the summer, so he was likely no more than 150 pounds. Yes, he had at one time been a New Jersey State wrestling champion, but nobody in their right mind would take on the approaching guy.

William stepped in front of me and pointed at the oncoming mountain. "I want you!" he said and went into a wrestler's stance.

The guy shifted his eyes from me to William, seemingly uncertain that William had directed his challenge at him. He'd probably never been challenged before and certainly not by some banty rooster. William threw his glove, showing absolutely no fear. Not an ounce. His eyes had become black pinpoints.

The mountain stopped and raised his hands. "Whoa! Whoa! Whoa! Take it easy. I got no beef with you."

"You and me. Let's go, big boy," William said.

The guy actually backed up. Incredible. "I just wanted to make sure the kid was all right."

It was apparent to me that the guy's intent was to make sure I was all right. William, however, was in fight-or-flight mode.

"William," I said. "It's okay. It's okay. William." Then a thought occurred to me. "Shutter," I said. William jerked his head and looked at me. "It's okay," I said.

It took a few seconds before William's pupils contracted and his eyes returned to blue. He looked confused, as if uncertain where we were, as if he had gone someplace else.

Eventually order was restored. The umpires called a forfeit. Both teams took a loss. Guys picked up hats and gloves and walked off the field with buttons ripped from jerseys, welts that would become bruises, and bloodied knuckles and noses. The worst of it was a cut over our center fielder's eye, which guys fixed with a butterfly bandage from an emergency medical kit the ball field kept.

We went to Village Host and relived the incident until everyone calmed down or had enough beer to forget it.

As night settled and guys departed with their girlfriends and wives, William sat alone at a table smoking a cigarette and drinking his beer. Monica, his girlfriend, was not there this night. William sat with his head against the wall, as if taking everything in. He looked at peace, but when he lifted the cigarette to his mouth, his hand shook more violently than I had seen to that point.

I took a seat on the wooden bench across the table from him.

William rolled his head and smiled at me. He was high. "Vincenzo," he said in a soft voice.

"Thanks," I said.

"For what?"

"Taking on that guy."

William shrugged. "Turned out it wasn't much of a fight."

"Why'd you do it?" I asked, interested in his rationale. "I mean, the guy was huge."

William smiled. He kept his head against the

277

wall and took another drag on his cigarette. "Did I tell you why I joined the marines?"

"You said it was hot and there was no one standing in line at the marine recruiting office."

He laughed. "Yeah. That was one reason." He stubbed out his cigarette and sat forward. "I joined the marines because I believed they were badasses, and I figured if I was going to go into a fight, and I was, I wanted to go in with the meanest fuckers on the planet. I didn't want the guy next to me to hesitate when the shit hit the fan. I wanted someone I could trust to have my back."

"I understand," I said.

"No. You don't." His statement took me aback, sort of like when he told me I didn't know scared. "That's what I *thought,* but there was a lot I didn't understand. A lot I had to learn." He told me about the day he rode a bus to Parris Island for boot camp, and about a big southern recruit who thought he was a tough guy and ran into a drill instructor half his size and ended up doing countless push-ups.

"The rest of us figured if they could handle the biggest guy, they could do the same, or worse, to us."

"You wanted to stop the fight tonight?" I asked, not sure I understood. "That's why you went after the biggest guy?"

William smiled, like he hid a secret. "No. The

point was, I realized at that moment that we were no longer people. We were no longer individuals. We had become numbers, interchangeable parts that would fight as one. We weren't supposed to think about how big our opponent was, how strong, how many, or how much ammunition we had. We were marines. We did our job, without hesitation. We followed orders. We achieved our objective. Did I *choose* that guy tonight? Was I trying to stop the fight?" Another smile. "That's a good story, Vincenzo, and I won't stop you from telling it, but I'd be lying if I said I was. I wasn't thinking about how big the guy was or the consequences of what I was doing. I was trained *not* to think about consequences. I was trained to fight whoever was there." He stubbed out his cigarette and leaned across the table littered with pizza trays and empty beer pitchers. "The big guy was just there."

Like the California beach and the girls in bikinis had just been there, I thought. William didn't think about consequences, about his past, or about his future. He stayed in the present. I assumed the present was difficult enough.

PART IV

Paint It Black

May 10, 1968

The hardest thing to accept is that death is real. Forever. Permanent. I'd served as an altar boy at funerals and I'd seen bodies in caskets at church, but those people were already in the coffin. They were old. Some had been sick. I didn't know them. To me they had always been dead. They looked like wax replicas of people. They weren't real. So death wasn't real.

Not these marines. Not Kenny. And not the half a dozen I've watched die since we've been outside the wire. These marines are young. My age. I shared a barrack with them. I traded C rations with them. I humped with them. I went through boot camp with some, ITR with others. Back then, before we arrived in-country, we talked about our lives, where we lived, the high schools we attended, the girls we screwed. We talked about going out with our buddies, fixing up cars, cruising strips. Now I'm taking photographs of their dead bodies.

The concept of permanency isn't something I ever thought about. Why would I? I'm young and healthy and in great shape.

Ask a normal nineteen-year-old in New Jersey about death, and he'll say, "Why are you asking me?" We don't think we'll ever die, or even grow old.

But here, we die. Every day. We die and everything goes on, the same as before. I now know what Cruz meant when he said, "Don't make friends." It isn't personal, but someday I may be putting you in a body bag and it's easier if I don't know you.

It happens so quickly, death. One moment you're here. The next moment you're gone. Zipped up in a body bag and helicoptered out. The military doesn't give us time to process the death, because there is no time. They tell us to put it out of our minds. They don't want you thinking about it. Saddle up and move out. You're still here. You still have a job to do.

But I'm tired, man, and I don't have the strength to get the dying out of my head. I don't have the strength to hump eighty pounds of shit in this unrelenting heat and humidity *and* clear my head. I wake up thinking about death. I think about it as we hump. I go to sleep thinking about it.

Today was worse.

I stared at EZ, a Black kid from Georgia.

We called him EZ because everything about him was EZ. He was never in a rush to do or say anything. "Take it EZ," he'd say all the time and usually with a bright smile. EZ had boyish features, a square jaw, an EZ smile. That's how I'll remember him. "Relax. Take it EZ." EZ's real name was Eric Johnson. I know this only because I read his dog tags when we removed them, put one in a bag, and taped the bag to his wrist so EZ can be processed as a KIA. He's forever young now.

EZ stepped on a booby trap, a hand grenade, they think. Booby traps, Bouncing Bettys, toe poppers, ambush mortars. They're everywhere we hump. Every day, another guy loses a leg. If he's lucky, that's all he loses. The unlucky ones, like EZ, buy the farm. If it's a mortar, several marines may buy the farm. We heard of a 250-pound buried bomb taking out an entire platoon.

You think, *I'm lucky. I can still walk.*

But then you wonder how far you'll make it before you trip a wire or step on a Bouncing Betty. How far will you get before they blow up an ambush mortar, then cut you down with machine gun fire and RPGs? It gets so that you don't want to take that first step. You don't want to lift your foot off the ground for fear you've triggered an explosive. You want to stand in place. Stay safe.

Except you can't.

Saddle up. Move out.

It's mentally draining, not knowing with each step you take.

EZ had been humping directly in front of me, our line spaced three meters between marines for just this reason. When the explosion detonated, I thought it was incoming. The ground exploded, and EZ's body flew upward and to the left. I fell backward from the force of the blast, though most of the energy went the other direction, as did most of the shrapnel. Marines in front of EZ and behind me got hit, though not too bad. They're the lucky ones. They're going to the rear for a little R & R. Some may get to go home. I didn't get a scratch. Not a mark on me.

I grabbed my rifle and scrambled for cover until Cruz came down the line yelling that it had been a mine, not incoming. I rushed to EZ. His eyes were open but his whole body, what was left of it, twitched. The death throes. So much blood. I didn't know what to do. The corpsman came forward, tying off tourniquets, stuffing holes with gauze, and pumping EZ full of morphine for the pain. I held EZ's head and talked to him. I could see his eyes. I could see his pupils. He didn't look at peace like they tell us. That's just more bullshit. He looked scared.

"It's okay, EZ," I said. "You hang in there. They're going to fix you up and send you home and you'll take it EZ." I kept looking in his eyes. I thought it was better than looking at the wounds spurting blood. And then, I saw a wisp of smoke in EZ's eyes suddenly evaporate, like fog dissipating, and I knew EZ was gone. His body no longer twitched. His chest no longer rose and fell.

His spirit had left his body.

I saw his spirit leave his body.

We called for a dust off and we loaded EZ and the wounded onto the chopper, but we never acknowledged EZ was dead. We never do. We make believe EZ is one of the lucky ones, that he's going home to his family. We say, "Take it EZ," as the chopper lifts and departs. It's easier that way.

Saddle up and move out.

I humped. I didn't think about the fact that I didn't take any pictures. I thought about something else. I thought, Did EZ's mother feel something in that moment when his spirit left his body? Was she standing at the sink filling a glass with water while looking out at the backyard where her son played football with his brothers and feel a loss? Did she double over in pain, drop the glass in the sink and shatter it? Did she cut her finger on one of the sharp pieces and watch blood flow down the drain? Did she know it was her son's blood? That his blood and his spirit had departed this world, that her baby boy had just died?

Did she know?

Will my mother know?

CHAPTER 15

February 19, 2016

Elizabeth wanted Tadich Grill to be a surprise on Mary Beth's sixteenth birthday, but the confrontation with Beau had spoiled that part. We still had the car surprise, however, when we got home.

Our daughter, our baby, sat across the booth at Tadich with eyes as wide as her smile, in part because her big brother sat beside her. Beau had made the decision on his own to attend.

It wasn't anything Elizabeth or I had said. His sister's words had impacted him, and, with time to calm down, he knew he was being selfish. I was proud of him. He had made the right choice. He even had a present for Mary Beth, some gadget she could plug into the lighter of her car and listen to her music on her phone. The only thing Beau asked was that he be allowed to check the score of the basketball game on an app on his phone. Chris had also agreed to text Beau with updates. As it turned out, Serra was no match for SI this year, and no cheering section was going to change the outcome. The Padres were down twenty at the half and never got closer than fifteen. Chris's final text summed up the night.

We sucked. You made the right choice. Wish I

went with you to Tadich. Bring me home a steak. Ha! Ha!

Tadich did not disappoint. We had crab and scallops, filet mignon, and Caesar salads. For dessert we ate rice custard and baked apples, and the waiter had the chef specially prepare an off-the-menu dessert for Mary Beth, a chocolate brownie topped with vanilla ice cream and chocolate sauce, something she would routinely ask for when she was a little girl.

When we arrived home, the car was parked in the driveway with a large pink ribbon and bow. A handwritten sign in the back window said, **HAPPY SWEET 16, MARY BETH**. Mary Beth didn't believe it at first. She was ecstatic to have her own car, no matter how many miles it had on the odometer. We went inside and opened more presents, then Mary Beth went upstairs to call her friends. Elizabeth and I went into the family room and sipped port, a gift from a friend. Beau sat outside on the patio, texting, no doubt trying to catch up with Chris and their friends after the game.

"I'm proud of him," Elizabeth said, looking out the window at our son.

I nodded. "We've raised a pretty good young man. And young woman. When did we get to be so old?"

"Speak for yourself, Methuselah. I'm five years your junior."

"Why do you think I married you?" I said.

Elizabeth laughed.

"You put together a nice birthday for Mary Beth. One she'll always remember," I said.

"I told you, it's all about making memories."

"Why do you think I put on the Santa suit at midnight on Christmas Eve for all those years?" I said.

"Because I told you I wouldn't give you any Christmas sugar if you didn't."

I laughed. "Yeah, there was that."

She pulled away and gave me a look. "Something else motivated you?"

"Just the Christmas sugar," I said, and we kissed.

My phone rang and I reached for it. The caller ID was unknown, but the area code was local. I answered it.

"Mr. Bianco?"

"Speaking."

"It's Eric Rochambeau," he said. Serra's principal.

The name surprised me. "What can I do for you, Mr. Rochambeau?"

"There's been a car accident. I'm sorry. I'm wondering . . . I'm sorry, but the details are sketchy."

"What do you mean?"

"Is Beau home with you?"

I felt my knees go weak but managed to stand,

and I looked to the backyard, to where Beau sat texting.

"He's here," I said. "We celebrated his sister's sixteenth birthday tonight. What's happened? Why did you ask if Beau was home?"

"I'm sorry," he said. "I just assumed . . . Chris Carpenter was in a car with three other seniors. I just expected one to be Beau."

"No," I said. Then, "What happened?"

"A drunk driver on the 101 freeway swerved into their lane. Peter Oxford jerked the steering wheel to avoid the impact, but he hit the guardrail and flipped the car."

"Oh no. No," I said, tears welling in my eyes. "Chris? What happened to Chris?"

"What is it? What's happened?" Elizabeth asked. "Vince, what's happened?"

"Oxford was hospitalized in critical condition with head and back injuries," Rochambeau said. "The two seniors seated in the back seat walked away with bruises and cuts."

"Chris," I said again. "What happened to Chris?"

"I'm sorry," Rochambeau said. "Chris didn't make it. I don't know the details."

His words blurred, something about Chris sitting in the passenger seat because he was too big to sit in the back, about initial reports that he had hit the ceiling and snapped his neck. The car did not have airbags.

I listened, but I stared into the backyard, at Beau. He had moved to the back door. I gave the phone to Elizabeth. "Vince," she said again. "Vince."

I went to the door just as Beau stepped through. "I can't get ahold of anyone," he said, and I hugged him. I hugged my son with every ounce of my being, with every bit of love in my soul, and I cried, knowing that it still would not be enough.

"Dad?"

Behind me Elizabeth sobbed. "Oh, dear God," she said, sinking into the chair. "Oh, dear God."

"Dad," Beau said, starting to resist my hug. "What happened?"

I looked at my son and I wished, more than at any other time in my life, that I didn't have to tell him what had happened, that I could somehow remove the pain I would inflict, and somehow inflict it on myself.

Beau looked frozen in place.

"There was a car accident," I said. "I'm so sorry, Beau. Chris is gone. That was Mr. Rochambeau on the phone . . ."

Beau gasped. His eyes widened with fear and panic. He looked like he couldn't breathe.

Elizabeth, instinct kicking in, rushed to her son. "He's hyperventilating. Get a bag."

I went into the kitchen and pulled open drawers. "Vince!"

I found the brown lunch bags, grabbed one, and handed it to Elizabeth. She had her hand on Beau's back. Our son was bent at the waist, gasping. "Beau, short breaths. Take short breaths."

Elizabeth put the bag to Beau's mouth and he took great gasps; the bag looked like it might explode with each exhale.

"I'm calling an ambulance," I said.

"Hang on," Elizabeth said. Beau's breathing gradually became more regular, but he still couldn't talk. Sobs choked his words.

My cell phone rang again, and I looked to where Elizabeth had placed it, on the table near my chair, in the light of the table lamp, beside William's journal.

I thought of EZ dying in William's arms, his life force slipping from his eyes. I thought of Kenny, who William had called Haybale, and who died from a one-in-a-million shot. I thought of the others who stepped on land mines and booby traps, and I wondered how anyone could ever accept the death of someone so young. How anyone could saddle up and move out as if it had never happened.

They couldn't, of course. No one could.

So William and those marines simply refused to accept death. Not just once. They refused death over and over and over. I looked again at Beau, his body sagging in his mother's arms, and I understood. For the first time, I truly understood.

And I wondered if reality had crashed upon my family, upon Beau, as it had crashed on William that summer.

Chris's death was tragic on so many levels, it was hard to comprehend. It seemed unreal, like we were all actors on a stage, waiting for the curtain to fall so we could drop that fourth wall and go back to being ourselves, back to our lives. I kept waiting for Chris to walk in the door with that big grin and give me an even bigger hug. "Hey, Mr. B.," he'd say. Chris had been like a second son to me and Elizabeth. He'd been at our house as much as his own during the past eighteen years.

But he hadn't been our son. Our son was home, alive.

I felt a deep regret that just days before, I had been thinking that Beau didn't yet understand loss, that we had made his life too easy, that he didn't even understand disappointment. I kept thinking of William Goodman's admonition that summer and about what he had written in his journal—that while he had never accepted death, he had also never avoided death. None of us could. Even though he'd made it home alive, death had followed him. I wondered if, in my anger and pettiness, I had somehow brought this loss upon Beau, as crazy as that sounded. But a lot of what William had written sounded crazy. And yet, it had all been true.

Elizabeth and I reached out to Art and Josephine but our calls went to voice mail.

As Beau's friends, and some parents, hurriedly came to our home, Elizabeth did what she'd always done. She fed them. At least, she put out food. No one ate much. No one drank. We barely talked. The young men, Chris's friends, hugged and cried. They looked stunned, disbelieving, uncertain what to do or to say. They weren't supposed to experience mortality, not at that age.

Seeing their pain made me think of my own experiences at their age, of driving home after I'd had too much to drink or getting in a car with someone drunk. I thought of how quickly my friends and I could have died, or killed others, maybe another high school student like Chris, who had his whole life ahead of him. Only by the grace of God had neither happened, but maybe, as with William and those other marines, I had only been fooling myself. "You don't cheat death," William said in the garage of that remodel during one of our talks. "You think you do, but you don't. Death finds you."

Eventually Elizabeth and I went to the hospital to console the parents of Peter Oxford. The Carpenters were not there. Chris's body had already been taken to a funeral parlor, and the Carpenters were making arrangements for their son's wake and burial.

We returned home. Just after midnight, Art

called my cell phone. I didn't know what to say. What do you say? He asked Elizabeth, Beau, and me to come over. We agreed.

After dropping Mary Beth at her cousin's, we drove to the Carpenters'. Art answered the door looking lost. He embraced Beau and the two men cried. "He loved you, Beau," Art eventually said. "Chris loved you like a brother."

"I loved him," Beau said.

Art released his embrace. "I was so relieved to hear you were not in the car, Beau. I thought you both died." Art looked to me. "Why wasn't he in the car, with Chris?"

"It's Mary Beth's sixteenth birthday. Elizabeth made plans. Beau chose to go to his sister's party."

"I didn't want to go," Beau said. "I wanted to go to the game, with Chris."

"I'm so glad you didn't," Art said, but he looked to have lost his train of thought, and I wondered if he was thinking what I had thought when I heard the news. If Beau had gone to the game, he would have driven Chris. Chris never would have been in Peter Oxford's car.

I thought of William's statement to me that the difference between living and dying was nothing more than dumb luck. Was he right? Had dumb luck saved Beau's life and cost Chris his?

Or was I looking at this all wrong? Maybe death wasn't following me. Maybe God had a hand in saving my son. Maybe Beau would have also been in Peter Oxford's car. Maybe God somehow intervened and spared Beau, spared my family. I knew William had lost his faith and his belief in God. He said God had abandoned him and the other marines when they needed him most. He said he'd been to hell, and nothing in eternal damnation could be worse than what he experienced in Vietnam.

But I did believe in God. Maybe more now than ever.

I believed, and I thanked God with every ounce of my being that he did not take my son. I know that was selfish to think in that moment, with the Carpenters grieving the loss of their son, but I couldn't live without my boy, and I wondered how Art and Josephine would live without theirs. How would they move forward? How else but with the grace of God? How had William moved forward?

How had the parents of all those young men?

Art wiped his tears and we followed him into the house. Josephine and their family—Chris's younger brother and two younger sisters and his aunts and uncles and grandparents—had gathered in the family and living rooms. We stayed for an hour or two. I don't recall. There was really nothing anyone could do but sit and console the Carpenters. After a few hours we decided to give the family some privacy and said our goodbyes.

Over the next couple of days, Elizabeth and I helped with the funeral arrangements, but it was Beau who organized the senior class to be altar servers at the funeral, perform the readings, and act as Chris's pallbearers. Members of the football team attended Chris's wake and his funeral with their white home football jerseys over their shirts and ties. The senior captains and coaches draped Chris's jersey atop his coffin. Beau spoke at Chris's wake, his tortured voice choked by sobs. He told the overflowing crowd how they all loved Chris, his sense of humor, his fierce determination on the football field, and how he always looked after those who were smaller than him, which was everyone. He told everyone that God must have called Chris home because he needed the best damn offensive lineman in the country to open holes for his running backs.

There wasn't a dry eye in the house.

At night, I could no longer read William's journal. I could no longer read about death. It was too raw. Too close to home. Too real. I set the journal aside, and I realized that was something William had never been able to do. He could not set death aside, so he did not accept death as reality.

Not until years after those deaths did reality come knocking, and death found William. He told me he felt guilty to have lived, to have made it home when so many did not.

I worried Beau would feel the same guilt, for not driving Chris that night.

I didn't want Beau to just move on, as William had been forced to do, without processing and coming to some understanding of Chris's death. I didn't want Chris's death to haunt Beau, the way death had haunted William, until he could no longer handle all the ghosts.

I asked, and Serra set up grief counseling at school. Beau and many other students attended the sessions daily. Father John Zoff, a retired priest, also talked Beau through his grief, and Elizabeth and I arranged for our family to see a grief counselor. Together we tried to make sense of a senseless situation.

It would be a process. I knew this from experience. My father's death, though expected, had been raw and painful. The first Christmas without him, his birthday, were melancholy. He had been a large presence in his family, and it was tough to have a celebration of any kind without him—weddings, the birth of a grandchild, baptisms. I always felt his absence. As the months passed, the melancholy faded, until, eventually, when I thought of my dad, I did so with a smile.

This would happen for Beau, but it was going to take time. Beau had lost a brother and a friend he saw every day. He would think of Chris every time he drove alone to school and drove home. He would think of Chris every Friday and Saturday night, at every game he attended, at graduation. He would feel his absence in class. He would feel a hole he might not ever completely fill.

I also understood better why William had been told to saddle up and move out. It was brutal and it was harsh, but it was because life does go on, which is why I assume William wrote in his journal, "Dying is hardest on the living."

I went upstairs the night of Mary Beth's birthday, and I asked her for the keys to the car we had just given her. She looked surprised, shocked, disappointed. "I'll buy you another car," I told her. "One with airbags."

Elizabeth and I did.

Sometimes you make your own luck; I had learned this from William.

June 10, 1968

We've been out on search and destroy for a month. There's been a lot of the former but not much of the latter. We hump in oppressive heat. Midday, the temperature is one hundred or more and the humidity matches it. It saps our energy. My uniform is stiff and white from dried sweat, and I can smell my own stench and the stench of those around me. We move, a listless, lethargic, silent column. I sweat more water than I can consume. I am constantly tired. The heat and the humidity, the loss of water, and the weight I carry on my back almost become too much. A part of me wants to just sit and give up, to give in to Vietnam, but Victor Cruz won't let me.

We hump up one hill and down another. We enter villages, most are recently deserted. We approach them carefully, with a forward team experienced in ambushes and booby traps. We go through them carefully, looking for rice, weapons, tunnel entrances. If we find anything, suspect anything, we burn the village to the ground. If not, we use the huts for shade to eat another C ration and rehydrate, and to sleep in spurts. It is the grunt motto. "Why stand when you can sit. Why sit when you can lie down. Why be awake when you can be asleep."

I can fall asleep standing up.

We have a good point man in Bean. He prefers to walk point. He told Cruz if he dies in the bush, he doesn't want to do so because some dumbass missed a trip wire or a mortar. In the bush, Bean sticks to the side of worn paths, if they can be found, and he searches before each step. The trails he finds, or cuts, are narrow and wet. Nothing ever dries beneath the thick bush. The bush sweats from the humidity.

Cruz tells us to remain evenly spaced, to not bunch up, but the bush has an eerie presence that causes men, even marines, to close ranks, especially at night.

We do not occupy the villages, or even the hills. We do not stay in one place long. Our mission is not to win terrain or seize positions. Our mission is to kill as many communists as possible. Each day this is reinforced, and with each marine we lose, I can feel something stirring deep inside me, an awakening of something dark that I have managed to keep caged, a malevolent force that seeks only to kill, that seeks revenge for the horrific conditions I must endure and the constant harassment that has taken so many of my brothers.

We have lost thirty-two men, eight per week, to booby traps and ambush mines. We've lost another three to heatstroke. Sniper fire harasses us. It can take us five hours to travel a mile. The sniper fire comes from the unbroken expanse of green that stretches from one mountain to the next, but we have yet to see the fabled NVA.

We hump through thick bush, climb rocks, wade waist deep through the boot-sucking mud of the rice paddies, and pull leeches from our bodies as we move from one checkpoint to the next so headquarters can keep track of us. Every so often you leave the bush and someone spots Charlie in a straw hat and black pajamas running in the distance. Probably the sniper who has been taking shots at us all day, but he's too far to hit. He disappears into the tree line and lives to snipe another day.

Late afternoon we hump to the top of a mountain. Our checkpoint. Some trails are so steep you look up at the boot soles of the marine in front of you. When the ground is wet, your feet slide and you grab at the undergrowth—vines and bamboo—to pull yourself up, but the weight of your pack makes you off balance. Guys fall, taking out marines below them, like dominoes.

Some marines don't get up. They just sit there with their gear, too tired, too mentally defeated. Cruz and the other squad leaders yell at them to motivate them, but it's like Cruz is telling them to lift a two-thousand-pound boulder, an impossible act. They don't even bother to try. You walk by them on your way up the hill. They stare into nothingness, like zombies, alive but without a soul. A half hour to an hour after we dig in atop our hill, the stragglers wander into camp, because nothing is more terrifying than being alone in the bush at night.

Once on high ground, the squad leaders set their perimeter. They direct us where to dig our foxholes for the night. I set trip flares and claymores and tie the cans with my marbles to the concertina wire. Then I dig my foxhole with my entrenching tool and fill the sandbags that will surround me. The ground can be like picking at cement, or it crumbles like sandstone. Everywhere, red ants and flies bite, and the relentless mosquitos fly up your nose and into your ears, searching for blood.

Marines digging foxholes unearth nests of scorpions and spiders as big as hockey pucks. I don't even look for the snakes anymore, unless I'm hungry.

Every time we stop for the night, Cruz instructs us to pull off our boots and socks to let our feet air out. So far, I do not have the jungle rot, though the rains will come, and when they do, Cruz says the rot is inevitable. We got another taste of the rain yesterday afternoon. The winds blew down from the mountains and clouds rolled in so fast I almost didn't have time to slip on my poncho. Within minutes Vietnam pissed all over us, a wicked downpour of such intensity you could hear only the water pinging against our ponchos and helmets. Just as quickly as they came, the clouds blew past, and the temperature is pleasant for the first time in weeks. It won't last.

I am often so tired I can't find the strength to chew, let alone take pictures, but Cruz also makes me eat. He won't let me sleep until I have eaten. He jabbers at me as the stragglers come in. "We aren't going to be like them, Shutter. We aren't going to quit. We aren't going to give up. Not here. Not in this shithole. We're going to hump. We're going to be grunts.

We're going to be marines. Then we're going home."

"Don't talk about home."

"You're going to come to Spanish Harlem, Shutter. You're going to come to my house. My mother is going to cook *empanadillas* and *pasteles* and we're going to eat until we're sick and throw up. Then we're going to eat more, just like the Romans." He cackles. "No more of these fucking C-rats, Shutter. We're going to eat real food. Then we're going to go out to the clubs and I'm going to find you a Puerto Rican girl. You have never seen women so beautiful."

"You think a Puerto Rican girl is going to want a gringo like me?" I say, humoring him. I no longer look like a gringo. My skin has gone from white to red to dark brown. I remember my first day at the firebase when Cruz said none of us were senators' sons, that we were all men of color. He was right.

"When you're with me, you are no gringo," Cruz says. "You are *mi hermano*. My brother. We'll drink and dance until the sun comes up. You wait. You'll see."

"Don't talk about home," I say again.

I sleep two hours. The third hour I'm on guard duty. I'm lucky to get four or five hours of sleep a night. When awake, I stare into a darkness so complete it is as if someone has taken a brush and painted everything black—the stars and the moon, the bush, the ground. But I no longer fear the darkness. I welcome it. In the darkness I, too, am hidden. I crave a cigarette, a nicotine perk to keep me awake, but in this painting, Charlie will see the flare of the match and the glow of the cigarette for miles.

So I paint it black. I paint it black and I stay hidden. And I wait.

I wait for Charlie.

CHAPTER 16

July 16, 1979

As the summer progressed, William talked more about Vietnam. Perhaps I had become William's confidant, the closest thing he had to a confessor. I don't mean to beat my chest as some hero; I was far from it. I didn't know enough about life, or the world, to have any meaningful or knowledgeable opinions about anyone or anything, which I believe is why William talked to me. He didn't have to maintain his pride or protect his image. I wasn't his parent or his priest, so he had no obligation to confess. I didn't judge him, so he had no reason to be defensive. I didn't expect him to be anyone, so he had no reason to be anyone but himself. He just needed to get those stories out, to purge an evil spirit. And I just happened to be there to listen, without asking a lot of questions, without condemning or trying to console, without approving or disapproving, without trying to minimize what had happened or what William had been through. I was the blank pages of a journal William could fill with the stories cluttering his mind, the ones that became the nightmares that haunted his sleep and led him to the bottle and the drugs. He could fill those pages honestly, without worrying about any commentary or requests for clarifications, without me judging him. He could just get the stories out and, maybe, I don't know, maybe feel a little better.

I liked to believe so.

Because, man, it was hard to listen to many of those stories.

"I made a mistake," he said one afternoon in the garage as the drywall was being installed in the remodel. "I gave up in school. After I lost my scholarships. I gave up, and I paid for it."

"Vietnam?" I said.

He nodded. "I could have gone to college."

"I know," I said.

"I don't mean the schoolwork. Hell, I could have done the schoolwork in my sleep. I mean, I could have paid for it. Like you. I told myself I couldn't, but that was just an excuse. It would have been difficult; my parents didn't have a lot of money with six kids, but I could have worked and taken classes at the community college for two years and then transferred to a university."

"Why didn't you?"

"Because I was a punk. I quit when I lost wrestling. I thought wrestling was my identity— the little guy who could wrestle like a snake. I was lightning fast, man. Students used to come to our matches just to watch me." He shrugged. "After the injury, I didn't have an identity. I became the fuckup, the guy who got stoned at lunch and screwed around in class. I stopped trying to get good grades and instead tried to get attention. The more my parents pushed me, the more I rebelled. I didn't fully understand the consequences of my actions until that afternoon when my dad handed me my draft notice and I realized I was going to Vietnam."

I thought of my jump into Ed's pool and my other stupid stunts. Was I after an identity? Would there be a consequence for me as there had been for William?

I also thought of a movie I'd watched with my dad, *On the Waterfront*. I thought of the scene in the car when a young Marlon Brando told his brother, Charley, that he could have been somebody, but that he'd never had the chance. That his brother had never looked out for him, and he'd turned out to be nothing more than a punk.

"Regret is so much harder to live with than failure," William said. "You got a chance to be somebody and to do something. Man, I envy you."

"I don't know. I mean, I'm class valedictorian. It's kind of embarrassing to say I'm going to community college."

"What are you talking about?"

"I got into Stanford, but my parents can't afford it. That's why I'm going to community college. I don't know."

William smiled. "Doesn't matter where you go to school. You'll make it. You'll reach your dreams."

"I wish I was as sure as you."

"You'll make it because you know what will happen if you don't. You'll end up working dead-end jobs like this, sweating your ass off breaking up cement and tearing off the roofs of houses, or humping one-hundred-pound bags of cement in the heat. Most of those guys going to those fancy schools never had to do what you're doing. They never had to work an honest day of labor in their lives or save their money to pay their tuition. They just expected their parents to do it for them. They don't know how most of the rest of the world lives. You know."

I hoped William was right.

Our morning routine changed as the sub-contractors worked on the remodel. Instead of driving to the Burlingame jobsite, I met Todd and William at Nini's Coffee Shop on Bayswater Avenue in Burlingame, just down the street from Todd's house in a neighborhood of single-story, two-bedroom-one-bath stucco homes built to house men coming home from World War II and hoping to join the workforce. Nini's was an old-fashioned, narrow diner on the corner, with a brown retractable awning, orange barstools, and tables that barely accommodated one but often seated four. The menu was written on the wall alongside photographs and memorabilia.

I usually arrived a half hour after Todd and William because I couldn't afford to buy breakfast. I ate at home. Todd and William were usually into their third cigarette and multiple cups of coffee by the time I arrived to get my assignment for the day. The first time I met them there, I followed Todd to the cash register and noticed that he pulled a toothpick from a container and stuck it into his mouth. The accessory I had deemed to be part of his tough guy image was just a tool to remove food stuck between his teeth. I laughed that I had given the toothpick so much more significance.

Most mornings, Todd gave William our assignment then left to bid other jobs. William pulled napkins from the dispenser on the table and drew intricate diagrams with dimensions. He laid the napkins on the table as he went, a step-by-step instruction manual on what I was supposed to do to prepare a jobsite while he bought tile, glue and grout, and other supplies. More than a few homeowners would do head turns when I pulled out those napkins and used them to rip out their countertops.

I worried about William. The shake in his hands had become more pronounced. I'd read that Parkinson's could cause such a shake, but I didn't think that was it. I'd also often catch William on a job with a distant, distracted gaze. He'd lost his joie de vivre, the chuckle in his voice that had kept the work site lively.

This morning I was to accompany William to a jobsite in Redwood City where Todd had contracted to retile a kitchen counter and back-splash. Todd wanted the project completed in a day so we could get back to the Burlingame remodel. My job was to make sure that happened.

I left my Pinto parked across the street from Nini's and jumped in the passenger seat of William's El Camino. Nini's was close to a 101 freeway on-ramp, a too-short span before cars had to merge into morning traffic. William punched the gas, and the El Camino leaped forward with a growl I felt in my stomach, like the feeling of going over a hill riding a roller coaster.

Just as quickly, William slammed on the brakes, narrowly missing a blue BMW that had changed lanes and cut us off. William laid on the horn, and just as quickly, the woman driving the BMW raised the middle finger of her right hand and flipped us off.

William didn't say a word. He didn't have to. The same dark look shaded his face as the night of the softball brawl. I felt the El Camino accelerate until its front bumper was within inches of the BMW's back bumper. The woman sped up. So did William. The woman tapped her brakes, William didn't. I thought we would plow into the back of her car. She must have had the same thought because she didn't try that again. She kept shifting her eyes from the rearview mirror to the side mirror. From what I could see, she looked young, with long dark hair, and afraid.

She took the next exit. William followed. She ran the stoplight at the end of the exit, turning right. So did William. A horn blared, the car on a collision course with the passenger side of the El Camino. I braced for impact, my stomach in my throat.

The car missed us.

William never glanced at me. Never said a word. His eyes, and his mind, were singularly focused on the BMW. The woman took a sharp left on a residential street. William followed. She took another right. William followed.

I didn't know what to say at this point, so I said nothing.

The game of cat and mouse continued. When we reached the El Camino Real, the woman switched lanes, cutting off cars. William stayed right on her bumper. After several miles she took a sharp right, then made a left and drove into a garage beneath an apartment building.

William followed her.

Now I was scared.

"William."

He ignored me. The woman parked the BMW in a stall by the elevator. Before she could get out of her car, William pulled behind her, threw the gearshift on the steering column into park but left the engine running.

The woman kept peering at the side and rear-view mirrors. I could see the terror in her eyes, and I knew she was contemplating making a run for the elevator. I didn't know what William might do, but I hoped she wouldn't run.

Her car door opened.

William opened his door. I almost said, "William, no," but the woman hurriedly shut and locked her door. William shut his door. I could see now the woman was crying, tears of fear.

We sat, at a standoff, for another minute or two that felt like ten or twenty. Then, slowly, the dark cloud lifted. William looked over at me, his eyes once again that crystal blue. He reached up, lowered the gearshift on the steering column into reverse, backed up, and drove from the building.

I let out a sigh and had to concentrate to keep my legs from shaking. I had a sick feeling in the pit of my stomach.

When we reached the El Camino Real, William lit a cigarette and took a drag, blowing smoke out the open window. After another drag, he looked over at me and his mouth inched into a grin. Then he said something I had never considered. "We just saved that woman's life."

I didn't ask how. He told me anyway. "Remember when I said you won't fail, because you understand what the consequences will be if you do?"

"Yeah."

"So does that woman. She'll never flip off another person as long as she lives."

I gave what he said some thought. "You scared the shit out of her."

"That was the intent. Better me than some guy who would have harmed her. People have been shot for less."

"What if she wrote down your license plate?"

He shrugged. "She didn't."

"But what if she did?"

He shrugged again. "What's she going to say?" He blew smoke out the window. "She's happy to be rid of me. In her mind, she doesn't want to provoke me and possibly relive the experience."

It had been a hard lesson learned for the young woman, certainly, but William was right. It was a lesson that might someday save her life. Mine, too. I have never flipped off anyone in the car. I've wanted to, many times, but the look of terror on that woman's face, even after all these years, remains as fresh as the day it happened. I told that story both to Beau and to Mary Beth when each got their driver's license, but the story doesn't have the same impact on them as it had on me, because they didn't experience what I experienced. They didn't see that raw, pure terror in the woman's eyes. Both said they would outsmart the driver—drive to a police station, or call 911 on their cell phone.

They're right, to a degree.

Cell phones have changed the landscape, but so, too, has the increased use of handguns.

"You could," I tell them, "except the guy might not be content just to follow you, as William did. And the guy might be certifiably crazy."

My children's reaction is proof that you must experience some things to fully appreciate them, and to not make the mistake of doing them again.

June 27, 1968

Cruz kept saying, "You don't find Charlie. Charlie finds you."

We stepped from the bush to a grove of elephant grass two meters tall and maybe twenty meters across to the next tree line. A fist went up from the marine walking point. Whippet. Cruz had insisted Bean take a mental break. The signal to halt was passed down the line. We dropped, waited, watched. No breeze blew the grass. No sound filled the bush. Late afternoon, the sunlight coming through gaps in the canopy were thin slants of green light filled with insects. We were being cautious. The grass is a good place for an ambush.

I waited for the hand signal to proceed. Instead, I got a signal that Whippet had eyes on three NVA. Within seconds I saw the soldiers marching through the bush to our right. Our lieutenant gave hand signals to stand down. Not to fire. Cruz told me the VC always march in threes. One soldier alone might surrender—*Chu Hoi* in Vietnamese. One might convince a second to also surrender, but one of three is likely a hardcore Ho Chi Minh true believer, and he will prevent the other two from surrendering.

True or not, I don't know, but three more VC came down the trail, so close I could hear their whispers. They gave no indication they knew we were there. More hand signals. This time I didn't need them. I could see a column of twenty, maybe twenty-five, NVA soldiers coming down the same trail. Now it was definitely on. There was going to be a brawl.

"Not good," Cruz whispered. Then he said, "No. No." But our lieutenant, Brad Dickson, he with a month of experience, signaled to open fire. He figured he'd found Charlie.

He was wrong. Cruz was right. Charlie had found us.

The column of twenty was just the tip of the spear, and the spear, we soon learned, was a company of NVA dug into the hillside across the elephant grass. The high ground. The column on our right had flanked us and placed us in the kill zone.

Charlie knew we were coming. The three soldiers served to give us a false sense of superior firepower.

Mines buried in the grass erupted. I dropped facedown into a shallow ditch.

All around me I could hear the pop-pop-pop of M-16s, the rat-a-tat-tat of machine gun fire as 7.62 mm rounds whistled overhead. Mortars and RPGs exploded. It was as if all hell had broken loose, as if Lucifer had opened the fiery gates and unleashed his demons. The tall grass provided no cover. Guys were getting hit, getting blown up, screaming "Corpsman" over the sound of war. I managed to get to my knees, lift my M-16, and open fire in the direction of the tree line. I fired on fully automatic, then dropped again, trying to get the goddamn rucksack off my back. I felt someone yanking on the straps.

Cruz freed me.

He was standing, as if oblivious to the chaos, like he was Superman and the bullets couldn't kill him. I yelled at him to get down, but Cruz stalked off, yelling orders, yelling at our machine gunners to open fire. "Sixties up! Sixties up!" He waved the mortarmen to return shells. We had been trained to unleash firepower and push through the ambush. Each rifleman who carried a 60 mm mortar round handed the round to the mortarmen and provided cover fire as they moved up. Our job was to keep the NVA occupied, but Charlie had a bead on us, and their mortars were exploding on top of us. I heard our radioman call in coordinates for the gunships and air strikes.

I couldn't tell a second from a minute or a minute from an hour. I just knew that I was popping off rounds—until I heard the rounds coming back at me, whizzing past me in the tall grass. Shit. We were sitting ducks.

Not this duck.

I switched to semiautomatic, fired three rounds, then belly crawled to a different, unoccupied spot. I fired again. Crawl. Fire. Crawl. I kept firing three-round bursts and crawling through the grass until I crawled out of it. I was positioned at a forty-five-degree angle to the hillside. I could see the NVA soldiers dug in. I switched again to fully automatic, and this time, with aim, I opened up. The hillside behind which the NVA had dug in popped. I saw NVA falling back and dropping down. I spotted the machine gun that was unrelenting, and I emptied another magazine. Then tossed two grenades. The machine gun went quiet.

Cruz shouted, and what was left of our platoon used the moment I had given them to let loose with everything we had—mortars and a hail of 7.62 rounds.

Overhead I heard the roar of incoming Phantoms before I saw them. I crawled back, quickly, toward my ditch. If our radioman's coordinates were off by even the slightest degree, the air-to-ground missiles would obliterate us. The tree line exploded in rolling balls of yellow-and-black flames. I felt the ground shake and the heat. After the Phantoms came the Cobra helicopters. They raked the hillsides with rockets, 20 mm bullets from the miniguns, and RPGs.

Within minutes, the shooting stopped. The NVA regiment, what was left of it, had pulled back into the bush. But how far and for how long?

Cruz came through the grass checking each marine. He grabbed my shoulder. "Shutter, you good?" He shook my shoulder. "You good, Shutter? Shutter?"

It took me a moment to come back from where I'd gone. I said, "I'm good," and I sat up. My muscles felt like I'd just run a twenty-six-mile sprint and I was still on the high from the adrenaline rush.

Cruz smiled and shouted. "Get out your camera, Shutter. Do your job. The *New York Times* is waiting."

My job? I didn't even know what that

was anymore, nor did I care. But I found my pack in the ditch into which I'd first dropped. The ditch that likely saved my life. I got out my camera, about to turn away, then stopped and looked down at that little culvert like it was a friend, and I snapped a picture to remember.

Marines were down. I don't know how many photographs I snapped of the dead and wounded. Too many. I looked through the lens of my camera and tried to convince myself I was making a movie one shot at a time, but I couldn't pretend anymore. It's like Cruz said. Vietnam is real.

There were too many dead and wounded to be medevacked out. They sent in an APC to break through the jungle. When it arrived, I helped load the wounded and the body bags, so many that the APC had to make multiple trips. The dead and the wounded retrieved, no marine left behind, I climbed on board, snapping pictures as we left the bush, back to where a perimeter had been established, where we could get medevac choppers in to fly out the dead and the wounded, and where we who had not died would remain through the night.

I put my name on the rolls of film,

slipped them into a bag, and put my lab buddy's name on it, then I handed the bag to a machine gunner on one of the transports and asked him to take the film to the lab at Da Nang. He assured me it would get there.

I worried all night that the NVA would return and overrun us, but Charlie didn't come. In the morning, Cruz told me we'd lost forty-two marines, with another fifty-eight wounded. Our battalion now consists of half of Alpha Company and half of Charlie Company. Bravo Company is no longer an effective fighting unit.

No time to mourn. We were told to saddle up and move out.

FNGs will be flown in.

Charlie's on the move again.

CHAPTER 17

July 20, 1979

Friday night I drove Billy and Cap to South San Francisco, picked up Mif, and stopped at Colombo's liquor store, where Scotty was now a manager. We bought a case of beer to take to a party. I had significantly reduced the amount I drank over the course of the summer. It wasn't any one incident but an accumulation of incidents: crushing rock with a hangover, standing in the puddle of water while holding the Skilsaw and the rebar with a hangover, and misstepping on a plank of the scaffolding and falling to the ground, also with a hangover. I had escaped injury, but like the puddle incident, my missteps had one thing in common.

Alcohol.

No, I hadn't been drunk, but I'd had too much to drink the night before.

I went into Colombo's to buy snacks, a bag of Cheetos, a bag of Doritos, and an assortment of munchies. On my way out the door, a guy, who appeared our age and about my size, walked in with a girl. I stepped out of their way, allowing the girl to pass, even holding the door for them. I didn't give him or the girl a second look or a second thought. At first blush he looked like a typical South City kid, a pseudotough guy in Converse tennis shoes, brown cords, and a blue letterman's jacket indicating he played football at El Camino High School. He gave me the stink eye but I ignored him.

We got in the Pinto and I drove away. Within a few miles, headlights appeared close behind me. The car pulled up to my bumper. I looked down at the speedometer. I was driving faster than the speed limit. "What's his problem?" I said, looking into the rearview mirror.

Heads turned, looking out the back window. The car was so close, it was clearly intended to send a message. I thought of William sending a message to the woman in the BMW, but I had not flipped anybody off. With parked cars on one side of the street and oncoming traffic on the other side, I couldn't pull over to let the guy pass. After several blocks, when traffic eased in the opposite direction, I figured the driver would pass me. He didn't.

"It's the guy from Colombo's," Billy said.

"What guy?"

"The guy who came in with the girl."

I checked my side mirror. Two people sat in the car behind me, but I couldn't identify either of them. "What the hell is his problem?"

"No idea," Mif said.

I took a right turn, onto surface streets. The guy followed. I made another right and drove down a steep grade. The guy pulled alongside me, punched the gas to get in front of me, then whipped his car into my lane. I slammed on the brakes, nearly hitting his car. Now I was pissed. With both cars stopped, I quickly got out. Unfortunately, unsophisticated when it came to fights, I slammed the door shut, temporarily trapping Billy and Mif in the back seat.

"What the hell is your problem?" I said as I approached the driver's-side window.

The guy turned and looked at me like I was shit on the bottom of his shoe. "What did you say to my girlfriend?"

The question took me off guard. "What?"

"What did you say to my girlfriend?"

I looked across the car to determine if I knew his girlfriend. I didn't. "When?"

"At the store," he said. "What did you say to her at the store?"

"I didn't say anything to her. I held the door open and let you both pass."

He pushed out of the car. By this time Mif, Billy, and Cap had exited the Pinto and approached. The guy stood the way William stood when taking on the behemoth at the softball game. Like he had no fear.

"One of you said something," he said to all of us.

"I didn't say anything," I said. "I let you walk in."

"What do you mean *let me?*"

"You saw it. Don't pull this bullshit."

"Bullshit?" the guy said and took a step forward.

I held my ground, and my gaze. His eyes were not pinpoints of black or laser focused. This guy was bluffing. "Yeah. Bullshit. Don't make up shit to impress your girlfriend."

He glared at me, but he didn't throw a punch. He turned to my friends. "Then one of you said something." They looked equally confused.

"Nobody said anything," Mif said.

The guy looked in the car. "Kelly, which one was it?"

The girlfriend got out of the car and came around the back. "Him." She pointed at Billy.

"I didn't say anything," Billy said.

"Are you calling my girlfriend a liar?"

"Call her what you want. I didn't say anything."

"Either you admit it and apologize or we're going to go at it right here."

I had been working hard, swinging sledgehammers, carrying lumber and hundred-pound bags of cement and grout. I still didn't touch 170 pounds, but I was in good shape and as strong as I had ever been. Maybe that's what encouraged me to say what I did. Maybe it was just the male hubris I had learned that summer from Todd and

William. Maybe it was my realization that the guy was bluffing, because I had seen a guy truly prepared for a fight.

"There's four of us," I said, volunteering my friends. "We'd kill you."

The guy stepped to me and slid off his jacket, throwing it on the hood of the car. "Yeah? One at a time. Who wants to go first? You got a big mouth. How about you?"

"You really want to do this?" I asked.

"You just said you'd kill me. Kelly, take the car. Go get Brian and Tim. Tell them where I am and what's happened. Tell them to bring the guys." His eyes didn't change, and I heard the lack of conviction in his voice.

The girlfriend moved to the driver's side of the car. I hadn't expected this.

"Hang on," I said to the girl.

She had a smug smile on her face, Farrah Fawcett beneath the curls. I realized she had put the guy up to this. She was testing him, his feelings for her, and enjoying it. He'd picked the confrontation to impress her, and now he had no way out. His bravado had backed him into this corner. He wasn't looking to fight. He was looking to save face.

I didn't care about losing face, and I didn't want to get punched in mine. I had no doubt Cap, Billy, and Mif would jump in, but then what? Where would the fight take us? Where and how would it end? And what purpose would it serve? I'd have to explain to my mom and dad why I had a black eye, a chipped tooth, or a broken nose. I stood to gain nothing from this confrontation, even if I won.

Just as William described the war in Vietnam.

I'd learned what tough guys really were, and I'd learned about real consequences talking with William that summer about a war we had no business fighting. I wasn't about to get into a random fight with a guy I had no beef with. I looked to the girlfriend and returned her smug smile.

Then I refocused on the guy. "What do you want?" I asked.

"What?" He seemed surprised by my question.

"What is it you want?"

"I told you. I want you to apologize to her."

"Okay." I looked to the girl. "I'm sorry if anyone said anything to you that was offensive. It shouldn't have happened. I apologize."

She lost the smile and squinted as if she did not understand English. Then she turned to the little tough guy, who looked equally confused but also relieved.

"Are we good?" I asked him, now ignoring the girlfriend.

He stared at me for a second, then turned to his girlfriend. Her brow furrowed like she was failing to solve a geometry problem. I cut her off before she could talk. "You asked for an apology," I said to the guy. "I gave her one. I'm not asking her. I'm asking you. Are we good?"

I'd given him control over the situation rather than emasculate him by talking to his girlfriend. If he was smart, he'd understand. After a beat he said, "Yeah. We're good."

I turned to my friends. "Let's go."

"Brad," the girl said.

"Get in the car, Kelly."

I held the bucket seat for Billy to slide in. The tough guy leaned against his car, head turned, watching me. His girlfriend went around to the passenger side and got in, sulking. She slammed the door. I looked at the guy one last time, and I thought of the army recruit William had described to me that summer, the one so easily indoctrinated that he would run into a wall over and over until he knocked himself out. And when he regained consciousness, his superiors would pin a medal to his shirt and he'd wear it with great pride, or maybe frame it and put it on the mantel, and never know that thousands of other guys had the very same medal, for doing the exact same thing, but not one of them had ever succeeded in knocking down that wall.

Tough guy gave me a small nod.

I didn't return it.

Inside the car, as we drove away, Mif said,

"Why'd you shut the car door? We couldn't get out."

"Sorry. I didn't think about it," I said. "Never happened to me before."

"We would have killed that guy," Cap said.

"Go get Brian and Tim," Billy said, mocking him. We laughed nervous laughter.

"Did anyone say anything?" Mif asked.

One by one, we denied it, and we rationalized that the guy had just been a South City punk trying to impress his girlfriend. We doubted he even had friends close by. We doubted he would have fought us. We doubted a lot, but what I did not doubt, what I knew for sure, was none of us stepped up to be first. In the past, my hesitancy would have eaten at my pride, but not now, not after working with William.

"Why'd you apologize?" Cap asked me.

I almost said, *It wasn't worth ruining the night over.* But that would have been a lie. "Because I didn't want to fight him," I said in a rare moment of honesty.

After a second, Mif said, "I didn't, either."

"Wouldn't have been worth it," Billy agreed.

"No sense ruining the whole night," Cap said.

Maybe speaking the truth was contagious.

August 1, 1968

I haven't written much the past month. I'm too tired by the end of the day, and in the mornings, I have to get prepared to move out. More of the same anyway. We hump. We find empty villages. We lose guys to booby traps and ambushes. We get in skirmishes and coordinate our own ambushes, but for now the NVA does not stay for long.

We've had reinforcements flown in. FNGs getting a lot of on-the-job training. Cruz spends a lot of his time just trying to keep them alive. The FNGs bring news. A lot has happened we did not know about. War protests at home have increased in frequency and size. Robert Kennedy was assassinated after winning the California Democratic primary and campaigning with a promise to end the war. I'm sorry he got shot, but I doubt he would have ended the war. I doubt all politicians. Westmoreland has been replaced, that much we knew—but apparently LBJ denied his call for two hundred thousand more troops. Looks like it's just us.

This morning we were given additional

time to get ready. We were awaiting orders. I took the time to just sit. Mornings are strangely beautiful, at least when it doesn't rain. The temperature is comfortable and the air clear and crisp. I sucked in each breath, savoring it like a cool drink of clean water. I could see color. The sky awakened with ribbons of red and orange, yellows, and fuchsia. The color is always welcome. It means I'm still alive. The rest of the day I'll see gray and brown and endless green. Tunnels of green.

I sliced off a piece of C-4 and lit it so I could have warm water to brush my teeth and heat my C rations. I can barely stomach anything now but the peaches and the pears.

I emptied my sandbags, found the tree against which I'd lowered my pack, slipped on the straps, and used the trunk to pull myself to my feet. We started with a steep descent to expansive rice paddies, green from the recent rain with just a hint of gold. Old people, their bodies as crooked as question marks, worked in the paddies. They didn't look up as we passed. They didn't acknowledge me. I wondered how they go on, like everything is normal, like we don't exist. How can they go on when marines are dying trying to protect them?

We approached their village, and I wondered if Charlie waited, watching, preparing for another ambush. We swept the village, but only found mama- and papa-sans, young girls, and children. Those not working stood in the door-ways of the primitive huts and watched me with looks of fear and hatred. There were no cheers of "GI number one."

I smiled to put the kids at ease, but they didn't smile back. The mama-sans quickly turned them away and ushered the children inside, like I was a stray dog who would bite.

I'm supposed to be here to save them, but I've come to realize they don't want me humping their mountains, stalking their rice paddies, and sweeping their villages. I'm not their friend or their protector, and certainly not their savior. I'm a foreigner. I don't look like them. I'm not built like them. I don't eat like them. I don't pray like them. I am the one who is different. This is their country. I am invading their home.

We asked where the VC were, but the answer was always the same. "No VC. No VC."

I wanted to believe them. I wanted to believe they were just farmers trying to survive, so we could move on and leave them alone, but then someone found a cache of rice. All this rice and there were only old men and old women, children. Who was all the rice for?

"No VC," they said. "No VC."

Someone found an AK-47.

My heart sank.

Someone was VC, which made every-one in the village VC. I knew what was to come. If body count is the measure of success, then the tendency is to kill anyone and count the body as an enemy combatant. It makes liars out of soldiers. It makes Viet Cong out of peasants.

We removed the villagers and burned the village to the ground, a village that had likely stood for a thousand years, through typhoons and cyclones and famine and disease. Some-one lit a cigarette and put a flame to straw and the village was gone in minutes. I didn't wonder where these people were going to live. I didn't think about what they were going to eat. I didn't care. They were just Charlie to me.

We marched them ahead of us because we thought they knew where the mines and booby traps were that would kill our marines.

I walked with them, and I thought, *All this time I've been looking for Charlie.*

All this time.

And Charlie has been right here, all around me, all this time.

CHAPTER 18

July 24, 1979

William and I returned to Behan's after a tile job one afternoon; William said his girlfriend, Monica, was again working late. Seemed she was always working late. Sipping a pint of Guinness while we awaited our food, I brought up the incident of the guy challenging me and my friends to a fight. I'm not sure why I brought it up. Maybe I just wanted to hear how William would have kicked the guy's ass and taught him and his girlfriend a lesson, like the lesson he had taught the woman driving the BMW.

Instead, William sipped his drink and asked, "What did you do?"

I contemplated making up a story, but only briefly. I got a sense William knew what I had done and that he would see right through any bullshit. After nearly two months working together daily, he knew who I was and who I was not. William, on the other hand, was difficult to know and difficult to predict, as were the things he would say. So, although embarrassed, I shrugged and told the truth. "I apologized."

William gave this some thought, but I couldn't read his expression.

"There were four of you?" he asked.

"Yeah," I said, starting to feel small.

"How big was he?"

Still shrinking. I had no doubt what William would have done. "Not much bigger than me. Probably weighed more, but not a lot."

More contemplation. Then William asked, "Did you say anything?"

"No."

"Did your friends?"

"They said they didn't."

"So why did you apologize?"

I let out a sigh. "To let the guy save face. I figured the girl put him in a corner."

"Of course she did." William laughed. Then he said, "Either that, or one of your friends said something."

"Maybe. I don't know. Maybe we should have taught him a lesson. I mean, two of my friends are big. Really big. They would have killed the guy on their own."

William nodded. "But nobody did."

"No."

"And nobody admitted they said anything."

"No."

"Shitty situation to put you in, if one of them did say something."

I shrugged and swiped at the condensation on the outside of my glass. "I didn't care."

"Yeah, you did," William said. "Otherwise you

wouldn't have brought it up, and we wouldn't be having this conversation."

I nodded. "Maybe."

"You might need new friends," William said.

And there it was. The reaction I could never predict. "They're good guys," I said, back-pedaling. "Like I said, I think this guy was just looking for a fight to impress his girlfriend. I think she put him up to it."

William nodded. "But the question is why? I think you already figured that out. Someone said something."

"Maybe," I said again. "But I wasn't going to fight the guy just so he could save face . . ." I paused. William waited. I shook my head. Why was I bullshitting? "The truth," I said, "is I've never been in a real fight." I shrugged and left unsaid the obvious.

William let almost a minute pass, staring at the people in the bar before he reengaged me. "You know the definition of a hero?"

I figured I could make up one on the fly. "Someone who acts without considering his own safety?"

"Someone too stupid not to consider his own safety and gets himself and other people killed," William said, sounding adamant.

Again, not the answer I'd been expecting. I let William's statement sit a moment, not quite certain what it meant. Finally, I just asked, "You think I did the right thing?"

"Never get in a fight if your heart isn't in it. You'll lose. Especially if the other guy has something to fight for. This guy did. His honor. You didn't. You'll get yourself and others killed."

I nodded. Made sense.

"It's like Vietnam," he said, although I had already deduced it. "None of us had our hearts in the fight. What was the point? Why was I supposed to care about a war in a country halfway around the world? How did it impact me? The government couldn't give us an intelligent reason why we were dying over there. They kept saying we were stopping the spread of communism." He frowned. "What does an eighteen-year-old care about the spread of communism?"

He doesn't, I thought, but didn't say.

William stared at me, as if looking straight through me. Then he asked, "Why'd you tell me that story?"

"I don't know," I said. "I guess I just wanted to hear what you'd say."

He nodded. "Was it what you expected?"

My turn to chuckle. "No."

"What did you expect?"

"I figured you would have beat the crap out of the guy."

William smiled, but it was pensive. Then he said, "Like that hulk at the softball game?"

"Yeah," I said, still chuckling.

"Only because fighting was what I was brainwashed to do," he said. "Listen, I didn't have a choice to fight or not fight. I couldn't back out or back down. My country put me in that position. Kill or be killed. Period. But you had a choice," he said. "And you made the right choice. The smart choice. And that takes a lot more guts than anything I did because I had to."

That made me feel good. For some reason, though, I said, "Sometimes I wish I was more like Todd, with that badass saunter of his."

William got quiet, a queer expression on his face. "You think Todd walks like a badass?"

"You don't? He saunters like Arthur Fonzarelli."

"It's not a saunter," William said. "It's a limp." William looked as though he was uncertain what more to say. Then he said, "He got it in Vietnam."

"What happened? If I can ask?"

William sipped his drink. "You can ask and since Todd told me, I'll tell you. Todd had been outside the wire for weeks on search and destroys. When he got back to his base, they rotated in a new lieutenant. Officers rotated out every six months, just when they finally had enough experience to know shit."

"Why?"

William sat forward. "Because Vietnam was the only war we had going on, and the military had promised all these guys if they went to officer candidate school, they'd get the chance to lead. So they rotated officers in and out as a way to get

343

them experience, except Vietnam was nothing like the classroom, and the VC were not like any enemy we'd ever faced. This was a guerilla war, and most of the guys rotating in didn't know shit and wouldn't until they lived through it. If they lived through it."

"Makes sense," I said.

William laughed. "It made no sense. That's the point. It was idiotic."

"So, what happened to Todd's leg?"

"Todd's platoon was supposed to get time off after they got back, but this twenty-three-year-old pissant firebrand out of West Point thought he was going to win the war on his own and he tells the platoon they're going back out, that Charlie's making another big push and he wants to beat Charlie to the punch. Nobody was buying the bullshit anymore. Todd said guys flat out refused to go, and this lieutenant threatened that anybody who refused to go would be sent to the military jail at Long Binh, which was a real shithole."

I just listened. I didn't feel it was my place to ask any questions.

"Todd only had three months left. He didn't want to end up in jail, but he said he had this strong feeling that if he went outside the wire again, he wasn't coming back. You get that feeling, a sixth sense. Todd said he was sure this ass was going to get him killed. The night before they were to go out, he was in his bunker, drunk and high and tripping. He took out this metal rod he kept in his rucksack and handed it to one of the guys in the bunker. Then he put his boot on a chair and told the guy to break his leg."

"Oh my God," I said.

William nodded. "This guy, also messed up, whacks the leg. Todd doesn't know how many times, because he thinks he passed out. Said he woke up on a stretcher with the lieutenant running beside him, yelling that he'd see to it that Todd received a court-martial and was sent to a military prison."

I had misjudged the saunter, just as I'd misjudged the toothpick to be an accoutrement of a badass. Far from it.

"What happened to the guys in Todd's platoon, the ones who went out?"

"They got ambushed. Half the guys died, including the lieutenant."

"Todd was right. He knew."

"We all knew," William said. "Over there, it was just a matter of when."

August 18, 1968

I was raised Catholic. I learned how to
pray the Our Father and Hail Mary and
the Glory Be so I could say the rosary. I
made my First Confession and my first
Holy Communion, and I was confirmed
at Our Lady of the Most Holy Rosary
Catholic Church. I went to a Catholic
grammar school and a Catholic high
school, and I went to mass Sundays with
my family. The marines are the first time
I've spent significant time with guys who
are not Catholic. In my platoon we have
Protestants, Lutherans, Baptists, Jews, a
few agnostics, Latter-Day Saints, even a
Muslim.

When I left for boot camp, my mother
gave me a gold cross on a chain to protect
me. I've worn it every day, and when I
first arrived in-country, I prayed every
day. I prayed all the time. You can't help
it.

At first you ask God politely. *Bless me,
God. Keep me safe.*

Simple prayers.

Then marines start dying, young men
just like you, young men who believed

with all their heart in the same God. Young men who prayed to the same God to protect them. I went from the simple prayers and requests to asking God to make sense of it, to make sense of all the young men dying.

I questioned God. *Why didn't you listen to them? Why did they die?*

My brothers are stepping on mines and booby traps and mortar rounds. They're getting shot up and blown up no matter how hard they pray.

I made deals with God.

If I live, I swear, God, I'll go to church every day when I get home. I'll become a priest. I'll quit drinking, quit smoking dope.

But my brothers continue to die, almost every day now. The NVA has resorted to guerilla tactics, and they're good at them. We can't even find them. The officers tell us it's because their numbers are dwindling, that we're winning. Really? Because every day I wake I see *our* numbers dwindling.

Then I got angry. I yelled at God.

Where are you? Why aren't you listening? Why do I even bother to pray if you aren't going to listen, if you're going to let guys die?

Still more die—friends you thought would never die are suddenly gone. I'm not any better than them, and worse than some, so I figure it's just a matter of time before my number's up. It's just fate. It's just bad luck. It has nothing to do with praying. Nothing to do with the guy upstairs. He isn't even here.

I understand now why Cruz told me not to make friends, but how do I not? I mean, I hump with these guys every day, we sleep together in foxholes, pull guard duty together at night, and shoot the shit. I don't want to know them, but I do. I know the names of the small towns from all over the country from where they came. I know their family members and their girlfriends.

They're just like me.

They pray, just like me.

And they die.

Maybe like me.

Finally, I gave up.

No more deals with God.

No more bargains.

No more prayers.

I'm not going to pray if you're not going to listen.

Like thoughts of home, I pushed the thought of a benevolent God out of my head until, finally, I stopped thinking about God altogether.

He simply doesn't exist.

Am I worried about hell?

I'm in hell. God can't send me anyplace worse than here.

And I don't need God. Because I don't care anymore. I don't care if I live or die.

I no longer fear death.

It no longer scares me.

It no longer has power over me.

I walk in the valley of death and I fear no evil.

Because I am the evil.

And that is an omnipotent feeling.

CHAPTER 19

July 26, 1979

As the subcontractors performed their jobs at the Burlingame remodel, I suspected I was no longer needed, and Todd would have been justified to lay me off. But I'd also come to learn that wasn't his way. I had worked hard for Todd and I guessed he felt a sense of loyalty to me. William told me one afternoon that I had saved Todd money on the remodel and it now looked like he would make money, especially after the owner agreed to pay more for upgrades he and his wife wanted.

Todd also bid tile jobs, kitchen and bathroom rip-outs, and other small remodels, even retiling around the trim of a partially drained pool. I performed the prep work on these jobs so William or Todd or both could arrive with materials and hit the ground running. It meant long days, but long days meant more money. It also meant I went out less with my high school buddies. They left for Giants games or parties while I remained at work. A couple had already left for school. Others vacationed with their families. I had stopped drinking during the week and felt better for it. I was also getting eight hours of sleep. By contrast, William's physical condition and his emotional state worsened. His clothes seemed to weigh on him, as did the work. He stooped, bent over, and he rarely called me Vincenzo. One afternoon when he took off his shirt, I was shocked at the muscle mass he had lost. He was also becoming unreliable. When William didn't show up at Nini's, Todd would drive back home to call him, while I waited in the truck. When Todd came out of his house, it seemed William always had an excuse.

On one occasion I expressed my concern about William's physical condition to Todd and asked if he was okay.

"Monica threw him out a few weeks ago," Todd said, referring to William's girlfriend.

"Where's he been living?" I asked.

"He's sleeping on some friends' couches and living in his El Camino," Todd said.

Nowadays the term "homeless" has a different connotation given the large homeless populations found in most cities, but the basics remain the same. William didn't have a place to live.

"I have a room above my garage," Todd said. "I'll let him stay there if he can't find anyplace else."

The following day, when William showed up at Nini's, he told me I should drive my own car to the jobsite, that he had errands to run after work. As I passed his El Camino, I noticed bags of clothes and other items. I felt bad that he was embarrassed. After what he'd been through, he had no reason to feel embarrassed about anything.

The jobsite was a master bathroom remodel in Redwood City. We found dry rot in the studding in the walls and the subflooring. Dry rot, I was told, cannot be ignored or go untreated. It starts with water intrusion that becomes a fungus that eats at the wood and worsens with time if ignored.

"It's like cancer," William said, using his boot to step on a weakened floor joist. His foot went through the joist like it was sawdust. "If you don't cut it out, it spreads and eventually destroys the entire structure."

I wondered if the same thing was happening to William, if Vietnam was rotting him from the inside, and I wondered what might happen if it went untreated.

We had a plan to treat dry rot. We showed the homeowner the problem and took pictures to document it, then we cut out the infected lumber and installed pressure treated studs and joists, which were resistant to dry rot, and replaced the subflooring. Because dry rot was prevalent in older bathrooms but hidden behind the walls and subflooring, Todd told his clients the cost would be billed on a time and material basis. That meant the owner paid for the materials, as well as William's and my hourly wages to perform the work.

Despite all this, it didn't mean the homeowner would be happy. People never were when the cost of a job increased. The wife on this particular job told us to stop work and called her husband, who we assumed called Todd. William and I sat outside in the shade of a large eucalyptus tree waiting for the papal blessing to continue. As per usual, I sat on one of our five-gallon plastic buckets, and William squatted on his haunches, smoking a cigarette.

"Whatever happened to that cute Italian girl in the house next door?" William asked. It was the first time he'd brought up Amy DeLuca in weeks.

"She went home to New York," I said again.

"Anything happen between the two of you? You looked like you were getting along at pizza that night."

A part of me wanted to tell William about that night, that Amy and I had returned to the house and the pool, but I knew Amy had just needed to get her mind off her ex-boyfriend, and I'd been a convenient distraction, nothing more. I also didn't get the sense William was all that interested. He was just making conversation and had something else on his mind.

"Nah," I said. "She was leaving that Sunday, and she has a boyfriend in Manhattan. She was just looking for something to do because her cousin's boyfriend was complaining they didn't get to spend any time alone."

"Too bad, Vincent. Nice Catholic Italian girl would have made Mama Bianco happy."

"How do you know she was Catholic?"

"Her family's Italian and she's from Queens. She's Catholic."

I smiled. "She was too old for me anyway."

"That's the best kind. They can teach you."

I laughed. "I'll bet."

William flicked his cigarette ashes.

I decided to ask William a question I had asked earlier that summer. "How come you don't wear your cross anymore?" I asked. "The one you said your mother gave you."

William sucked his cigarette. He'd previously said he lost the cross, but I didn't believe he had. This time, though, he said, "I gave it to a guy who had a use for it. I no longer did."

"Oh."

William took a moment, as if debating whether he wanted to say more, and in that moment I realized asking again had been a mistake, that William had lied for a reason. A part of me hoped he wouldn't tell me what happened, but then he said, "I told you Bean usually walked point?"

"Yeah," I said.

"Except some nights Cruz made Bean take a break and we'd switch off taking the point."

"Okay."

"We went out one night and it was my turn to take point, but Tommy, this guy from Minnesota, he asked me to switch because the next day was his birthday and he didn't want to walk point on his birthday. He said it was bad luck. So I said, 'Sure.' What do I care, right?"

"Right."

"We called Tommy 'Forecheck' because he was a big hockey guy. Played in college and the semipros, and he was talking about playing when he got home, said he had a tryout with the Minnesota North Stars. Big mistake."

"What?"

"Talking about home."

"Victor Cruz warned you about talking about home," I said.

William nodded. "Said *that* was bad luck. Forecheck had this freaky weird accent. He elongated his *o*'s. Minn-eh-soooota." William smiled, remembering. He took a drag on his cigarette and blew the smoke into the sky. I could smell the tobacco on the breeze blowing through the eucalyptus leaves. "We used to make fun of him, give him a hard time. He just laughed with us. Said we were the ones with the accents." William's eyes seemed to lose focus and he said softly, "Good guy."

He looked back up at me as if he had forgotten I was there. I was hoping he wouldn't continue, and I was trying desperately to think of another topic.

"This night that Forecheck asked to switch

355

point, we were humping the same patrol as the night before, and we'd all come back without a scratch. So I was thinking no big deal. I switched with him and I was walking at the back with Victor Cruz. It was so dark I could barely see Cruz, and he was only three meters in front of me."

William took another deep drag on his cigarette. His hand shook and the shake found its way into his voice. "I heard a sound, a click. We all heard it. Everyone froze because we knew that sound. We knew what was to follow. Cruz and I both dropped where we stood."

"Was it a mortar?"

"No. An incoming mortar whistles. This was a Bouncing Betty. You know what that is?"

I nodded. William had told me about Bouncing Bettys. I didn't want to hear the rest of the story.

He told me again. "You step on the trigger. Click. It explodes an ordnance buried nearby. But it doesn't just explode. It bounces, about chest high. Then it explodes shrapnel, to do maximum damage. I'd heard that click enough to know to drop, and hope the shrapnel goes past you instead of through you. This night it missed me and Cruz, but a dozen guys at the front of the line got hit. The rest of us hunkered down, waiting, in case it was an ambush and the NVA opened up. When they didn't, we attended to the wounded. I was thinking about how lucky I was to have not walked lead that night. I was looking at all these guys who'd been hit, and I didn't have a scratch on me. Good luck for me, right?"

"Shit yeah," I say.

"Then Cruz asked, 'Where's Forecheck? He was walking lead.'"

I felt nerves in my joints, like I needed to stretch.

"Cruz and I went to the front and started looking for Forecheck, but it was so dark, no moon. We couldn't see shit. We couldn't find him anywhere. The lieutenant, he didn't know shit. So Cruz was telling everybody to be careful because if there's one booby trap, there's usually more. The Vietnamese wanted you to think the mines were anywhere and everywhere, so you'd get paranoid."

He pulled again on the cigarette. It looked to me like his eyes were moist.

"Anyway, it's like Forecheck vanished, just ran off into the jungle. I was looking at the blast, and I figured out the direction of the force of the explosion based on the guys who got hit and the plants and shit, and I shine my light up into a tree . . ." William looked like a guy who had taken a blow to the gut and had the wind knocked out of him. "I looked up and . . . there was Forecheck . . . pieces of him . . . in the tree." William looked like he might cry. I didn't know what to say. After a beat, he continued, "Cruz looked at me.

Neither of us said anything. Then the lieutenant, an FNG, he said, 'Someone needs to climb that tree and bring him down.'" William stubbed out his cigarette and blew out the last breath of smoke. He didn't look at me anymore.

I felt sick.

"There's wounded all around, but Cruz and I didn't get hit, and this lieutenant, he and Cruz didn't get along. He said, 'Get him down, so his family has something to bury.'

"Cruz looked at him and said, 'What's the point?'

"Lieutenant said, 'Forecheck is Catholic. Catholics have to bury a body.'

"Cruz said he'd do it, but I was the reason Forecheck was in the tree. I switched point. All of a sudden, I'm not feeling so lucky. I said, 'No. I'll go up.' So I climbed the tree . . . and I peeled Forecheck off the branches . . . what was left of him . . . so we could zip those pieces in a body bag so his family had something to bury."

William paused. His eyes remained unfocused. I knew he'd gone back to that night. "When I climbed down, I was washing Forecheck's blood off my hands with water from my canteen, and my cross, which I wore around my neck with my dog tags, was dangling, and I thought that being Catholic didn't do Forecheck any good, and it just made things worse for me. I snatched the cross, yanked the chain off my neck, and put it in the bag with what was left of Forecheck. Then I told Cruz, 'Anyone asks, I'm not Catholic. I'm nothing. Nobody has to climb a fucking tree to pull me down.' "

I couldn't speak. I didn't say a word. I just sat there, numb to everything, while William stood and walked to his El Camino.

PART V

Take Me Home, to the Place . . . I Once Belonged

September 24, 1968

I'm writing this journal entry from a hospital bed. They flew me from the bush to the Ninety-Fifth Evac Hospital at Da Nang. That should tell you two things. One, I got hit. Two, I'm still alive.

We were ambushed, again. It would be easier to write about the days when we weren't ambushed. It seems so frequent now. We've lost so many guys. As for Charlie Company, First Platoon, only five of the original thirteen from my squad were still there. Me, Cruz, Bean, Whippet, and Dominoes, though Whippet isn't there anymore either.

The NVA hit-and-runs were constant, but they also stood and fought. A week ago the RPGs exploded as we neared a village on the other side of a stream. I lay flat on my stomach behind a downed tree and sprayed on fully automatic until Cruz came down the line yelling for us to shoot semiautomatic—three-round bursts—to save ammunition.

"I'm hit. I'm hit." The voice coming from my right sounded disbelieving and angry. "Corpsman!" I recognized

Whippet's voice, but heavy and persistent machine gun fire prevented our corpsman from moving up, and we couldn't provide enough suppression.

I forgot everything my mother told me about not being a hero, about blending in. I guess I reacted on instinct, the way a parent wouldn't hesitate if his kid got hit. I moved to the sound of Whippet's voice, firing as I went, and found Mr. Gung Ho, Mr. "I'm going to kill me some Cong," screaming like his leg was blown off. Not his leg, but a portion of his right boot. I grabbed him and drug him back through the bush. It happened in an instant. The blink of an eye. Before you could snap your fingers. It felt like someone shoved my shoulder and knocked me backward, off my feet. I tumbled down a slope and me and Whippet fell. The bullet probably saved my life. I didn't even know I'd been hit. It must have been the shock. I got up, went to Whippet, and finished dragging him behind the log.

The corpsman made his way over and I was shocked when he stuck me, not Whippet, with a needle of morphine. That's when I realized I'd been hit.

Cruz helped to remove my vest. He was kneeling over me, putting pressure on my shoulder until the corpsman could stuff the wound with gauze and put a field dressing on it. The way Cruz was looking at me, I was sure I was going to die.

"You and me have a date in Little Havana, Shutter."

"Don't talk about home," I told him. Strange thing. I wasn't scared. I wasn't afraid. I felt an odd sense of peace.

"We're going to dance all night, Shutter. The Puerto Rican girls are going to love you."

Cruz felt the pockets of my vest. He looked puzzled, then looked at me like he'd just found a bar of gold. He pulled out the Tiger Chewing Tobacco tin. The one Longhorn gave me. The one I kept in the upper left pocket of my flak jacket, and in which I kept this journal and this nub of pencil. One more thing Charlie had to penetrate to kill me.

Only he couldn't.

Cruz fell back against the log laughing and showed me the tin. He ran a finger over the dented corner. Then he laughed again. "Longhorn saved your life, Shutter. He saved your life. The bullet hit the corner of the tin and deflected just enough. It missed your heart and hit just below your collarbone, in the meat of your shoulder."

"It went through clean," the corpsman agreed.

Cruz said it again, this time to himself, as if not believing, as if he needed to hear it said out loud to believe it. "It deflected and went clean through. You are one lucky son of a bitch."

But I didn't feel lucky. I didn't feel a thing.

I stayed behind that log until the fighting ended and the NVA melted back into the bush. The morphine wore off and I felt a searing pain. They called in a dust off, loaded me and Whippet and the rest of the injured, and flew us out.

The doctor who treated my wound also said I was lucky. I showed him the dent in the tin can and told him what had happened, that I'd kept the tin in my vest pocket and it had deflected the bullet just enough to knock it off target. He smiled, but he wouldn't say for sure my theory was correct, not without the bullet.

"Although," he added before leaving my bedside, "the wound does have an upward trajectory, which would indicate you may be right, about the tin deflecting it."

I didn't know if he was serious or just humoring me. Maybe he figured there was nothing wrong with a marine believing he had a lucky talisman. I'd seen grunts with anything from rabbit's feet on chains to a necklace of VC ears. And each swore it was good luck, at least up until the day he died or, like Longhorn, his DEROS came up and he made it home.

The doctor likely figured, *Let him believe what he wants.*

What's the harm?

CHAPTER 20

April 17, 2016

Elizabeth and I both sensed that since Chris's death, Beau was searching for something, his own identity, perhaps. He had become more open to leaving the Bay Area to go to college, and he had applied to LA schools and schools on the East Coast. Elizabeth wasn't happy about it. She kept asking Beau why he wanted to go back east with so many wonderful schools in the Bay Area.

Beau said he just did.

Elizabeth also did not want Beau to play football, but Beau had looked into attending football camps, including two in Los Angeles. I told her in private to let Beau go through the process. I rationalized that football could get Beau into a school that might otherwise be a reach, but that it was unlikely he would get on the field his freshman year anyway. He could then quit but stay in school and get his degree. Schools used student-athletes all the time. Student-athletes could also use schools. If the school didn't like it, too bad.

I was more concerned that Beau's motivation to play had something to do with keeping Chris's memory alive. I thought of William, and his comment that sometimes you just have to live through things to truly understand them. I'd experienced something similar when my father died. Friends had lost parents, and while empathetic, I hadn't understood the pain that could accompany that loss until my own father died.

I also did not want Beau to play college football. Most of his high school years were just before the CTE studies came out, before the movie *Concussion* with Will Smith hit the big screen. Elizabeth and I didn't know what we didn't know. Beau played the game undersized, but relentless, and he'd paid for it with injuries. He'd already had the one concussion. We hoped he would quit, but Beau had to make that decision for himself.

Beau and I jumped on a plane to Los Angeles, rented a car and a hotel room, and went through the recruiting process, which was an eye-opener. When we showed up at the first camp, I could see Beau's nerves in his demeanor. Big, athletic players surrounded him. To make matters worse, the first thing the college recruiting team did was instruct the recruits to remove their shoes and shirts to get weighed and measured. They then handed each recruit a T-shirt with a number on it and herded them out the door to the practice field to be timed in the forty-yard dash and cone drills.

As I sat with other parents sweltering on metal

bleachers and slathering on sunblock, I watched this process and felt sick to my stomach. I remembered the passage in William's journal about his indoctrination into the US Marines, how he had been treated like a piece of meat, all individuality stripped away, everyone handed the same gray sweatshirt and sweatpants with a number that would be his new identity.

I looked down at the field and watched Beau going through another drill, doing bear crawls, rolling, getting to his feet, shuffling left, right, forward, back, then running to the back of the line to prepare for the next drill, and I realized that Beau, too, was a commodity for the coaches to mold and make bigger and stronger, and to indoctrinate on how to think and take their orders at face value. I worried about my son, my boy.

When Beau finished the camp, we went back to our hotel. In the morning we would drive down the I-10 freeway, and he'd perform at a two-day camp attended by coaches from multiple schools. I refrained from saying much to Beau about the camp that afternoon or the upcoming camps, except "Do your best and don't worry about the rest."

When Beau came out of the shower, I asked him how he felt the camp had gone. He told me he didn't think the coaches even noticed him.

"I was just a number," he said, and I marveled at how my son had become so intuitive. We talked about grabbing some dinner, but Beau, a kid never cheated out of a good time, immediately got on his computer and after a few minutes said, "The Dodgers are playing."

I loved baseball, always had, and I'd never been to Dodger Stadium, home of the Los Angeles Dodgers. I could check it off my bucket list. And seeing a game with my son would be priceless. I only recalled attending one game with my dad, at Candlestick Park, to watch the San Francisco Giants and Willie Mays. *Create memories,* I heard Elizabeth say.

When we arrived at the stadium, I approached the ticket counter. Tickets ranged in price from expensive to very expensive, but you could buy bleacher seats in the outfield for just ten dollars.

"Let's just get those," Beau said, and I knew he meant it.

"No. We might never see another game here," I said to Beau, though inside I had a deeper debate. I was working a job I was not passionate about. At the very least I would enjoy the opportunities the money allowed me to afford for my family.

I bought two tickets three rows behind the first base dugout. The temperature was heavenly, hovering around eighty degrees.

Neither Beau nor I had eaten, so before getting to our seats, we bought Dodger Dogs, fries, and Cokes. Beau had a big smile on his face when we reached the seats, and we asked a guy sitting behind us to take our photograph. That photograph remains on a corkboard in my home office with the ticket stub.

We settled in to watch batting practice and eat, wiping mustard from the corners of our mouths. Yasiel Puig, the Dodgers' right fielder, launched baseballs high into the air and far over the center field wall. Each crack of his bat hitting the ball sounded like a gunshot that echoed against the stadium's still relatively empty seats.

Vin Scully stood on the field and I was just about to point out the Dodgers' iconic announcer when Beau said, "I don't want to play anymore." He turned and looked at me. Even behind the sunglasses I could tell he was fighting tears.

"What?" I said, though certain I had heard him correctly.

"I don't want to play football anymore. These people . . . they don't care about me, Dad. I'm just a number to them."

And there it was. As was so often the case, Beau had reached his own conclusion, seemingly without my help. I became a parent thinking of all the things I would teach my son and my daughter. I never realized how much I would learn from them. I knew then my son would never be a piece of meat. He would never be a number.

Because that was my son.

He was not me.

He was a better version of me.

"Why are we down here then?" I asked, not because I was bitter about the time spent or the cost. I wanted to hear my son's explanation, his rationale. "Why did we come down for these camps?"

He set his Dodger Dog in his lap, which was when I knew things were serious.

"I thought I wanted to play, you know, for Chris—because he and I talked about it so much. But Chris would be the first person to tell me to play for myself or don't play at all. Besides, it won't be the same without him. I won't be making plays behind him."

I smiled. William had been right. Beau had to have this experience to truly understand Chris would not be with him.

"Sometimes I think I was supposed to be in the car that night," Beau said, tears rolling down his cheeks from behind his sunglasses.

"It wasn't God's—"

"Don't," Beau said softly. "Don't tell me God has a reason for everything; there's no reason for someone so young to die. Chris was only eighteen. He had his whole life ahead of him."

I took a breath and thought again of William's journal. "Did I tell you about the summer before I went to college?"

Beau shook his head.

I told Beau about William and Todd, what they had been through and how neither believed in

God. "They said they stopped believing because when they needed God, he wasn't there."

"I feel that way now," Beau said, wiping his tears.

"I know," I said. "But I do believe. You know why?"

"Why?"

"Because I was there that moment you were born, and the moment your sister was born. So I know, firsthand, there has to be a God to make something so beautiful as you and your sister, to give me and your mother such incredibly precious gifts." I paused to let that sink in. "Every time someone so young dies, Beau, like Chris, it's a shock because it's not just a loss of life, it's a loss of potential—what that life could have been. The death of someone so young shatters the illusion we all have at eighteen—the illusion that we're immortal, that we're never going to grow old, that we're never going to die."

"That's what I thought," Beau said. "I thought Chris and I would go to the same college, work and live near each other our whole lives, that our children would play sports together. I just never thought he wouldn't be part of my life."

"I know," I said. "But we don't know God's ways. Maybe, perhaps, God spared you a greater tragedy down the road. I'm not making excuses. I'm just saying, we don't know." I thought of something else, something my older sister had once said. "You know, I used to complain about all my ailments, all my worn-out joints, until one day, your auntie Susie said to me, 'Well, the alternative to growing old is a lot worse, so count your blessings that you're old enough to have worn out a knee or a hip or a shoulder.' Growing old is a privilege, Beau, not a right. I thank God every day that I wake up. I thank him every day for your mom, for you, and for Mary Beth."

"It doesn't bring Chris back," Beau said.

"No. It doesn't. That's the hardest part about death. It's permanent. It's final. But Chris will not have died for nothing if you learn just one thing from his death, if you learn that life is fragile at any age, and that every day is a gift. His death won't be for nothing if you learn to celebrate each morning that you wake, take a breath, and realize you're still alive and the day is filled with endless potential."

Beau was silent for a moment. His hot dog sat in the paper tray in his lap, partially uneaten. After a minute he said, "That's why I have to go away. To grow up. You know that, right?"

"Is that what these camps are about?" I asked.

"I'm not running away from Chris's death, Dad, but I need to go away for a while and find myself. I can't do it at home. It's nothing against you and Mom; you've always given me everything I needed to succeed, but now I have to succeed on my own, without you, without Chris, without everything I need. I have to find out if I can stand on my own two feet."

I felt the pang of loss but put it aside to think of my son. "I understand, Beau. I was your age once, and a lot less mature. You will stand on your own two feet."

"You're not upset I'm going away? Because it sure seems like Mom gets upset every time I mention a school in LA, or out of state."

I took a breath. "I'll miss you, Beau, because I love you. Your mother loves you. You and she have always had a special bond. You should take pride in that. Some parents can't wait for their kids to go away. Not us."

"I never knew growing up could be this hard."

"Just be happy you have the chance. So many, for so many reasons, never do."

I recall looking at my son in the bright Los Angeles sunshine, with the smell of hot dogs and popcorn and beer all around us, and I realized my son would not go to school in the Bay Area. It wasn't Chris's death and the difficulties that followed that had led Beau to his decision, though they certainly had been a factor. It was just time for Beau to go. And it was time for Elizabeth and me to let him go. Time to let him live through his own experiences and grow up. It was time to let him find the man he would become, the type of man he wanted to be, the type of person he wanted to be. I realized no one was better suited to choose what was best for Beau than Beau. And I took some pride in that. Elizabeth and I had raised a good young man.

I smiled. "Let's enjoy the game. Tomorrow we'll go to the beach."

"What about the camp tomorrow?"

"What about it?"

"You paid for it. You paid for the airfare and the hotels."

"Have you ever been to a Southern California beach?" I had been many times as a young man while attending UCLA law school, but I was thinking of William's story at this moment.

"No."

"Trust me, you won't be disappointed. It's sunshine and bikinis."

I smiled, though tears pooled in my eyes, thankfully hidden behind sunglasses so my son would not feel guilty about what he had to do, so he would not make a decision to please his dad or his mom, or Chris. I wanted him to make a decision to please himself, and along the way, I hoped—no, I was certain—he'd find the man he wanted to be, a man of whom his mother and I would be more than proud.

But oh, letting him go hurt.

And it would for a long time.

November 14, 1968

I never thought I'd say this, but I miss the guys, though there aren't many left from when I first flew into Firebase Phoenix. It's just Cruz, Bean, and me now. Dominoes finished his tour. Whippet is headed home. They couldn't save his entire foot. They amputated three toes. Last I saw him, in this hospital, he was hobbling on crutches.

After being in the bush for months, things in the rear don't seem real. I can't sleep at night; the beds are too soft. Most times I sleep on the ground. It's also too quiet. I can't hear the rhythm of the bush. I can't hear the insects, the buzz of the mosquitos that tortured me, or the persistent rains that came as regular as the mosquitos, every morning and every night. I feel out of place. I go to the bathroom and they have toilets with seats and toilet paper. They have showers with hot water and soap. My body is clean for the first time in months. I no longer smell like the bush. I got my hair washed and cut, and I shaved, just to fit in with everybody else.

In the mess hall I eat real food from real plates with real utensils. I ate real eggs. I hadn't had real eggs in seven months. I drink from cups, fresh brewed coffee and clean water, not the shitty stuff we'd drink from the rice paddies with iodine tablets. My utilities were thrown away. I wear freshly laundered ones. I stepped from the shower this morning and I saw my naked reflection for the first time in months. I don't look like me. I don't look like the marine I didn't recognize in my bunker mirror before I went outside the wire on my first lurp. I'm twice removed from the person I once knew. I can see my ribs and my collarbones. I can see my chin and jawbone. My eyes are sunken, like a cancer patient after months of chemotherapy.

I don't have a weapon. I don't have my M-16 or my .45, and that makes me really feel naked. I don't have to be on guard twenty-four seven, watching my back and the backs of the guys around me. I also don't have my camera. I assume it was turned in here at the lab.

I can't get used to it here. I sat eating at a table in the mess tent and someone dropped a tray behind me. I slid under the table for cover. People in the mess hall looked at me like I was crazy. They're the ones who are crazy. Don't they know what's happening out there? They're living in their castle here while young men are dying in the bush.

I walk the base and I feel like I've landed on the moon. The base is a city, with tens of thousands of people and everything you could possibly need. I walk past dental clinics, restaurants, snack bars, a woodshop, a post office, a swimming pool. They even have basketball and tennis courts, a golf driving range, a laundromat, and a bank. At night there are nightclubs and bowling alleys. I mostly stay away. I keep mostly to myself.

I visited my buddy in the photo lab, and he gave me more photographs. He said I had some great stuff. He said they'd run in *Stars and Stripes*, but I had stuff good enough for the papers back home. Maybe a book. I thanked him for saving me copies. They are good. Real. They show the real Vietnam. They show marines in the bush injured and dying, not this facade they've erected here in the rear. This isn't real. This isn't Vietnam. I look at the pictures and I think, *If I can make it out of here alive, if I can make it back home, maybe I really do have a chance at one of the newspapers.*

Okay, maybe not the *New York Times*. Maybe that's as unreal as this base. But maybe the *Jersey Journal*.

I talked to the PFC in the rack beside me. His nickname is Pee Bucket. No joke. He said he was in one of the shitters when his post got mortared and the entire shitter fell over with him in it. He came out with his pants around his ankles. Somebody said he smelled like a pee bucket and the name stuck. Why he told the story to me, who knows?

Pee Bucket is going home. He lost his left leg below the knee to a land mine. He was supposed to fly out today, headed to some place in California where he's going to get a prosthetic leg and learn to walk again, but he missed his flight out. I don't have to ask him why he missed his plane. I know why. He's scared to go home. He doesn't feel like he belongs there anymore. He belongs here. He has a job here. What's he going to do at home, without a leg?

I think the same thing about my own situation. I once had a calendar to count down the days in-country. I think I wrote about that. I no longer count days.

I've become used to the grunt life. I've become used to living in the bush. There's a rhythm to it. I'm on my own with my brothers, what remains of them. Nobody can get to you. Your parents can't tell you what to do. Your employer can't tell you what to do or how to do it. Even the military can't get to you. What are they going to do if I refuse an order? Send me to Vietnam? Send me out on search and destroys?

I smiled at that thought. I can't believe I've missed the bush.

Captain Martinez came to see me—my first captain at Firebase Phoenix. Corporal Cruz got hold of him and let him know I'd been wounded. Martinez said that based on my combat experience and my injury, I could finish out my duty here, in the rear. Martinez asked if I could type. He needs a clerk. I thanked him and told him I'd have to think about it.

It sounds crazy, but I believed that I belonged in the bush, and I couldn't leave it, not without Cruz.

CHAPTER 21

July 26, 1979

A car approached, and I was happy to have a distraction from William's story about pulling Forecheck from the trees. A silver Mercedes wove along the wooded driveway and parked. A man, presumably the husband, stepped out. He was a big guy, maybe six foot six and stout. I could tell from his expression, and the way he disregarded William at his El Camino and then me, that he wasn't happy.

William and I followed the husband into his torn-up master bathroom, though my mind kept slipping back to the story William had just told me about pulling bits and pieces of his friend Forecheck out of a tree.

"Why can't you just fill in the rotted areas with wood putty? Why do you have to replace it?" the husband asked William. This guy, Eric something, was an insurance agent, but that didn't stop him from throwing around construction terms like Christmas Catholics throw around Hail Marys and Our Fathers at holiday masses, without any real understanding of the meaning behind the words.

"Dry rot is a fungus," William said. "You have

to cut it out. If you patch it, it will keep spreading and get worse over time. You'll have a new bathroom, walk in one day, and step through the floor."

Eric made a face like he didn't believe it. "Why didn't Todd tell me it would cost this much?"

"Todd couldn't have known how much it would cost. You can't know when the walls and the flooring are in place."

"Well I'm not paying that much to fix it. Come up with another solution."

"There are no other solutions," William said. He sounded bored, or tired.

"I'll talk to Todd when he gets here."

William and I went back outside until, eventually, Todd showed up, Eric came outside, and the debate started all over again—until Eric could no longer ignore reality: clearly damaged plywood, joists, and wall studs. He switched tactics and blamed Todd for not putting the expense in his bid. He said the contract reeked of a "bait and switch."

Todd remained calm and held his ground. "That's why it's a contingency item. It's bad luck, I'm sorry."

Bad luck. I thought again of Forecheck. I couldn't help but look at Eric like he was the biggest jackass on the planet. This was a bathroom. It was only money. Nobody had died. Nobody had been blown to bits in a tree.

"I told you about this potential when I bid the job," Todd said.

"He did tell us," the wife said.

Eric ignored her. He must have been a real joy to live with. "It seems like a convenient way to inflate a bid."

Todd shrugged. "If you think you can get someone to fix the dry rot for less, you're welcome to do so, but I won't guarantee the work if I don't approve the fix."

"I'm going to have to think about it," Eric said.

Todd shrugged. He turned to me and William. "Pack everything up. We're done here."

We went to the driveway, and I immediately put all the tools in the buckets. I could hear the husband and wife talking. She wanted us to do the work, but the husband was trying to save face, the way the South City kid had tried to save face with his girlfriend that night he'd picked a fight he couldn't win. After less than five minutes, the husband backed down.

"Okay. Fine. Do the fix. But keep all the receipts so I know what the materials cost, and my wife is going to keep track of your worker's time. This job doesn't need two guys." The husband looked at me. "How much does he get paid?"

"Five bucks an hour," Todd said.

"Five bucks? That's more than minimum wage. He's a kid."

The husband said it like I was ten years old. He was early thirties at most.

"He's not a kid," William said suddenly. "He's eighteen."

Eric turned to Todd. "Fine. But my wife will track their hours." He stormed off, lowered himself into his Mercedes, and drove away.

Before leaving, Todd opened the glove box in his truck cab and handed William a Polaroid camera. "Document everything before you close it back up," he said. William and I did so.

The next morning, William and I returned to the jobsite to do the tile work. This time we drove together in the El Camino, which looked to have been cleaned of William's stuff.

We worked all day, mixing mortar, letting it set to a certain firmness, then cutting and laying tile. The wife decided she wanted a geometric design in the back wall of the shower, and William drew out several options on sheets of paper. The guy was gifted, an artist. She picked a complicated design, but William never hesitated to accommodate her, though I knew it would be more work cutting and fitting the tile together. I got the impression he enjoyed doing the creation and seeing it come to fruition.

When we finished, late in the day, William wiped off the grouted tile with a sponge and put the sponge into the bucket. The wife walked in.

She took one look and was ecstatic. You would have thought we had installed solid gold tiles. She kept saying how beautiful it had all turned out.

The husband drove up as I put the tools into the buckets and put the buckets into the back of the El Camino. He looked to the house. "You guys are finished?"

"Yeah. William's inside with your wife settling up."

The guy hurried inside. Given the wife's professed love of the tile job, I was not surprised when William quickly came out the front door. What did surprise me was the look on his face. I had seen that crazed look once before, in the seventh grade. Barry Hickman. I still remember his name. He had come to school with a near beer, strutting around the schoolyard like he was a big deal. I don't know what compelled me, but I bullied Barry, and as more students bullied him, I couldn't apply the brakes. I upped the ante. I knocked the still full can of near beer from his hand and walked away. Someone shouted my name, and when I turned, Barry barreled toward me at full speed, his arm cocked as if ready to throw a baseball, but not a baseball, the can of beer. He rushed at me so quickly the leather soles of his shoes had no chance to stop him on the asphalt, and he slid, which is the only reason the missile he unleashed didn't smash me in the face.

I can still hear the can whizzing past, just inches from my head. The terror did not end there. It was just beginning. Something had snapped in Barry. An animal came at me, eyes bulging, his pupils pinpoints of black, teeth bared, face flushed. I did the only thing I could think to do. I spun like a bullfighter. The raging bull blew past me, slid again, and this time Barry fell on his ass. I grabbed him in a headlock before he could get up, and I held on for dear life. My classmates implored me to kick Barry's ass, but I wasn't about to give Barry another shot at me. Truth was, his expression, what I had provoked in him, scared me.

And I was scared by William's expression now. His eyes were not flat and lifeless. These were Barry Hickman eyes. Animal eyes. Eric had flipped a switch, and in an instant, William had snapped. He pulled the sledgehammer from the bed of the El Camino, pivoted on the heels of his boots, and stormed back toward the house.

I dropped the tools.

Not good.

Eric stood at the door with a hand up, as if that would help. I figured a guy his size wasn't used to being challenged, but he was being challenged now. In a big way. He said something like, "If you don't agree, you can take me to small claims court."

Was this guy nuts? Small claims court?

William was about to take his head off with a sledgehammer. Eric had no clue what he had provoked.

"Where do you think you're going?" Eric dropped his hand. When William didn't stop, Eric became the matador before the bull, and I think the idiot finally realized what he had sowed. Too little, too late. Eric made his next statements while retreating, presumably to shut the door, but William arrived too fast, the lightning-quick high school wrestler. He drove his shoulder into the door and knocked Eric back. No hand, and no door, was going to stop William.

Eric shouted as William stormed down the hallway. "Hey. Hey! Where the hell do you think you're going?"

I followed William. I'm not sure exactly what I thought I could do, but I was following the man code. You didn't leave your buddy hanging. Eric turned to me as I stepped inside the house. He had that look of uncertainty and fear etched on his face. "What is he going to do?" he said.

I can't believe I could even speak, or what I said, but I said, "He's going to get his money's worth."

The wife looked stricken, crying and shouting. "Eric! Eric, just pay him. Pay him!"

Eric kept calling William's name, kept trying to reason with him as he rushed down the hall behind him. "Hey! Hey, I'm talking to you! Hey! Hey, where are you going?"

William knew where he was going and so did Eric. William stepped into the bathroom and raised the sledgehammer, about to take a huge chunk out of the beautiful shower design.

The wife screamed, but now her words had a bite of anger, directed at her husband. "Goddamn it, Eric, pay him!"

None of it had any impact on William, the raging bull. Just as the sledgehammer was about to fall, the husband shouted, "You swing that hammer and I will fucking kill you."

And that was it.

Things moved in slow motion.

William spun on his boots and redirected his aim from the floor to Eric. Fight or flight. Live or die. William chose to fight. I thought of all the stories he had shared with me that summer. I thought of all the occasions he said he had lived because of luck, while others had not. I thought of him telling me that his ass only stopped shaking when he no longer cared if he lived or died. And I knew what William was capable of.

So did Eric.

The husband's eyes widened. His wife's hands moved to her face, covering a silent scream. I did what William had done when Whippet got shot. Something I would not have done at the start of the summer. I moved on instinct. I stepped toward William and I gripped the sledgehammer.

"William. No," I said.

William's eyes shifted to me, to Eric, back to me. He looked as if he had no idea who I was, who Eric was, or where he was.

"Don't do it," I said. "William. Don't do it."

The weight of the sledgehammer gradually lessened. Color returned to William's eyes. His face slackened, like melting wax.

"He isn't worth it," I said. "Let it go."

I turned to Eric, who opened his mouth, and I cringed, certain he would say something even more stupid, but to my relief, fear got the better of him. "Okay. Okay. I'll pay!" he said. "I got my checkbook right here. I'll write it for the amount in full."

He held the checkbook out in front of him like he was holding out the Holy Grail, imploring William to take it. He spoke slowly, carefully, as if speaking to someone who did not speak English. "I'll pay in full. Okay? I'll pay in full."

William looked frozen in time and place, but he wasn't in Redwood City, California. I knew he'd gone back to Vietnam, to a firefight in the bush, a firefight like the ones he had described. William lowered the sledgehammer, and I felt my stomach drop and my knees weaken. I took the sledgehammer and let out a breath I didn't realize I had been holding.

Eric stepped backward, down the hall. "Get me a pen," Eric said to his wife, watching William as if he were a stray dog who might bite. "Get me a pen."

At the kitchen counter, the wife handed Eric a pen. His hands shook so violently he could hardly hold it. He wrote the check, ripped it from the checkbook, and handed it to me, as if fearful he might not get back all his fingers if he handed the check to William. His handwriting was almost illegible, but he'd paid the amount in full.

I nodded to William. "Let's go."

I looked at Eric and his wife, both dazed and stunned and scared, not quite sure what they had just witnessed. It had not been of this world, not behavior they could relate to. It had been pure adrenaline, coming from someone who knew the true meaning of a battle for survival. The couple huddled together in the entryway, watching us go. Again, I don't know what possessed me. Manners. Hubris. Smart-ass. Whatever it was, I just couldn't help myself. As I stepped from the house, still carrying the sledgehammer, I said, "Nice meeting you both."

And I closed the door.

Outside, I threw the sledgehammer in the bed of the El Camino, pulled myself into the passenger seat, and turned to look at the house. My first thought was Eric would call his bank and cancel the check, but I quickly dismissed it. Like the woman who had flipped off William, Eric wouldn't have the guts. He knew if he did, he'd always worry William would come back and take the house apart with that sledgehammer, blow by blow. He now knew William was capable of just about anything.

I did, too.

And it scared me, the quickness with which William had gone from zero to ten, the way Barry Hickman had gone from laughing and smiling to crazed animal.

We drove the El Camino Real in silence. I didn't dare say a word. After a few minutes, William looked over at me. The pinpoint black eyes were gone, and his cheeks no longer flushed. His jaw had relaxed. He smiled as if the entire incident never happened. He'd just as quickly gone back to zero.

I felt uneasy in the car with him. After weeks working beside him every day, I felt like I didn't know him, not really. I knew a facade, the guy William wanted me to see. He didn't want me to see the guy clearly in pain. The guy shrinking before my eyes. He didn't want me to see the real William.

After a few minutes, William chuckled and said, "Nice to meet you both?" I laughed with him, but inside I wasn't laughing. It's hard to ignore reality when reality is about to hit you like a sledgehammer.

And the reality was, had I not been there, William would have killed Eric.

I believed with all my heart that William would have taken a life, and I knew, in that moment, it would not have been the first. William had been trained to kill. That's why he stayed alive. That's why he sat beside me. He had survived. Because he had killed the guy trying to kill him.

December 2, 1968

I spent Thanksgiving at Da Nang, went to a strip club, drank a lot of beer, and ate turkey with dressing and mashed potatoes smothered in gravy. The meal was supposed to remind us of home. I didn't let it. I ate the meal like it was any other. I didn't think about the holiday, or what my parents and my siblings were doing at home.

I got a Purple Heart. Imagine that. An officer came through the hospital and awarded the Purple Heart to each of us who had been wounded. I know what the Purple Heart means, what it will mean to my mother and my father. It just doesn't mean much to me. The officer went down the row of wounded. He even gave a medal to Abramowitz in the rack at the far end of the hall. Thing is, Abramowitz wasn't wounded. He's here because a Vietnamese hooker gave him a bad case of the clap. We all held it together until the officer left. Then we laughed so hard I nearly rolled out of bed. They came back a day later and took back the medal and Abramowitz got dressed down.

He'll tell you it was worth it.

I thought so, too.

When the Thanksgiving weekend came to an end, I went back to the lab and got my Pentax camera and more canisters with my photographs. They told me I could stay in the rear and shoot dignitaries and ceremonies, but I turned them down. I turned down Captain Martinez also, at least for now. I told him I wanted to finish out with Cruz, that I'd like for the two of us to leave the bush together. He said he understood and that he'd hold the clerk position for me.

I was put on a transport back to Firebase Phoenix, and, man, was Cruz pissed when I got off the chopper. He threw a punch and swore at me, said he had called in a favor, that the war had ended for me. Then he refused to talk to me.

Rumors spread that Whippet and I had shared a foxhole together. Some of the guys also knew I'd shared a foxhole with Kenny, a.k.a. Haybale, way back when I first arrived. I was also humping just behind EZ when he stepped on the land mine, and I had switched point with Forecheck.

Word now is Shutter is bad luck, not

somebody to hang around or make deals with. They say death follows me.

After taking a few hours to calm himself, Cruz spoke to me. I told him what I had told Martinez. I told him that Martinez promised to hold the clerk's job for me. I also told Cruz what the doctor said about Longhorn's tin maybe being good luck.

"Maybe, Shutter," he said. "Maybe. But next time, don't take the chance. Don't be a hero. Just keep your head down."

Don't be a hero.

I could see my mother with a clarity I had not allowed myself to experience since I stepped on that bus to boot camp at PI, South Carolina. I could see her standing in front of me, her hair pulled back in a clip, wearing her maroon dress, pearls strung around her neck. I could even hear her voice for the first time since I left for Vietnam.

Don't stand out. Just blend in. Blend in and come home.

And it hit me. *What the hell did I just do?*

I turned down the clerk's job and asked to come back *here?* Cruz was right. The war was over for me. I had survived. I had lived.

Oh my God. I felt a rush of anxiety and desperation. What the hell had I done? What the hell did I do? *What the hell did I do?*

I am going to die in the bush, and I had a chance to leave it for good, alive.

I wonder if all those things—being beside Kenny and EZ and Whippet, switching point with Forecheck—I wonder if all that wasn't bad luck but good luck. I wonder if the God I no longer believe in used Longhorn's Tiger tin to save my life.

Did you even think of that? Did you? No. No, you didn't.

I took Kenny and spared you.

I had EZ step on that land mine and made the shrapnel fly past you.

I took Forecheck so you could live.

I had Longhorn give you the tin to protect you from that bullet.

You're so bitter and angry, you missed all the signs.

What did you do? You threw it back in my face.

You came back.

What have I done? Oh, God, what have I done? I have a feeling, a premonition. My luck has run out.

I want to go home. Oh, God, I want to go home.

Too late. You had your chance.

Home. I thought about it. Truly thought about it for the first time since I arrived, and the thought scared me, more than any I have had since I arrived, because of what Cruz said.

You think about home, and you're about to die.

CHAPTER 22

August 10, 1979

Friday night would be the final outing of the summer for our rat pack—me, Mif, Cap, and Billy. Then we'd leave for college and go our separate ways, though I wasn't going anywhere, not for at least two years. Mif and two other high school friends had moved to Cal Berkeley for fraternity rush and freshman orientation. They all had pledged a fraternity previously pledged by Serra graduates we knew well. We were to drive to their apartment in Berkeley with Donny Keaster. Donny had graduated Serra the year before and was playing football at a local community college. I didn't tell my parents I was headed to Berkeley to attend a fraternity party. I simply said I was going out and would spend the night at Billy's.

As we drove through the city to the Bay Bridge, I noticed Donny drove with his hands in a weird position on the steering wheel, noon and six o'clock. I leaned forward from the back seat. "What's wrong with the steering on your car?" I asked over the sound of Ted Nugent blasting so loud the speakers crackled. Nugent had achieved cult status with Serra guys. He claimed he deliberately failed his Vietnam draft physical by taking drugs, eating junk food for days, and crapping and pissing in his pants, earning a 4-F status.

"It's all screwed up Vinny B.," Donny shouted back at me. "I have no idea."

"Can you drive like that?"

"You get used to it."

Except it didn't look like Donny had gotten used to it. It looked like he was fighting the steering wheel, and we kept inching from one side of the lane to the other. This was not good. We had stopped at Scotty's liquor store and picked up a case of beer for the drive over, and a dozen empty cans already littered the car floor. I had nursed just one, but Donny had downed three.

We made it to Mif's apartment in Berkeley. They sublet it from Serra guys who rented it the year before under rent control in liberal Berkeley. Mif and two other friends paid almost nothing for it, but free would have been too much. I had envied them having their own place, but after seeing the squalor, living at home was looking better and better.

We walked from the apartment to Greek Row. The streets, sidewalks, and lawns were packed with college students. Because we were with fraternity brothers, we got into Mif's house, though only after doing Jell-O shots at the door, which were so strong they nearly made me puke.

"Everclear," Mif said, which was grain alcohol. Billy acted as if he had downed the shot, then spit the Jell-O onto the lawn. I wished I had done the same thing.

Mif and the other pledges were put to work and seriously abused. The rest of us didn't fit in, and it soon became apparent that while this had sounded like a good idea in theory, it would not be one in practice. I knew few people, had no allegiance to the school, and therefore had few subjects in common with anyone. As the night wore on, we lost Mif and the other pledges, and I lost interest.

When the police showed up, we took that as a cue to leave. Billy, Cap, and I walked with Donny back to his car. Donny was so drunk he stumbled from one side of the sidewalk to the other, the way he steered his car on the freeway. Cap also was in no shape to drive. When we reached the car I said, "Donny, let me have the keys."

Donny refused.

Billy also asked for the keys.

Again, Donny refused. "Nobody drives my car but me."

"I can drive," I said. "I didn't drink." I'd had just one beer and the Jell-O shot hours before.

"Get in the car or you're walking," Donny said, swearing.

"Donny, let him drive," Billy said.

"It's my car. I drive. You want a ride, get in. Otherwise take the bus."

We could see there would be no reasoning with Donny. Billy looked at me. "What do we do?"

My first instinct was to not get in the car. My first instinct was to call a cab, despite the significant expense. I could afford it. I also thought of going back to Mif's apartment and spending the night on the couch. We could have done a lot of things. But I also knew that letting Donny and Cap drive home was a death sentence for the two of them, and maybe others.

I couldn't let them make the drive without being there to at least keep Donny alert. I couldn't bear the thought of letting them go and later learning they had died in a car accident, maybe killed others, but I also had a premonition—a premonition that if I got in that car, I would not live.

"I don't think we have a choice," I said.

Billy remained hesitant. "I'll go if you're going. Try to keep him awake."

"That's my plan," I said.

Donny nearly sideswiped several parked cars before we even reached the freeway. Cap, in the front seat, fell asleep. I was in the back with Billy, both of us imploring Donny to pull over so one of us could drive. We kept talking to him, trying to keep him alert. Donny drove so erratically it was a miracle we were not pulled over. I kept hoping we would be.

As we drove across the Bay Bridge, I looked over at Billy. He had cinched the drawstring of the hood of his sweatshirt so tight he couldn't see.

"What are you doing?" I asked.

"I don't want to watch us die," he said. And I could tell by his tone he meant it.

I wondered if I had pushed my luck too far, if I was going to die. Why did I get in the car? What the hell was wrong with me? I didn't have a death wish. I wanted to live. And in that moment, I realized something else. My ass was twitching, uncontrollably. At first it felt like a muscle spasm, but it gradually worsened.

I now knew scared.

I sat forward. Every time I'd see Donny's head nod, I'd flick his ear. He was so drunk he didn't know it was me. He just kept swiping at the air, as if a bee were annoying him. His ear was beet red, but he was awake, battling to keep the car straight.

By some miracle we reached the 280 freeway south, and by an even bigger miracle, we came to the Trousdale exit. Donny's chin dropped to his chest and I flicked his ear.

"Take this exit, Donny. Donny, take this exit. Donny!"

At the last moment, Donny lifted his head and swerved to take the exit, traveling too fast. He hit the brakes, sending the car into a slide. We spun, how many times I do not know. I just remember feeling totally helpless, centrifugal force shoving me into Billy and both of us against the car wall. The car bounced, nearly tipped, and came to a sudden stop with a thud.

It took a moment to get my bearings. We were at the bottom of the exit. We had slid into the dirt and tall grass and hit a barbed wire fence and several wooden fence posts, uprooting them.

I looked over at Billy, whose eyes were the size of saucers. Then I looked to Donny and Cap. Both were passed out.

I could hardly catch my breath. I leaned forward and pulled the door handle next to where Cap slept and shoved the seat far enough forward for Billy and me to get out. Cap stirred but did not come to.

"What do we do?" Billy asked.

If we called the police, Donny would get busted. I was so pissed at him for not letting one of us drive, I didn't care. Except I did care. I could not let him wake up and drive again and possibly kill someone. I leaned back inside the car, turned off the engine, and removed the car keys. I was about to throw them into the tall grass, but Billy stopped me. "Give them to me," he said. "Donny will call me in the morning when he wakes up. I'll tell him what happened and that I have his keys."

"Billy, I'm sorry. We shouldn't have gotten in the car."

Billy shook his head. "They'd be dead if we hadn't. We did the right thing."

We jogged down Skyline Boulevard and split at Hillside. When I reached the top of the steep hill leading down to my house, I paced back and forth, fingers interlaced atop my head, my chest heaving and in pain, struggling to suck in air. I couldn't catch my wind. I couldn't breathe. I sat down on the pavement along the edge of the road and lowered my head between my knees, thinking I might pass out or throw up. I kept seeing Forecheck hanging in the trees, only it wasn't Forecheck. I didn't know Forecheck. The person in the trees was me.

Bad luck.

That's what kills most guys. Just bad luck.

Fifty-eight thousand young men.

What each would have given to have had just one more day, I thought. What their parents and their families would have given to have them come home, for just one more day. I thought of William in the garage on the Castillo remodel. *Growing old is a privilege, not a right.*

I knew now what he meant.

"What the hell are you doing?" I asked myself. "What the hell are you doing?"

I thought of my mother and father getting a bag with just pieces of me to bury, what that would do to them. This wasn't funny anymore. This wasn't a story to repeat at school the next day so we all could share a good laugh.

This had been beyond idiotic.

We all could have died.

Worse, far worse, we could have killed innocent people who had just happened to get in their car and, unbeknownst to them, driven straight toward a bunch of drunk high school kids.

Just bad luck.

"Bullshit," I said. It wasn't bad luck. It was complete and total selfishness.

I choked back sobs. I didn't know if I cried because I had somehow managed to survive and had made it home, or because I now truly understood what William meant when he said so many would have given anything to be in my position. I wept bitter tears at the top of the hill. I wept until I had no more tears to shed. I did not want to die. And I did not want my stupidity to be the cause of anyone else's death.

When I calmed, I stood, took a few deep breaths, and walked down the hill to my home. At the bottom of the hill I looked up at the second-story balcony, at the darkened french doors and the bedroom windows, and I thought of my parents, sound asleep, getting a phone call in the middle of the night and knowing before the police officer on the other end said a word that I had died. I thought of my mother. I thought of the mothers of all those marines William had told me about.

Would my mother ever recover?

It was time to put Peter Pan away, forever.

It was time to grow up.

I didn't turn the deadbolt with stealth, as I had done earlier that summer when I drove home from Ed's graduation party. I didn't try to be quiet or trick my mother into believing I was in bed, asleep. I never had. My brother had told me my mother knew I'd come home past my curfew and had snuck into bed. I hadn't fooled her. I had just been foolish to think I had. With four older siblings, I could try few things she hadn't already experienced. She likely kept quiet because it was enough that I was home, safe.

I'd only fooled myself that night.

I stepped inside and shut the door. My mother's bedroom door opened at the top of the stairs and she stepped onto the landing. "What are you doing?" she asked. "Do you know what time it is?"

"I'm sorry, Mom," I said. "I'm so very sorry."

December 12, 1968

Cruz is a short-timer, which means I'm a short-timer, if Captain Martinez keeps the clerk's position open.

Cruz has less than a month in the bush. Then, we'll both get on a Huey back to Da Nang. He'll process out, and I'll turn in my M-16 and my Pentax for a typewriter, or maybe I'll shoot dignitaries posing and pretending like we're winning this war. We ain't. We're just existing, some of us, anyway.

After I get home to New Jersey, I'll meet Cruz in Spanish Harlem. New York isn't going to know what hit it.

We'll both make it out of the bush, out of the Nam.

We'll both escape this hell.

I say it. I think it.

I don't believe it.

CHAPTER 23

August 13, 1979

I spent a quiet weekend at home, and Monday morning I met William and Todd at Nini's. I never got the impression William had said anything to Todd about Eric or about the sledgehammer, so I also kept my mouth shut. I did learn from Todd that William had moved into the room above Todd's garage until he found a place of his own.

William and I were sent back to the house in Burlingame to perform a massive cleanup around the property. When we arrived, William was quiet. I asked William how Todd had made out on the remodel, but he only shrugged, remote. It being just the two of us, I decided to ask if he was all right.

"Yeah. Why do you ask?"

"You don't look good, William. You've lost a lot of weight and . . . Look, it's probably none of my business—"

"It's not your business."

"Okay," I said.

After a few minutes William said, "Don't worry about me. I'm a survivor. Worry about yourself. You don't know shit. The world is playing chess

411

and you're playing checkers. It's going to piss all over you."

"Okay," I said again.

William didn't speak for another minute or two. I figured I'd pissed him off. But I didn't care. Someone needed to ask him if he was okay. We walked around the site picking up spent nails and scraps of lumber and filling a blue dumpster.

"I'm drinking too much and I'm doing too many drugs."

William made the statement without looking at me. Then he squatted, as he always did, but this time he brought both hands to his face, as if in prayer. I noticed the tremor. His eyes were moist. "I can't get things out of my head. I can't forget. I could always forget. I could always put shit behind me, tell myself, 'That's no big thing.' File it away. Now I can't. I can't seem to forget."

"Can you get help?"

"I made a call to the VA in Napa," he said. "I've been thinking about checking myself in."

"I think you should, William. If it could help." As I said it, I wondered what the hell I knew, and I half expected William to explode at me. He didn't. He simply nodded, several times.

"I called," he finally said. "I have friends who had their claims denied because they'd been home for too long, but now they're taking guys. They're calling it post-traumatic stress disorder." He took a breath, and I sensed he was struggling

412

to hold himself together. "Sometimes I wonder."

"About what?"

"Why I made it home."

I was about to tell William he came home because God had plans for him, but he no longer believed in God. "It was just luck," I said. "That's what you told me. You got lucky. Nothing to feel guilty about."

He rocked, slightly, as if in a rocking chair. "Did I tell you about Victor Cruz?"

"Yes," I said.

"No." He shook his head. "Did I tell you about him not coming home?"

Oh shit, I thought. I had assumed Cruz made it home. "No."

"It was after I got shot. After I recovered and went back."

I knelt in front of him.

"I went back to my platoon. I could have taken a clerk's job in the rear, working for my former captain, Dennis Martinez. Cruz had called in the favor, but I didn't take the job. I didn't want to leave Victor in the bush. I returned so we could watch each other's backs. So we would leave together."

This much I knew. William had told me this, but I didn't say anything. I just let him talk.

William shook his head. "Cruz was pissed. He said the war had ended for me, that I shouldn't have come back. That's when something clicked.

I could see my mom. I could see my house, my home, my brothers and sisters, my father. I could see them all clearly when before I couldn't. And I knew I'd made a mistake going back into the bush."

Again, William had told me this. He had told me he thought his luck had run out, and he had a premonition of death. "What happened to Cruz?" I asked, gently nudging him forward.

"Victor was close to his thirty-day DEROS, a short-timer. He wasn't supposed to go outside the wire anymore. He was going to ship back to Da Nang and shine a seat with his ass. We got word we were going back out to secure a hill for the ARVN. It was supposed to be a walk in the park. Secure it, let the ARVN move in, and come back. Victor and I would leave the bush, and I'd take the clerk's job. When I went into the bunker, Victor was packing, I thought, for the rear."

William looked at me through moist eyes.

"What did he say?"

"He said he was going out with me. He said that was the deal, that we would leave Firebase Phoenix together. I told you, right? About how I was going to meet him in Spanish Harlem, that we were going to eat until we threw up, then dance until dawn."

"You said you didn't talk about home, that was one of the first things Cruz taught you."

"He did. He'd say, 'Don't even think about

home, Shutter. What good is home going to do you? You're here now. You're in Nam.' He used to say it would jinx me to talk of home."

William took a deep breath and exhaled. I got a sense he wanted to tell me something more but was struggling with where to begin. "What happened, William?"

"Our company got orders to take this hill," he said, starting to repeat himself and to stutter, words blending together. "It was supposed to be just a few days outside the wire. Just take the hill and come back. Cruz didn't have to go. Cruz was a short-timer."

"It's okay, William. Slow down."

But he didn't slow down. He spoke rapid fire, holding back tears. "He went to our captain at the firebase and said I had a clerk's job waiting for me in the rear, but the captain wouldn't release me unless he had orders. That's why Cruz went out again, because of me. Because the captain didn't have orders for me to fly to the rear."

I didn't like where this was headed. "William, you don't have to . . ."

He grabbed my left wrist with both his hands. "Cruz and I were in Charlie Company. Alpha Company went up the hill midmorning. Bravo wasn't there. I don't remember why not."

I did. It was the ambush he'd told me about. The one in the elephant grass that had wiped out much of Bravo Company.

"One hundred meters from the summit, an NVA regiment had set an ambush. They had dug in and waited for us to get close. Too close to call in air support."

"A brawl," I said, remembering what William had called it.

"That's right," he said. "A brawl. The NVA opened up with RPGs and machine gun fire. AK-47s. They unleashed hell and cut Alpha Company to pieces. We could hear the men screaming, but the hill was steep, and it had been raining all the time. Every time we sent men up, guys slipped and slid down. They couldn't get up. Those who did, the NVA cut them down, too. This went on for hours. The men screaming, moaning. Officers kept sending us up. More men died. We had no way to get to them. We couldn't call in artillery, not even the Cobras. We had to just wait until the NVA melted back into the bush. But they didn't. This time they didn't.

"The wailing got to be too much. Cruz couldn't take it. He said he was going up. I told him not to be a hero. I told him to blend in. Don't stand out. My mother said that. 'Blend in. Don't be a hero.' He and I just had to get back to the firebase alive. We just had to make it back, but he couldn't take the thought of good marines dying on that hill."

William took another deep breath, this one in a burst, like he was having trouble breathing.

"Are you all right? William?"

"As the sun set, Cruz said, 'Let's go, Shutter.' I told him no. I said I wasn't going up that hill to get myself killed, that I'd had this feeling ever since I'd gotten back to the firebase that my luck had run out. I told him I never should have come back, that the guys were right. They said death followed me. I told him what he always told me, that he should keep his head down. He said he couldn't. He couldn't leave them." Another breath. "I came back for him. I never should have come back. If I hadn't come back, if I had taken the clerk's job, he never would have been out there. He would not have felt compelled to go."

William cried and lowered his head, hugging his knees. I didn't know what to do. I thought of calling Todd.

"I'm sorry," I said. "But the captain—"

William spoke as if he didn't hear me. "In the morning, the NVA pulled out and what was left of us made our way up the hill. I kept looking for Cruz as I climbed over bodies on the trail. I kept waiting for him to step out from somewhere and call out, 'Shutter. Do your job, Shutter.' But I couldn't find him. He wasn't on the slope. He . . . He . . . I didn't find him until I reached the top. Victor had made it to the top of the hill. The only one. He'd made it. Just Victor. Guys from Alpha Company who were still alive said Cruz pulled them to safety . . . that he killed a dozen NVA. They said he shot his M-16 until he ran out of ammunition. He grabbed rifles off the dead, emptying them. They said he didn't stop until he'd made it to the top. They said he crawled when he couldn't walk, that NVA bodies lay on the ground where he'd finally stopped moving. A brawl. They said it had been a brawl."

"He took the hill," I said.

William nodded, fighting back tears. "We put the dead in body bags . . . Victor. We sent them out in choppers. I wanted to go with Cruz, but the lieutenant wouldn't allow it. He said he needed every man because we were spending the night atop that hill. I didn't have a choice. I had to dig in. It was the longest night of my life. I didn't sleep. I wished the NVA had come. I wished I could have killed them all, for Victor."

He shook his head. "I remember the sun coming up. I remember the sun coming up and the lieutenant telling us to saddle up."

"You left?" I asked, uncertain I understood him correctly. "I thought—"

"We packed up and humped down the hill. The South Vietnamese never came. I don't know what happened to them. That's the hardest part, that Cruz died for nothing." He lowered his head. More tears. "I never wrote this in my journal. I couldn't. I never wrote about what happened to Cruz." William looked up at me, openly crying. "I never told anyone. I never told anyone that I let Victor go. That I wouldn't go up the hill with him. I should have gone with him."

I was about to tell William that he made the right choice, the difficult choice, but then I realized that William wasn't just talking about going up the hill with Cruz. He was talking about dying with him, that he should have died with Corporal Victor Cruz, USMC, that day, that a part of him wished he had died, that it would have been better to have died that day than it had been to live with the guilt.

I did not know what to say, so I said nothing. William's head fell forward, against my shoulder, and he sobbed.

PART VI

The Finish Line Is Six Feet Under

December 22, 1968

While I waited on the clerk's job in the rear, Charlie moved toward the cities. In October, President Johnson ended Operation Rolling Thunder, the bombing of North Vietnam, and the politicians have been pulling out marines to entice the Viet Cong to restart peace talks. We abandoned Firebase Phoenix and were redeployed to provide security in the cities, so the South Vietnamese army could better concentrate on fighting.

Not likely. Just more bullshit.

They said we're leaving Vietnam. The FNGs told us the protests back home had intensified. I didn't really care. I didn't believe I was going to make it home. I spit in good luck's face. I spit in God's face. Payback will be a bitch.

We were in a city just northeast of Da Nang, going door to door, hunting Charlie. M-16s and AK-47s traded bullets. RPGs and rockets were flying and exploding all aroundme.

In this chaos a Jeep appeared, driving like hell. The driver slammed to a stop to talk to some marines. One marine pointed to where I was standing behind a truck. The driver looked in my direction, then floored the Jeep and popped up onto the grass.

"William Goodman?" he asked. He was terrified. His utilities were clean and he was clean shaven. He was rear support. He'd never been in the bush. Unlikely he'd been in any firefight.

"Yeah," I shouted over the sound of an RPG exploding and the rattle of automatic gunfire. I was alternately firing my M-16 and taking shots with my Pentax.

The guy in the Jeep kept slumping lower in his seat. "You're leaving. Get in. Chopper's taking off."

I shook my head. "You got it wrong. I got about three months."

"I got orders from Captain Martinez to find you, take you to the chopper, and make sure you get your ass on it. He said to tell you that is an order. Chopper's leaving. Get in."

I was being sent to the rear, to the clerk's job. More good luck? It would never happen. The God I no longer believed in wouldn't let it happen. I was paralyzed by my confusion. A blow to my shoulder knocked me back to reality. This big Pole looked at me like I was crazy. We called him Cheesesteak because he was from Philadelphia.

Cheesesteak yelled at me, "Shutter, get in the fucking Jeep, man. Don't be a hero."

I got in, still unsure.

We drove through the war, machine gun fire and exploding RPGs, and I kept thinking I was going to get hit. I was going to die. I couldn't outrace death. It was right behind, following me. I was not meant to leave the Nam. I was meant to die here, punishment for spitting in God's face, for coming back. Punishment for Victor Cruz.

We reached the helicopter pad at a field base and I climbed on board. Just as we were about to take off, marines hurried to the chopper carrying a body bag. They slung it on board and I noticed there were two others.

Death follows me.

I raised my camera and snapped pictures as the Huey's blades thumped and the chopper lifted off. I kept waiting for it to get hit, for the Huey to pitch and roll and crash, but we departed, and the Huey flew me to Da Nang. The minute it touched down, the air base was shelled, just like when I arrived. God was not about to let me go that easily. He was mocking me.

Do you hear me now, William? Do you believe in me now? Too late. You're too late.

I would not make it to the rear.

I got off the helicopter, but I was not taken to Captain Martinez. I was processed quickly, though not for the clerk's job. I was processed home. I was handed my final pay. I was too stunned to tell the processing sergeant I still had about three more months. I didn't say anything. I turned in my Pentax. They told me they would deliver it to the lab. I turned in my M-16, my .45, my helmet, and my flak jacket, though I kept the Tiger Chewing Tobacco tin with my journal. I would have given the tin to someone in my platoon, paid forward the good luck, but it was too late for that now. I was given clean utilities and told to quickly change. The sergeant told me that normally he'd have a lot of paperwork for me to process out, but there had been a lull in the shelling, a window to take off, and if I wanted to leave, I had to do so now. I didn't have my photographs or my ditty bag. They were with my squad. The sergeant processing me handed me the forms to fill out on the plane, and I was rushed outside with another marine.

My legs were leaden. I was trying to run but I could hardly move them. I didn't believe I'd make it to the stairs. I expected to get blown up by a mortar.

When I reached the bottom of the ramp, I was so tired I could barely climb. I'd humped for miles with eighty pounds on my back, but it felt as if I'd used every ounce of adrenaline. I had nothing left in reserve. My legs had ceased to function. I was helped up the ramp stairs by two marines. I expected to get hit. Even when I was on board, strapped into a seat, I didn't believe the plane's wheels would leave the ground. A shell would hit the plane and I would die on board.

Death follows me.

The pilot wasted no time. We barreled down the runway and I felt the wheels leave the ground. We ascended, nearly vertical, to get out of antiaircraft range. I waited to hear an explosion, expected to see one of the engines out my window burst into flames, to feel the plane jolt violently, and for Vietnam to pull me back, refusing to release her grip.

But there was no jolt.

There were no flames.

The plane ascended, and soon, through the rain, I saw the blurry South China Sea. I realized it was not raining. I was crying. I looked around the plane. It was maybe half-full with guys who looked like me— dark skin, dirty hair, beards. Everyone on the plane was crying. Tears of joy. Tears of sorrow. Tears of disbelief.

It hit me: all the guys not on this flight. Kenny, Forecheck, EZ, Victor Cruz, and a dozen others, a thousand others, tens of thousands.

I felt guilty to be going home, to have lived.

There were no stewardesses. No hot dogs. No Cokes.

Nobody talked. Nobody said a word.

I cried until I fell asleep.

CHAPTER 24

August 23, 2016

Elizabeth remained active to keep her tears at bay. She pulled new sheets over the blue twin mattress—a simple task made more difficult because our son had elevated his dorm room bed six feet off the ground. Beneath it we had positioned Beau's desk and a compact refrigerator Elizabeth bought so Beau could keep food in his dorm room. I suspected it would be used more for beer, though I didn't say this thought out loud. I said the arrangement provided more floor space, which was at a premium.

I grabbed a sheet corner to assist with the task and noticed how soft and luxurious it felt. I checked the tag. "Egyptian cotton? We don't even have Egyptian cotton on our bed at home," I said to Beau, who smiled.

Elizabeth had spared no expense at this parting of the ways, not that the luxuries had dulled her pain or mine any. She snapped the sheets over the mattress as if it had offended her, and she beat the two goose-down pillows like punching bags to fluff them. Her blonde hair fluttered with the rhythmic oscillating fan she had placed near an open window, but the breeze did little to alleviate the heat and stuffiness. The temperature had been the first thing to hit us when we stepped into the room, the smell a close second. It smelled like someone had spilled a gallon of lemon-scented Lysol. We left the door open to air out the room, and we could hear excited freshmen celebrating this beginning, their first year out from under the parental thumb. Adults.

They had no idea.

Elizabeth set the pillows at the head of the bed, then pulled up the blue goose-down comforter; she'd matched UCLA's school colors—powder blue, gold, and white. Now she lamented that it all seemed rather precise and bland. I didn't have the heart to tell her the bed covers would soon be beneath a cascade of unwashed laundry, books, papers, and food wrappers. She compared Beau's side of the room to that of his roommate, whom we had not yet met, and whose décor was anything but bland. Above the *Star Wars* bedding the roommate had neatly pinned wall-to-wall *Star Wars* movie posters. For the next nine months, Beau would awaken to a black-clad Darth Vader, Luke and Leia holding blasters, and Han and Chewie, the Wookiee, beneath the *Millennium Falcon*.

My son had given me a concerned look when he'd first stepped into the room. "What the hell?" he said.

Mary Beth laughed at both the décor and at

her brother's seeming misfortune. I didn't want Beau to prejudge a person he had not yet met. A college roommate, I knew, was like a spouse. The room would be the home to which they both returned for the next nine months. What was that saying about not having the ability to choose your family?

Apparently not your freshman roommate, either.

Beau had spent an entire day answering questionnaires about his likes and dislikes, his habits, his hobbies, the music he listened to, how late he studied, and how early he woke, so the school could pair him with someone with similar habits and interests.

At least in theory. I was relatively certain Beau had never written the words "Star Wars" in any answer.

Ever the good soul and optimist, Elizabeth said, "It's a bold statement. He must be confident in who he is."

Elizabeth had been, as expected, melancholy since leaving home the prior day to make the long drive from Northern California to Westwood. She did not see this trip as a beginning for Beau, but as an end; she was losing her firstborn, her baby boy.

"You didn't bring anything to put up on your walls," Elizabeth said.

"It's fine," Beau said, pacifying his mother's

concern. "I have a bulletin board, and I brought some family photographs to put up." He looked at the desk clock. "You should get going. I have an orientation at three."

To remind him, three young women stopped by the room to walk to the orientation with Beau. My son wasn't rushing us, but he was moving on. Beau needed to get away, and I understood why. He needed a fresh start, a place where he wouldn't be reminded of what had happened, of death. He needed a place far enough away that he couldn't be called home to every family function or crisis. Life had punched Beau in the face, as it had punched William Goodman and Todd Pearson. He was recovering in his own way.

It was part of growing up. It was part of realizing you don't know a damn thing about the world, that at times, you weren't even playing the same game.

I had said goodbye the night before we left Burlingame, as Beau and I reclined on the leather sofa in the family room watching a *Seinfeld* rerun. Elizabeth had gone to bed to read, and Mary Beth was out with her cousin. I had wanted to say something from my heart, but I struggled to find the right words. Then I thought of William's journal, which I had not yet finished, though I neared the end. The entries provided perspective, as William's stories had provided me with perspective before I, too, went off to college.

"You're a good man," I said, lowering the volume on another George Costanza tirade. "You've become a good man. I'm proud of who you've become."

Beau put down a bowl of ice cream, sensing—or perhaps dreading—this father-son moment. "Thanks, Dad."

"I've already been to college, and I have no desire to go back. I can't live in your dorm room. You'll have to figure out things on your own, just as I did. You'll have to determine who you are, the man you're going to be. You'll have to decide if your word stands for something or rings hollow. You'll have to decide if you will treat women with dignity and respect, whether you're the guy who gets drunk at every party and does something stupid he wakes to regret."

Beau nodded and with solemnity said, "Which were you?" He chuckled nervously, then added, "I won't be that guy, Dad."

I was rushing, trying to beat my tears. I thought of a conversation I had with William in 1979. "You'll have to decide if you'll have a relationship with God, and what that relationship will be. I hope you do."

I was going to tell him the rest of his life is both a long time and the blink of an eye, but Beau knew that also, from harsh experience. Instead, I said, "What you choose to do with your life is now up to you. Find your passion. Then find a way to make a living at it. Do so, and you'll never work a day in your life. Most of all, remember that it takes a lifetime to build a reputation, but only a moment to destroy it."

I paused again, to press back tears.

"And always, always remember, Beau, that you are loved."

"I know, Dad. I love you, too."

I do not recall my father saying those three words to me, though I know he loved me. Words were just not his way. I saw his love when he dropped us at school each morning and then drove to the pharmacy to work those long hours, in the way he watched our grammar school basketball games after mass, then hurried home to work on the cars so my older siblings could drive to school. He had given his life to us. A father at twenty-one. Six kids by the time he turned thirty.

But man, I had always wanted to hear those three words from him.

I wanted my son to hear them from me.

"I love you, too," I said.

In the dorm room, Elizabeth and Mary Beth gathered and flattened the empty cardboard boxes. Mary Beth looked as distraught and uncertain as Elizabeth, though for an entirely different reason. She no doubt contemplated that she would be the lone child at home and would be living life under a parental microscope. Outside, cars lined the dorm's circular drive. Young men and women dressed in shorts, T-shirts, and flip-flops walked the sidewalk wearing expensive sunglasses and broad smiles. Camp college was underway, four years ripe with potential and possibilities. We carried the cartons that had held my son's life to the car, and I slid them into the back while my wife said her goodbye.

Elizabeth wore sunglasses, but they did not hide the tears that ran down her cheeks. She had her arms around Beau's neck, stretched onto her toes, whispering in his ear. Her baby boy was a man.

And he was leaving home. Leaving her.

I remained stoic, for my son's sake. When at last Beau had hurried off, we got into the car. Elizabeth sat in the back seat, willingly giving the front seat to Mary Beth. In the rearview mirror I watched her stare out the window as Los Angeles slipped away, and we drove through long stretches of brown nothingness, silent.

I held it together, mostly. Grief would come over me like a rogue wave. My stomach muscles gripped, and I emitted forced, choked sobs.

"Dad. Are you all right?" Mary Beth asked when the first wave struck, thinking perhaps I was having a heart attack.

Unable to speak, I nodded and waited for the wave to roll over me.

Elizabeth did not ask if I was okay. She knew

the pain, and she knew, better than anyone, that the only salve was time.

As I drove those many miles home, I ruminated on the months before my son's departure for college, and I thought also of the summer months before I went to college. Though the circumstances had certainly been different, the waves that hit Beau his senior year of high school had provided him a radical and harsh new perspective on life and death, just like the waves that had hit me.

December 24, 1968

My plane landed in Tokyo to refuel for the flight to Seattle, but I never left my seat. A flight crew got on and the stewardess told me I had time to get off the plane to stretch my legs and buy some food. I declined. I was not going to tempt fate by getting off the plane until I landed safely in New Jersey.

The plane was refueled, and ten hours later, we landed in Seattle. US soil. From Seattle I flew to Newark, New Jersey. It was all happening so fast, thirty-six hours from Vietnam to stateside. In Seattle I had to deboard and change planes. I went into an airport bathroom. I realized I hadn't washed Vietnam from my body, though I had changed into my laundered utilities before boarding the plane in Vietnam. My hair was unkempt and my face unshaven. I looked like hell. I'm sure I smelled worse, given the looks I received. I tried to wash using paper towels. A guy approached the sink beside me. My skin tingled with the anticipation of a confrontation.

"Did you serve?" he asked.

I nodded.

"Thank you," he said.

I turned and looked at him, uncertain what to say. He smiled and stepped past me.

I fought back more tears.

I reached my gate. I hadn't called my mom and dad to tell them I was on my way home. "Home." It sounded like a foreign word.

I looked for a pay phone just as I heard a woman's voice over the loudspeaker. She advised that the flight to Newark was boarding. I was not about to miss it.

Six hours later, I was in the back seat of a taxi. The taxi driver was Asian. He kept glancing at me in the rearview mirror, the way people in the airport terminal glanced at me, the way the people in the villages glanced at me, like I was a rabid dog that would bite. Like I didn't belong. The taxi driver was driving fast. Everything was whizzing past the windows. I leaned forward to check the speedometer. He was driving the speed limit. Sixty-five miles per hour. After so many months of the slow crawl of humping, the sensation of speed was terrifying. I thought he was going to crash. I thought he was trying to kill me.

I thought of the irony.

Death still followed me.

Minutes from the airport, he exited the freeway and drove me through Elizabeth's business district. Just like that, I was home. I'd made it home. People walked the sidewalks. Cars drove the street. Everything was the same. The faces of the people. The houses. The buildings. The businesses.

But I didn't recognize any of it.

I didn't believe any of it was real.

It was a forgery. Vietnam was real.

I told the taxi driver to pull over. He looked at me in the rearview mirror.

I told him again, "Pull over."

The fare was $6.23. I threw a twenty-dollar bill at him and got out. Money meant nothing to me. I walked the streets in my utilities. Defiant. Seeking a confrontation. People stepped out of my way. They stared as I passed, no doubt wondering if they knew me, thinking, *He looks familiar.* No one greeted me. No one else thanked me. No one said a word.

I wanted to grab the approaching man by the collar of his suit jacket and ask him if he knew what was going on in the real world. I wanted to tell him, all of them, that young men, their sons, were dying in the bush every day, that they were being shipped home in boxes. Nobody looked at me long enough for me to speak. I was not real. I was a ghost. I was an imitation of the young man who left this town. I'd had no time to decompress. Nothing to prepare me for my return to civilian life. They'd just thrown me back, like an unwanted fish, and told me to swim. OJT.

I stepped inside a bar and took a stool at the far end, away from everyone. I didn't know what time it was. I didn't care. The bartender approached. I asked for a beer. The bartender asked to see my ID. I looked at him like he was joking. He stared back. I wanted to lean across the bar and rip his throat out. I wanted to scream at him, "Do you know where I've been?"

"You can't be in here if you're underage," he said. Then he turned to walk away.

"Are you joking," I said, not about to give him the satisfaction of getting out my ID. My uniform should have been enough. "Seriously?"

He turned back. "It's the law."

"So is sending me to a foreign country to kill. None of you had a problem with that."

"Take it up with your congressman," he said.

"My congressman sent me!"

"Then your senator. I don't really care. Just get the hell out of here before I call the cops."

I almost dared him to make the call, but I was tired of fighting. I was done fighting.

I left the bar. As I walked, it started to snow. I stopped and looked around at the businesses. Christmas decorations in windows. Colored lights along the exteriors, and Christmas music emanating from inside the stores. The temperature was suddenly cold. From where I'd been, it was freezing. It felt so good.

I started the long walk home.

I could do it.

I'd humped for miles through streams and rice paddies and over mountains. The hardest part is getting up off the ground and taking that first step. Then you take another, and another. You walk away from where you've been, toward your next checkpoint. I tried not to think, not to dwell on where I'd been, on the past. I tried to forget it all. It was irrelevant anyway. I didn't take terrain or villages. I just kept moving.

So I would keep moving now. I walked on, away from the past.

A car horn honked.

I looked over.

The car had slowed. The passenger leaned out the side window as if he were about to jump from the car. He had long hair, a droopy mustache, and the middle finger extended on both hands. His spittle hit the toe of my boot.

The past, I thought. Like death, it had followed me home.

CHAPTER 25

September 7, 2016

Two weeks after returning home from dropping Beau off at school, Elizabeth had gone into the bedroom to watch one of her shows and Mary Beth was out with friends, so I sat down in the recliner in the family room and turned on the lamp. I wanted to read the remainder of William's journal alone, with just William.

His note had asked me to read the entries in order. I had honored his request. It had not been easy reading. I stopped for a period of time after Chris's death. I had tried to start again, but each time I had to put the journal down. I could now imagine what it had truly been like to be eighteen years old and to have lived through what William had written about. A part of me didn't want to read the end, didn't want to read again how everything had turned out. It was enough, for a part of me, to know that William had made it home alive and, after some bad times, that he had found his way, that he had married and, hopefully, lived a good life.

But he'd sent me his journal for a reason. He couldn't throw it out, and he didn't have anyone else with whom he could share his stories. I felt as if I owed it to him, for everything he had taught me about growing up that summer, what he had taught my son. I owed it to him to finish the journal.

I opened to the final entry, and I noticed immediately that it was written in ink, not pencil. The writing also was not as scribbled. It did not appear as rushed. This entry had been added after the other entries. Well after.

Vincenzo,
I'm glad you've come this far. I hope you will come just a little farther.

The personal greeting from William jarred me. Its immediacy made it eerie, as if William had been watching me all this time, as if he knew all along that he intended to give me his journal, that he had more to tell me.

It's important to me that you know the truth and, hopefully, after reading this, you will understand. I was nineteen years old. A boy really. A boy whose humanity, values, and sense of himself as a moral, righteous person had all been compromised. The war took that from me, more than anything else that it stole. I lost all understanding of myself, everything my religion and my parents

444

had taught me. I had a hell of a time getting it back. I had PTSD that summer we worked together. Many GIs didn't know about PTSD then, because so little was known about its effects. The VA kept turning away all these GIs with the same symptoms—quick to anger, suffering with anxiety and panic attacks, having flashbacks and nightmares, eating disorders, and substance abuse. We didn't know then that PTSD symptoms can remain dormant for years, until triggered by an event. I don't know what triggered mine. Everything, I guess.

In Vietnam, killing became very impersonal. We never called the people "Vietnamese." They were "VC" or "Gooks," "Chinks" or "Charlie." You didn't feel like you were killing a person, though of course you knew you were. Much of the time outside the wire, you didn't see the guy you shot, so we told ourselves we didn't kill anyone. At least I did. Those times you did see the bodies, you told yourself it wasn't a bullet from your rifle. It was someone else's bullet. You didn't really know.

Except I did.

One time.

It haunts me.

I told you the story. But not the whole story. You deserve to hear the whole story. The real story. The truth. I hope you will understand. I hope you will forgive me.

I set the journal down and I looked beyond the ring of light cast by the lamp, toward the hall that led to the bedroom where Elizabeth watched her show. I thought I wanted to read William's journal alone, with just him, as had often been the case over the past year.

Now, I wasn't so sure.

The lamp shone like a lone streetlamp on a deserted street. But for flashes of blue television light on the hall wall, the rest of the room, and the house, was dark. And the dark had always scared me. I didn't know why. It was one of those weird things. Even in my own home, the place I had lived for two decades, the darkness caused my imagination to flare and, at times, to run wild. I thought it was just an idiosyncrasy, but one night when I went to shut off the hall light, Mary Beth called out to me from her room. "Can you leave it on?"

"Why?" I asked, peering in the door.

"It's my night-light," she said. "I'm afraid of the dark."

So maybe it was a genetic fear. All I know is that I would have been terrified in Vietnam, as William described the night, in darkness so black you couldn't see your hand in front of your face. But I knew it wasn't the darkness that scared me this night. I was scared about what awaited me on the final pages of William's journal, what he called "the real story" and "the truth." I worried about why he hoped I would forgive him.

I wondered if anyone else knew what I was about to read. Had William's wife known? Perhaps. A close friend, doubtful. Everyone's past contains things we are not proud of, skeletons in our closets that we do not share, not with strangers and not with those we love and who love us. We fear that to do so will change their perception of us, and their belief in who we are.

But William didn't really know me in 1979 when we worked together, not in any detail, and over this past year, as I read his journal, I wondered if that was why William had told me about Vietnam, why he shared his journal with me. I was not his spouse or his friend. I was not even his peer. The journal would not color my perception of him because, like Beau and his freshman roommate—by chance paired together for nine months—William and I had been paired together by chance and we would never see one another again.

I went back to the journal.

We were on patrol December 12, 1968. We were told to take this hill, secure it, and turn it over to the ARVN. Hill 1338. I will forever remember the number.

We'd humped all day. Usually we cut our own path to avoid the land mines. Alpha Company took point. Charlie Company, my company, was in the rear. It was just me and Victor now. Bean had rotated back home. Forecheck was dead, and Whippet had been injured and sent home.

Cruz wasn't supposed to be with me. He was a short-timer—under a month before his DEROS. He was supposed to be on a Huey headed to Da Nang to file papers and avoid paper cuts before he shipped home. He wasn't supposed to be on a lurp. He was there because of me. He was there because I turned down the clerk's job at Da Nang that he had set up for me, because I had come back for him, so we could leave the bush together. He was out in the bush because of me.

As we humped, I kept my gaze down, searching for booby traps. I was worried, but more so for Cruz. Every step he took, I expected it to be his last. I expected to hear a boom and then nothing.

Cruz would just be gone.

As we humped, Cruz kept talking about going home to Spanish Harlem, about me coming to meet his huge family. He kept saying we were going to eat Puerto Rican food until we threw up, then go to the clubs and dance with the senoritas until morning, then do it all over again. I couldn't understand why he was breaking his first rule—don't talk about home in the bush—and I kept telling Cruz to shut up, to not talk about home. But he wouldn't let up. He kept describing the party until I could see it in my head and taste and smell the food. I could also see the senoritas. I could see their tanned skin, dark eyes, the sexiness of their hips and their calves, the curve of their breasts beneath their sweaters. I could smell their perfume and feel their bodies up against mine, their fingers playing with my hair. It was one of the most vivid visions I'd had of home since I arrived in Vietnam, and though I tried, I couldn't push the vision from my mind.

The terrain steepened. The trail became thick with vegetation. It had rained hard the prior night and early that morning. Seemed like it always rained now. We all had trouble getting our footing. The red mud-clay was, at times, up to our ankles. Alpha Company went up the hill at roughly four p.m. I figured we'd make it to the top and set our perimeter. We'd dig in. In the morning we'd turn the hill over to the ARVN and leave.

What I didn't know, what none of us knew, was that an entire NVA battalion, an estimated five hundred men, were dug in atop the hill and along the southern side—a reverse L. It is a classic ambush tactic, and we were in the kill zone.

AK-47s opened up on Alpha Company along with rocket-propelled grenades. The NVA knew we had superior firepower and superior air support, so it waited until we got to terrain where the APCs and the tanks couldn't help us, couldn't come up the hill. It waited until we got so close we could see one another. Too close to call in air support.

It was a brawl. A street fight.

Machine guns tore up the jungle, cut down men and plants. RPGs exploded. Alpha Company never even had time to drop their packs. We could hear the wounded wailing, but every time men were sent up the hill, the NVA cut them down. We couldn't overwhelm them with superior firepower, not this time. We were trained to fight our way through the ambush, but without the firepower, without footing, that was a futile act.

At dusk the NVA didn't evaporate into the bush. They continued to fight.

They fought all night. Charlie Company tried, but we couldn't get up the mountain, couldn't reach the dead and the wounded. I hunkered down halfway up the hill and expected Cruz to hunker down beside me. He was going home, to the party, to the food, to the senoritas. But Cruz wouldn't hunker down.

"I'm going up, Shutter," he said to me.

"What?" I shouted. "No. No you'll die."

"We all have to die."

"No," I said. Then I broke the first lesson. "We're going home to New York. We're going to eat your mother's cooking and dance with the senoritas in the clubs."

Cruz smiled. "It's not real, Shutter."

"What?"

"I made it up." He shrugged. "My mother died of breast cancer when I was twelve. My father is in prison. It was a blessing. He used to get drunk and beat me and my brothers. I didn't get drafted. I volunteered at seventeen to get out of there, and I reupped 'cause there's no place for me to go. There is no home. This is home now. The marines are my home."

I was trying to process this, trying to

understand it, but I couldn't, not with the battle raging.

"What about the senoritas?" I asked. "What about dancing until dawn?"

"I can't go home, Shutter. If I go home, the gangs will kill me. I'll be unemployed. I'll have to deal drugs and I'll end up in prison like my father, if not a grave."

"You can come to New Jersey," I said. "My mother will cook for us and we'll go to the clubs in New York."

Cruz smiled. "I got to go up that hill, Shutter. I'm a marine. I have to bust through."

"Then I'm going with you."

"No," Cruz said. "You have a family. You have a home. You have a mother and father who care. That's why I made up all that stuff, so you didn't lose sight of going home."

"I'm coming," I said.

I turned for my rifle and helmet, and Cruz hit me in the back of the head with the stock of his M-16. At least that's what I later deduced. By the time I came to, he'd gone up the hill.

By dawn the NVA had evaporated back into the bush. We found thousands of spent rounds but we didn't find a single NVA body. Not one. Alpha Company went up that hill with 137 men. Seventy-six died. Forty-three were seriously wounded. Most of the dead were shot in the head at close range. Ears were missing. Eyes had been gouged out. Ring fingers had been severed. Charlie Company lost seven men and had another ten wounded.

Those of us still alive crawled out of our foxholes stunned and dazed. The jungle looked like a huge blaze had burned through it. The foliage had evaporated, and ash blew in the breeze and fluttered to the ground like dirty snowflakes. It was hard to breathe; the air was toxic. Bodies lay scattered everywhere. Marines were putting them in body bags and lining them up for transport.

I looked for Cruz. The soot and dirt and sweat had changed their faces; I didn't recognize anyone. I wondered if I was somehow in the wrong place, if a bomb had blown me to another hilltop. I had to stop and look each marine in the eye, try to put a name with a face. I had to ask, "Cruz?"

They shook their heads.

I moved on.

When I couldn't find Cruz among the living, I searched the dead. I searched the bodies being put in body bags. Cruz was not among them.

The top of the hill was barren. No buildings. No bunkers. No foliage. Charcoal sticks and craters remained from the many bombings over the many months. Just one marine lay atop the mountain. Just one marine reached the top. Just one had punched through.

Victor Cruz.

His eyes were closed. He looked at peace, like he had lain down to sleep. He had all his limbs. I didn't see bullet holes in his body. I thought maybe he wasn't dead. I hoped he'd just been knocked out, that the bombing knocked him out. I patted his cheek, at first just a tap. Then harder.

"Wake up," I pled. "Wake up or they're going to ship you home with the dead."

But Cruz didn't wake up. He didn't open his eyes.

Marines grabbed my arm to stop me from hitting him. I broke free and I sat down beside him.

Cruz took the hill.

He made it to the top.

And that's where he died.

I removed his dog tag and the contents of his vest, and I put them in a plastic bag that I taped to his wrist. For who? I don't know. I helped put him in a body bag and I whispered, "I hope you're home, at a party, that you eat until you puke, and you dance until the sun comes up. And I hope you do it again the next day, and the day after that, and the day after that."

Then I zipped the bag closed.

I looked up from William's journal entry into the darkness of the room, and I wiped the tears from my eyes. I thought of William, of the story he told me that final day at the remodel. He told me he chose not to go up the hill with Cruz, and I had always thought that was why he felt guilt, why he could not leave the war behind. I thought of my son, at the Dodger game, telling me he thought he should have been in the car with Chris.

But now William had said that wasn't what happened, and I was wondering, Did Cruz actually knock William out? Or was that just what William wanted me to believe, so I didn't think poorly of him for not going up the hill?

But why would William care now?

Even if it were true, if Cruz knocked William out, why then would William have felt so much guilt to have survived? I looked back to the journal and turned the page. There was one more entry, also freshly written. Also in ink. But there was no new date.

The story continued, and so did I.

After the bodies were helicoptered out, we climbed down the hill. The ARVN, the South Vietnamese, never came. At dusk we took a short break in a field of rice paddies.

I sat alone, the only remaining marine left from my original squad. Nearby sat three marines smoking a joint. They shook their heads. "Shutter," they said. "Take our picture."

I was not thinking much anymore. I'd forgotten I still had the camera. I raised it and snapped their photo. They had soot and dirt in every crack of their visible skin, which otherwise had no pigmentation. It was gray. They didn't look like men. They looked like ghosts, walking dead. They didn't smile. Though only in-country a couple of months, they already had the lifeless eyes I'd seen in so many marines, like their souls had already left their bodies—the way EZ's soul left his body.

One of them pointed across the paddy. Far in the distance a mama-san was bent over, working in the shin-deep water as if it were just another day. We'd just lost all these marines. We'd lost Victor Cruz. And she just went on with her life, like nothing happened. The guys watched her from across the paddy. One of them, I don't remember who, it doesn't matter, said, "I'll bet Mama-san is VC."

"Sure as shit," said another. "They're all VC. I'll bet she gave us away, gave the NVA time to ambush us."

I looked up and saw her in the distance, small and fragile, just a shadow really, her cone-shaped hat and white shirt against the fading light.

"What do you want to bet I can hit her?" one of the guys said.

I heard someone say, "Don't bother. You're just wasting ammunition." And I realized it was me. I was not thinking, This is an innocent woman. I was thinking we shouldn't waste ammunition.

The first guy took a shot. Mama-san never looked up. She never looked over. She just kept working.

The second guy shouldered his rifle, shot. Missed.

The third guy also missed.

They looked to me. Like I was one of them. But I was not one of them. I was not like them. I was not going to shoot at an old woman.

I looked to the old woman, and suddenly I was hovering over this shell of a marine I no longer recognized, this marine I did not know. I watched as he raised the barrel of his M-16 and put the stock to his shoulder. He's not going to pull the trigger, I told myself. He was just going to put the sights on her and pretend to pull the trigger. He was not going to shoot an innocent woman.

She was a dark shape against the fading light and the red horizon. Too far. She was too far to hit.

He squeezed the trigger.

The old woman fell over.

I lowered the rifle and looked to the three soldiers. No one said anything. No one's facial expression changed. They stood and fell out, humping across the rice paddies, past the old woman's body. As we passed, they never looked over at her. They didn't care.

But I looked.

I saw the face.

Not an old mama-san. A boy. Maybe seven or eight years old. A child.

His eyes were open, staring up at me, pleading for an answer. Why?

I had no answer.

I didn't know why.

I see that young boy's face every day.

He walks down the streets I walk, sits in a passing car, plays soccer on the soccer fields with other kids. He eats in the booth next to me in restaurants, sits in the movie theaters I attend, stands in line when I wait for anything. I see him at night when I close my eyes. I see him in the morning when I wake. I see him in the shower and in the mirror when I shave.

He is death.

Death follows me.

The young boy haunts me. He has a right.

I took his life.

He's taking mine.

CHAPTER 26

June 17, 2017

I drove down to Los Angeles to pick up Beau after he completed his first year at UCLA. There had been some talk of him staying in LA, about a job working with a friend at a golf course, but ultimately, Beau decided he wanted to come home. Elizabeth had too much going on at work to make the drive, and with Mary Beth still in finals, we thought it best that Elizabeth stay home and keep Mary Beth on track.

I helped Beau carry his belongings to the car. It wasn't much. I was amazed at how little one could live on, the simplicity of college life. It made me think of William again, what little he had in Vietnam. Beau's freshman roommate, whom I had never met, had already checked out, leaving just the elevated bare mattress and pinholes in the wall where the *Star Wars* movie posters had hung.

He and Beau got along fine but they weren't close friends and didn't socialize. After nine months living together, they headed for home, and with an undergraduate student population of forty thousand, it was unlikely they would see much of each other again.

"You ready?" I asked Beau.

"Hungry," he said, which was always his answer. "Can we hit Tommy's on the way home?"

"What's Tommy's?"

"Oh, Dad, you have not had a chili cheeseburger until you've had Tommy's."

I didn't have the heart to tell Beau that because of a weird iron issue with my blood, I had become primarily vegan. And this was one of those opportunities when I figured a chili cheeseburger with my son would have a far greater impact on my memories, not to mention my cholesterol and fat levels, than on my iron count. And I wasn't about to pass up an opportunity to create a memory.

We ate the burgers at an outdoor bench in glorious sunshine, then jumped in the car and headed for home. I kept waiting for Beau to turn on the radio and use the aux cord to plug in his playlist, but he never did.

"Did I ever tell you about my final drive home from law school behind my buddy Thomas?"

"No," Beau said.

"I had an afternoon final, but Thomas waited so we could drive home together. I didn't finish the test until close to five o'clock. We should have just spent the night, but we were both anxious to get home. We came out of these mountains and descended into tule fog."

"What's tule fog?" Beau asked.

"Tule fog is a thick ground fog, like driving through pea soup. The headlights on my Ford Pinto could barely pierce it."

"Shit, really?"

"We should have pulled over and stayed in a hotel. Not that either of us had any money, but we had credit cards."

"Why didn't you?" Beau asked.

Good question. By the end of law school I was twenty-five years old and couldn't blame an undeveloped frontal cortex. I had a girlfriend, but more importantly, I wanted to get away from law school. It had been three difficult years, and I wanted to put it in my past. "We should have," I said, "and I hope that if you ever find yourself in a similar situation, you have enough sense to do it."

"Seems logical," Beau said.

"It does," I said, "but I wasn't thinking logically. I just wanted to get home and see my girlfriend."

"This the girlfriend you broke up with the next year?" Beau asked, smiling.

"Same one," I said. "The next morning Thomas called and told me to turn on the news. The tule fog had caused a fifty-car crash that night and, by what we could judge, it happened just ten to fifteen minutes behind us. Twelve people lost their lives. Thirty people were hospitalized."

"Shit," Beau said again.

"Do you know why those people died and we lived?"

"Luck," Beau said, shrugging.

I nodded and thought of that line from the Harry Chapin song, but my boy was not just like me. I had no doubt he would have stayed in a hotel. I'd like to believe I had something to do with that, but I think Chris's death had more to do with it.

"But here's the thing. We had the chance to make our own luck. We had the chance to pull over and get a hotel or, at worst, to sleep in our cars until morning—so did all those other people who didn't and lost their lives. Don't forget that. Sometimes bad luck is really dumb actions or inaction. You can make your own luck by making smart decisions."

Beau looked out the window. "I could have been better at that this year," he said.

There had been the phone call home after Beau's first-quarter finals when he learned he had earned two Cs and a B-minus. There had been the poor girlfriend choice that had also ended badly, and a fight at a UCLA football game that resulted in a black eye and a trip to the hospital.

"It's part of growing up," I said. "Hopefully, you learned from the experiences, so you won't go through them again."

His spring quarter, Beau pulled two As and a B-plus.

I almost said, *At least you had the chance to make your mistakes and live to talk about them,* but I realized I wasn't the best person to tell Beau how lucky he had been. The best person was a guy just about the same age as Beau, who had flown across the country to Los Angeles chasing a girl, and decided to stay for the sunshine, with no humidity. A guy who appreciated those small blessings.

"I have something for you to read," I said to Beau, and I handed him William's journal.

"What is it?"

I gave his question a moment of thought. "It's a book about life as an eighteen-year-old young man, about growing up and growing old."

"Sounds interesting."

You have no idea, I thought.

Neither, it turns out, did I. Not fully.

EPILOGUE

August 26, 2017

It is prophetic, I suppose, my landing at the Seattle-Tacoma airport fifty years to the day after William wrote his first journal entry. Despite having traveled all over the world, I have never been to the Pacific Northwest. I've never seen the reason, though my good friend Thomas now resides in the Emerald City.

I get my rental car. I figure this is one of those glorious mornings I've heard about in the Pacific Northwest. At ten in the morning the temperature is comfortable. Not a cloud in the sky. I lower the window. The chill feels invigorating.

My destination is a place called Issaquah, which I'm told is twenty-two miles northeast of the airport and it should, according to the GPS on my phone, take me roughly half an hour to get there, though I have arrived smack dab in the middle of traffic.

I plug in and find a second route; this one avoids Seattle and weaves its way south around the southern tip of Lake Washington, but I soon find the 405 freeway a rolling parking lot. I sit back and relax. I'm not in any rush. I do not have an appointment. Some things are better discussed in person than over the phone.

I make my way east on the I-90 freeway. Traffic lightens. I will arrive before noon. Before, I hope, William has started his day, whatever that entails. I know little about him, which sounds odd to admit. An internet search revealed that he worked as a drug and alcohol rehabilitation counselor at a VA hospital in Seattle, which means he worked with veterans. He gave back. A property records search revealed he owns a home in Issaquah with a woman I assume was the wife he mentioned in the letter that accompanied his journal. An obituary in the *Seattle Times* indicated his wife died of cancer, as he wrote, and was survived by a daughter from a prior marriage. William's LinkedIn profile provided that he retired not long after his wife's death.

I could not find a phone number, neither a landline nor a cell phone. I'm uncertain whether I would have called. Even now, I'm not quite sure what I will say to William. I can't very well say *I was in the neighborhood and thought I would stop by.* But I don't think I will have to say much. I suspect he will know why I have come. I hope he understands.

The woman's voice on my GPS instructs me to take the Front Street exit and proceed south through a quaint commercial district of one-story brick and wood-slat buildings. It looks like an old mining town, but with modern amenities. I stop at the only stoplight in town, which gives me the chance to look around. A theater. A Subway sandwich shop. A hardware store beside a cannabis store. A pharmacy and a grocery. I can see William walking these streets, far from his memories, happy. At least I hope he's found happiness.

I proceed out of town and pass one-story houses that have become home to dental practices, an architectural firm, a State Farm Insurance office. Farther out I pass apartments, a Lutheran church. I wonder if William ever found God again. Front Street becomes Issaquah-Hobart Road and the density of houses declines and the space opens to trees and lush green lawns. Another mile and the GPS voice tells me to turn right. I proceed down a gravel road with white fencing and drive to a one-story clapboard home. A car sits idle in the carport. The home is a sky-blue color with a white porch railing. A porch swing hangs motionless from two metal chains. The front door is white with two asymmetric colored-glass windows in the corners. I am struck by the quaint and peaceful setting.

I push out of the car before I have the chance to talk myself out of this encounter, and make my way to the front door, which I find ajar several inches. I can see inside. The hardwood floors glisten, inlaid with a mosaic design running along the edges of each room, the pattern uninterrupted by any furniture.

The door creaks open, and I step inside to the smell of freshly painted walls and redone floors. The staircase is directly ahead of me; the wallpaper leading up the stairs is an old-fashioned country pattern. To the right, a lamp hangs over an empty rectangular dining room. To the left, the centerpiece of the front room, is a white brick fireplace. I can see William seated there, reading, his wife nearby. I can see holiday gatherings, a family sitting down at the table to eat a Thanksgiving meal. I realize I am embedding William in Norman Rockwell paintings from the book on the coffee table in the front room of my home.

My heart is breaking. *I'm too late,* I think.

"Can I help you?" A woman approaches from down the hall.

"I'm sorry," I say. "The front door was open. Are you related to William?" I think perhaps she is the daughter William wrote of in his first letter to me.

"No. I'm his real estate agent."

"I didn't see a sign. Has the house sold?"

"Last weekend," she says. "I took the sign down today. We had seven offers in two days, every one of them over the asking price." Real estate inflation has come to Seattle, along with traffic. Good for William. She puts out her hand, which I shake. "I'm Dawn Richards," she says. "Are you looking for a home in Issaquah?"

"No. I'm just visiting from California. I was hoping to find the owner, William Goodman. I knew him many years ago. Looks like I'm too late."

"He had a motor home. He and his wife. She passed about two years ago. He fixed up the house, hired me to put it on the market, and took off. He left instructions to put his money into a bank account."

I smile. "He didn't say where he was going?"

"I don't think he had any set plans. He signed the papers remotely on my company website, and I deposited the money into an account in town. How did you know William?"

"I worked with him almost forty years ago on a construction crew. I haven't seen or talked to him since."

She gives me a puzzled look, clearly intending to ask, *Why, then, are you here?*

"A couple years ago he sent me a letter, with a journal he kept while in Vietnam. I finished reading his journal and hoped to speak to him."

She squints, as if having trouble believing my story. Then she says, "Did you say you live in California?"

"Yes."

"Burlingame?"

"Yes," I say, intrigued by where this is going.

"You're not . . ." She pulls out a white

envelope from her storage clipboard. "You're not Vincenzo, are you?"

I laughed. "Vincent," I say. "Vincent Bianco. Though William used to call me Vincenzo."

She gives a soft chuckle, shaking her head as she hands me the envelope. "William asked me to mail this after I sold the house. This is really too strange."

I recognize the same scribbled handwriting from the manila envelope sent to me almost exactly two years ago. As before, American flag stamps adorn the upper-right corner. As before, William did not provide a return address. "He asked you to mail this after the house sold?"

"Yes," she says.

I pause. William didn't want to talk about what he wrote in his journal. I can understand why. I've read a lot about Vietnam veterans, and what I've read is that many won't talk about their experiences. There are many books, but most veterans keep to themselves.

"You look like you're on your way out. I don't want to keep you."

"I have another showing. I have to lock up, but you're welcome to sit on the swing or porch steps to read his letter, if you like."

"Thanks," I say. "I'd like that."

I step out onto the porch. Dawn Richards closes the front door and deadbolts it. It feels like she is closing a life lived. "Do you know anything about the people who bought the house?"

"A young family," she says. "They're moving out of Seattle and want more room, more land. They want to slow down and spend time with their children."

I can imagine a young boy riding a bike in the yard, a young girl in a dress on a swing fastened to a limb of the oak tree. More Norman Rockwell paintings. My ideal of a bucolic existence, one without wars. One in which the family would walk into town to eat a meal, catch a performance at the local theater, and walk home again, the boy kicking a can. A life I could imagine from my youth. One not constantly interrupted by cell phones or social media. I have a thought and yell to Dawn Richards, who is just about to get into her car. "Did William leave a cell phone number?"

She looks up. "Not with me."

"An email address?"

She shakes her head. "No."

I smile and wave. Then I sit on the porch swing, and I think again of that Norman Rockwell painting. Now I'm in it. It is why I came to the Northwest, I suppose. I just wanted the chance to know that William is okay, that he's led some semblance of a good life. Maybe that's why William has left his home, taken to the road in his RV, so he can remember the good life he had here, with his wife, and won't have to watch it deteriorate in his old age. Another family will have the chance at that bucolic existence.

As Dawn Richards's Subaru pulls onto the gravel drive and back to the street, I sit on the porch swing and watch her go. The cables creak under my weight. I swing gently and imagine William and his wife sitting here on a warm summer evening with time having no meaning, just existing.

I debate whether I want to open his letter and read the final words William has written, whether I want to spoil the beautiful life I have imagined. In the end curiosity wins, as it always does, and I carefully tear off a small strip from the end of the envelope and pull out the letter. Two photographs fall into my lap, facedown. One is older, I can tell by the framing. I turn it over. It is faded, but unmistakable. It is a picture of me, Mike, and William in our Northpark Yankees uniforms, the trophy we won that summer resting on a table at the Village Host restaurant. Mike is in the middle, wearing a battered straw cowboy hat, his blond hair flowing beneath it. William is on the right, his dark hair equally long, his face tan. William is smiling and holding up his index finger. I am on the left, kneeling, also with a finger extended, also smiling. My hair, too, is parted in the middle and falls below my ears. The '70s. The fashion decade we'd all like to forget.

I turn over the second photograph. It is a picture of a man I hardly recognize, but for the mischievous sparkle in his blue eyes. William. His hair, what he has left, is nub short. He is no longer the lean young man in the prior picture. He has put on weight, though he is not fat, just thicker with age, as am I. He stands on this same porch, his arm around a woman, the porch swing behind them. I can tell by their embrace, the way she leans into him, turning slightly so that her left arm can reach across his body and hold him, that they love one another. That they are in love.

I set both photographs on my lap, overwhelmed with emotion. A part of me smiles. A part cries. A picture is worth a thousand words, but I'd still like to read William's.

I open the letter.

Vincenzo:
By the time you read this, I will be gone. Don't panic. I have an RV. LOL.

I'm selling the house and taking to the road, as I did so many years ago when I lived in my El Camino. By comparison, this will be luxurious.

I've decided to see the United States. I don't want to sit in this home alone. I don't think it would be good for my psyche. It's been lonely since my wife's death. I've tried to fill the days hiking in the mountains near our house, fishing the streams, gardening out back, but I've come to realize that I'm just killing time, the way we used to kill time in Vietnam. We killed time until we died.

I don't want to kill time. I don't want to die. I want to live—however many years I have left. I owe it to Victor Cruz and all the others who didn't make it home, who never got the chance to grow old. I'm going to go see the national parks in Utah. I've taken up photography again. I took one of those MasterClass courses on the computer with Annie Leibovitz. I couldn't do it for many years. I feared I'd put my eye to the lens and see all those horrors I witnessed through that lens so many years ago. But I didn't. I saw only the beauty of nature and of the living.

Speaking of photographs, I have two for you. The first I hope you recognize. That was taken at the Village Host in Burlingame the night we won the league softball championship. You, me, and Mikey. I found a scrapbook when I was cleaning out my things, downsizing before the move. I never threw it out. I'm glad I kept it. I wish I had kept my medals. I would have liked to have shown my grandkids.

I think I wrote when I sent the journal that I have a daughter from Cheryl's first marriage. That's my wife's name. Cheryl. Her husband was a Vietnam soldier who didn't make it home. We met at grief counseling at the VA. My daughter was just eight when Cheryl and I married, so I raised her as my own. She has three children. Her oldest, a boy, is about the same age as you in that picture. He's a bit of a wild child, but a good kid. I'm hoping I can talk some sense into him before he heads off to college. Boys that age are too easily forgotten. We simply expect them to pass from their teenage years into manhood, with all its responsibilities, without any help. It's a tough transition. Nobody hands you an owner's manual that explains

1. how to be a man,
2. how to be a husband, and
3. how to be a father.

Everyone just expects you to do it.

So . . . What else?

I'm going to keep another journal, the second one in my life. And I haven't had a drink or a drug in thirty-seven years and counting. Sober and happy.

I've forgiven God.

I didn't really have much choice if I

wanted to be sober, but I realize now it was the right thing to do. My beef wasn't with God, it was with the war. It took a long time to figure that out, though. I had to forgive myself first. If you read my journal, you know why. I hope you did. But I realize that when I wrote that final entry I left you in a bad place, a hopeless place that I once inhabited. That wasn't fair. I've come to realize that no situation is hopeless unless we let it be.

I take responsibility for what I did. If I could take back that one moment in time, I would. But I can't.

I had to find a way to live with it. To live with that young boy. Years of counseling helped. He's still around, though he no longer haunts me. I no longer fear seeing him. He is my moral compass, my conscience. Whenever I get angry, he's there to calm me. The way you did that day when you stopped me from swinging the sledgehammer at whatever that guy's name was. Whenever I want a drink or a smoke, he's the consequence of going down that rabbit hole again. He's pushed me to lead a good life, to make amends, and I've tried. I worked with other veterans fighting similar demons for almost four decades. I like to believe

I also taught them how to turn a foe into a friend.

I imagine I'll have a conversation with that boy when, hopefully, I reach those pearly gates. I imagine he will be there to greet me, I hope with a hug and not a fist.

I will finish my twelve steps in the afterlife. I will make amends with him and his family.

You gave me that chance, Vincent, when you listened, and when you stepped in front of that sledgehammer and kept me from ruining what was left of my life. Because of you I met my wife and my daughter, and I found myself. I hope you know that.

Todd Pearson. I wonder if you've thought of him? I looked him up. Step eight in my recovery—make a list of all the persons I have harmed and be willing to make amends. Turns out Vietnam killed Todd and he didn't even know it. Died of cancer from Agent Orange in his forties, like so many other veterans. I spoke to his wife—he divorced and remarried.

Well, I've rambled long enough. And now I need to ramble along.

I hope this letter finds you well. If you ever talk to Mikey, please give him my best. And, you never know. I just may drive this RV up to your front door one day and honk the horn. I hope you won't mind seeing an old friend.

I think of you as a friend, Vincenzo. And I thank you for being there and for listening. You have no idea what it meant to me.

Peace. Semper Fi.
William

PS. If we do ever see each other again, I want the true story of what happened with that Italian girl from New York that summer. I know you didn't tell me the truth, and I applaud you for your discretion. But I'd still like to know.

I lower the letter and look out at William's yard. I don't cry. I smile.

I'm happy for William. It's what I needed to know, why I came. I needed to know he was all right. I do have one disagreement. This will not be his second journal. It will be his third.

I was also William's journal that summer so the stories didn't, maybe, drive him crazy. He told me his stories and, maybe, I don't know, maybe he felt a little better.

I like to believe so.

I'm glad he told me about Todd, but sad, also, at his ending. Some years after working for Todd,

I, too, had searched for him. I went by the house on Bayswater, where he no longer lived. The post office had no forwarding address. Likely he moved out of the house when he and his wife divorced. Years later, I looked him up again, this time using the internet, though I figured the chances of Todd being on social media were slim to none. None. I never did find him. Now I know why, and I can also shut that door. He is another life lost to Vietnam, a name that hopefully will also be etched on the black granite memorial in Washington, DC.

Maybe someday I will write that book William suggested, that owner's manual for young men. Maybe I'll catch that dream, of being a writer, for both of us.

Or maybe I'll just tell the story of William, of Vietnam, and the summer of 1979.

Maybe.

ACKNOWLEDGMENTS

There is a saying we writers hear bandied about: "Write what you know." Most writers I know say the better adage is "Write what you're interested in." Stories such as *The World Played Chess* and *The Extraordinary Life of Sam Hell* come from the heart. As I explained in my acknowledgments in the latter book, I have never had ocular albinism and I was fortunate to only have been bullied in one instance that I can recall. But I do have a brother with Down Syndrome, and the subject of bullying and what it does to both the bully and the victim interested me. So I researched it, and in the process, I found Sam Hell and ocular albinism.

The same is true with this novel. First, it is a novel, not a memoir. I never served in Vietnam or in any branch of the US military. The Vietnam War, however, always interested me. I don't know why exactly, much like I don't know why Elvis Presley interested me. Maybe because they were a part of my life. I was born in 1961 and, like Vincent, graduated high school in 1979. I do recall, as a young boy, watching the news at night and seeing the helicopters in Vietnam, the soldiers fighting over there, the wounded, and the dead in body bags being flown from the bush. I recall thinking about how young those men were, how their lives had been cut so short. I watched the protests on television and felt the protestors were justified, but I worried that our country was being torn apart.

Mostly, I recall being interested. The war captivated me, particularly the thought that so many young men and women were being sent halfway around the world to fight not an invader—like the Nazis—but a political theory. Communism.

I graduated from high school in 1979 believing, like many young men, that the world was my oyster, and my future, limitless. My sister's boyfriend did get me a job working on a construction crew with two Vietnam veterans, and I did get the education of a lifetime over that summer. Like most Vietnam veterans, the two men didn't talk much about their experiences. Stories usually came when we were out drinking a few beers. They would open up and tell me what it was like to one day be an eighteen-year-old living in America and, seemingly, the next day be in the jungles of a foreign country, with a foreign climate, fighting against a foreign enemy you didn't know and didn't have anything against who was actively trying to kill you. Neither man understood the war, or his place in it, how it would have any impact on his life or the lives of Americans in general. They both said no one ever could offer them a good explanation as to why they were supposed to shoot and kill Vietnamese people living in Vietnam. Both expressed the feeling that they were the foreigners and that their presence never felt justified. What also struck me were the similarities between these two men, despite differences in age, branch of service, and experience. One was a marine, the other, army. For men still young, they seemed old to me that summer, and fatalistic. They did not believe in God, they drank too much—in my opinion—they were quick to get into fights, and when they did, they usually picked the biggest opponent. They seemed to live day to day, like they no longer trusted the promise of a future.

Mostly, though, I recall they were good men.

My work on the construction team that summer, and thereafter during every break from school, helped finance my college tuition at Stanford. I could not have afforded to attend had it not been for that employment. My boss could have let me go any number of times when the work got too light, but he never did. He always found work for me, and he always paid me. I have tried to find him, without success, to thank him for what he did for me. I hope someday I have that chance.

In college, I found the book *Nam* by Mark Baker, true stories of men and women who served in Vietnam. I read it cover to cover, then a second time. I still have my first edition. The stories fascinated me, in part, because I felt as though I had heard so many of them that summer between high school and college. I rushed to find other books and read accounts equally as raw and honest. I watched *Apocalypse Now* and *Platoon* and *Full Metal Jacket* and many other movies on the Vietnam experience multiple times. I watched *The Deer Hunter* just once, but I have never forgotten it.

When I set out to write this novel, I had no intention of writing about Vietnam. I intended to write about that critical moment in every boy's life when he goes from being a boy to being a man. There is no set timetable, but it seems the moment society expects this transformation to occur is when the boy graduates high school. We are expected to go off to college and come home a man. Or go off to work in the real world or join the military and magically understand what it means to be a man, a husband, and a father. There are no classes to help us. At least, there were none in 1979. Most of us, I assume, learn by emulating the men we know. Mostly I emulated my father, a good, decent, and moral man.

I also emulated a big brother who came into my life when I was in the eighth grade, a young counselor. Chris took me under his wing and helped me to grow up. He liked to say, "There's no owner's manual."

And I emulated the two men I worked with that summer. I did not have a choice. They did not treat me as a boy and did not allow me to act as one. They did not have that luxury when they were my age. They depended on me to be at work every morning on time to do my job and get the work done, because they knew the dire consequences that could occur if one man failed to do his job. They expected me to earn my paycheck. And they relied on me because they needed me to be reliable.

When I sat down to write this story, I told my friend Dale what my intent was, and he responded, "It's like that adage. The world played chess while I played checkers."

I had never heard it, so I looked it up.

Sometimes we know so little, we are not even playing the same game everyone else is playing. Chess is complex and strategic and requires that we think several moves ahead of our opponent. We need to map out our future and be prepared to make unexpected deviations when necessary. In 1979, I was still deciding whether to jump the checker in front of me and get crowned. That summer changed me.

When I realized my novel was really about three men—Vincent, the father of an eighteen-year-old son; Vincent, the eighteen-year-old boy; and William, the marine—I knew I had to do a lot more research, but that was okay because the subject interested me. I read more than a dozen firsthand accounts of soldiers serving in Vietnam.

I read articles, treatises, and military papers on the marine experience in Vietnam. I watched just as many movies and documentaries, including Ken Burns's legendary documentary. Neither William nor Todd is any one person; they are an amalgamation of the stories I heard in 1979, the stories I read, and the stories I witnessed on television, in theaters, and on my computer.

Even with all that information, I knew I had more work to do. So I called up a friend of mine, Gunnery Sergeant Bob Mannion, a United States Marine, who served during Vietnam, and I asked for his help. Bob, who is also a talented writer, never hesitated. He sent me manuals and documents to help me understand the marine experience in Vietnam, and he read my manuscript front to back multiple times, making sure I got the weapons and terminology correct, the marine procedures accurate, and the Vietnam experience, hopefully, authentic.

I owe Bob a huge debt of gratitude. I am certain I got some things wrong simply because I misinterpreted what he told me. Those mistakes are mine and mine alone.

I also want to thank Joe, my son. It was Joe who suggested the book would be stronger if I could re-create an authentic Vietnam experience, and do so through a journal documenting a soldier's powerful tour of duty. Joe has helped me now with three novels. He sees things at a ten-thousand-foot level, and his observations and suggestions are usually spot on.

I have had the chance to go to Washington, DC, half a dozen times in my life, and each time I go, I visit the Vietnam Veterans Memorial. I run my hand over the names etched in the black stone monument, and I try to remember those etchings are more than just letters. Those etchings represent real people who lost their lives far too young—deaths that forever changed the landscapes of their respective families, possibly this country, and maybe the world.

This novel is written with the utmost deference and respect to all those men and women who fought in Vietnam on both sides, as well as the Vietnamese people who lived through it. That includes my father-in-law, Dr. Robert Kapela, Major, United States Army Medical Corp on ground as medical doctor and recipient of the Bronze Star for his "meritorious achievement in ground operations against hostile forces" from May 1969 to May 1970. I have never had the chance to visit Vietnam, but Joe and other family members have, and each has said, to a person, that there are no finer people.

The racial slurs in this novel are not mine, and they do not represent me or the way I think or what I believe. They are far, far below the moral and ethical education I received from my mother and father. They do not even belong to the soldiers who uttered them. The racial slurs were part of the psychological warfare the military used to dehumanize the enemy so soldiers could kill other soldiers and not consider the reality of their actions. This, unfortunately, is a tactic that has been used throughout history, not just during the Vietnam War, or even limited to wars.

www.npr.org/2011/03/29/134956180/criminals-see-their-victims-as-less-than-human

www.lassennews.com/racism-and-war-the-dehumanization-of-the-enemy

May we never forget, so we never again have to experience it.

I wish to thank Meg Ruley and Rebecca Scherer at the Jane Rotrosen Agency for their continued guidance and support. Thanks also to Jane Berkey, the agency founder, who took me out for a drink during one particularly difficult moment in this writer's life and told me to keep going forward, that things would work out. She was right. They did work out, largely thanks to the agency's incredible guidance.

Thanks to Danielle Marshall at Lake Union, my publisher, for her unwillingness to accept anything but my best. She read the first draft and told me I could do better, though she was kind about it. She was right. I worked with my longtime developmental editor, Charlotte Herscher, and together we improved the manuscript. Charlotte never lets me forget what readers expect when they buy one of my novels, and I'm grateful to her for pushing me.

Thanks to Sean Baker, head of production, and to Nicole Burns-Ascue, production manager. I absolutely love this cover and all the covers of my novels. They tell the story so well. Thanks to Dennelle Catlett, Amazon Publishing PR, and to Erica Moriarty, Kyla Pigoni, Lindsey Bragg, and all the others who tirelessly promote my work. Thanks to Jaye Whitney Debber, production editor, and Valerie Paquin, copyeditor. Thanks to Jeff Belle, vice president of Amazon Publishing, and Mikyla Bruder, publisher, and associate publisher Hai-Yen Mura. This is quite a team and I'm humbled to be part of it.

Thank you to the two men I worked with that summer of 1979 who inspired this work. Thanks to my former brother-in-law, Rick McHale, who got me the job and the education of a lifetime. Thank you to my high school buddies for allowing me to use their likenesses and some of our stories. I want to emphasize again, however, that this is a work of fiction. My high school buddies have grown to be great men who, though I live far away, I still consider my good friends.

Thanks to my mother, Patty Dugoni, who gave me my love of reading and writing. I didn't fool her that night I snuck home and jumped in bed. She just let me think I did.

Thanks to my daughter, Catherine, and to my

wife, Cristina. You've helped me to achieve a dream come true.

Last but never least, thanks to you, my loyal readers, for your continued support. Your emails have been heartwarming, intelligent, and inspiring. This has been a difficult year for all of us, but this book helped me put this experience in perspective. Most of the young men who served in Vietnam served for a full year. Marines served thirteen months. Those who served in World War I and World War II served much longer. They were separated from their families, their country, and their jobs. They awoke each day wondering if it might be their last. And the Vietnamese people endured more than fifty years of war.

Heroes. Every one of them.

RESOURCES

I know the Vietnam War experience is highly personal for each of those men and women who served. What I have attempted to capture and re-create in *The World Played Chess* is one fictional marine's experience based upon the stories two veterans told to me during the summer of 1979 and thereafter and all the firsthand accounts documented in the books, articles, treatises, and military papers on the marine experience in Vietnam, as well as movies and documentaries. These resources are set forth in the attached list. Any mistakes are mine and mine alone.

Documentaries

The Vietnam War, ten-part series, directed by Ken Burns and Lynn Novick, 2019.

Articles and Journals

"Combat Photographer: Vietnam Through the Lens of Marine Corporal William T. Perkins, Jr." by Frank Blazich, October 12, 2017, https://americanhistory.si.edu/blog/combat-photographer-Vietnam.

"The Psychological Effects of the Vietnam War," Edge, Josh Hochgesang, Tracye Lawyer, Toby Stevenson, War & Peace: Media and War.

"US Marines in Vietnam Vietnamization and Redeployment 1970–1971," Graham A. Cosmas and Lieutenant Colonel Terrence P. Murray, US Marine Corps (USMC), History and Museums Division Headquarters, US Marine Corps, Washington, DC, 1986.

"US Marines in Vietnam, The War that Would Not End 1971–1973," Major Charles D. Melson, USMC, and Lieutenant Colonel Curtis G. Arnold, USMC, History and Museums Division Headquarters, US Marine Corps, Washington, DC, 1991.

"The Marines in Vietnam 1954–1973: An Anthology and Annotated Bibliography," second edition, History and Museums Division Headquarters, US Marine Corps, Washington, DC, 1985.

Books

Bing West, *The Village*, Pocket Books, 2003.

Dan Brookes and Bob Hillerby, *Shooting Vietnam: The War by Its Military Photographers*, Pen & Sword, 2019.

Don McQuinn, *Targets: A Vietnam War Novel*, Raven's Call Press, 1980.

Jim Ross, *Outside the Wire*, Stackpole Books, 2013.

Mark Baker, *Nam: The Vietnam War in the Words of the Soldiers Who Fought There*, Berkley Books, 1981.

Michael Herr, *Dispatches*, Vintage International, 1977.

Philip Caputo, *A Rumor of War*, fortieth anniversary edition, Picador Henry Holt, 1977.

R. C. LeBeau, *Donut Hole: A Marine's Real-Life Battles in Vietnam During 1967 and 1968 Marines, First Force Logistical Command Clutch Platoon*, 2019.

Tim O'Brien, *If I Die in a Combat Zone*, Broadway Books, 1975.

Tim O'Brien, *The Things They Carried*, Mariner Books, Houghton Mifflin Harcourt, 1990.

William F. Brown, *Our Vietnam Wars: As Told by 100 Veterans Who Served*, Booknook.biz, 2018.

Movies

Apocalypse Now
Born on the Fourth of July
The Boys in Company C
The Deer Hunter
The D.I.
Forrest Gump
Full Metal Jacket
Good Morning, Vietnam
Hamburger Hill
Platoon
Tigerland
Uncommon Valor
We Were Soldiers

BOOK CLUB QUESTIONS

1. Have you ever realized you have never really walked in someone else's shoes—similar to Vincent and the jungle boots? How do William's stories on the construction site affect Vincent's worldview as a young man?

2. Did you or anyone you know serve in Vietnam? What do you know about the war and America's reception of the soldiers who returned home?

3. Vincent pulls his son out of an important football game to protect him. How does his relationship with William and reading his journal influence that decision? When Beau ultimately gives up the sport, do you agree with his decision and reasoning?

4. When William experiences death, losing Haybale so early in his combat experience, how do you think that affects his psyche? Is that a defining moment or is he torn down gradually?

5. Why does William fight to bring honor to Haybale's kill?

6. How does William's photography shape the way he sees the war?

7. When Vincent compares his inability to throw out his plaques, awards, and degrees to

William throwing away his medals, what is Vincent afraid of losing?

8. Vincent's first sexual experience is based on an innocent lie. Do you think he regrets this? Why? How does this compare to William's experience?

9. Can William's loss of friends in combat be compared to Beau's tragic loss of his friend Chris? Why or why not?

10. Do you agree with the lesson William perceives he teaches the reckless BMW driver? Or is this another manifestation of PTSD?

11. When Vincent backs down from the fight on the road with the young man from the convenience store, what do you think informs his decision?

12. Loss of faith is a theme in the novel. How does William reclaim his faith in goodness, humanity, and himself? What about Beau? Vincent?

13. How does William reconcile himself with the horrors of what he has seen and done? With the loss of Cruz?

ABOUT THE AUTHOR

Robert Dugoni is the critically acclaimed *New York Times*, *Wall Street Journal*, *Washington Post*, and #1 Amazon Charts bestselling author of the Tracy Crosswhite police series, which is set in Seattle and has sold more than seven million books worldwide. He is also the author of the Charles Jenkins espionage series and the David Sloane series of legal thrillers. He has also written several stand-alone books, including the novels *The 7th Canon* and *Damage Control*; the literary novel *The Extraordinary Life of Sam Hell*, *Suspense Magazine*'s 2018 Book of the Year, for which Dugoni won an AudioFile Earphones Award for narration; and the nonfiction exposé *The Cyanide Canary*, a *Washington Post* best book of the year. Several of his novels have been optioned for movies and television series. Dugoni is the recipient of the Nancy Pearl Book Award for fiction and a three-time winner of the Friends of Mystery Spotted Owl Award for best novel set in the Pacific Northwest. He is a two-time finalist for the Thriller Awards and the Harper Lee Prize for Legal Fiction, and a finalist for the Silver Falchion Award for mystery and the Mystery Writers of America Edgar Awards.

Robert Dugoni's books are sold in more than twenty-five countries and have been translated into more than thirty languages.

Website: www.robertdugonibooks.com
Twitter: @robertdugoni
Facebook: www.facebook.com
/AuthorRobertDugoni

Center Point Large Print
600 Brooks Road / PO Box 1
Thorndike, ME 04986-0001 USA

(207) 568-3717

US & Canada:
1 800 929-9108
www.centerpointlargeprint.com